# REDEMPTION

## KATHRYN BARRETT

OMNIFIC PUBLISHING
LOS ANGELES

Omnific Publishing
1901 Avenue of the Stars, 2nd floor
Los Angeles, CA 90067
www.omnificpublishing.com

First Omnific eBook edition, October 2014
First Omnific trade paperback edition, October 2014

The characters and events in this book are fictitious.
Any similarity to real persons, living or dead,
is coincidental and not intended by the author.

Library of Congress Cataloguing-in-Publication Data

Barrett, Kathryn.
    Redemption / Kathryn Barrett - 1st ed.
    ISBN: 978-1-623421-35-9
    1. Contemporary Romance — Fiction. 2. Hollywood — Fiction.
    3. Scandal — Fiction. 4. Fortune — Fiction. I. Title

10 9 8 7 6 5 4 3 2 1

Cover Design by Micha Stone and Amy Brokaw
Interior Book Design by Coreen Montagna

Printed in the United States of America

To all the friends along the way<br>
who've encouraged me and inspired me,<br>
and to my family,<br>
who have always supported me.

# ᏢROLOGUE

From the *Los Angeles Times*

HOLLYWOOD EMBRACES ITS OWN AS SCANDAL DEEPENS

Thousands of mourners gathered in Beverly Hills today to hold a candlelight vigil after the shocking death of one of America's most beloved screen actresses. Not since the death of Marilyn Monroe has such an outpouring of public emotion been seen, and while police have quickly concluded their investigation, the rest of America continues to ask why.

There was blood on her hands. Blood and something else her mind wouldn't acknowledge. She couldn't focus in the soothing, protective haze that was fast numbing her to reality.

Claire stared at her blood-spattered hands, glowing eerily under the glare of the brute lamps used to illuminate the set. *Why didn't someone turn them off?* she thought dully. *Someone needed to turn off the lights. They were so bright…*

She concentrated on that thought as the noise swirled around her, urgent voices, the approaching whine of a siren. It must have been close by, waiting in case of an emergency. That happened, sometimes. People got injured on the set, prop guns went off accidentally. Even blanks could do damage, she had heard, if fired at close range.

Someone had wrapped a blanket around her bare shoulders, but still she shivered under the bright lights. *Someone really should turn them off. They must use massive amounts of electricity.*

The practical thought calmed her. Absently she estimated the cost per kilowatt hour—a similar question had appeared on her Management 480 final last month. Two thousand kilowatts each, someone had said. The electric bill would be enormous. Someone would be in trouble when the bill came due and red ink spilled.

She rocked back and forth on the floor of the greenhouse, no longer conscious of her surroundings. No one noticed her in the commotion.

Her hands clutched the blanket, smearing blood on the wool. *She would have to wash her hands.* The new worry scratched on her brain. If her mother saw her with dirty hands, she wouldn't be allowed any dinner. And if her father found out how her hands had been dirtied, there would be hell to pay.

*Hell.* She had been there already, been born there. But she had escaped—hadn't she? They wouldn't send her back. Her breath caught, tangled in fear. Would they?

Her head tilted, and a low keening sound emerged from deep in her throat.

"Someone get her out of here—Jesus Christ, Clarissa! She's covered in blood!" The disgusted voice penetrated her consciousness. That was a voice she knew, a voice she had come to trust. Why did it sound so shattered now?

"For Christ's sake, get her out of here!" The voice was more urgent. "She shouldn't be here! Oh, God, Hayley—" The words broke in a sob, but Claire knew her own tears would never fall. She didn't cry, not ever, no matter how much she hurt inside.

When they led her out, a proud little smile lingered on her lips and the blood had already dried on her hands. The flash of light from the camera made her blink, and suddenly, she knew where she was. But she couldn't remember what had happened, why she was naked under the scratchy blanket that covered her shoulders.

But a part of her did know. Her lot in life, she had learned, was to constantly atone for the sins of others. The devil wanted its ugly price paid again and again, and she was the one chosen to pay it.

# CHAPTER ONE

From the *Philadelphia Inquirer*

Famed financier Connor Forrest, recent buyer of Kaslow's Department Store, has appointed Claire Porter as Vice President, Finance, of the twenty-four store chain. Ms. Porter, a six-year veteran of the Forrest Group staff of market analysts, was reportedly the driving force behind the addition of Kaslow's to the FGI portfolio.

"I have complete confidence in Ms. Porter's ability to keep a tight rein on the expenditures of the company, while at the same time advance the store's operations into the next decade," Forrest commented through a spokesperson.

No further details were provided regarding Ms. Porter's background.

Suede-covered heels tapped a staccato rhythm on the floor, a patch work of marble imported over a century ago from Italy. The sound echoed against the mahogany ceiling panels four floors above, where a pantheon of Roman gods reclined, carved by a commercial artist whose name no one could remember.

Claire took a deep breath. The earthy scent of foliage, dampened by an early morning sprinkling, blended with the factory-fresh odor of new merchandise to create a unique fragrance.

*The smell of new money mixed with old,* she thought, dodging an outstretched palm frond.

The last time she had made her way through the rotunda of Kaslow's Department Store, shoppers were scurrying through the spoked aisles, gleaning the latest markdowns. At the edge of the mosaic-tiled fountain in the center sat the weariest of the lot, some with daredevil toddlers dangling over the sparkling water.

Today only a quiet goddess greeted her, a bronze figure posed in an uncomfortable-looking arc in the center of the now calm fountain. Claire averted her gaze from the too-knowing eyes as she approached. Could the goddess of Fortune possibly be considered a religious icon? Perhaps it wasn't entirely appropriate for the store's image.

But she could just imagine the headlines in tomorrow's paper: "Kaslow's New Owner Dumps Heavenly Relic Along with Pension Plan; Employees Hold Talks with the Antichrist."

*Rule number one: Choose your battles.*

She gave the silent figure a conciliatory glance as she skirted the fountain. Below the surface of the water, an assortment of coins lay scattered like fall leaves. At the end of the week, they'd be collected and sent to the Make-a-Wish Foundation, where some good might actually come from the spare change tossed into the fountain.

Claire wasn't prone to the practice herself. She'd learned early on that the only wishes that came true were those accompanied by sixty-hour work weeks.

Though, if ever there was a time when she could use a run of good luck, today—the first day of her new job—would certainly be the moment to call in a few favors from whichever gods granted such things.

Well-honed lore maintained that Kaslow's fountain really did possess magical properties. Countless tales attested to that fact—one couple had even been married near the fountain where they claimed to have wished for, and found, their true love.

She had to admit it was a fantastic marketing gimmick.

She passed a display of orange-and-black socks, ties, and other Halloween-inspired accessories. The fountain's legends had originated with Earnest Kaslow, the retail genius who founded the store in 1890. Claire had read about him when she'd plotted the buyout of Kaslow's. The founder of the store, a true merchant prince, had possessed retail savvy unequaled by even R.H. Macy.

Claire paused in front of the elevator. A little of that savvy would come in handy now. Despite the majestic surroundings and the rich display of merchandise, the store was losing cash like an Atlantic City gambler on the down side of his luck. Claire intended to dam the flow. Job security for all employees had been assured in the original offer, yet she was determined to curb runaway executive salaries and limitless expense accounts along with other undue expenditures.

*This* was the battle she'd chosen — and one she was determined to win.

She punched the ivory elevator button, then tightened her grip on her briefcase. An image of her first day of school, an ordeal even if she hadn't been dressed in leftovers from the church collection box, flashed across her mind, then quickly rejoined other, darker images she refused to acknowledge.

The elevator pinged. Gleaming brass doors parted silently, and Claire stepped inside, hoping the welcome awaiting her on the seventh floor would go as smoothly.

More likely, she'd be greeted as warmly as an IRS audit.

She frowned, remembering the article in today's *Philadelphia Inquirer*. It had been just a small blurb, really, announcing her appointment to the board. Though it wasn't her first brush with publicity, she still hated seeing her name in print — even her real name — and a photo that wasn't unfocused and blurry. There was always the chance that someone would recognize her.

Although that hadn't happened in ten years.

She smoothed her tight chignon of "crow feather" hair, as her mother had called it. Not a single strand had dared to escape its confines, and without checking, she knew the Lancôme she had applied that morning was flawless. Long ago she had learned the art of camouflage. Ninety-nine percent of attitude was acting, something she had once been told she was good at.

The never-let-them-see-you-sweat philosophy had served her well over the years, and today it would be her number one ally. When all escape routes were blocked, she could stand her ground with the best of them.

She allowed herself a tiny smile of triumph. It would take more than a boardroom of overstuffed executives to rout Claire Porter, she told herself, the pinging tune of the elevator cheering her on.

After all, what could possibly happen that was worse than what she had faced before?

In a far corner of the rotunda, near a crowded display of gloves, a man aimed his Nikon at the elevator doors and snapped the shutter, capturing the image of a dark-suited woman just before she disappeared into the elevator.

Then he glanced at the fountain, where a ray of sun glinted off the figure in the center, causing the bronze eye to wink at him.

He stopped, blinked, then shook his head.

As he turned and walked away, a spray of water surged to life from behind the goddess, showering her bronze head and anointing her with a stream of purified liquid from somewhere below. The water cascaded over her outstretched arms, then fell into the pool below, where it was stirred by underwater jets that kept it flowing.

The wheel of fortune had just spun into motion.


Claire jotted a final note on the tablet in front of her, then glanced around the boardroom.

She recognized most of the department managers from her previous meetings with management. Chester Wheaton was Vice President of Merchandise. She knew his easygoing exterior hid a sharp mind, which would be crucial in carrying out the retail strategy Kaslow's would have to adopt if it was to remain competitive. Stanley Adair ran the Marketing department and seemed to have all the initiative of a contented housecat. Fortunately he was due to retire next spring.

Five minutes after the meeting was supposed to begin, Evan Kaslow walked in. He was slated to take over the president's office after his uncle retired, but Claire wasn't so sure he was the best choice. He had a reputation as a corporate Casanova, and the last thing Kaslow's needed was a sexual harassment suit.

And now that Bernard Kaslow's successor would be chosen on the basis of skill rather than family pedigree, Evan would have to earn his way to the executive office.

Which might explain his sour expression as he greeted her. "I see the Black Knight has finally joined our ranks."

Claire swallowed a sigh. A business blogger had dubbed her the "Black Knight" after FGI put in its white knight rescue bid for Kaslow's. She thought it made her sound like some sort of medieval mortuary director, hardly the image she was hoping to portray.

Evan narrowed his gaze, eyeing her black Donna Karan jacket as if it were a knockoff from H&M. "At least you're dressed for the part. But shouldn't you be buying your business suits at Kaslow's now that you're on the board?"

She leveled him with the impassive smile she'd perfected long ago, when girls at school mocked her knee-length dresses and clunky shoes. "Hello, Evan. I hope to have a chance to check out the styles in Ladies' Corporate Wear later. But I thought it more important to get our balance sheets back in the black first."

Evan's confident look faded. As Vice President of Stores, he bore part of the blame for the financial losses Kaslow's had sustained. Claire intended to see that each branch pulled its own weight from now on.

Claire congratulated herself on the easily won skirmish. Not bad for the first board meeting, but she had a feeling that when she announced the restructuring of the store's pension plans, she'd have more than her wardrobe to defend.

Jackie Prescott, the public relations director, breezed into the room, the scent of Chanel floating in with her. "Sorry I'm late," she said. "But when you hear why, you're going to die. Absolutely die." A smug glance traveled over the assortment of executives at the table as she sank into the only vacant chair. When her gaze settled on Claire, Jackie's wine-colored lips tightened into thin cracks. "Oh, hello, Claire. Did you see the announcement in yesterday's business section? They wanted more background information, but I didn't have any in my file." Opening a floral notebook, she added, "You seem to have been born when you came to work for the Forrest Group."

In some ways she had, but Claire wasn't about to share that with Jackie.

"Yes, I did see it. I thought it was fine. It's not my background that counts, after all." She was grateful the mention had been brief. The unexpected publicity had unnerved her, although the article had been buried beneath a story on the local housing market.

Claire wondered what Jackie was doing at the board meeting—she wasn't technically a member of the board. Perhaps she planned to prepare a statement on the changes expected at Kaslow's—at least, the changes Claire hoped would occur. The board would still have to agree, and though Claire, as the unofficial representative for Connor Forrest, was a force to be reckoned with, there was no guarantee her plans would be implemented if they didn't pull their own weight.

Connor's system of checks and balances, she reflected with a smile.

The room stirred as Bernard Kaslow arrived. Nine minutes late, Claire noted. He was the spitting image of the portrait of Earnest Kaslow on the wall, minus a set of fluffy sideburns.

As he settled at the head of the table, Jackie leaned forward, filling Bernard in on her news, no doubt. Finally, he nodded and glanced up. "The details will have to wait until later, Jackie. I'm sure we'll need some good news after we hear those numbers from Finance." He frowned at Claire. "I hope the picture's not as grim as some of the rumors floating around here seem to indicate."

Claire thought she detected a warning in his voice, but she ignored it as she rose from her seat. "Hardly. As you all can see from the sheets I've passed out—the new budget proposals, along with next year's earning projections—the financial picture could hardly be described as 'grim.' I think with some creative belt tightening—" she glanced around the room, noting a few relieved expressions, then continued "—we can all manage to live within our means for the next year and at the same time keep up the image of quality this store is known for."

For the next twenty minutes, she outlined a detailed financial forecast for the company, one that differed vastly from the haphazard accounting her predecessor had favored. During his era, department managers had asked for, and generally received, their budget amounts. During hers, she would tell the departments what they were allowed to spend. The change would take some getting used to and would put a few backs up, but she was prepared to be firm.

"And finally," she said, her gaze resting on Bob Berry, director of human resources. His broad face was smiling, since his budget would actually be increased. "You'll notice I've earmarked funds to be used to establish a corporate childcare center on the premises. Currently there is no adequate daycare in the area, and after the center is in place, it will double as a drop-in childcare facility for our customers. Thus, the purpose is twofold: an employee benefit, in keeping with Forrest Group policy on the West Coast, and an incentive to bring in affluent suburban shoppers, many of whom have young children.

"As you can see," she finished, "we plan to keep the emphasis on Kaslow's as a shopping experience, a place to be entertained—but only when that entertainment enhances sales, rather than entertainment purely for entertainment's sake."

Jackie jotted a note in the floral notepad. "Oh, dear, looks like no more free concerts in the rotunda on Thursdays."

"On the contrary, Jackie. The concerts are a relatively low-budget item and seem to bring in the sort of customers we want. However, we can't afford another bridal extravaganza like the one last spring. The 'wedding' alone cost half a million dollars, and our bridal department is only a small part of our total operation."

Jackie gave her a frosty glare. "Some of the best families in Philadelphia were there—the Stedwells, the Van Ostermans—even the mayor!"

"And did any of them buy wedding dresses?" Claire asked, knowing the answer.

But Jackie ignored the question. "You obviously have no understanding of how these things work. Word of mouth is the most important form of advertising."

Claire calmly pulled out a sheet of paper containing sales figures broken down by department. "Sales in Bridals were actually down last spring, due to changing demographics as well as the labor problems of one of our manufacturers. Not even the most aggressive marketing can change that. People aren't having big weddings anymore. A focus on less extravagant—"

"You're a financial manager! What on earth do you know about marketing?"

Claire refrained from pointing out her dual Master's in Marketing and Finance had well-prepared her for her current position. "My job is to maintain the bottom line. The benefits must outweigh the costs. Give me solid proof of a publicity proposal that meets that criteria, and I'll be all for it."

Jackie smiled triumphantly. "Ah! I have one right here." She pointed to her notepad. "I've just been on the phone with Marty Baker. It's still waiting approval on their end, but GrayWolf Productions wants to use Kaslow's as a location for the film they're shooting here in Philadelphia this winter."

Claire could only stare at her, mute with shock.

"GrayWolf?" someone on the other side of the table asked as Jackie continued to beam.

"They're an independent production company. This will be their first film, but they're definitely legit. I talked with someone in the

Philadelphia Film Commission this morning, and they've been given permission to shoot on location at some of our historic sights."

Claire gripped her pen, wondering desperately if there was a roll of antacids in her briefcase.

"Who's starring in this film?" Chester asked.

"For now that remains a secret — though I've heard Ben Affleck's name mentioned," Jackie said with a cagey smile.

Claire glanced around the room, noting the mounting enthusiasm. Even Bernard was beaming approvingly.

Apprehension lodged somewhere near the pit of Claire's stomach as her worst fears materialized. No, not her worst fears. This qualified as a distant second, maybe even third.

She took a deep breath and held up a hand to ward off the buzz of excited questions. "Hold on. What exactly have they asked for? Permission to film outside the premises?"

"Oh, no, they want to film interior shots here — it may require closing the store for a couple of days, but the compensation they've mentioned would more than make up for lost revenue."

"Absolutely not." The words were out of Claire's mouth before she could contain them. Every head turned toward her.

"Closing the store is out of the question," she continued. "There is no way to compensate for inconvenience to our customers, not to mention the possibility that something could be damaged."

*Or someone.* She tried to keep the thread of desperation out of her voice. "And there's also the matter of Kaslow's reputation to consider. If the film contains scenes with graphic violence or sexual content, it would undoubtedly offend many of our customers."

"Oh, there's no need to worry about that," Jackie said. "I've been told the film will most likely be rated PG. It's a light romantic comedy, something along the lines of *Pretty Woman*. And they'll be taking out an insurance policy to cover any damages to our premises."

"But we can't close the store," Claire said firmly. "Regardless of what sort of financial incentive they're offering."

Evan clicked his pen as if loading a weapon. "They could always shoot around our store hours. We are closed on Sunday mornings, Saturday evenings. Surely they could get in then."

"Marty did mention that possibility," Jackie added.

But a few hours would hardly be time enough to set up for a scene, much less complete the numerous takes necessary to shoot a few seconds worth of film footage. Claire said nothing, though, her mind busy sorting objections into neat piles she could deal with.

Jackie went on. "They've asked permission to use some of our merchandise as props. They're willing to pay extra for that, as well as cover any damages. They'd also like to negotiate with our restaurant for catering while they film here. That would certainly make up for some of the lost revenues." She tossed a gloating look in Claire's direction, then added, as if cementing the deal, "Filming starts in January, which is one of our slower months."

Claire closed her eyelids briefly, wondering if there were some god somewhere she had somehow offended. Perhaps she should have thrown a few pennies into the fountain this morning. No, she quickly amended, it would take more than pennies—quarters, perhaps, half dollars…Series EE treasury bonds…

She opened her eyes, focusing on the woman whose Chanel was beginning to smell like a withered floral arrangement. Between that and the stale cigar smoke, she felt as though she could barely breathe.

"As much as I hate to sound like a spoilsport," she began, "there are, however, several considerations, aside from the most obvious financial ones. There is absolutely no guarantee that any film starting out as an innocuous romantic comedy won't end up overflowing with gratuitous sex and violence—scripts get rewritten all the time. We simply can't have Kaslow's reputation, as well as our premises, exploited."

She glanced at Bernard Kaslow as she spoke, hoping the implied threat to his own good name would concern him. "Our customers won't want to shop at a store that's been the scene of—whatever sort of mayhem they decide to film here. And shutting down the store even for one day would be tantamount to hundreds of thousands of dollars in lost sales, as hundreds of customers take their business elsewhere—possibly for good."

Jackie looked taken aback by Claire's reaction. "Are you actually suggesting we should turn down the opportunity to have our store featured in a film? Think of what *Miracle on 34th Street* did for Macys!"

"I'm suggesting we give the matter some thought—from a financial standpoint rather than an emotional one. The lure of Hollywood is strong, I realize." No one knew better than she how strong it was. And how destructive. She swallowed, trying not to appear as desperate as she was.

"Now, Claire, I think you're blowing this all out of proportion," Jackie began. "Perhaps your priorities are—" she glanced at Bernard Kaslow, who had listened to the discussion without reaction "—not with Kaslow's at this point," she finished, a shrewd look on her face.

"On the contrary," Claire bit off, turning to Bernard for support. "Surely you agree it would be…unwise…to allow our location to be used without knowing more of the details. If they can't provide them, we shouldn't sign a contract."

He nodded his head thoughtfully, his chair creaking in rhythm. "You're certainly right, Claire, to have concerns." His gaze shifted to the portrait on the wall, as if wondering what his legendary ancestor would do.

The face in the portrait gazed back, a crafty look in the painted eyes.

Bernard cleared his throat. "We'll do what we can to have all your questions answered. Jackie, why don't you set something up with our attorneys and Claire, let them meet personally with these movie people. I'm sure once all the questions get answered, we'll all agree this is a good idea—after all, there's always room in the budget for some free publicity, isn't that right?" A satisfied smile appeared on his face, and his eyes glowed with excitement.

*Probably seeing his name in lights*, Claire thought, fighting the urge to swallow.

"Of course, Mr. Kaslow. I'll set that up right away." Jackie scribbled a note with her hot-pink pen.

Just the thought of meeting with anyone from Hollywood, or wherever the independent production company was from, made Claire's stomach roil. But if she insisted on squelching the idea totally, without a legitimate reason, more questions would be raised than she wanted to answer.

Hiding her apprehension, she nodded. "All right, then. If they can provide more information, I'll be glad to hear it. But I warn you, it would take a lot to convince me this is truly in Kaslow's best interest."

Or her own. She closed her notebook with a final thud and left the room.

Back at her desk ten minutes later, Claire tore at a fresh roll of antacids with shaking fingers. Not a good start, she thought, crunching two peppermint-flavored tablets at once. She had definitely chosen a battle, though not exactly the one she'd gone into the boardroom prepared to fight.

She leaned forward and began massaging her temples. Her gaze traveled over the few personal items she had placed on her desk: a crystal jar packed to the brim with gourmet jelly beans she never ate; a clay mug molded into a lumpy face, an assortment of pencils sprouting from its brown hair; and a silver picture frame.

The photographs encased in the double frame caught her attention. Her son's third-grade school picture, and another of him in a blue uniform, proudly clutching a soccer ball. She would have to call the local league and find out if there was a team in their neighborhood. As compensation for leaving San Francisco, she had promised to sign Tripper up for the sport of his choice, despite knowing the logistics involved would be a nightmare.

She wondered how his first day at his new school was going. Hopefully better than hers. Mr. Gonzalez, his teacher, had assured her he would have no trouble adjusting this early in the year. The fact that Tripper had a male teacher was a plus, in Claire's opinion. As a single mom, she had always made an effort to seek out male role models for her son, and Mr. Gonzalez had hardly raised an eyebrow when she responded with a terse "there's no father" to his question about the blank line on the enrollment form.

Fatherless kids were probably as common as untied shoelaces in schools these days.

Remembering the catastrophe she still planned to avert, she straightened, mentally tucking the part of her life labeled "motherhood" back into its compartment. She picked up the phone and summoned her office assistant, resisting the urge to pop another antacid into her mouth.

"I'm going to need rental rates for downtown commercial space," she said when Joan appeared. "And call the Philadelphia Film Commission and get a list of location fees for anything filmed here in the last three years. Then I'll need projected January sales for our downtown store, plus a list of employees." As she spoke, she jotted down each idea, each objection, and like a general with a foolproof battle plan, she felt her doubts all but disappear.

Joan lifted her eyebrows. "I heard they were thinking about filming a movie here, but I thought it was just another rumor." Then she grinned. "Last year, I heard Denzel Washington was in the store, getting the royal treatment. Turned out it was the fire inspector."

"Well, hopefully this will amount to nothing but a lot of smoke." Claire made a final note on her pad, and then she ripped off the page and handed it to Joan. As she turned to leave, Claire remembered: "Oh, by the way, I was told you're expecting a baby."

Joan glanced back at her, her look of surprise mixed with apprehension. "Yes, around March."

Claire's smile was warm. "Congratulations. I've made sure Personnel upgraded you to a permanent employee. You'll be covered under the family leave policy that went into effect this month." In the past, Kaslow's had often hired "temporary" workers for long-term positions in an effort to avoid paying them benefits, a practice that, in Claire's opinion, stank.

Joan seemed stunned. "I was told this job was classified as temporary. I thought I wouldn't be eligible for benefits."

Claire shook her head. "From now on, seasonal workers will only be hired in the retail side. Here in the corporate offices, we'll make every effort to hire permanent employees—and give them full benefits."

Joan's face broke into a smile. "I also heard a rumor you were trying to get a childcare center here."

Claire nodded. "Yes. Although we're not exactly sure where it will go."

"I know the perfect place—that old theater on the eighth floor. No one uses it anymore."

"That sounds feasible. I'll make a note to look into it."

Then, as Joan left, Claire's smile faded. She knew Joan wasn't married, a fact that, subconsciously at least, had probably prompted her to transfer her from reception to the position as her office assistant. She knew all too well the difficulties a single mother faced. If it hadn't been for her grandmother's support all those years ago, freely sharing her retirement pension as well as her time babysitting after Tripper was born, Claire never could have made it on her own.

She shuddered to think what the alternative would have been.

She turned to the work on her desk. The past was just that, and fortunately, she no longer needed to worry about where the next diaper was coming from. Now all she had to do was outwit this latest trick of Fate.

"Mom, are you sure I'm your son?"

Tripper's question stopped Claire in her tracks on her way to the refrigerator. She glanced over to where he sat at the pine dining table, staring at his school photos. They'd been taken before they left San Francisco and had just arrived in the mail. His face bore a puzzled look of introspection, a look she had often noticed. She assumed it was the inevitable result of being the only child of a single parent. Sometimes there was just too much time for thinking.

This time, though, his bout of nine-year-old introspection had backed him up the wrong path.

She laughed and answered lightly, "Of course you're my son, silly. You certainly aren't my daughter."

"Mo-om!" he protested, rolling his eyes at her attempt at humor. "I'm serious. We don't even look alike. Your hair's a lot darker than mine, and your eyes are—" he looked up at her face for confirmation "—sorta gray," he declared, then continued with his comparative analysis. "And you're not very tall for your age. I'm already almost your height. I bet I'll be a lot taller than you one day."

The incontrovertible proof of his mistaken parentage was offered solemnly, with all the thoughtful reasoning of a genetics expert.

"Hmm. You know, you're right," Claire agreed with mock seriousness as she took a seat across from him. "We look nothing alike. There was probably a mix-up of some sort at the hospital." She tilted her head, pasting a thoughtful look on her face, and mused, "Maybe my real son is out there somewhere, wondering why on earth he looks nothing like *his* mother."

Tripper heaved an impatient sigh. "You know what I mean." He gave her an accusing look, then said with blunt accuracy, "I look like my father, don't I?"

Claire's heart took a quick dive. He rarely brought up the subject, and she had begun to hope his questions would eventually cease altogether. She looked away, pretending to study the credit card bill that had arrived in the mail. "I suppose you do resemble him," she prevaricated, hoping to steer the discussion away from awkward territory. Carefully she refolded the bill, then inserted it into its envelope. "I need to start dinner. And it's past time for your homework, isn't it?" she said, rising from the table.

But this time, Tripper wasn't letting her off so easily. "How come you never want to talk about him?"

She was about to put him off again, but the sight of him looking up at her, his green eyes filled with confusion, sent her around the table toward her son instead of the refrigerator.

"Oh, Tripper!" Guilt tugged at her heart. "It's not that I don't want to talk about him; it's just that…there's nothing to tell. I've told you before, I hardly knew him." She tunneled her fingers through his hair, a maternal gesture that reassured her as much as it did him. She wished for the hundredth time the answers were simple enough to be understood by a nine-year-old, wished even harder she could assuage her guilt with a simple explanation.

"It doesn't matter who your father was or whether you're a dead ringer for him. You're an individual, Tripper, not a reflection of your parents." She believed that strongly and more than anything wanted her son to share that belief—even more than she wanted him to stop asking questions she wasn't prepared to answer.

Tripper stared stonily at her midsection, refusing to meet her eyes. He had heard this before, and Claire knew he had questions—and not just about his parentage, but hers as well, a subject she definitely wasn't going to discuss with him.

She nudged his chin up gently and gazed at him, his eyes finally turning toward hers. She resisted the urge to go all "sappy" on him—nine-year-old boys hated to be embarrassed more than they hated missing basketball shots at the rim.

"And as for who you look like," she said, smiling, "it wouldn't matter if you had green hair and purple eyes, you're still my son. I distinctly remember giving birth to you, so don't get any ideas about going off to join the gypsies.

"Now, why don't you cut out one of those pictures so I can take it to my office? We can mail the rest to your friends in San Francisco. Then you need to get started with your homework." With a last warning glance over her shoulder, she opened the refrigerator door and began looking for dinner ingredients.

# CHAPTER TWO

"Oh, hell." Matt Grayson stopped short at the sight of the two naked women lounging next to his swimming pool.

"A.J.!" he hollered, ignoring the beckoning looks cast in his direction. "Are these yours?" he demanded as a shorter, dark-haired man appeared, balancing three cocktails in his hands. He looked like the bed he had no doubt just crawled out of: unmade and rumpled.

"Oh, hey, Matt. I thought you were at your office."

"I am at my office. I'm working at home today." Matt nodded toward the two women. "These left over from last night, or did you recruit a new batch? And why are we serving them drinks at this hour of the morning? It's not even lunchtime," he said, taking the glass nearest him and sniffing its contents.

A.J. squinted against the full morning sun. "They're breakfast mimosas. You want one?"

"No thanks. I see you're still celebrating," Matt said dryly, the bubbles in the drink erupting as he swirled the liquid. The ink on A.J.'s divorce papers was scarcely dry, a divorce A.J. hadn't wanted. Matt realized he had simply turned to booze and bimbos in an attempt to dull the pain, but there was a limit to self-indulgence. Matt had served time in the same institution, and when his time was up — six months, to be exact—his family had, lovingly and firmly, pushed his butt squarely back into reality.

And now, ten years later, Matt was as immune to the insidious disease of self-indulgence as he was to diphtheria, though all around him in Hollywood it seemed to flourish. Hard work, he had found, both in the gym and on the set, worked a lot better than any drug yet invented.

He dumped the drink into the pool, then tossed a couple of beach towels to the perfectly matched centerfolds posing on his redwood lounge chairs.

"Time to go, ladies." Matt hooked his thumb toward the door. "And be sure and pick up your clothes on the way." He plucked another goblet from A.J.'s grasp, gave it a frown, then poured the pale liquid into the deep end. He would have to get the damned pool cleaned now. No telling what refuse had ended up in there during the impromptu party A.J. had thrown last night. Matt had stayed away, preferring the company at the billiard bar he had just opened to joining in his houseguest's party.

One of the women paused in front of him on her way toward the door and trailed a nail suggestively across his chest. "A.J. said you might give us an autograph later," she purred. "Leonardo DiCaprio once signed his name right here." She stroked her right breast suggestively. "Too bad you don't have an 'i' you could dot," she said, punctuating the words with a sexy giggle.

Matt tucked his tongue into his cheek and pretended to be intrigued by the suggestion. "Why, that's real smart of you, knowing how to spell my name and all," he said in his best Montana drawl. "But I better warn you—there's a female inside who's the real jealous type, and she's got teeth that can rip through shoe leather." He gave the silicone breast in front of him a look that could pass for regret, then took the towel still dangling from her hand and draped it over her shoulder. "You'd better hurry—she's almost finished with her breakfast."

Not sure if they'd just been insulted, the two blondes—at least one of them was a natural, Matt noticed—scurried off, throwing an identical pair of pouty looks over their shoulders as they disappeared inside.

Matt gave a sharp whistle, then shouted, "Sadie! Come on, girl, let's go for a swim!" A biscuit-colored missile of fur came charging onto the patio, aimed straight toward him, pink tongue dangling from the grinning mouth. Matt grabbed Sadie's front paws as they reared up, gave them a wag, then set her down firmly. "Watch that, or I'll start looking into obedience school!" he warned, meeting her adoring gaze head on.

"And a minute ago you were threatening to sic her on…" A.J. scratched his unshaven chin thoughtfully. "You know, I can't remember what they said their names were. Started with an 'S,' maybe. Sherry…Cherry…Did they look like twins to you?"

Matt sighed as Sadie splashed into the pool, spraying water on his pants leg. "Oh, hell. You've got to get a grip on this. Why don't you go call Maggie, see if you can get the kids this weekend? I've got to go to Philadelphia. You can have them over here."

A.J. shook his head, a morose expression crossing his face. "She's taking them to Carmel to meet his parents. The wedding's next month."

"Aw, fuck," Matt swore sympathetically. Thank God he had learned his lesson when it came to women. They had no equal when it came to ruining a man's life, and until he found one that he was sure wasn't capable of sending him to a shrink, he would fork out his affection on sloppy-tongued canines and women like Annie, whose interest in him was purely sexual.

"Oh, what the hell," he relented. "Let's have a beer. It's almost lunchtime anyway. I've got a meeting later, though — Karen and Marty are coming over. We're deciding on the locations for *Lyin' Hearts* before I head out east."

"Already? I thought you didn't start filming until after Christmas."

"Yes, but we need to know where we'll be shooting so we can pin down the schedule. Once the contracts are signed, we can start planning shots, draw up the storyboards."

A.J. shook his shaggy head in mock amazement. "Contracts? Storyboards? You're gonna lose your street cred once TMZ figures out America's Hottest Actor isn't just another pretty set of pecs. Steven Spielberg know you're horning in on his territory?"

"For now that's still our dirty little secret. At least until we pull the wrapper off GrayWolf."

A.J. let the glum look settle. "Next thing, you'll be a movie mogul and politicians will want to crash our parties."

Matt laughed, then whistled for Sadie. "I'll go get that beer. You want one, or are you planning to drink that sissy stuff?"

"Yeah, sure, I'll take a beer," A.J. said, then tipped up the glass and swallowed the rest of the mimosa. "Just getting my vitamin C," he muttered, following Matt inside.

Behind him Sadie scrambled out of the pool, her morning swim over as suddenly as it had begun. She paused for a fierce shake, painting the smooth Mexican tiles with pool water, then hurried after the man in her life.

Matt's office looked more like that of a cattle baron than an A-list actor. Only a few relics of his thirteen-year career hung on the walls: a movie poster from *Night Hawk*, the first film he had starred in; a framed photograph of him with Robert Redford, taken at the signing of environmental legislation designed to protect stretches of the Western mountain ranges; and a framed copy of his very first review, in which his performance was compared unfavorably with that of the bird playing opposite him.

Behind the Mission-style desk, Matt leaned back, studying the location photos in his hand. Marty Baker, the location manager, looked on, eager for a reaction, while Karen, the production designer for *Lyin' Hearts*, took the photos that Matt handed to her, glancing at them. She'd seen a similar set already from Marty's updates.

Though most of Matt's roles so far had been heavy on action, *Lyin' Hearts* would be a change of pace. A romantic comedy, it would rely on wit rather than weapons to make an impact. And not only was Matt starring in the film, but his fledgling production company had chosen this project for their first picture, and he had given himself the task of directing.

His balls were definitely on the block. He'd be risking his credibility for a low-budget, high-brow comedy. But the script was worth the risk, the film Matt envisioned worth protecting from outside scrutiny before it even got off the ground.

Amazingly, they had managed to keep news of the project from the press so far, which is one reason they were meeting in Matt's home instead of his office in Burbank. Officially, he was "taking a much-needed break from filming."

As an independent, their budget was low. So low, in fact, Matt himself was working for merely a share of the profits. If word got out that last year's top-drawing actor was even associated with the film, the budget would have to be bumped up, as everyone from suppliers to the film crew would demand a larger chunk off the top.

The pile of photos on the desk was growing as Matt examined, then discarded each one. He looked up, an eyebrow lifted in mild surprise. "I won't even ask how you managed to get into the ladies' room, Marty," he said. "Just tell me if it's as big as it looks. I hate shooting in cramped quarters."

"You could build a theme park in there," Marty replied. "And I've already asked for permission to use the chairs as props."

Matt studied the photograph closer. The delicate chairs — French Provincial was his uneducated guess — would provide the perfect contrast for the rough character he played in the film. He tossed the photo to Karen. "What do you think about that? It would save us some money on set decoration, wouldn't it?"

Karen was responsible for the total look of the film, from the design of the sets, to the wardrobe, makeup, and hairstyles of the actors. Matt intended to let her have the final say. Having been on sets where directors constantly second guessed every decision, he had decided his strategy would be to hire the best and then let them do their jobs.

Karen barely glanced at the photo. "They'll do. And that fountain there…" She pointed to another photograph, lying face up on the table. "I think it would be perfect for Scene Twenty, where Luke and Jane have the argument."

"It would have to be rewritten, but you're right, it would be the perfect backdrop." Matt glanced at the photo. "What's it supposed to represent, anyway? Some kind of goddess?"

"Fortuna, Roman goddess of Fortune."

"Is that right?" Matt grinned. "Let's hope she's smiling on us. I think we've got our prime location right here, Marty. Get the contracts signed. I want to be able to get in the place next week while I'm in town."

"We'll have to film in the evening, after the store's closed. I tried feeling them out about shooting in the daytime, but unless we blow our budget — "

"No problem. The shots will all be indoors, anyway." It would be hell on the crew, but sometimes after-hours shoots were necessary, especially for low-budget films. "Why don't you schedule it for the first few days we're there? We'll all still be on California time. That'll give us a cheap edge."

Marty nodded, jotting down the instruction on his notepad.

Just as quickly, the rest of their decisions were dispensed with. Marty and Karen left, leaving Matt alone with Sadie, who snoozed under the desk. Though he knew pre-production was a crucial part of the process, he itched to get the actual filming underway. It wouldn't begin for another two months, right after Christmas. If he was lucky, he could get in a few weeks at his ranch in Montana, the place he still considered home. The beach house in Malibu, an honest-to-God bachelor pad now that A.J. had moved in, was more a shelter for strays than home.

His latest stray was starting to wear on his nerves. A week in Philly wouldn't be so bad, provided he managed to keep his presence there a secret. To avoid attention, he had recently begun sporting the occasional disguise. With a week's worth of beard stubble, a pair of dark Ray Bans, and a baseball cap pulled low over his brow, he could pass for nondescript. Plus, the name "Roscoe Arbuckle" on the guest register never stirred interest at the better hotels.

He propped worn lizard-skin boots on the desk. He could just imagine the field day the tabloids would have if they knew he had played host to two naked nymphets last night. Though he had developed a Teflon skin over the years, he still hated the invasions of privacy that dogged him.

That was one reason his relationship with Annie worked so well. As a gospel singer who'd recently gone country, she had no wish to have her name associated with Hollywood's former bad boy. Consequently, she had worked harder than he to keep their affair a secret.

Contrary to popular belief, he'd never been as totally lacking in morals as everyone had assumed—not that it mattered much anymore. The scandal that had erupted in the early days of his career had turned out to be only a momentary stain on his reputation, dismissed with a "boys will be boys" shrug.

He had even managed to forgive himself, though occasionally, usually after a few beers, he still reflected on the whole sad affair.

The phone on his desk buzzed. It was Pam, his assistant. "I've faxed you the latest rewrites, and your press agent called. You're on *Letterman* next month—I went ahead and made the travel arrangements.

Oh, and the new *GQ* comes out around then—you're on the cover, remember? Should I call security and have them send over more bodyguards?" she added, her voice only half-joking.

Matt sighed. With fans sometimes thick as deep-woods mosquitoes, he had reluctantly begun traveling with a couple of beefed-up "friends."

"Just make sure my trip to Philadelphia stays under wraps—at least until the contracts get signed."

"You got it. We'll put out that you're in Montana at the ranch. One more thing—Laura Hayes called." Laura was his co-star in *Lyin' Hearts*. "She wants to talk to you about living arrangements on location. She's having trouble finding a place. I told her the house you rented had a couple extra bedrooms—"

"Sure, if she wants to bunk with me that's fine. I won't be around much anyway. Most of our locations are only available during odd hours. Just make sure she knows the press will have a feeding frenzy if they find out."

The thought of sharing digs with Laura didn't concern Matt. An easy friendship had already sprung up between them during their previous meetings. He made a point of not getting involved with his co-stars—nothing like a hard lesson learned.

After hanging up, Matt took the pages that had fallen from his printer, and started reading. Before he could get through the first page, Marty called from his cell phone. "Matt, you're not going to believe this."

"Try me."

"Kaslow's is balking. Apparently they've got some new tight-assed executive who objects to the idea of letting in the likes of us Hollywood degenerates."

"Send them the pages of the script that are set in the store. That should set their minds to rest. Just make sure they don't know who all is associated with this. If they think I'm involved, they'll have visions of explosions going off in Housewares."

"All right. I'll be meeting with them next week. If they don't go for it, I don't know what we'll do. There's really no other suitable place."

"They'll go for it. Offer more money if you have to—though with the publicity they'll get from this, they should be paying us a promo fee. Didn't you say they were close to declaring bankruptcy?"

"Actually, they've just been bought out. It's apparently the new owner's representative on the board who's throwing the objections at us."

"Find out who it is. We'll woo him if we have to."

"Her—it's a woman. Hey, maybe you should take a shot at it—"

"I trust you, Marty," Matt said dryly. "Do whatever you have to; just get it finalized by next Friday. I want to get in there before I leave Philadelphia."

"I'll see what I can do," Marty promised, then hung up.

The photos Marty had taken were still scattered on his desk. Matt gathered them up, intending to save them for Karen, who would use them to draw up the storyboards. Her job was crucial to the film's success. The look and feel—the *mise en scene*—was as important in this film as the characters. And this place was the perfect location to convey that. Even from the photos, he could see that Kaslow's exuded the kind of image called for in the screenplay.

Gleaming woodwork, elegant chandeliers, that huge fireplace in the men's department—all quietly proclaiming "Establishment," and all of it painted over with a thin layer of snobbery.

That attitude was the real villain in this picture and what had originally attracted Matt to the script. A lighthearted comedy on its surface, yet underneath it poked at certain attitudes of society with a subtle viciousness. The plot was simple, a Cinderella story turned on its heels.

Matt would play the down-and-out Luke, discovered sleeping in the ladies' lounge by Jane, a Main Line debutant. In a plan to fool her overbearing parents, Jane recruits him to be her "fiancé," and a farce ensues, a quirky twist on *Pretty Woman.*

Matt's attention caught on the photo in his hand. In one corner was the image of a woman, a severe figure dressed in black and clutching a briefcase. Probably an employee, he figured, and then an idea occurred to him. He picked up the phone and called Marty.

"Why don't we offer to use their salespeople as extras? They know the routine, and if it sweetens the deal…"

Stuck in Santa Monica traffic, Marty agreed. "Hey, after five years of location scouting, believe me, I've learned a deal can never be too sweet."

# Chapter Three

Claire gaped at the contract on her desk. GrayWolf had actually offered to cast some of the store's employees as extras! When word of that enticement leaked out, everyone from shoe clerks to janitors would be clamoring to be in the film. She could even imagine some of the board members preening before the camera.

And there were more incentives: Kaslow's name would be featured prominently in the film—Claire made a note to have them define "prominently"—as well as listed in the credits. In addition, they had asked to use the store's fixtures and merchandise as set decorations and props. Claire didn't need to ask for a definition there. Technically, a "prop" was anything an actor actually touched, while a "set decoration" was merely an object that appeared on screen.

Their costume designer would provide many of the clothes the characters would "try on." For a moment, Claire wondered if they would consent to feature only the brands the store carried. Then she shook her head firmly. She had no intention of actually allowing this intrusion, despite the very attractive terms of the contract.

And besides, Kaslow's would make a comeback financially without the help of Hollywood. Already, Marketing was working on some of the ideas she had brought up in their meeting. Though

Claire had been careful to refrain from appearing to butt in, her influence, as the person who effectively controlled the budget at Kaslow's, was considerable.

Joan stuck her head in the door. "This just arrived. It looks like the script for that movie." Her eyes were eager as she set the package on Claire's desk.

"It's only the scenes they want to shoot here," Claire explained. "When is my meeting with their representative?"

"Tomorrow at nine a.m. Are we going to sign the contract? I heard they're offering roles as extras to the employees."

"We haven't decided yet. And I believe they were only interested in using our sales associates—for authenticity," she said, her eyebrows raised skeptically. "Even then, there's hardly any guarantee that anyone will get screen time. Most film footage ends up on the editing room floor." Instantly she regretted the words. She was beginning to sound like the resident expert on motion-picture filming. "Would you get Garrett Brown on the phone? I want to hear what our legal department has to say about this."

"Certainly, Ms. Porter," Joan said and with an air of stifled excitement left the room. More than once during the last week, Claire had noticed Joan, a wistful look on her face, stuffing a movie magazine into her desk after her coffee break. Claire wished she could spare her the disillusionment. A career in Hollywood was about as glamorous as that of a Women's Wear mannequin.

After she was gone, Claire picked up the script and began reading. Occasionally a reluctant smile tugged at her lips. It really was a romantic comedy and, if she was any judge, a well-written one. Odd, she thought, that an unknown production company was producing a script of this caliber.

She tucked the pages under a spreadsheet of last week's sales figures. So far, every discreet inquiry she had made into the identity of GrayWolf Productions had come back unanswered. No one seemed to have heard of them. Claire was beginning to get the impression it was an upstart production company without a credit to their name. Hardly a threat to her peace of mind, but one she still wanted to keep out of her store.

The phone on her desk buzzed. Claire spoke with Garrett Brown, who agreed the contract was generous, though unusual. Apparently the identity of a filmmaker wasn't normally listed on the location contract, just the name of the production company entering into the agreement.

There were still plenty of questions, though. With a glance at the script, Claire reminded Garrett of their meeting tomorrow with Marty Baker. She only hoped the answers would show the deal to be more disadvantageous than the board could allow.

The traffic in Philadelphia was just sliding into a smooth rhythm after its rush-hour staccato. Matt glanced up from his notes as the car slid to a stop at a red light. He was touring locations with Jackson Li, the photography director.

The driver motioned toward the left. "Robert Indiana's *LOVE* sculpture."

They'd received permission to film one of the closing scenes there, in Logan Circle. As Matt gazed at the large red letters, the director's vision he had been honing all week kicked in.

"You know, Karen ought to talk to the weatherman, try to arrange a layer of snow for when we film there. What do you think, Jack?"

"Save the cost of special effects making the canned stuff," Jack said, then added thoughtfully, "And you're right: a white background would focus attention on the actors in the scene, highlight the stark letters of the sculpture." He gave Matt an appraising look. "You've got a good eye. You sure you've never done this before?"

Matt laughed. "No, but I'm still only one step ahead of the doubting Thomases. One misstep, and I won't get a job directing a used-car commercial."

His phone buzzed. Matt glanced at the screen, saw Marty's name, and answered.

Marty's voice was bleak. "I've gone to the line with the cash offer, Matt, ponied up every possible incentive, and still no dice. Kaslow's won't budge." He sounded like he was holed up inside a foxhole, armed with just an iPhone. "Their point woman, the CFO, is like some sort of accounting wizard. I swear she's got the last fifty years of Philadelphia location fees memorized, along with a few other facts and figures I'd never heard before. Even their attorney is starting to feel sorry for me."

Marty was as good at negotiating locations as anyone in the business, so Matt was surprised to detect a bit of awe in his voice as he continued, "The woman just reeks 'cool disdain.' You ever try to reason with a block of ice?"

Matt laughed. "You need to up the offer?" He quickly calculated. The cost of finding a new location, not to mention recreating the look that already existed at Kaslow's, would be more than double what they were offering.

"I don't think she'll go for that. She seems to think we're trying to shoot some kind of low-budget porn film. *Attention Kaslow's shoppers: Sex for sale on the fourth floor. Get it while it's hot.*"

"I sent the script—"

"Yeah, she says they get rewritten all the time."

"Well, that's true."

"Look, you said the cat will be out of the bag soon anyway. Any chance you could come by here, spring her in advance? Reassure these suits we're on the up and up?"

Matt sighed. He turned to the driver. "How far are we from Kaslow's?"

"It's just a few blocks from here, on Market."

"Then let's head over there. Marty says Kaslow's execs are still balking, and I'm ready to get something signed. If they won't come on board, we'll have to talk to Macy's."

"The nearest Macy's is in New York," Jackson informed him.

"Oh yeah? Think they'd consider moving?"

Matt sighed, then told Marty he would be there shortly. He'd handle the negotiations himself, cut through whatever bullshit the execs were giving Marty. As much as he hated throwing around his star status, sometimes it was the easiest way to pry open doors.

While they waited for Marty's boss to show up, Claire returned to her office to retrieve another copy of last year's sales figures. She had gone into the meeting armed to the teeth with objections, in the form of location rates, replacement costs for the valuable store fixtures, even estimated childcare expenses for the employees who would have to stay late to restore the premises after the film crew left.

When she returned to the conference room fifteen minutes later, she noticed a few office assistants fluttering near the door, their voices pitched high with nervous excitement. On the sofa in the reception area, a brawny man sat holding a cup of coffee. Claire ignored the commotion and strode into the room, clutching her rolled up sheaf of papers like a rocket launcher.

She spared a brief glance toward the newcomer. Instead of the short, balding, movie-mogul type she had expected, the man relaxing at the table was well-built. He half-reclined with panther-like grace, one denim-clad leg crossed over the other, his firm jaw carpeted with a casual stubble of light brown beard, his face shadowed by a low-slung sports cap. Before his identity could register on Claire's suddenly sluggish brain, she heard him speaking.

"We're planning to film in quite a few Philadelphia landmarks: the Art Museum, Independence Hall. Might even manage a quick set up at the Liberty Bell." His lips curved up in a lazy smile while the sound of that warm, deep-set voice washed over Claire with the viscosity of honey. She had heard it before. On the late-night talk shows, before she could change the channel. Once at the movie theater, when a trailer from one of his films was shown.

And occasionally in her dreams. The sound of that voice, that mouth, whispering to her…

A cry of alarm escaped her lips.

Every eye in the room focused on her. By sheer force of will, she gathered her scattered wits, commanded her heart to stop racing.

*Never let them see you sweat,* she repeated to herself, the words like a mantra in her frozen brain.

Somehow, her shaking legs carried her to the nearest chair. She sat staring sightlessly at the papers in her hand, frantically wondering if ten years was long enough to effect a sea change in one's appearance.

Not only was her name different, but surely there was no trace now of the naïve girl she had once been. Her appearance had altered drastically in the ten years since Matt Grayson had last laid eyes on her: No more fat-rollered curls rioted over her shoulders. The fresh-off-the-farm face she had been born with now bore a layer of expensive cosmetics. Her shabby jeans and T-shirts had been replaced by trim silk suits. And, even more importantly, her demeanor was no longer that of a shy, awkward ingénue. Clarissa Peters had transformed into a polished, sophisticated businesswoman, a new woman entirely, from the sleek chignon at her nape to the blunt tips of her pumps.

Matt Grayson would never recognize her.

Even so, she slipped the silver-rimmed reading glasses dangling from the chain around her neck onto her nose.

As the introductions were made, she could almost feel him staring at her. She composed her features in a mask of anonymity and lifted her gaze, confident her eyes held no sign of recognition. That bit of acting came easily, but then, it always had.

She met his stare, cool, composed, allowing no hint of fear in her expression. Across from her, his green eyes tunneled through the shadow cast by the cap's bill as he stared at her. Her tension mounted as she waited breathlessly for him to recognize her, and when that first moment passed, she breathed the tiniest sigh of relief.

She could pull this off, she realized, lowering her gaze to the papers in front of her once more. That is, if she could manage to ignore the pounding in her chest, the trembling of her fingers, and the fluttering of her stomach, unprepped by antacids.

Of course, Matt Grayson was probably used to that sort of reaction from women.

She heard Garrett Brown continuing the introduction. "Claire is new to the board here and has some concerns I'm sure you can address."

Before she could respond, Matt spoke up. "I'm not sure I can answer all her questions. Our production manager handles most of the financial decisions. But I think I can set your minds at ease regarding the content of the film. As Marty told you, this isn't an action adventure. It's definitely a kinder, gentler, picture. Think *Bridesmaids*. I brought a copy of the script." He pointed to a blue bound manuscript on the table. "No four-letter words, no guns, not even a nude scene."

Claire swallowed the bile in her throat and found her voice. "Scripts get rewritten all the time, Mr. Grayson. What guarantee would we have that something that starts out as innocuous as…as a Disney film doesn't eventually end up filled with scenes containing gratuitous violence or sexual content that we might find inappropriate?"

The atmosphere in the room chilled. Even old Earnest Kaslow, from his vantage point on the wall, seemed to be chiding the room's occupants.

Across from her, Matt twirled the cap he had pulled off his head. Then he gave her a slow smile, warming the chill in the air.

Claire looked away, not wanting to meet his eyes. Perhaps she was laying on the objections too thickly…Would he suspect anything?

But he answered her question, his voice as patient as when he'd coached her all those years ago. "We're not planning to film a sequel to *Showgirls*, Ms. Porter. *Lyin' Hearts* is a romantic comedy, the kind of film you could take your mother-in-law to see. It'll most likely snag a PG rating." He gave a brief synopsis of the film, the same studio pitch he'd have given to a producer—if he hadn't been producing the film himself.

Claire frowned. "All the same, you have to understand, Kaslow's is a well-known and respected name here in Philadelphia. You're proposing to use that name in your film, not to mention our premises. The potential for damages alone—"

Marty broke in, pointing to the unsigned contract in front of him. "We've agreed to take out a substantial insurance policy. That's standard practice when filming on location."

"Insurance wouldn't even begin to cover the cost of repairs should any of the store's architectural features be damaged, Mr. Baker. Many of our store fixtures were designed over a hundred years ago especially for Kaslow's flagship location. They are literally one of a kind."

They could attempt to recreate the look in a studio—preferably a studio in Los Angeles, three thousand convenient miles away. It would be expensive, but compared to what she was prepared to hold out for, it would be a bargain.

"What if we double the offer?" Matt Grayson said with a determination that surprised her. "Plus, we'll triple the amount of insurance we take out, and someone from the store can remain on the set to make sure we don't break anything."

"That certainly seems reasonable…" Garrett Brown began, looking toward her for approval.

She steeled her gaze. "It's out of the question. The disruption involved in turning our store into a movie set, even after hours, as you've proposed, would simply be too great. And as you can see…" She held up a few of the papers in front of her. "Even at double the amount, your offer is substantially low when compared with location rates paid on similar productions—by more prominent film companies."

"We'll triple it."

Then, before she could raise another objection, he went even further. "And we'll give you a point share of the profits. It could amount to a windfall, after foreign release, video sales, et cetera."

Marty Baker stifled a groan. And Claire wanted to scream. There was no way she could turn down such an offer—not without bringing unwanted questions, unwanted attention, to her own reasons for wanting Matt Grayson to stay as far away from her and her store as possible.

But then he added the coup de grace: "Plus, the store gets a prominent mention in the film. In fact, the script's being rewritten right now to include a scene set in the rotunda near that fountain, which I understand is some sort of local landmark."

Claire took a deep breath, briefly toying with the idea of strangling the goddess of Fortune. She managed a tight smile in his direction. "That's quite a generous offer. Still, there is more at stake here than money, Mr. Grayson."

"You're right—your store has a lot more than cash to gain. Just ask the folks along the Snake River in Idaho—tourism's booming ever since they filmed *A River Runs Through It*. And I hear property prices in Notting Hill have soared since Hugh Grant and Julia Roberts made out there."

Then he added dryly, "I doubt Kaslow's reputation would be hurt by being known as the place to meet members of the opposite sex."

Claire glared at him. She wanted to take his easy assurances and wrap them around his neck. The old anger, the almost forgotten hurt, began to creep through her. Her eyelids lowered. Then, before the images could come back full strength, she lifted her gaze and saw Matt Grayson watching her, a thoughtful expression on his face.

Suddenly, she knew she had to get out of there before ten years of camouflage melted away like the tip of a glacier, before Matt Grayson saw through her own disguise like glass and shattered her existence just as easily.

She gave him a stiff smile. "I can assure you that Kaslow's board will consider your request carefully. If you'd like to submit an amended copy of the contract, along with whatever script changes you propose, we will certainly take a look at it. I can't guarantee, however, that it will meet with approval." She stood up, surprised when her trembling limbs held firm. "Now, if you'll excuse me, I have work to do. I'm sure someone will escort you out." As she retreated, practically rushing from the room, she could feel their burning glares like a blowtorch aimed at her backside.

The men at the table cleared their throats. Matt wasn't sure what impulse had prompted his offer, unless it was an urge to overcome her objections in the quickest way possible. Cutting through the executive bullshit had given him a certain satisfaction, even if it had exploded the budget he'd been tending carefully.

Beside him, Marty stared forlornly at the contract in front of him, as if it had suddenly turned into a death notice. The attorney for Kaslow's finished noting the changes on the copy in front of him, then closed his pen with a satisfied click.

Matt stared after the woman who'd just left the room, feeling a prickle of awareness inch along his spine. Something about her didn't ring true, as if she were miscast for the part of uptight executive. His mind kept wanting to picture her in a different role…

Suddenly, he remembered why she looked familiar. The photograph that Marty had taken, the one with the woman dressed in black. It was the same woman, except, in the photo, he could have sworn her face had registered the faintest tinge of fear.

His lips curved into a satisfied grin as he stood to leave. Whatever had her running scared that day had obviously been outgunned, he thought, remembering her unwavering face from across the table.

Or else she was just a damned good actress.

In the relative safety of her office, Claire sank into the chair behind her desk. She braced her throbbing temples with fingers that still shook. The last person she had ever expected to see — in the flesh, that is — had just waltzed into Kaslow's as if he owned it. Matt Grayson, here in Philadelphia. In her store.

She took a deep breath. Now it was more imperative than ever to keep GrayWolf out of Kaslow's. If Matt Grayson recognized her… surely he would have said something if he had. Or was he as anxious to avoid stirring up the bad memories as she?

For her, it would mean her hard-earned reputation in shambles once again. Her position on the board was tenuous enough as it was;

if anyone realized the new executive at Kaslow's was better known for her exploits in the bedroom than the boardroom, her position would become unbearable. The respect of her coworkers was vital to her success. But one word from Matt Grayson…

And her reputation would be ruined, again.

Claire never doubted that she bore some blame herself for the disastrous events that led to her public disgrace. It had been her decision, after all, to go to Hollywood.

And her decision to sleep with Matt.

No, she had never blamed Matt for the aftermath — the horrible publicity that had resulted after the tragedy, most of it aimed at the "bimbo" who, with her "wiles," had lured the fiancé of America's sweetheart to her bed. Claire doubted she had ever possessed any wiles, but it was true she had been infatuated with Matt Grayson, and he had no doubt realized that and taken advantage of it. She really couldn't blame him.

After all, hadn't she done the exact same thing, only in the boardroom? Taking advantage of a company's weak position — their "fiscal naïveté" — was exactly what had landed her here. In a job that, ironically, had resulted in her coming face to face with Matt Grayson again after all these years.

Fortunately, though, Matt hadn't recognized her. Remembering his hardheaded insistence on using Kaslow's for the location of his film, she realized he had been more interested in getting what he wanted than in identifying the person across from him.

Clarissa Peters, for all her notoriety, had obviously failed to make much of an impression on Matt. Claire could almost feel insulted but for the fact she had so much to lose if he did recognize her.

Of course, she had changed so much. Not just physically, but inside. She could hardly believe she had once been that inexperienced girl who had fallen into Matt's arms.

So trusting, even though life had already taught her that people were rarely what they appeared. But she had thought Matt Grayson was different, a prince to her sleeping princess. A prince with so much to teach her, things she had been so very eager to learn.

Little did she know it was a poison apple she had been given, and she was not Snow White but the Wicked Witch, as the press had called her, making a mockery of the name Matt had once playfully called her on the set.

It was a bitter lesson, but she had learned it well.

Big juicy apples had rotten centers, the seven dwarves were on strike, and Prince Charming was already taken.

Best to rely on your own wits, she told herself as she stuffed folders into her briefcase and, for the first time in memory, left her office early.

# Chapter Four

From the refrigerator in his hotel suite, Matt snagged a beer, then settled on the down-stuffed sofa in the sitting room. The dark, rich brew quenched a thirst he hadn't realized he had. After a day spent previewing locations, readjusting the shooting schedule, and haggling with ornery executives, he had earned his paycheck, more so than on the days he spent filming in jungles and deserts.

He had gotten more than he had bargained for at the meeting with Kaslow's execs. Or maybe he had given more. Somehow he had found himself making concessions he had never intended, letting his emotions cloud his good sense. That was why he had cut short his football career at the University of Montana in favor of acting. In a clutch, Matt had always gone with his instincts, rather than the carefully arranged game plan the coaches had drawn up.

Now his instincts had him blowing his budget before filming had even started, all as a result of a boardroom duel with a hard-hearted hombre in a designer blouse.

The voice of the woman at Kaslow's still echoed in his mind, tapping at a long-ago memory. He often forgot faces, but voices stayed with him. The inflections, the accents, their unique rhythms. The way they reflected the speakers' moods.

And her mood had definitely been testy. He could still hear the chill in her voice, a chill that was mirrored in the ice floes of her eyes.

The voice from his memory, though, was softer, less distinct than the one challenging him in Kaslow's boardroom. Filtered by a southern drawl, slightly husky — that low-pitched purr that accompanies sexual satisfaction.

He closed his eyes, sliding deeper into the sofa, letting the images, the sounds, seep back into his memory. That voice moaning, a sexy little catch in the throat. His own voice groaning in response. A gasped, "Oh, Johnny."

His eyes flew open. *Johnny.*

"Oh, shit." His eyes narrowed as he stared unseeing at the beer in his hands. Vanessa. No, her name wasn't Vanessa, and his wasn't Johnny. Vanessa and Johnny were the doomed lovers they had played, roles that had eventually mirrored actual events all too eerily.

The image of her face, and more, appeared suddenly like a photograph in his mind. That hair, the black untamed wildness that smelled like honeysuckle. Eyes like soft gray suede. A smile that turned her cheeks into rose-tinted apples and his insides to jelly.

He raised the beer to his mouth again, remembering. It had been a long time ago. Ten years, he figured. What was Clarissa Peters doing now? What had ever become of her?

Then recognition struck, bright as a kick light. The hair was scraped back and lassoed with a clasp now, her eyes granite hard but still gray. Her face was leaner; the lips stiff, not nearly so inviting. But the voice was the same. Oh, it certainly used different words now. Harder, stronger, more confident. But ten years and a thick layer of sophistication couldn't alter vocal chords, and he distinctly remembered her voice whispering against his throat.

The wide-eyed innocence he had found so appealing was gone, but then, that was to be expected. There had been a time when he even believed it had never been there, that it was all an illusion that had roped him in like a bleating calf.

Now she possessed more potent weapons. Her seat on Kaslow's board put her directly in a position to stop him from filming there.

He stared at the beer bottle in his hand. It all added up — why she had been so determined to thwart their plans. If Claire Porter really was who he thought, then it was no wonder she didn't want him around. She had obviously changed her name, altered her appearance and mannerisms enough so that no one would recognize her.

He wondered how she had managed to make it so far up the corporate ladder. But then, one of the things he had been drawn to was her intelligence.

His eyes narrowed. Thoughts of today's skirmish faded as he wondered just how to confront her with his knowledge. First thing tomorrow morning, he decided, he would call on the former Clarissa Peters. They were long overdue for a morning-after squaring of accounts.


The next morning Claire had just begun to imagine she was in the clear when the phone rang. She picked it up, and her heart skipped a beat as she recognized the voice on the line.

"This is Matt Grayson," he said, as if she could mistake that voice. "I was wondering if we could meet."

"I don't think that would be a good idea, Mr. Grayson."

"Call me Matt. After all, you used to, *Clarissa.*"

At the sound of the name, her throat closed up, her hand clammy on the receiver.

He knew. She didn't say a word, couldn't, and then she swallowed and cleared her throat. "I—I think you may have misheard. I-It's Claire. Claire Porter."

He gave a short laugh. "Cut the crap. It took me a while, but I finally figured it out. You're Clarissa Peters. Though, I have to admit, you've changed. A lot."

"I really can't talk now—" she began, but he stopped her.

"Then tell me when we can meet."

"That—that would be inadvisable."

She heard him sigh. "A phone call, Clarissa." He emphasized the name. "That's all it would take. I could find out where you live, show up on your doorstep—the husband doesn't know, I take it."

"I don't have—" Too late she realized it might be better to let him think she was married. "You seem to be misinformed," she said firmly. "I'm not this Clarissa—who did you say?"

For a moment, the line was silent, and she was beginning to think he had fallen for her ruse, but then he spoke. "Then tell me why you're so damned eager to keep us out of your store."

"That's very simple. It's a bad business decision. As I explained yesterday, the inconvenience, the possibility of damage…" Her voice trailed off as she scrambled for another reason.

"Ah yes," he said, smooth satisfaction in his voice. "You always were concerned about the bottom line, weren't you, Clarissa? That's the only reason you agreed to take your clothes off for the camera, if I recall correctly. You wanted more money."

Now it was her turn to be silent. Finally she spoke, her voice bitter. "You've got your facts wrong, Mr. Grayson."

"I don't think so, *Miz* Peters."

"It's Porter," she said, feeling an urge to sharpen her claws on his flesh. "And I would appreciate it if you would keep your suspicions to yourself. This has nothing to do with the current transactions."

"It has everything to do with the *current transactions*. And no, I can't promise you I won't blow your cover — unless you agree to meet with me. How about, say, in an hour? My hotel room?"

"No."

He sighed. "Then I'll call your boss — that would be Mr. Kaslow, wouldn't it? Mention I knew you once — " Claire heard him chuckle over the phone. "Implying of course, that as a former *girlfriend* and all, you're probably not the best person to negotiate with me on this."

She swallowed, feeling trapped. But then, she reminded herself, she had gotten out of worse scrapes before. "All right. I'll meet you. But not at your hotel room." She thought quickly. "The store doesn't open for another hour. Come to the service entrance on Tenth Street; take the freight elevator to the seventh floor. My office is just past the elevator entrance. If anyone asks, you can explain you're checking out the location for…storage."

"All right. I can be there in fifteen minutes."

"Twenty," she said, just to be obstinate. And to give herself more time to compose herself.

"Twenty minutes," he agreed, and for a moment, Claire remembered how easygoing he had once been. Apparently she wasn't the only one who had changed.

Twenty minutes later, Claire stood gazing out the bare window behind her desk. She had sent Joan off on an errand that should keep her occupied for an hour. And, fortunately, her office was located near the end of the corridor, near the freight elevator — in fact, she used it often when she was in a hurry. There was little chance Matt would run into any of the other store personnel on his way here. Still, she felt as if she were inviting a mountain lion over for breakfast.

Maybe she should have faked her own death…

*Stop it*, she told herself. This was just going to be one of those "haven't seen you in a long time, how've you been" kind of things. He'd probably try to twist her arm over the contract, but she'd had her arm twisted before, to no effect.

She sat behind her desk, staring at the open door as she composed her features. When she heard the heavy clang of the elevator doors, her throat went dry.

She could always move to Mexico…Surely there were cultural advantages to living in a foreign country. And they did have soccer there. Tripper could easily learn Spanish—

*Oh, my God, Tripper!* Her gaze flew to the photograph on her desk. She could hear footsteps in the hall as she grabbed the frame with a shaking hand. But before she could open a desk drawer and shove the damning evidence inside, Matt appeared at her door.

Claire hid the frame in her lap. She looked up at Matt in the doorway, her expression carefully blank. He *had* changed, she realized, filled out, grown broader, his features more handsome with another ten years added to his age. As he walked toward her desk, wearing jeans that looked more suited to the range than to the office, she realized one thing about him hadn't changed: He still exuded sex appeal the way most men sweat. Effortlessly, gracefully—and to Claire, at least, dangerously. Though she was in absolutely no danger of falling for his brand of sex appeal again. As she had discovered, on the few dates she had found time for in between climbing the corporate ladder and raising a son, she was now practically immune to the appeal of the opposite sex.

She gave him the same smile she would give her dentist and, without a trace of nerves, said, "I see you were able to find it with no trouble."

"Yeah, I'm starting to feel right at home in freight elevators. I've been using the one at the hotel."

"Why all the secrecy?" She opened her desk drawer and as unobtrusively as possible slid in the photograph frame while he sat in the chair across from her desk.

He settled his green gaze on her. "That's funny. I was just about to ask you the same question."

Claire looked away. She had rehearsed her answer, yet now, the words seemed to have been spirited away by a band of butterflies. "I don't know what you mean," she finally said.

"Clarissa Peters. That's who you are. Or should I say 'were?'"

Claire shook her head. "I was never Clarissa Peters."

Before she could explain, he pounced on her statement. "Come on. You've changed a bit in the last ten years, I'll admit, but I never forget a voice." Dark amusement crept into his gaze. "Especially one that's whispered sweet nothings in my ear."

She resisted the urge to toss the jar of jelly beans at him. Instead, she tossed him a frosty glare. "Clarissa Peters was a stage name. I never intended to have an acting career, so I invented the name. The acting job was simply a way to earn some easy money—at least, I thought it would be easy." The bitter thought twisted her lips. What a naïve ninny she had been. "It was supposed to help with expenses for grad school."

"I remember you told me you wanted to go to grad school. MBA, right?"

She nodded.

"So you were really 'Claire' all along." He seemed satisfied with that. But his next words were a shock. "I tried to contact you."

"Oh? Whatever for?"

"What do you mean, 'whatever for'? To see if you were all right, to see if you needed anything—"

"What on earth could I possibly have needed—except anonymity?"

"Hell, I don't know. I just know I tried, and your agent said he didn't know how to get in touch with you. I even tried calling all the Peters in the Oklahoma City directory."

Claire refused to feel any satisfaction at his words. There had been a time, briefly, when she would have given anything to hear that he had been concerned. But now, the words were too late. "Well, that's very touching," she said coldly.

Matt's eyes remained level, and for a second, she thought she saw regret. "You really have changed, haven't you?" he said quietly.

Claire didn't reply.

He looked away, taking in the well-trimmed office. A painting of the store hung on one wall, along with her master's diploma. Then she saw his eyes rest on the credenza, at a photo of her brandishing a tennis racket.

"It looks like you've done pretty well for yourself."

"Well enough," she agreed.

"I never would have pictured you here." He shrugged. "I thought you were…more of a country girl, maybe. Not so many hard edges back then."

Claire raised her eyebrows. "You hardly knew me 'back then.'"

"I wouldn't say that." He grinned wickedly. "I thought we got to know each other pretty well, in fact."

Claire couldn't tell if he was mocking her. "Having sex with some-one hardly constitutes 'knowing' them—not in the usual sense of the word."

"Maybe you're right. I didn't even know your real name, much less anything else about you. As I recall, I did most of the talking when we were together."

She shifted her gaze, remembering against her will. It was true, she had encouraged him to talk about himself. And she had listened, wide eyed, as he shared anecdotes about his family back in Montana. It was as if he were talking about life in the Australian outback, so different was the life he described from hers.

She lifted a shoulder. "I suppose I was something of an introvert."

"An introvert?" He laughed, incredulous. "The next day you were taking your clothes off for the camera!"

"On your advice, I might add!"

"I agreed with the director that it was crucial to the scene. But you could have refused. No one would have blamed you."

"Oh, for God's sake! How can you be so hypocritical?"

"*I'm* hypocritical? You were the one acting as if you had never taken your clothes off in front of a camera." His lips twisted in irony. "Imagine my surprise when all those photos turned up."

"They were doctored! I've never posed nude before!" She felt color flame along her throat. "I modeled lingerie—demure bras and panties for a staid department-store catalog."

Her hand covered her mouth as she remembered the shame, the mortification she'd felt when she'd seen what the tabloids had done with those photos. It was those photos, taken during a modeling gig to earn extra money, which had landed her the role of Vanessa. The photographer had mailed them to his friend, a Hollywood agent. A few weeks later, Claire found herself on the set of *Bed of Roses*, filling in for an actress with a drug problem, and she was as unprepared for the minor role as she'd been for an affair with an up-and-coming actor named Matt Grayson.

When Matt spoke, his voice was quiet. "So you got screwed. First by me, then by the press."

"That about sums it up," she said lightly, swallowing the bitterness.

"For what it's worth," he told her, "I had no idea they had come down so hard on you. It was a while before I got around to even reading the papers. When I finally did, they had already crucified you — us," he amended.

Claire closed her eyes, wishing he would stop digging up memories better left buried.

"We were both branded with the scarlet A, weren't we?" Matt laughed. "Despite the fact Hayley and I weren't even married."

She hadn't known of his relationship with Hayley James at the time she met him; she was shocked when she read about it in the papers later. She hadn't wanted to believe it, but remembering the last time she had seen Matt, slumped in the chair at the police station, so racked by grief he hadn't even noticed her, Claire had no choice but to accept it. It had hurt at the time, but after reading the full account of their love affair in the papers, she had understood. Or thought she had.

"There were rumors, later," she said finally, curiosity getting the better of her. "That you had been married in Vegas. Before the film began."

He chuckled, shaking his head. "And last month I was supposedly shacking up with Snooki," he said, then sobered. "Claire," he continued, earnestly, "there are a lot of things you don't know, things about my relationship with Hayley."

She waved a hand, as if batting a pesky fly. "It doesn't matter. It was a long time ago. Believe it or not, I've managed to forget all about it," she said with a careful little laugh.

"Oh yeah? All of it?" He gave her a calculating look, and she realized he was a more experienced opponent than she'd thought yesterday. "That's why you don't want us here, isn't it? Because you don't want it all dredged up again."

She gave him a cool look. "There are lots of reasons I don't want your film crew in my store. Most of them have nothing at all to do with what happened ten years ago."

"Come on. It's a damn good deal for your store," he argued. "Especially after the perks I threw in yesterday."

"I disagree. Just the thought of having a film crew in here…" She shuddered. "My God, the potential damage to the premises alone is—"

"The only damage you're worried about is to yourself," Matt declared. "You've built a nice, tidy life here, haven't you? And now you think all that will come crashing down around your pretty little ears."

"Oh, please. I can do without the sexist comments."

"Sexist comment?" He started to protest, then lowered his voice suggestively. "Honey," he drawled, "if you want to hear a sexist comment—" He lingered for a moment on the V of her neckline.

She could feel her cheeks stain pink. She wanted to scream but settled for sending him a look designed to chill boiling lava.

He leaned over the desk, his green eyes too warm, too knowing. "What happened to you? Where's that passionate, vibrant creature who melted the camera lens every time she let out a breath? What happened to the warm-blooded woman I couldn't seem to keep my hands off of—even though I knew I should?"

He raked a hand through his hair in frustration. "Goddamn it, Claire, you used to be a living, breathing woman, not some…bloodless statue that belongs in the art museum."

"How dare you," she said, holding her voice still despite her trembling knees. "What right have you to come here and accuse me of lacking something—some vital ingredient—when you're the one who obviously lacked any kind of morals? You slept with another woman when you were engaged to be married—"

"That's not true," he said, cutting her short. "We had talked about marriage, sure, but that was before—" He stopped, as if reluctant to divulge all the details of his and Hayley's relationship, a relationship that had been dissected thoroughly in the press after her death. "Oh, hell, what difference does it make now?" He turned away, his gaze landing on the painting of Kaslow's fountain.

"None whatsoever," Claire said briskly, wishing he would leave before any more damage was inflicted. "As I said, I've put it all behind me. Gone on with my life. I would prefer to have no more reminders."

He turned to face her. "Sorry, but I'm not going to disappear, at least not for the next few months. I've got a film to make here. After that, I'll be crawling back to the 'den of iniquity' you seem to think I inhabit. All I want is a few days' access to this place."

Claire could only stare at him, astonished.

"I'll make sure I stay out of your way," he went on, ignoring her outrage. "No one from the crew will realize who you are. Hell, it took me a few hours to catch on, you've changed so much."

"You honestly think I would let you—"

"You're not the only one on the board. The others seemed more than ready to sign on the dotted line."

It was true, she knew. Especially after they got a glimpse of the reworked contract.

He noticed her hesitation. "It's a great deal for Kaslow's. And I'm sure your lawyers have been over that contract like bees on a honeycomb. As soon as your board approves it, I'll be out of your hair."

She closed her eyes, a feeling of resignation creeping through her. There really was no argument she could make, at least not one that would be convincing. And with the stakes so high, much higher than he knew, she couldn't afford to raise his suspicions further.

But maybe she could salvage a guarantee.

She tilted her chin, giving him a calculating look. "I don't want the press anywhere near while you're filming. We've just gone through a rather unpleasant buyout here, aside from the fact that I would prefer for personal reasons to remain…anonymous."

"No problem. I was planning on having a closed set anyway."

"And everything else we discussed?"

He raised his hand, as if swearing. "Every last 'i' dotted."

"And you'll keep absolutely quiet about…our past relationship? I mean you'll tell no one, not your best friend, your mother, your girlfriend—"

He gave her a sheepish look, then admitted, "I was bluffing earlier about calling your boss. Your secret's safe with me. Although I still think we ought to…" He paused but then apparently decided to ignore any impulse to dig deeper. "I'm not going to blow your cover. You've got my word on that."

She believed him, though she couldn't fathom why. There was just such an honesty about him, a non-negotiable code of ethics, and when she remembered that she was the one on shaky ethical ground, she blinked.

"You keep your end of the deal, and I'll have the contracts signed today."

"Great. I'd like to get inside tonight, after the place closes. Look around, set up shots."

She only had to think a moment before agreeing to the request. The sooner he got out of town, the sooner she could breathe easy. "I'll make sure there's someone to let you in. I take it there's no more need for secrecy?"

"Actually, as long as you can keep this to yourself, I'd appreciate it. As soon as word gets out I'm involved in this project…" He shrugged. "All hell tends to break loose. You know how it is."

Unfortunately, she knew all too well. She agreed, then rose from her desk to escort him from the room. As he passed her secretary's desk, she called out from the doorway. "Matt."

He stopped, his hand on the door.

"I…I just wanted to say…this is probably a little late," she said, settling her gaze somewhere in the vicinity of his knees. "But I just wanted you to know…I'm sorry. About Hayley. I read that she was… pregnant when she died."

"You didn't have to read it. She made it pretty clear just before—" He stopped, a bleak look shadowing his face. "Remember? You were there too."


When he was gone, Claire stood frozen by the door. Then she whispered to no one: "No, really, Matt, I don't remember."

# Chapter Five



Claire looked around the conference table, noting the attentive demeanor of the other board members. It was the first board meeting of the new year, and finally, she felt she'd been accepted as a real member of the team, not just a watchdog for the Forrest Group.

She had counted only one yawn, one surreptitious glance at a watch, and one nervous fidget since she began speaking. She settled her gaze on Bernard Kaslow at the head of the table and directed her remaining comments to him.

"If we want to capture the shopper's attention, we have to offer exclusivity. They can always get similar products at a lower price from the discounter selling out of a concrete box. But if they want a shopping experience that includes our own unique amenities — concierge service, designer chocolate kiosks, free alterations, customer delivery, comfortable chairs in the retail areas — then we have a chance at grabbing them.

"And if we offer exclusive products," she continued, "a brand of jeans no one else carries, or a line of cookware not stocked in the other department stores, for example, we can count on a return visit. But our buyers must have first-hand knowledge of what the customer wants, to prevent future markdowns that are killing our profit margin."

And that was the bottom line. The different department heads were so often intent on maximizing their own department's performance that they forgot the reason they existed in the first place. Claire saw it as her job to make them aware of the overall picture whenever possible, a task that often overlapped boundaries. At various times she found herself expounding on the intricacies of marketing, the esthetics of store design, or the finer points of customer service, but she constantly emphasized the bottom line.

"Aren't we shooting ourselves in the foot by operating Kaslow's Closet at our downtown store?" Chester Wheaton asked. "Our customers have to know they can sooner or later find an item marked down in the basement."

"I agree." Evan Kaslow sent a snide smile around the table. "We're giving customers a mixed message: Shop our store for quality, and buy your bargains in the basement."

"Yet it still gets that price-oriented customer into the store," Claire replied, resisting the urge to recite the retail statistics she'd learned in Management 101. "She may browse through the basement, but when she sees what exciting things are happening upstairs, she'll stop and linger. Spritz on our exclusive perfume, schedule a visit to the fifth-floor spa, sit in our comfortable chairs and enjoy the string quartet on Thursdays. Shopping at Kaslow's is still the best entertainment in town."

"That will certainly be true this week," Bob Berry inserted. "Too bad we can't leave the store open while Matt Grayson is filming here. That would bring the customers pouring in."

Chuckles of agreement echoed around the table.

Claire's reply was sharper than normal. "Stargazers, not customers. More interested in getting an autograph than checking out our new spring apparel."

The head of security, Leon Griffin, looked up. "That reminds me…We've got a potential problem as far as security's concerned.

There'll be upwards of a hundred of their crew roaming the premises. They're providing their own security, but they don't know the first thing about inventory control. I'm afraid our merchandise will start walking out of here."

He addressed his comments to Claire, who, as a result of the successful negotiations in October, was now the unofficial point person for any concerns regarding the filming. She didn't mind; in fact, she preferred having at least some measure of control over the operation.

"Make sure the most expensive items remain locked in their cases," she answered. "And our CCTV will be up and operating, I assume?"

Leon nodded. "The problem is, they want access to the whole building. They'll be holding the extras in our auditorium, using our lounge areas and fitting rooms, moving equipment in our service elevator — there's no way to monitor the entire situation, even with closed-circuit TV."

"Post security personnel outside the main entrance and lock the other doors. If anything suspicious leaves here, have them demand to check it out. Remember, these aren't customers we have to worry about offending," Claire pointed out.

Evan spoke up. "You seem to have a poor opinion of anyone associated with Hollywood. I guess for someone who grew up in… Oklahoma was it…?" He lifted his brow in question. "It all must seem very…depraved."

Claire gave him a cool look over her wire reading glasses. "You'd be surprised the degree of depravity I've seen in the boardroom, Evan. Which is exactly why I don't trust anyone, regardless of whether they're from Hollywood or Antarctica, to stroll around millions of dollars of merchandise unsupervised."

"Then you'll be happy to know I've asked my secretary, Lee Ann, to stay late to keep an eye on things."

Claire sighed. Lee Ann was hardly equipped to put a stop to an invasion of army ants, much less shoplifters. And if the office gossip she'd heard was true, Lee Ann was mainly interested in sleeping her way up the corporate ladder.

"Then make sure she has a pass. No exceptions, not even for employees." Claire shut her notebook with a thud that, she hoped, indicated the discussion was over.

Shortly afterward, Bernard Kaslow ended the meeting, and Claire tucked her pen into her briefcase. The next week would be a logistical nightmare, for the film crew as well as store personnel. She cringed at the thought of the cast and crew traipsing through the hundred-year-old corridors, but most of all she dreaded the presence of the film's star. Her number one concern would be to stay out of his way and hope he in turn stayed out of hers.

On the way out, she was stopped by Evan. "Got a minute? I want to talk about the new Atlantic City store."

"There's not going to be a new Atlantic City store. We discussed that in our last board meeting, and it was voted down. Remember?"

"It was voted down because you were against it. A word from you…" He trailed off, the cold smile on his face not as charming as he no doubt meant it to be.

"That's not true. Yes, I presented information that convinced the majority of the board members that it was a foolhardy idea at this point, but I was hardly the only voice in opposition."

"Still, if you were to change your mind…"

"And why would I do that?"

"I've worked up some new figures — new sales projections, building estimates — that you really should see."

Claire frowned. "Send me a copy. I'll take a look at them." She began to move away, but Evan took a step back, blocking her path.

"I'd rather discuss this now. In person." The smile was gone, replaced by a tense frown.

"I'm sorry. I don't have time now to hear what should have been presented a week ago, if your figures are even valid." She resisted the urge to step back, out of the range of his cologne. Evan was a bully, but she didn't give in to bullies. Not anymore. "As I told you then, we can't afford another capital outlay at this point, not with the Cherry Hill store still not showing a profit. Plus, the board agreed to put our building funds into the Market Street renovations."

"I really think you'll regret your decision." A thin film of sweat clung to his upper lip. Desperation didn't sit well on his Armani-clad shoulders.

"It was the board's decision," Claire pointed out. "Take the case up with them. I'll take a look at the figures, but right now, I'm busy," she said sharply, then moved around him.

Evan had been unusually vocal in backing his pet project, so much so that Claire wondered if there were another reason he was so desperate to have the Atlantic City store added to the Kaslow's chain. Perhaps it was the proximity to the casinos — she'd noticed his taste for risky gambles in the past.

But Claire took risk management very seriously, which was why she'd be glad when the next week, and the risk that Matt Grayson posed to her life, was over.

"Print it," Matt called from his spot next to the video assist monitor. This was the third take of this particular setup and the first one in which the extras had hit their marks. So far, things had gone well. And it was only midnight.

Laura was giving a great performance as the snobby Jane. That elegant nose seemed to tilt upward, as if drawn by a magnet. Eventually Jane's demeanor would mellow, after a few days in the company of "Luke."

Laura glided over to him, still in character. "Matthew, you simply must let me do that again." Then her voice dropped to its normal tone. "My stupid heel caught on the edge of the carpet."

"You were out of camera range. I saw it. But we'll do it again anyway for close-ups." He turned to one of the production assistants hovering nearby. "Heather, get that carpet taped down. We don't want any accidents."

Laura leaned against a marble column and looked around. "This place is fantastic, isn't it?" she said, taking in the opulence. "And the men's department — that fireplace is amazing. Are we going to have it lit for our scene there?"

"Sure are," he said, watching the camera operators return their equipment to the original positions. "And we've already alerted the fire department — and supplied the folks upstairs with plenty of aspirin. I imagine the thought of us playing with matches in their flagship store is giving them headaches."

Laura eyed him with interest. "I heard you had to do some pretty fancy negotiating to even get us in here."

He shrugged. "I think they had the idea we'd wreck the place." He watched a member of the crew carefully place duct tape on the underside of the carpet — probably worth thousands, he figured, hoping the fears he mocked didn't come true. He could just imagine the glee with which Claire would bill them for the damage.

Laura laughed. "They must have thought we were filming a sequel to *Jungle Fever… 'Retail Hell.'*" She threw out an arm in a dramatic gesture, barely missing a nearby display of hats. "I can see it now: You have a shootout with the bad guys on the escalators, then lunge over the cosmetic counter just in time to save me from the evil perfume spritzer."

Matt chuckled at her enthusiasm. "Write the screenplay. Maybe it could be a sequel to *Lyin' Hearts.*" Then he noticed that Mimi, the assistant photographer, had moved the close-up camera in place. "Places," he called, then walked over to peer through the camera's viewfinder. "Perfect. Cue the extras. Heather, we want quiet on the set. Sound—you're on."

Mimi snapped the electronic clapboard to begin the next take.

It was seven a.m. when they finished the scene. They had spent over nine hours setting up and filming for what would probably be less than five minutes screen time. It was a crucial five minutes, however. It established Laura's character as a young woman of discriminating tastes and the wealth to back them up.

Laura was nothing like her character. And though Matt was enjoying her company, he felt no romantic stirrings for her. In fact, if he had had to choose a little sister, she would have been his first choice. Laura, too, seemed to look at him more as a friend and adviser than a potential shower partner.

As he walked back to his makeshift dressing room on the third floor, he couldn't keep his thoughts from skipping back to another young actress, who had once looked at him with similar trust. But that innocent admiration had quickly erupted into more, flaring up into a fierce passion that still gave off a thin wave of heat, even after ten years. No other woman had ever affected him like that, so instantly and completely.

As the elevator doors opened, he wiped a hand over his face, disgusted with himself. It was useless feeling lust for a girl who no longer existed. All traces of Clarissa had been wiped out and replaced by the stern executive upstairs. At least, he thought they had. Somewhere underneath those tailored business suits and the prissy coiffure, was there a passionate woman itching to get out?

He smiled at the thought, though a part of him wanted to head for her office and shake the starch right out of her. The sane part of him, the part that had learned long ago not to follow those wild impulses, warned him not to. One film had already been shelved because he couldn't keep his hands off Claire Porter, and he wasn't about to risk this one.

Besides, he was thirty-six years old, too old to react like an awkward adolescent hard up for girls. He should call Annie, see if she could fly out and spend a weekend in Atlantic City—naked.

He passed by the windows overlooking the city street below, just coming to life. Heather had told him snow was in the forecast. That should cool his jets—plus, the second unit could get the outdoor shots they needed. Obediently, his mind turned back to the business at hand, but it was a while before his body remembered he was no longer wild about Claire Porter.

And lingering in the back of his mind were a dozen questions he still wanted answered.

# Chapter Six

"You are the type of woman we had in mind when we developed this fragrance. Very elegant, *trés chic.*" M. Lemond gazed across the table at Claire, an appreciative gleam in his eyes.

The representative from the French perfume maker was living up to the reputation of his countrymen. Claire ignored his heavily accented flattery and moved her fruit plate to the side, replacing it with her notebook. They were having a breakfast meeting in the sixth-floor restaurant.

An exclusive deal to sell a new line of fragrance was a retailing coup. Not only would such a deal establish Kaslow's cachet among East Coast retailers, but the expenses were shared by both the manufacturer and Kaslow's, making the product one of their most profitable.

Claire normally wouldn't have been the sole representative from Kaslow's at this meeting, but Evan Kaslow had cancelled at the last minute and Monsieur Lemond couldn't reschedule. The possibility of getting exclusive rights to market the new perfume from famed perfumier Mme. Bendel was too tantalizing an opportunity to let slip, so Claire had offered to meet with Bendel's representative by herself.

The financial details had been worked out with no problem; it was the marketing aspects that he insisted on controlling.

She jerked her attention back to what he was saying.

"You see a very elegant woman at the office, who is perhaps, how do you say, not so uptight at home?" His dark eyebrows raised suggestively over a pair of frankly admiring eyes.

She smiled and refrained from mentioning that flattery would get him nowhere. What she wanted to hear was how they intended to cooperate with Kaslow's when it came to promotion. "Our Marketing department has come up with several ideas," she began. "Full-page ads, samples enclosed with credit card bills—"

"No, no, no," he interrupted. "That is out of the question. We don't want our product associated with such an unpleasant experience as opening a bill."

Claire hid a smile. He did have a point, not to mention the fact that credit card bills often went straight to accountants, who weren't likely to purchase expensive perfume for their clients.

Monsieur Lemond stroked his thin mustache. "Macy's has offered to display our product at the store's entrance. They've also invited our signature model to launch the campaign," he informed her.

With a cool nod, Claire volleyed, "And we'll do the same, except…" She recalled an article she had read in *Advertising Age*. "Perhaps the entrance is not the best place to make an impression. When people walk in off the street, the first thing on their minds is finding the location of the item they've come to purchase. It's while they're browsing the aisles that a well-placed product display has the potential to capture their attention, maybe spur an impulse purchase. While they're searching for the hard-to-find gift, a small kiosk featuring your perfume may be just the thing."

He looked interested. "Perhaps you are right."

"And"—Claire went out on a limb—"why don't we have Madame Bendel herself visit the store for the kick-off promotion? I'm sure the local press would be interested in covering the event." And Jackie would turn cartwheels across the boardroom at the prospect.

Monsieur Lemond hesitated. "I'm not sure Madame could be persuaded to come to America. She rarely leaves Paris these days."

"Of course, it was just an idea." But Claire wondered if there were some way to sell Kaslow's to the famed perfume maker. Her gaze swung behind M. Lemond to the window, where she could see production trailers and vans lined along the street like stranded railroad cars. Kaslow's flagship store had sold itself to the producers of *Lyin' Hearts,* much to her dismay, with the help of a few photos and a video the location manager had filmed. Perhaps the same method could be employed to entice Mme. Bendel. Never underestimate the power of video—and maybe this time, it could work to her advantage.

"How about if we sent her a video of our store, showing the layout and the architectural features that make Kaslow's unique? That would surely convince her that we have a location worthy of her presence."

Monsieur Lemond looked doubtful. "But I do not have time to make such a video, unless you already have something?"

Claire gave him a tight smile. "I think I can get something. You're leaving this afternoon?"

"Yes, for New York. I'm meeting with the representatives from Bloomingdale's."

"I'll have something in your hands by then," she promised, crossing her fingers underneath the table.

On the way back to her office, she cursed her own impulsiveness. There was no way she could have someone professionally document the highlights of Kaslow's, not in time to sway Monsieur Lemond before Bloomingdale's pitch. But a video already existed, one created by someone more experienced in these things than anyone she could find on short notice.

She couldn't call Matt. That was out of the question. However, she mused, stepping into the elevator, she could have Joan phone Marty Baker. Several times he had phoned her office to discuss details, and Joan had eagerly taken care of his requests.

And of course, she would offer to pay.

Hopefully the video would be enough to convince Mme. Bendel that she had to have her product sold exclusively in Kaslow's. And, if it spurred a visit from the reclusive perfumier…Claire gave an inward shrug. For that coup, she would get on her knees in front of the goddess of Fortune herself.

An hour later, she picked up the phone to hear Matt's voice.

"I hear you want a favor."

"Yes, if you still have the video that Marty made."

"Yeah," he said, "I've got it. At least, Karen has. She's the production designer."

There was a moment of silence over the line, and Claire couldn't help but notice he hadn't exactly agreed that she could have it. "I told Marty we would be happy to pay whatever it would cost to have a DVD copied. It would be great if I could get it by this afternoon."

"Oh, I imagine that could be arranged," he said, and this time she was positive of the note in his voice: The other shoe had yet to drop, and when it did, she was pretty sure he would make her pay for sticking it to him during their previous negotiations.

She sighed. "Okay, how much do you want?" she asked bluntly.

He laughed. "I'm wounded, Claire. You actually think I would be so petty?"

"Sure. If the shoe were on the other foot…"

"You mean you wouldn't hesitate to screw me—figuratively, of course."

She gave a hard laugh. "I won't answer that. Just tell me, can I have the video? As I said, the store would be happy to reimburse you for expenses."

"I'll give it to you," he said. "This afternoon. On one condition."

She waited.

"I want you to come by my trailer and pick it up."

She swallowed an exasperated groan. "That would be foolish. I can have someone deliver it and save us both the trouble."

"Forget it. I want to talk to you, in person. And lunchtime is good for me."

"That's—it's—out of the question."

He upped the ante. "Did I happen to mention our footage was shot with a high-definition, stereoscopic 3D infrared recording which made up for the low light?"

"I'm sure it's adequate."

"We've also got some great stills I'll throw in as extra incentive."

"That's very tempting, but I can't—"

"You know," he mused aloud, "as soon as I saw what a classy operation Kaslow's was—on film, anyway—I knew no other place would do."

Claire sighed. "Look, I'm sure you'll agree it would serve no purpose for us to meet."

"Wrong. There's a lot we need to talk about, things you should have heard a long time ago. All I want is to sit down and talk. Get some things off my chest."

"Then call a shrink. I really don't have time for this." She fingered the trackpad on her desk, bringing up the spreadsheet she'd been adjusting, an estimate of the sales the Bendel account would bring in.

"Twenty minutes. That's all I want," he cajoled. Then his voice hardened. "I mean it, Claire. I want to see you. For your sake as well as mine." She heard him sigh. "For a long time, I felt guilty as hell about what happened, and I knew all the facts. I can't help but believe you felt the same way."

"I've put it behind me. And I suggest you do as well."

"No, you haven't, and for the same reason I've never been able to forget. You feel responsible, just like I did. And I had more information than you, knowledge about what caused Hayley's death. Information the public never found out. I think it's time you heard for yourself what she was going through, why she turned that gun on herself—"

"I have no desire to hear anything about that day." Claire clenched the phone, resisting the urge to toss it across the room. "It can't possibly do anyone any good to rehash the event."

"Ever heard the expression 'The truth shall set you free'?"

"I consider myself perfectly free, at least, as long as no one here realizes who I—was."

"Somehow, you don't strike me as the type to ignore unfinished business."

"Oh, our business was finished, all right." A bitter note crept into her voice as she eyed the photo frame on her desk. Reason number one, she reminded herself, why their business had to be finished, before anyone else was hurt.

"I disagree," he said firmly. "I think you need to hear what I've got to say. You deserve to know all the extenuating circumstances, circumstances that had nothing to do with either of us. Meet me somewhere, anywhere—"

"No. I can't."

He sighed. "Claire, believe me, I wouldn't drag this up if I didn't think there was good reason. I was eaten up with guilt, at first, for what happened. It was a long time before I could live with myself, at least in a sober state. I have to believe you had a few pangs of guilt yourself—or else you're as cold as you'd like everyone to believe."

She refused to let him goad her. "I've dealt with it, Matt, a long time ago."

"I have a meeting with Karen at Kaslow's tomorrow afternoon. We could have dinner later, wherever—"

"I'm not meeting you anywhere. I told you."

"Scared?" he taunted her softly.

"Of course not. I simply see no need for us to meet."

"Then do it for me." His voice warmed with persuasion. "There are some things I need to unload, so to speak. I thought I had it all worked out, but since seeing you that day, I've been—" He paused, and Claire heard him sigh. "Hell, I don't know. I just think if I fill you in on all the facts, we both might be able to finally put it all behind us."

Even over the phone, Claire could hear the scarred-over hurt in his voice. She reminded herself that whatever pain and anguish she had endured, his must have been much worse. Even after ten years, it had obviously not completely diminished.

When she spoke, her voice was softer. "Oh, Matt, there's no reason for you to still feel guilty over what happened. We were both young. And impetuous."

"I told you, I don't feel guilty—at least not about what happened to Hayley. It's you, Claire. You got the short end of the stick. And unless I'm way off base, I think that experience changed you. You're different now, and I think the treatment you had at the hands of the press was partly responsible. I'm to blame for some of that. I could have said something, cleared you of any blame, but I kept my mouth shut."

She wanted him to stop talking, stop dredging up memories best left buried, but he seemed to have some need to make up for the ten-year-old hurt.

"And I *was* the one who talked you into that nude scene, remember?"

"I was old enough to know what I was doing. I don't blame you for that, if that's what you want to hear."

"No. This is about what I want you to hear, things you need to know." Then he changed tactics. "Listen, I can be pretty persistent, or so I've been told often enough, and I've got six more weeks to hound you. All you have to do is give me an hour or so. You can pick the time, the place."

She sighed. Dealing with persistent males was becoming her specialty. Sometimes it was best to give them what they wanted, she told herself, and at least this wouldn't involve millions in cash the store couldn't afford. And maybe if she gave him an opportunity to ease his conscience, he would keep his distance.

"All right," she agreed reluctantly. "I'll meet you tomorrow." She thought for a minute. His presence at the store could easily be explained, and as point person for the project, she had the perfect excuse if they were seen together. "How about the theater? It's on the eighth floor, behind Floor Coverings. No one will be there; it's been closed off due to renovations. If you're spotted, no one will think anything."

"Sounds good," he agreed. "And the DVD's on its way. You should have it any minute now."

Claire hung up the phone. By now she should have realized: Matt was as incapable of holding a grudge as he was of flying to the moon. Whatever else he could be accused of, he always played fair.

But of course, he had no idea just how seriously she had wronged him.

# Chapter Seven

Snowflakes landed on the windshield of Claire's Volvo, reminding her of the crocheted doilies that had been scattered about her grandmother's house in Oklahoma. The windshield wipers made determined passes at them, while from the radio, the local weather report promised Delaware Valley residents six to ten inches, the first significant snowfall of the year. Fortunately, Claire thought as she negotiated the slick roadway, the association fees at her condo development included snow removal.

Beside her, Tripper peered out the window, cheering on the flakes that were rapidly covering the ground. "Hey, Mom, do you think I could make a snow fort?"

"If it snows much longer, I imagine you could make an igloo," Claire replied, glancing over at him at as she turned into their drive. School would likely be closed tomorrow. She would call Estelle, the housekeeper she had hired for occasional babysitting as well as housework, and see if she could spend the day with Tripper.

"David says he made a really cool fort in his backyard last year when it snowed. Could I stay with him if school is closed tomorrow?"

"I'll give Estelle a call. If she can't come, we might consider it."

"Hey, can we make snow ice cream for dessert? I bet David's mom knows how."

"I'm sure she does." Claire smiled at the additional plug for David's house. Her son could be relentless when he wanted something—like someone else she'd dealt with today.

But she wouldn't let thoughts of Matt occupy her now. She had already resolved to deal with that issue later, after Tripper had gone to bed and she had a warm cup of tea. She pulled the car into the garage and got out.

Briefcase in one hand, she picked her way to the mailbox and retrieved the mail, grateful she'd had the foresight to wear boots that morning. Coming back up the drive, she pretended not to see Tripper duck behind the corner of the house. When the snowball hit her shoulder, she obligingly let out a surprised cry. Then she wedged her briefcase between her knees, scooped up a handful of ammunition, and returned fire.

Minutes later, the impromptu snowball fight ended when Claire held up her hands in surrender, laughing as she cried, "Uncle!"

"Rematch this weekend," she promised as they walked toward the door. "Provided the temperatures remain low, like the Weather Channel predicts."

Inside, Tripper tossed his backpack on the table and raced out the door again before Claire could even remove her coat. Wishing she could stay home with him herself tomorrow, she reached for the phone and rang the housekeeper.

Estelle was apologetic between sniffles. A severe cold had her "laid up."

Torn, Claire hesitated before calling Mrs. McCall, David's mom. Candace was already watching Tripper on Friday, when school was cancelled for a teacher in-service. And she had agreed to drive the boys to basketball practice after school. She hated to ask for another favor. But rescheduling her meetings would be difficult, and she knew Tripper would prefer to spend the day with his friend. Maybe she could thank her later with something from the store, like a basket of gourmet food items or a gift certificate to the spa.

She dialed their number and soon had arranged for Tripper to spend the day with David. Before she could hang up, she had to endure Candace's excited chatter. "I couldn't believe it when I heard. Matt Grayson filming a movie at Kaslow's, of all places!" she gushed. "I saw him in *Jungle Fever* last week. Tell me, is he as gorgeous in real life?"

That was something Claire had tried not to notice, but, doubting Candace would buy that, she settled on a noncommittal answer before hanging up. The reminder of the public's obsession with celebrity made her grateful once again that she had managed to shield her son from the effects.

She just hoped she could continue to do so. If anyone found out his mother had once had a one-night stand with Matt Grayson, he would find himself the butt of jokes, or worse. The normal life they now led would certainly be nothing but a memory.

Eight weeks — if she could manage to lie low that long. She stuffed a handful of unopened envelopes into the slot marked "unpaid bills" on the desk in the kitchen. Her day of reckoning might eventually come, but for now, she had avoided the thing she dreaded most: telling her son the truth about her past.

She had kept the details from him deliberately, a conscious decision to spare him from knowing the circumstances of his conception. On the day he was born, she had made a vow to herself, a vow that he would never know the depths to which she had fallen before he entered her life. How did one explain to a little boy his mother had had an affair, suffered a cruel and public punishment, and as a result of one sleazy episode had given birth nine months later to a beautiful baby boy?

She smiled, remembering the warm surge of joy that accompanied the news she was pregnant. It might have been a self-destructive thing to wish for, but for such a brief time, she had wanted to have Matt's baby.

It was only later, when her grandmother had crushed the joy with reality, that she had doubts, doubts that had fled the moment she held her baby in her arms.

He was so tiny, so perfect, so undeserving of the scorn sure to be heaped on him. She would keep him in innocent ignorance, even if that meant lying to him — a sin she had often committed. She learned long ago the difference between white lies and dark ones. White lies saved your skin; dark lies could damage your soul.

From the kitchen window, she watched Tripper prospecting the backyard, attempting to gather the dry powder into a large enough ball to form a snowman. He had yet to learn the intricacies of snow, and she wouldn't be much help there. In east Texas, where she had spent her childhood, snow had been about as rare as Swedish cars on the highway.

Claire's gaze grew distant, and her lips tightened in a frown. Snow might have been rare, but a thick layer of permafrost had flourished around her heart. It was only when she had finally broken free, moved to Oklahoma and the shelter her grandmother's house offered, that the ice encasing her soul had thawed.

That was why Matt had gotten in so easily, all those years ago, and how he had stolen past her defenses.

But now those defenses were firmly shored up. There was no way he would be able to tunnel past them tomorrow.

A shiver ran down her spine, shaking her from her musings. She tapped on the window, gave Tripper a cheerful smile and a "ten more minutes" signal, then started dinner.

Later that night Claire awoke drenched in sweat, stifling a scream of terror. She was choking, drowning as the weight of the water above pushed down on her. Blurry faces laughed at her through the blue haze above, accusing fingers pointing downward. A strong hand gripped her neck, forcing her to remain underwater.

She gulped oxygen into her lungs, biting back sobs of fear. The red LED display on the clock switched to 12:33. Moonlight leaked from the edges of her bedroom window, covered in heavy rose-colored draperies that matched her bedspread.

It was a dream, a nightmare. The first one in a long time.

Slowly, she wrested control of her racing pulse, concentrating on deep breaths. She heard the sound of the furnace clicking on, then its steady reassuring hum.

Maybe Matt had a point: Unresolved guilt could play havoc with one's sleep.

Sighing, she got up and went across the hall to check on Tripper. He was sound asleep under his Lakers bedspread, his sleep undisturbed by her scream or by the pictures of bats he had recently added to his bulletin board.

She picked up the book still spread open on his bedcovers, smiling as she saw the cover. His dreams were probably filled with Jedi Knights and lightsabers. She poked a bookmark between the pages, then set it on his bedside table.

His life was as normal as she could make it. She felt a touch of pride. She *had* done a pretty good job raising him. She didn't regret her choice to do it alone.

Occasionally she had wondered, what if *her* mother had made the same choice? Rather than give up her infant to the Reverend Porter and his wife to raise, what if her birth mother had kept her? Then she shook off her thoughts. Regrets were useless, a fact she would point out to Matt tomorrow.

She still couldn't believe she had agreed to meet him. But perhaps he was right: the horrible guilt she had felt over Hayley James's death had once caused her to disappear into anonymity. She remembered the measures she had gone to in order to prevent anyone learning it was quiet, unassuming Claire Porter, straight-A college student from Stillwater, Oklahoma, who was now Public Tramp Number One, the catalyst behind the death of America's sweetheart.

Of course, there was one person who *had* known and wasn't surprised that Claire Porter had turned into a whore, just like the woman who gave birth to her.

A shudder ripped through her. Claire stood up, forcing unpleasant thoughts back into her subconscious.

But dreams, she had found, had a habit of coming back.

# Chapter Eight

Kaslow's third-floor men's department was lit up like the Second Coming. Stand-ins, extras, and various members of the film crew milled around like nervous penitents, waiting for the director to create chaos from order.

The set decorators didn't have to work much to enhance the clubby atmosphere. Reeking with masculine elegance, the location was already a perfect backdrop for the scene. Behind the mahogany counter, a wall of ties formed a rich silk mosaic. Leather chairs waited stoically for inhabitants, and in the corner, a warm glow from the fireplace unfurled onto the polished wood floors.

A rack of suits, like a row of headless executives, stood off to one side. Boxes of shoes—Gucci wingtips, Bally loafers, Bruno Magli slip-ons—were casually piled nearby. On top of the polished table, a trio of stiff shirts on disembodied torsos looked like targets.

The camera had already surveyed the area, filming the requisite "set-the-scene" shots that could be spliced in during editing. A tense edginess hovered in the air. As he left the dressing room, Matt felt the familiar tightening of his own nerves. He welcomed it, knowing the performances of the entire cast would benefit from the tension.

Preparing to slip into character, he was unusually quiet. A makeup bib hung around his neck, and nearby, the makeup tech kept a wary eye on him. His stand-in had already completed the light check.

He watched as orange-red flames danced around the logs in the fireplace. It was never used due to strict fire codes, but Marty had obtained permission from the powers that be to light the massive twelve-foot structure. A fire marshal was on hand, along with several Kaslow's employees, though the one person Matt half-wanted to see was nowhere in sight.

Soft strains of Beethoven filled the air, taking the edge off the tension. Matt preferred upbeat rock, but in honor of the store's ambiance, he had chosen the classics.

This would be a complicated scene. They would shoot it roughly in sequence, with the rapid changes of wardrobe shot later in the dressing room. There would be a series of reaction shots, close-ups of Laura critically appraising her creation, a blond Svengali to his *Pygmalion*.

He had already discussed camera angles with Jackson. The camera operator was scanning the script for any last-minute changes. The script supervisor had a digital camera ready to photograph the sets after each successful take. With a fine eye for detail, she would ensure continuity from take to take, setup to setup, scene to scene. If his tie was loose in one take, it would have to be in the exact same position in the next shot, or else they would have to show him altering it.

"Places!" Mimi called.

The makeup artist dabbed his nose and removed the makeup bib, and Matt strolled over to his mark. The actor playing the sales assistant joined him, and after a quick lighting check, Mimi called for quiet on the set. Suddenly, the tension transformed into action.

For the next four hours, "Luke" pranced, postured, and preened; in tweeds, in wool blends, in a cotton undershirt and trousers. He slipped from one designer suit to another, from sport coats to casual sweaters, from pleated slacks to jeans. He admired himself in the wide triple mirrors. "Jane" looked on, made pretty little pouts of dissatisfaction, motioned for him to turn around, and then sent the poor salesman scurrying for more.

They shot the few lines of dialogue from the script. For several minutes at the end of one take, Matt and Laura improvised while the cameras continued to roll. Matt held up a Bruno Magli loafer and eyed Laura hopefully.

"Do they have it in glass?"

Laura snatched the loafer from him. "Talk to your Fairy Godmother. I've got a limit on my Visa."

Matt relaxed, out of character at last, and tossed an arm around her shoulders. "Okay, that's a wrap. You did good. I think that was our best take, but we'll wait until we view the dailies to decide."

"Whew." Laura fanned herself with a hand. "This place is steaming. Is it just a rumor, or is it really snowing outside?"

"No rumor. We've postponed the scene in the rotunda so we can shoot the ending in Logan Square in the snow."

"Well, at least we'll cool off."

Just then one of the store employees approached, and Matt prepared to answer yet another request for an autograph.

But this one wanted something more. She licked her lips and eyed him like a confection. "I'm Lee Ann Ellison, from the executive offices of Kaslow's," she said.

Matt remembered being told she was Evan Kaslow's secretary when she'd been listed as an extra.

"I was wondering if there was anything I could do to make things easier for you." She looked him directly in the eye, her message clear. "We aren't all as unaccommodating as some of our board members."

In response, Matt turned to the assistant director, who had just appeared at his side, a murderous expression on her face. "Fran, weren't we looking for someone to oversee the cleanup crew? This very accommodating woman just offered to help out."

The woman's jaw dropped as Fran took her arm. "I told you we should have hired professionals," Fran muttered to him, then hustled her away.

Matt sighed, weary to the bone. A big scene always took a lot out of him, and pulling double duty made him feel like a trail rider in a rodeo. He couldn't forget that the ultimate success of the film rested on his shoulders this time, but the responsibility felt good. He had picked up a thing or two over the years, lurking on movie sets. Never one to return to the trailer after the director called, "cut," he had watched and listened instead.

An assistant handed him a cup of coffee. They would block tomorrow night's scene in the ladies' lounge, and then he hoped to grab some sleep before his meeting with Claire.

Claire was late getting in the next morning. Though the snow plows had made short work of the eight inches of snow, traffic moved slower on the expressway, and her thirty-five-minute commute stretched into an hour. The delay gave her time to reflect on her upcoming meeting with Matt.

She would let him speak his piece. Then she would offer what little absolution she could, pat him on the back, and send him on his way. A good plan, provided he asked no questions for which she had no answers—at least, no straight answers.

Her usual parking slot was taken up by the production trailers and equipment trucks, a concession ironed out in the location contract. She parked across the street, then forged her way through piles of slush that lined both sides of Market. By the time she arrived at the employee entrance on the north side of the building, the hem of her gray wool skirt was flecked with mud.

The doorman let her in, cheerful as ever, despite the frigid air that poured into the building each time the door opened.

"Good morning, Marcus." She paused to stamp her boots on the dark-green floor mat, carefully avoiding the gold K emblazoned in the center. "You've been here all night, haven't you?"

Marcus Gaines was one of the store personnel on duty while the film crew occupied the building.

"Yes, ma'am," he replied. "I sure didn't know making movies was so much work." He shook his head. "It always looks so easy, up on the screen, but those movie people spent one whole night just making that poor woman walk through the third floor. I could've told 'em, don't nobody spend that much time shopping nowadays. In and out, that's what they do now. Just in and out, all the time in a hurry." He shook his head again at the perfidy of today's shoppers.

Claire smiled. "You're right. Our market researchers could probably learn a few things from you about changing customer habits." She stuffed her gloves into her bag, then made her way across the rotunda, where she ran into "those movie people." She stepped aside as several grips lugged equipment past her, then noticed the crew members huddled under the palms near the fountain. Matt and a few others she didn't recognize were deep in conversation.

Apparently the enemy was just breaking camp. Claire searched the foliage for possible cover, but she was caught in the open.

Matt looked up. His bloodshot eyes locked on to her from twenty feet away. "Claire," he called, breaking away to amble toward her. "I was just going to call you," he said when he reached her. "We need to reschedule the shoot we had planned tonight. It might mean an extra day. I hope that's not a problem." He glanced toward the entrance, where a few lagging snowflakes still fell on a determined stream of traffic. "Mother Nature's decided to smile on us, so we have to take advantage, shoot a snow scene out in Love Park." He leaned wearily against the trunk of the palm branching out overhead. It offered a hint of seclusion.

She had forgotten the effect he had on her senses. Ten years ago, her heart had swelled with infatuation when she saw Matt; now she was better able to control her skittering pulse.

She glanced down, not wanting to be caught in the web of his gaze. "Your contract included the possibility of extending your time here. It shouldn't be a problem, though I could call legal and make sure."

"Do that. You can let me know when we meet—in twenty minutes? I just need to get cleaned up, grab a cup of coffee—"

"All right." She glanced around to make sure no one was in earshot. "You know how to get to the theater?"

"Yeah, but I have a better idea. We just finished blocking the next scene, but I need to go back and do a quick run through, as long as the store will be empty another hour or so. Why don't we meet there? It's the perfect place—no one would overhear a conversation."

Claire frowned. "You're supposed to be filming in the second-floor ladies' lounge."

"That's right." He flashed her a grin. "It's perfect. Think of the symbolism…We can flush away the past, so to speak."

Claire shot him a skeptical look, but she had to admit the idea was a good one. The ladies' room was about as private as they could get, at least until the customers showed up in an hour and a half. There weren't even CCTV cameras mounted there. "The janitors will be there—"

He shook his head. "We're responsible for cleanup, remember? Our people took care of that an hour ago, after we struck the set in the men's department." He took her silence for agreement. "I'll meet you up there—say, nine sharp?"

At her reluctant nod, he walked away, flexing his shoulder muscles as if working out the kinks. Claire's gaze followed him, almost against her will, watching as he was swallowed by the loose-knit entourage lingering near the entrance. Then she turned and hurried past the fountain. This time, the goddess of Fortune merely smiled benignly as she passed.

Claire swabbed at the splatters on her wool skirt with a damp towel, hoping Matt would find a way to enter the ladies' lounge discreetly. His crew had done their cleanup well; no lingering signs indicated the recent descent of a movie crew. A smile tugged at her lips as she envisioned the scene they would film here. How incongruous Matt Grayson would appear, a testosterone-drenched cowboy, hiding out amid a pastel harem.

Kaslow's Ladies' Retiring Room, as it had always been known, was spacious enough to bivouac a small army. A sitting room, separate from the modern restroom area, held several comfortable sofas and a dozen dainty chairs standing ready to assist with any overflow. On the pink brocade walls were a series of prints depicting Kaslow's transformation to a modern department store. Claire found them fascinating but knew that they were scheduled to be replaced by floral prints during the renovations.

The door opened, and Matt strode in, somehow not as out of place as she had imagined. The preponderance of pink only seemed to emphasize his maleness.

His rugged good looks didn't seem to be affected by a sleepless night. But then, all-nighters were probably routine in the circles he traveled in.

He flashed her a sample of his thousand-watt smile, the same one that slayed women in their seats before the big screen, but instead of swooning, Claire crossed her arms and gave him the same look she'd give a contrary executive.

"You look like you've just swallowed a mouthful of that rose-scented soap," he said, pausing in front of her. "Relax. This isn't going to be as bad as you think." He reached out and touched her cheek. She could feel them flood with heat.

She lifted her chin. "I still don't see the need for this. We said everything we needed to in my office, when you were here before."

"No, we didn't. For instance, I don't even know what you've been doing these last few years. You aren't married — I've gathered that much. Tell me, how have you been?" He pulled out a chair, inviting her to sit.

Stiffly, she took the seat he offered, though exchanging chitchat was the last thing she wanted to do. The plan, she reminded herself, was to give him a figurative pat on the back, then politely and firmly suggest that he never call her again.

"I've been fine," she told him. "As you pointed out last time we met, I've done well for myself. Put the past behind me."

"I have to admit I still have a hard time picturing you in a board-room. I don't mean that as sexist. I consider myself an enlightened guy most of the time. But my memories of you…" He shrugged, then dropped into the seat across from her, stretching his legs out in front of him. "You just seemed so young."

"I *was* young. Twenty-one."

"I guess so. That makes you…what, thirty-one now?" He gazed at her quizzically.

"Thirty-two," she corrected him.

"That's right. You told me your birthday was in October. On Halloween, right?"

She blinked. "Yes, it is. I'm surprised you remember."

She shifted uneasily in her seat, feeling unprotected without a desk in front of her. Despite his friendly remarks, she didn't trust the conversation to keep to safe channels.

Matt linked his booted ankles and gazed at her thoughtfully. "I remember quite a lot about that week," he told her. Then, as if he'd rehearsed the best way to rattle her, he added, "I remember meet-ing you. Expecting to see another starlet with more ambitions than scruples, and instead finding a shy accounting major who just hap-pened to be a natural-born actress. And I remember our date, when we went to that little diner. You told the waitress to bring a birthday cake, as soon as you found out it was my birthday. Chocolate, wasn't it?" The smile he gave her could have melted granite.

Claire averted her gaze. "If this is going to be a game of 'remember when,' I don't want to play."

He gave a short laugh. "You don't want to be reminded we were once attracted to each other? Is that it?"

"It was a long time ago and has absolutely no bearing on our present circumstances," she said tightly, focusing on the flocked wallpaper.

"Come on, Claire. Our present circumstances are a direct result of what happened. If we hadn't been so goddamned attracted to each other…Christ, we practically did the deed right there on the set."

"I didn't come here to have my youthful indiscretions thrown in my face." She moved to get up, and he put a hand out to restrain her.

"I'm not blaming you for anything. Certainly not our 'youthful indiscretions,' as you call it. You have to admit, though, the chemistry went both ways. I didn't seduce a woman who wasn't interested."

"I'm not saying you did!" Claire turned, finally, and faced him. "But I hardly knew what I was getting into. I had no idea you were involved with Hayley James. I never read the tabloids—at least not until my picture started selling them."

He released her arm and gazed at her skeptically. "Everyone in America knew we were living together. You mean you had no idea?"

"None." She laughed bitterly. "And not everyone cares what goes on in Hollywood. I was busy trying to finish my degree. The opportunity to act in the film practically fell into my lap. I told you then, remember, that I had never acted in front of a camera. That's why you offered to 'give me a few pointers,'" she said, a mocking edge to her voice.

But she couldn't blame him. She'd been eager, hadn't she, to know everything he could teach her, not just about acting, but about living—and loving. He had made her feel, for the first time in her twenty-one years, like someone special, someone put on the earth for a reason, rather than a mistake. Someone deserving of love, even if it was only the physical kind.

Matt shrugged and said wryly, "I know pro ball players who'd have acted with more propriety than I did." Then he sobered. "It was a bad time for me. I'm not trying to excuse everything that happened, but Hayley and I had just had a big fight. She was in Vegas, getting an abortion. At least, that's what she told me. Turned out she didn't go through with it."

Claire looked away, not sure she was entitled to hear the intimate details of his and Hayley's life together. But somehow she realized he needed to explain, to confess, as if he knew she was the least likely person to condemn his actions.

His gaze focused on his boots as he continued, his voice ragged. "I wanted her to keep the baby, even though I knew a kid was the last thing she needed. The last thing *we* needed. But I still thought…" He swallowed, the planes of his face twisted in remorse at the memory. "Hell, I don't know. I think somehow, deep down, I thought I could be like my big brother, Mark. They had two kids, were expecting a third. They seemed like the perfect family. So fucking normal, so un-Hollywood."

He laughed in self-derision. "I wanted that—with Hayley, with anyone. But it was too much pressure for her. I didn't know this at the time, but she was ill. She had a mental illness. Bipolar disorder. She never told anyone." He made a scornful sound. "I guess she thought it would hurt her 'image.'"

"Oh my God!" Claire covered her mouth in shock, filled with sympathy for the woman whose life had been portrayed as ideal. A mental illness—and the stigma—could have ruined her career, as it obviously had her life.

"She had quit taking her medication. Maybe because of the baby." Matt shook his head ruefully, slumping lower in his seat. "She wasn't herself, I can see that now, but back then, I just thought she was working too hard. I tried to get her to take some time off. That was another thing we had it out over. I didn't think she should do *Bed of Roses*. But she refused to hear of me going off to do a film without her. She had never been the jealous type, so I was surprised. Annoyed by it, I guess. I told her she was just being paranoid."

"As it turned out, she had good reason," Claire said quietly. "My God, when she heard the rumors—"

Matt shook his head. "Before filming even began, it was all over between us. I was sleeping on the couch at that point. When she went off to Vegas, I told her I was moving out just as soon as the film was finished. We agreed to be civilized about it, not let it affect our work." He shrugged. "At least, I thought we had agreed."

"Somehow I don't think she expected you to jump into bed with the first woman who came along."

"I didn't expect to, either. Not with you or anyone." He gave her a wry look. "But you have to admit, things got a little heated between us. Even that first night, while we were filming our first scene together."

Claire blushed, remembering. And their "chemistry" had been obvious to everyone, she had realized later, prompting the rumors—rumors that had eventually made their way to Hayley's ears. "Things never should have gotten out of hand. Especially since you knew she was due to show up the next day."

"I didn't care. Sure, that was callous of me. Maybe I wanted to hurt her." He made a derisive sound. "I'm sure a therapist could have a field day analyzing my motives. But I had already realized our relationship was dead in the water. I guess, subconsciously, I wanted to end it with a clean cut."

"Oh, you did that, all right." Claire laughed humorlessly.

Matt leaned his head on the back of the seat, gazing unseeingly at the crystal chandelier that hung above their heads. He didn't say anything for a long while. Claire wanted to comfort him, offer absolution somehow. But when it came to erasing guilt, the only lesson she knew was a harsh one. Living with it was easier.

Finally, he spoke. "I went back home. Punished myself every way I could." His lips twisted at the memory. "Stayed drunk most of the time, dared every hothead in a hundred-mile radius to use me as a punching bag."

He pointed to his nose, glancing at Claire. "See that? Ran into a beer bottle, unfortunately before it got drank. Second time I broke it, I don't even recollect how." He gave her a tired grin. "But at least I was too far gone to feel any pain."

Claire had noticed the slightly crooked slant of his nose years ago, while examining his face on a magazine cover as she waited in line at the supermarket. It didn't seem to have adversely affected his looks; if anything, it gave an edge to a face that was almost too perfect.

She looked away, determined to get the meeting over.

"We both behaved despicably. A little guilt was in order."

"Yeah," he said slowly, as if he was exhausted. "I was the world's biggest scumbag. And you…" He looked at her. "They were even harder on you. Those photos—"

There was one, Claire remembered seeing, taken immediately after the shooting, of "Clarissa" being led away, a blanket tossed around her shoulders, a chilling smile on her face. It had led to rampant speculation that she had seduced him, even plotted Hayley's death. Ironically, she didn't even remember that day. Her mind had erased all the gruesome images, the same way it had protected her in the past. Many times as a child, she'd awakened not knowing where her bruises came from.

But she remembered seeing Matt at the police station later, remembered how he'd looked away from her.

"Tell me something, Claire. Why did you do it? Why did you sleep with me?" Matt asked bluntly. "I never believed all that garbage they said in the papers, about you sleeping your way to the top. One of them even implied you set me up, that you wanted Hayley to find out about us." His voice was harsh, the accusation creeping through.

"I didn't," she said in a flat voice. "I told you I didn't know you were living with her."

"Then why? Why did you go to bed with me, a man you hardly knew? And why did you run off afterward? You could have contacted me. Instead, you slunk away in the middle of the night like some pay-by-the-hour whore."

The blood drained from Claire's face. She closed her eyes, trapping the hurt beneath her eyelids.

But he'd given her the perfect opening, and like a fencer spotting an exposed vein, she took it.

"No, I wasn't really a whore. I just played one on TV," she said with a raw laugh. "You see, it was all an experiment — 'on-the-job training.' Method acting taken a bit too far." Her voice was stained with ten years of bitterness. "I realized I was in over my head. I was totally inexperienced — with acting. I didn't know how I could possibly play the part of your mistress. So I decided I would become exactly what the script called for. Your lover." She gave an offhand shrug, then dragged her gaze from the rose-patterned carpet to eye him, completely emotionless. "I figured for that role, you would be the perfect teacher."

Claire had planned exactly what she would tell him, justification for sleeping with someone she barely knew. She had even convinced herself it was true.

Matt didn't say anything, just looked at her with those startling green eyes. His irises were shot with gold, Claire noticed absently, just like Tripper's.

Then she twisted her lips in a brittle smile and added the kill shot: "It was all an act, Matt. I even told you I loved you. Remember?"

For a moment, he was silent, staring at her as if she'd just uttered heresy, and then he gave a harsh laugh. "Jesus Christ. They were right. You were every bit the cold, calculating bitch, weren't you?"

She didn't bother to agree. She could tell from the look on his face he believed her.

He shook his head derisively. "All this time, I had convinced myself you were just a sweet, innocent kid. A kid who got caught up in something she couldn't control, didn't expect."

"I was," she admitted. "And I hate that, not being in control. So I did what I always do. I tried to gather all the information I could, as efficiently as possible. That was all it was, my 'attraction' for you. I needed you to get me out of a tight spot. I had no idea anyone would get hurt, and I've regretted that ever since, but I don't beat myself up with the guilt." She gave him a plastic smile, ignoring the devastated look in his eyes, knowing he would easily recover from any blow to the ego she was capable of inflicting.

"Now, I think we've said everything we needed to." She stood and looked down at him. "We can walk off into the sunset, no looking behind us. Roll the credits, hit the lights."

He didn't say anything, just looked up at her, an unfathomable expression on his face.

"I wish you good luck with your film, Matt. I really do. I'll try to make it as easy for you as possible. And afterward, you can go back to California and forget I ever existed."

She turned and walked away, her heels leaving little scars all over the roses.


Matt sat there after she was gone, feeling raw and drained. Used, he realized, used years ago, not so much to propel her career but to save her the embarrassment of appearing foolish in front of the camera. It shouldn't hurt so much, he told himself. It wasn't as if his trip to the top hadn't been accompanied by his fair share of users.

But this was more personal. He had been convinced that what she'd felt had been real, that the passion they shared was honest.

He remembered the shy little look on her face when they had brought the birthday cake, how she had pretended not to know where it came from. The twinkle in her eye that gave her away. There had been no doubt in his mind then that she was really as sweet as she looked.

And later, in bed with her, their lovemaking had been so tender, so innocent. It was the first time a woman had ever cried with him, though she had sworn they were tears of joy.

No, his mind had never accepted the fact that their affair was as sordid as the press had made it out.

Or was that just his guilt, trying to justify an act that ended up destroying a woman he had cared for?

He shook his head. Hell, he was going to wind up in a therapist's office after all. Wearily he pushed himself up from the chair. He wasn't used to prolonged bouts of self-pity, preferring action to stewing over a problem.

But there was nothing he could do, no way to put Claire Porter under a microscope and detect her true feelings. She was probably immune to truth serum, and there was no way to relive the past.

As he reached the door, a thought struck him. How many times had he done exactly that? Each time he reviewed the dailies from filming, he was essentially reliving events that had occurred hours before. A record of his hours with Claire still existed, in a film vault somewhere, fragments of footage stored originally as evidence in case of a lawsuit. It had to be there still, an unfinished story waiting to be told.

He opened the door, a plan of action brewing in his head. There were few people he trusted to be completely discreet, and one of them owed him a favor. A.J., he decided, was about to earn his keep. Personal indiscretions aside, Matt knew the lawyer in him was as closemouthed as a tick when it came to his client's activities, and he would be even more protective of his friends.

He'd call A.J., have him dig up the footage from *Bed of Roses* and send it here.

Then he would see exactly what the camera saw during those two days of filming, unedited and unvarnished. Claire could dodge her emotions, and his questions, all she wanted. But the camera had caught her performance, and if he had learned anything during his career, it was how to judge a fake.

# Chapter Nine

For the next two days, Matt managed to push the confrontation with Claire out of his mind. The film took up most of his time—there were still script revisions to approve, shooting schedules to coordinate, and a dozen last-minute problems to deal with.

He'd hardly had time to walk Sadie, so today he'd brought her along on his daily run. He was beginning to wish he'd left her with his brother Mark. With four kids in the house, she'd have had no shortage of exercise.

Dodging a heap of gray snow on the sidewalk, he wondered what his family would say if they knew he was once again in the proximity of That Woman. He'd never tried to explain to them just why he had gotten mixed up with Clarissa—Claire, he reminded himself, slowing his pace as he turned the corner. He wasn't even sure himself. Was he such a poor judge of character? Could he have misjudged her so much?

But he had been in the middle of a painful breakup and susceptible to a sweet smile.

At his door he stopped, exhaustion slumping his shoulders. Had Kaslow's previous owners experienced the same punched-in-the-gut feeling he'd felt when she'd hung him out to dry, all nice and tidy in the ladies room?

Snow White, it seemed, had grown a thorny hide along with a new hairstyle.

After a quick shower, Matt walked into the office. A FedEx package lay unopened on the desk. He tossed down the script revisions he'd meant to read and ripped open the envelope. A DVD was inside. As A.J. had explained over the phone, the entire footage from *Bed of Roses* had been transferred to tape and a copy given to the officers investigating the incident.

He glanced at his watch. He had an hour before he had to meet Jack to review tomorrow's shots, and fortunately Laura was meeting with Wardrobe this afternoon. He went to the rec room in the basement, where a TV hung on one wall.

He inserted the disc into the player and settled on the sofa opposite.

The total running time was less than an hour. The director had had an unerring eye when it came to deciding which take to print; consequently, only a few scenes were repeat performances. The first few minutes were master shots of the set, taken to ensure proper placement of props later. Halfway into the tape, the first scene with "Vanessa" came into view.

The camera caught her running to him, the action unnecessarily drawn out on the unedited footage. They met, exchanged a few words, and then he was crushing her to him.

Matt realized then what everyone had meant when they used the word "chemistry." It was as if a magnetic force existed between the two people on screen, an invisible bonding agent. Pheromones, perhaps, that tugged at gazes, that tenderized each touch, each caress. A substance that could be scooped up and bottled and used to melt camera lenses.

Then came another shot of the same setup, a close-up this time. Matt stared at the lovers on screen. He remembered this take. For the first time in his career, he had totally forgotten the presence of lights, cameras, and the other crew members. He'd just let the feeling overtake him. He had told himself later it was acting, the best bit of acting he had done, but the truth was he hadn't faked a damn thing.

What was on the screen wasn't chemistry. It was honesty.

He watched the scene unfold, struck by the differences ten years had made in Claire. She had been so young, only twenty-one, though he knew women that age whose years showed on them like worn dollar bills. There was something fresh, untried about her—untested, yet somehow knowing. A distance, even then, as if she were merely observing.

He remembered the comments from several of the crew members later, after the disaster on the set, when the scandal had started to creep around them. Jumping on the slander wagon, they had called her snooty, claiming she looked down her nose at everyone else. Though Matt was convinced it was shyness that had set her apart from the rest of the cast and crew, the words had done their damage. Claire was branded a stuck-up bitch, as well as a homewrecker.

Neither reputation was deserved.

The scene ended, and he pressed the pause button. He knew what was coming up, but now he wasn't sure he wanted to view it.

He rubbed his fingertips lightly against the soft buttons of the remote control, staring at the frozen image of a clapboard on the screen.

He knew the camera was not the impartial judge some thought. The image it produced was subject to the visions of the director, the cinematographer, the cameraman. The angles, the lighting, the screens used to soften the edges — all of it could change the tone completely. Even the most passionless scene could be artificially enhanced, setting a completely different mood.

As an actor, he had trained himself to look beyond the special effects and get to the emotion, or lack of it, in the acting itself. It was an annoying habit. He could hardly watch a performance without dissecting it, looking at every nuance, each expression, with the critical eyes of an Academy voter.

So now when he pressed the play button and watched the screen, he viewed it dispassionately. An observer, not a participant.

It was easy to see what was going on in this scene.

It hardly registered that it was him. A younger, leaner version of himself, entwined with a younger, softer version of Claire.

The camera lens was in soft focus. But it did nothing to dim the passion that flamed between the two lovers on the rich loam of the greenhouse.

Matt watched as Johnny slipped his hands over Vanessa's shoulders. He had forgotten skin that white existed. Skin that soft. His hand moved to her breast, covering it from the harsh glare of the camera. He had used his body as much as possible to shield hers, knowing how nervous she was. Her flesh had trembled when he touched her, and Matt had imagined himself soothing a frightened mare, trying to give his mind something to focus on besides the erotic feel of the woman in his arms.

It hadn't helped. His body had responded to her as naturally as his lungs took in air.

The urgency between them built with each frame. Each camera angle captured a new aspect of desire. Matt realized now that what he was viewing wasn't at all what the tabloids had luridly depicted. It wasn't sordid or ugly. It was poignant, not pornographic.

Even unedited, the film clearly showed a scene evocative in its beauty, in its human passion. Hands reaching, touching tenderly, caressing. There was no sound, so he didn't hear the moans, the sighs, the intake of breath when he touched her — there, on the soft pillow of her belly.

As an actor, he could see the moves he had made to simulate passion. As a lover, though, he knew the result wasn't simulated. After she lost her nervousness, it was as if she became another woman beneath his hands. Her eyes closed, she let herself go, let herself enjoy his caresses. Let herself feel. The look on her face — wonder, joy, as if she had just discovered a new species.

Could it have been true? What had her life been like up to that point? She hadn't been all that experienced, he felt instinctively, yet she hadn't been a virgin. Or had she? How would he have known, after all, unless she had told him?

He remembered visiting her immediately after the take. She had seemed confused at first, endearingly attentive to his stumbling apologies. And later, in her hotel room, he had taken it a step further — at her invitation, he remembered. But the shyness with which she had tried to hide her body, did that belong to the same woman who had told him coldly she was only interested in an acting lesson?

Her explanation, that she had gone to bed with him simply to help her learn her role, didn't ring true. They had already filmed the scene, and though the director wanted to add more the next day — mostly close-ups and reaction shots after Hayley's character caught them "in the act," the bulk of the scene was already a wrap.

Claire was lying to him. Lying to keep him at a distance. Maybe lying to herself for the same reason he had been tempted to: guilt.

Damn it, she had no reason to feel guilty. What they had done was perfectly natural, perfectly human.

The scene on the screen ended, and Matt pressed the off button. He had no desire to see what came next.

And besides, he already had his answer. As well as more questions.

"Here's your coffee and the latest issue of *Chain Store Executive*. There's an article on private-label merchandise you might want to check out. Page twenty." Joan placed her offerings on Claire's desk.

"Thanks." Claire glanced up as she reached for the coffee, then noticed Joan's trim maternity suit. "That's a nice outfit," she commented. "Maternity clothes have certainly improved in the last ten years. Did that come from the store?"

Joan beamed. "Sure did. That was a great idea, moving the maternity department right next to Infants."

Claire tapped the magazine in front of her. "There was an article in here last year on the resurgence of maternity wear. With more working mothers-to-be who can afford designer maternity fashions, it seemed a timely idea."

"I guess it was a lot tougher back when you were a brand new single mother." Joan sighed. "As I keep telling myself, if you could do it, then so can I." She glanced down and gave her belly a fond pat. "This little guy is gonna have it lucky. I never dreamed when I came to work here there'd be on-site daycare up and running by the time he made his appearance in the world."

"That should be soon, shouldn't it?"

"Another month, and I'll start training my temp." Then she pointed to the calendar on Claire's desk. "I've marked it on your calendar. Don't forget, you have a meeting with Evan Kaslow at nine to discuss store renovations. I sent him a copy of your budget projections, so be prepared for fallout."

Claire made a face. "I plan on wearing a hard hat. The Atlantic City store was his pet project, but there's no way we can justify the expansion to the stockholders, even with his new figures, as well as the renovations for our downtown store. He'll just have to accept it."

"Speaking of stockholders, you have a conference call scheduled with Mr. Forrest at one. After that, you're free until three, but I'll be out this afternoon—doctor appointment."

Joan left, and Claire spent the next hour preparing for her meeting with Evan.

As predicted, he took the news of his project's demise with more than a little resentment.

"I believe this shows an appalling lack of foresight on your part," he told her later when she joined him in his office, and then he added, "and on the part of our new owner. The Atlantic City market is a logical expansion location for a company like Kaslow's."

"I disagree," Claire replied. "Our market projections there don't indicate a need for a high-end retailer. If Kaslow's were a discount store, then yes, I'd say damn the torpedoes, full speed ahead. Presently, however, Boscov's is filling our niche, and until—"

"It sounds to me like you're just afraid to jump in the ring and compete with the big boys." Evan glared at her from behind his desk, his hand nervously tapping the Mont Blanc pen against the blotter.

"At this point, jumping in the ring would be foolish. Kaslow's needs to concentrate on winning the contests we're already involved in. As I've said repeatedly, our current customer base must be satisfied before we try to conquer any new markets."

"I guess the rumors weren't true," he said.

"What rumors?"

"Our aggressive new financial manager isn't so aggressive after all. Maybe Jackie was right. Maybe your priorities are—"

"With the stockholders," she said firmly. "Who happen to care only about the bottom line. Once we shore that up, then we'll consider expanding our markets. Until then, forget about Atlantic City."

Claire turned and left the room, shutting the door behind her with a determined click. She was sure she had made the right decision and equally sure Connor Forrest would back her up.

That was confirmed during the conference call with him later. "I'm really impressed with the numbers I'm seeing from Kaslow's," he told her. "Keep up the good work out there. By the way, how's the film coming along? No major explosions?"

"As far as I know, everything's gone smoothly. It's all done at night, so there's been little inconvenience. They should wrap it up tomorrow evening." And as she said the words, Claire could almost feel her stress level pulse back to normal.

The freight entrance of Kaslow's was deserted, and Matt was able to slip up to Claire's office unnoticed. There was no one in the outer office, so he approached her opened door silently, then watched her unobserved for a moment.

The number-crunching executive behind the desk looked so different from the woman in the video, he almost forgot why he had come.

Her head was bent over her desk, and with a pencil eraser, she poked the buttons of a serious-looking calculator. The pair of silver-rimmed glasses she had worn before were perched on the end of her nose.

Through the window behind her, he saw a chunk of ice fall to the ground.

She must have heard the small sound he made. Still engrossed in her figures, her head inched upward by slow degrees, her gaze clinging to the figures on the calculator before settling reluctantly on him. She blinked, and then her gray eyes darkened before they frosted over and she frowned. Matt wasn't sure if she were more annoyed at being interrupted or by the fact that it was him doing the interrupting.

He ignored the lack of welcome and walked in, shutting the door behind him. "I have something for you." He tossed a package onto her desk, then settled himself casually against the edge.

Claire gave the envelope a cursory glance. "If that's a script revision, we have a very efficient interoffice mail system. You could have given it to any receptionist."

"I don't think that would have been a good idea. If that got into the wrong hands, we'd both have hell to pay."

The envelope bore the unmistakable outline of a DVD. Claire eyed it again, frowning as if it contained a request for a budget increase.

"I'm not interested in seeing the finished product, if that's what that is."

He shook his head. "This isn't *Lyin' Hearts*." He waited a beat, watching her for reaction. "It's from *Bed of Roses*. The unedited footage."

"Are you — oh, my God, have you lost your mind?" She half-rose from the chair and jerked the wire frames from her nose so she could glare at him unimpeded.

"You never did get a chance to view your screen debut, did you?" He nodded toward the package. "There it is, in Technicolor. Transferred to DVD for your viewing pleasure."

"You sadistic son of a—" She broke off stiffly, then breathed in through nostrils that flared ever so slightly. She was clinging to her composure like the string of a helium balloon, fast floating away. Matt decided it was time she lost it.

He braced his chin with his fingers and eyed her appraisingly. "I've been critiquing your performance," he told her. "After all, I was your teacher. I figured I should at least see how my star pupil measured up."

He saw her flinch, a movement that would have been imperceptible to all but the most observant.

"Don't tell me you watched that. What kind of sick person are you?" she said in a flat voice, then folded her glasses with a disgusted click, her movement controlled.

Too controlled, he decided. Giving her a calculating look, he crossed his arms and replied, "Sure I watched it. It's really too bad the picture was never finished. Your performance—if that's what it was—deserved an Academy nomination. Hell, I don't think I've ever worked with anyone quite as good as you." He raised his eyebrows in a mock salute.

The tiny quiver in her chin was the only clue that she was upset, and even that disappeared when he let his gaze linger on it. As if on cue, she found her voice. "I'd appreciate it if you'd leave my office. Now." With a wave of her hand, she dismissed him as if he were a copier salesman. "And take this—this piece of filth with you when you go." She wrinkled her nose at the package on the desk.

The glow from her desktop computer abruptly went black as he looked at her, ignoring her instructions. Instead, he baited her once again.

"Filth? I prefer to think of it as educational. A documentary. We could call it *The Birth of a Woman*."

She tapped a pencil on the desk. A typical Claire gesture, he thought: *Tightly Reined Fury.*

"You really should get over this obsession you have with the past." Her eyes narrowed with just the right touch of disdain.

He wanted to applaud her performance. Instead, he agreed with her. "You're right. I am obsessed. But when the past doesn't jive with the present, I feel compelled to find out why. Your story doesn't ring true. All that was garbage you told me, wasn't it? Sleeping with me just to learn your part—"

"The only garbage is this video! It's going straight in the trash—or better yet, I'll burn it." She reached for it, but his hand got there first.

"Watch it first. I dare you." His eyes met hers over the desk. "What are you so afraid of?"

"I'm not afraid of anything."

"You're lying, Claire." Leaning nearer, he continued. "That woman in the video…tell me, where did she disappear to?" His eyes traveled down her body, what he could see of it, encased in the gray wool of her dress. Past the white collar at her throat, over the trim buttons down the front, to where the sleeves ended in snowy white cuffs at her wrists. Her hand trembled ever so slightly.

He brought his gaze back to her throat, where a strand of pearls disappeared beneath her collar, rising a bit with each breath. She was flustered, he realized. The imperturbable Claire Porter was nervous as hell. The signs were so subtle he would have missed it, except he had been trained to notice the slightest evidence of emotion. The knowledge gave him a tiny thrill of victory, a reaction he wasn't sure he wanted to examine.

He turned up the pressure. "I remember how hot it was —"

"It was the lights," she said sharply.

"The lights, hell." He laughed deep in his throat, then looked deliberately at her lips. "Someone had given us peppermints just before shooting began, remember? I remember tasting it — when I kissed you."

Her mouth tightened.

"And your hair…it kept getting caught on my face. I remember it smelled like shampoo. Not all flowery, just clean. Like you."

The pearls against her throat jerked as she swallowed. Her lips parted, as if she were going to speak, but no words came out.

"You had this sexy little intake of breath," he continued, "and you shivered, like you were cold, every time I touched you."

She gave a similar shiver now. His voice dropped to a lower register.

"I remember what it felt like — your skin. Soft as the rose petals in that greenhouse."

She found her voice. "Still remember your lines, I see."

He laughed, and the tension that had been coiling in his gut eased. "They were pretty corny, weren't they?"

Claire relaxed back in her chair, her composure settling around her once again like a wool blazer. "You've got your own movie to make. You should be making it, not trying to resurrect the past."

He knew she was right. Even now he should be viewing yesterday's dailies. But here he was, compelled by some force beyond his control, trying to shake her from her self-imposed exile. Unfreeze her, jog her senses awake.

"What happened ten years ago…it was as if you were asleep, emotionally and sexually. And when I came along, forced you to feel something, you couldn't stand it."

She just listened attentively, as if he were reciting the stock quotes.

"You ran away, hightailed it out of there. It wasn't just the publicity—you found out real life is a pain in the ass. Feelings are messy, people get hurt. So now you just avoid it altogether. Shut yourself up here like an executive Rip Van Winkle, letting life pass right by you." He waved a hand over the desktop, the motion disturbing the reports she had been reading.

Her face hardened. "You don't know anything about my life."

"I know you're scared to death someone's going to come along and make you feel again. You punched the wrong number into your calculator once and ended up with the wrong answer. But it's not the end of the world. People make mistakes, put their lives back together. They get forgiven, Claire. They forgive themselves."

"For God's sake, I don't need your pop psychology. I have better things to do."

"Like what? Get your next report written? Slash somebody's budget? Give someone the ax?"

She glanced at the open desk calendar. "Actually, I've got a meeting with the Marketing department. In half an hour."

"Tell the Marketing department to go to hell. When's the last time you just let go, had fun?"

"Yesterday, as a matter of fact," she replied smugly.

"Oh? What did you do, read the comics before the business section?"

"No—"

He raised one eyebrow. "Chewed bubblegum in a board meeting?"

"Of course not," she said, frowning.

He looked aghast. "Don't tell me you wrote in your checkbook with purple ink."

She gave him a quelling look. "As a matter of fact, I have a very full and rewarding life. Not that it's any of your business," she added snidely.

"Ah, but it is my business, Claire. You see, I've been beating myself up regularly for ruining your life. So if your life isn't ruined, I'd really like to hear about it."

The look she gave him was almost pitying. "Maybe you should take your own advice. Forgive yourself. You didn't ruin my life, Matt. But if you don't stay out of it and leave me alone…" She let out a sigh, an agitated little breath that he loved, that somehow sounded sexy coming from her lips.

Matt looked away, shoving his fingers through his hair. He had come up here to see if she was the same woman on the tape, to throw it in her face, make her admit she felt something for him once. All of a sudden, that seemed pathetic. Women regularly propositioned him, showed up naked in his backyard, for Christ's sake, and here he was panting after a woman who had told him more than once to go to hell.

It either said something about his perseverance or indicated how long it had been since he had been with a woman. He almost grinned. *That* was a problem he could do something about. He'd call Annie, see if she could come out. He didn't need to be here, pestering Claire like a twelve-year-old.

He looked out the window behind her, across the rooftops covered with snow, past the icy branches in Rittenhouse Square, to the Schuylkill River in the distance.

Inside, the central heat was on, but it felt colder than the twenty degrees outside.

"You're right," he said finally, picking up the package on the desk and weighing it in his hand. "There were two people who died that day, weren't there? Only one was mourned by the public. The other just quietly disappeared."

Claire was staring at the mug on her desk, a misshapen thing that looked out of place among the professional flotsam of her desktop. An odd little smile tilted the corners of her mouth, and she said quietly, "She didn't have a choice. It was midnight. Cinderella was due back at the hovel. The fairy tale was over."

He laughed. "Oh, there's always a choice," he said. "Maybe the prince would have bought her another glass slipper."

She shook her head, then smiled wryly. "Instead she got herself a job and bought herself a pair of Ferragamos. Not a bad deal, I'd say."

"Ah, Claire." He shook his head. "Somehow I don't think she managed to buy herself the happily ever after part. I get the feeling she got a part in *Sleeping Beauty* and she's asleep in some castle, waiting for the prince." He started to hum "Some Day, My Prince Will Come."

Claire scoffed. "Well, at the risk of ruining a perfectly good metaphor: This castle's changed ownership, and I'm now the resident witch. And as you pointed out, I have people to fire and budgets to trim. So, if you've done what you meant to, go on and make your movie. I've got work to do." She looked at her watch. "I have to finish this estimate before my meeting with the Marketing department—in twenty minutes."

"Yeah, sure," he said, masking his disappointment. What did he expect, after all? She was right. This wasn't a fairy tale, it was real life, and happy endings didn't exist.

But he couldn't help wishing he could manufacture one for Claire, like he could on screen. Because, despite everything, he still felt that he had wronged her somehow.

But clearly the lady didn't want him, or his apology, anywhere around.

He looked at his watch. "All right, I'll get out of your hair. I'm supposed to view the dailies for the *Pygmalion* scene in an hour."

"The what scene?"

He smiled. "*Pygmalion*. Luke's transformation, from cowboy to stockbroker. You remember Julia Roberts in *Pretty Woman*? Same principle, with the sexes reversed."

He turned to leave, but her voice stopped him. "You're forgetting something."

He paused, his hand on the door.

"Take that—" she nodded at the package still lying innocuously on her desk "—and burn it. I don't ever want to see it again."

He hesitated. "It's pretty flammable. I could get scorched."

"I'll loan you my oven mitts."

Matt smiled. A woman whose gaze could freeze flames probably didn't need oven mitts, but he'd take the video anyway. It had done its job.

# Chapter Ten

Somehow, Matt never got around to calling Annie. Not even the thought of hot sex, the kind with No Regrets written all over it, could erase the erotic vision of Claire Porter sitting behind her desk, brandishing a No. 2 pencil and a touch-me-not attitude.

Was he just hankering for the forbidden fruit? The one woman who told him "no" in no uncertain terms? Or was it possible Claire Porter was getting under his skin again after all these years?

He hoped it was the former. The last thing he needed now was a woman whose idea of a good time was watching the stock quotes—and not the ones from the Crider County Stock Auction.

Hell, he thought as he strolled into the kitchen of the townhouse he shared with Laura, Claire Porter probably didn't even own a decent pair of jeans.

Laura looked up as he entered the room. "Well, here he is, the 'Quintessential Guy' himself," she announced. She was perched on the counter eating ice cream, the latest issue of *GQ* open next to her. She took another bite, then let out a moan of rapture as she slid the spoon from her mouth.

Matt eyed the half-empty ice cream carton in her hands. "You planning to eat all that?" he asked, ignoring her comment. The woman in front of him was slim as a reed, but he couldn't resist adding slyly, "You'll never fit into that evening gown if you do."

Laura smirked and jabbed the air with the spoon. "Ha. Lynn told me I had to gain a pound if I didn't want it to slide off me." She dug out a chocolate-covered nut. "Eat your heart out, Cover Boy."

Matt frowned. "Don't you have something better to read? Like your script? Scene twenty-seven was rewritten yesterday."

She shrugged. "I'll have it by the time we get around to filming." She would too. As Matt had quickly discovered, Laura was a professional right down to her coral-painted toenails, now dangling prettily from the counter where she was perched. "How were yesterday's dailies?" she asked, rooting around in the carton for another brazil nut.

"Good. We won't have to reshoot the scene at the Reading Market, either. Got it right the first time."

"Too bad. I was hoping for another trip there. Those cookies…" She closed her eyes and gave a little sigh of pleasure. "Pure chocolate heaven."

He chuckled, shaking his head ruefully. "It's a wonder we have anything left in the refrigerator around here."

"That's right—you're supposed to be bulking up for your next role, aren't you?"

He nodded. "That's one reason I scheduled the fashion plate scenes early in the shoot. In two months, I might look more like a heavyweight fighter than a wealthy stockbroker."

"Oh, you shouldn't worry. According to this article, you have the amazing ability—" Laura held the magazine aloft and began to quote: "'to appear equally at home on a horse as in a Porsche; as comfortable wearing Levi's as wearing Armani. And as graceful on a basketball court playing a pickup game as handing out Academy Awards.'"

Matt dismissed the charges with an elegant lift of his eyebrows, then pulled a leftover steak sandwich from the fridge.

"Speaking of basketball, I'm getting tickets to a Lakers' game in a couple of weeks. Wanna go?"

"Me? I don't know a free throw from a field goal. And I thought you had sworn off public places after that photographer snapped you on your run."

"For a chance to see the Lakers, I'll brave it. Besides, I've made a deal with the local media. They lay off me while I'm here, I hold a press conference when this is over," he said, unwrapping the sandwich.

Laura gave an unladylike snort. "Huh. That's like sharks agreeing to lay off the tuna."

Matt laughed, then ripped off a bite of his sandwich.

"Oh, Annie called. She said her concert this weekend was canceled and she wanted to come out here, maybe meet you in Atlantic City. She said you had mentioned getting together sometime during the shoot."

Matt winced. "Damn. I haven't called her since I've been here."

Laura gazed innocently into the ice cream carton. "She might have mentioned that."

Matt sighed. "I'm too busy this weekend anyway. I'll just have to call her and explain."

"I'm sure she'll understand." Laura said, tossing the empty ice cream carton in the trash.

She probably would, Matt realized.

If he called her now, explained he would have to spend the weekend shooting the scenes they had rescheduled due to the snow…The problem was, it would be a lie. Yes, they would be shooting, but he could work around that. It was his feelings for Claire that were the real problem.

Briefly, he wondered what Claire's reaction would be to a wild weekend in Atlantic City—but then decided to save the image for midnight, when he had time to savor a fantasy.

He set his plate in the sink and glanced at Laura, who had been watching him with an interested expression on her face. He nodded at the notepad near the phone. "That Annie's number?" he asked, realizing he had to be straight with Annie. She deserved that much.

He gave Laura a wry smile. "The Quintessential Guy is about to become the Quintessential Asshole."


Two days later, Claire strolled through the store on her way to her office, noting the signs of the newly begun renovations around her. She had developed the habit of walking up the escalators, which remained frozen until the store opened at ten. She appreciated the exercise, as well as the opportunity to view the selling floor, free of customers at this time of morning.

Kaslow's was getting ready to shed its skin. The store would undergo a complete makeover, including a floor design incorporating the latest retail trends.

Along with its new decor, Kaslow's would acquire a new logo, with packaging and advertising to match. A new look all around, to reflect the new ownership.

If everything went on schedule, most of the renovations should be completed by March. Just in time, Claire thought, hurrying down the corridor to her office, for the *Scandal* debut. Provided Mme. Bendel approved the choice of Kaslow's as the exclusive East Coast distributor.

Maybe the trade she had made with Matt wasn't such a bad deal. And, as filming at Kaslow's had wrapped up without a hitch, she had to admit, not only were her fears groundless, but the potential profit for the store could turn out to be rather tidy.

When she reached her office, there was a surprise waiting. A bouquet of pink roses sat on her desk, with a note attached. Claire peeled off her gloves and opened the small envelope, smiling as she read: *The castle's all yours again. Thanks for everything, Matt.*

And the postscript: *You're invited to a special "premiere," 8:30 a.m. in the theater.*

Joan popped her head in. "Aren't they beautiful? They arrived first thing this morning. And there's going to be a special screening of the footage shot here. Jackie set it up."

"That's nice. You go ahead," Claire told her, unpacking her brief-case. "I need to outline the annual report."

"You're not going?" Joan looked crestfallen, and Matt's words came back to Claire. Was she turning into a spoilsport? It *would* be fun, she realized, to see what the almost finished product looked like. And to see if the store really was shown in its best light. She glanced at her watch. "Well, maybe for a minute," she relented.

Joan's smile widened and she patted her growing stomach. "Good. I hear there's even going to be popcorn."

When she wasn't actually eating, Joan was usually thinking about food. Claire smiled as she stuffed her handbag under the desk. "My grandmother always said a healthy appetite meant a healthy baby," she said, wishing her grandmother were still here to dispense her homespun advice.

Claire slipped into the theater just after the hastily edited film montage started. She couldn't help laughing as she watched—if the outtakes she was watching were any indication, the movie would be a hit. That could only be good for Kaslow's bottom line, she told herself.

Before the selection of clips was over, she felt a movement behind her and a voice whispered in her ear. "How about meeting me on the roof later? We could make a snowman."

Startled, Claire glanced back. Matt's face was limned with light from the entrance, and for a moment, she was star struck.

Then her senses returned. "The HVAC equipment is up there. By now the snow should be filthy."

He chuckled, then leaned close to whisper in her ear again, and the touch of his breath on her neck made her want to shiver. "I promise not to put any down your back."

For an instant Claire found herself tempted. Playing in the snow with Matt…

But that was foolish. Not only was she not dressed for frolic, but she had no desire to encourage a relationship with this man. Or any man, she reminded herself.

There was already a man in her life, and he was at David's house, home from school again while the teachers held an in-service. "Sorry," she told Matt. "But I have bills to pay. We're getting ready to start renovations in earnest, now that you and your crew are out of our hair."

He reached out and looped a strand of her hair behind her ear, and this time Claire couldn't halt the shiver that raced down her spine.

"Did you get my flowers?"

She nodded. "Yes. They were very beautiful." Then from the speakers at the front of the theater, she heard his voice, complaining about the glass slipper he had been given. She arched a look at him over her shoulder. He smiled back.

"If it can make a curmudgeon like you laugh, the rest of the world doesn't stand a chance," he murmured against her ear.

Scattered laughter erupted from the small audience that had gathered as the rest of the outtakes were played—bloopers that normally were edited out of the footage and reserved for celebrity roasts, Matt told her. Then the screen turned blue and the show abruptly ended.

Around them, people began filing out of the theater. A few stopped to congratulate Matt, including Bernard Kaslow.

"You see there, Claire?" he said. "Nothing to worry about. Just good, clean entertainment." He thumped Matt on the back, and then Jackie was next in line with effusive praise. Claire found her exit blocked, the wall on one side and a line of expectant fans on the other.

Matt came to her rescue—and his own. "Claire was just telling me about the renovations getting underway here. In fact, she offered to give me a tour before the store opens." Then he took her by the arm and forged his way through to the entrance of the theater, ignoring the gaping expressions of several disappointed employees.

Claire found herself in the elevator before she could mount a protest.

He leaned back and gazed at her from across the interior. He looked no different in person, she realized, than he had up on the screen, and she knew his persona had little to do with makeup and costumes. It was Matt, solid, sure of himself, with his wide-legged stance and easy laugh, and altogether too tempting when he wanted to play.

But Claire reminded herself again: Playing with Matt was not on her agenda.

As usual, he plowed right over her objections.

"What do you say? I'd really like to see what you're planning to do to this place. It's already quite an impressive building."

"All right," she agreed. "I'll show you around. But the tour ends on the first floor. Before we open at ten." At the entrance to Kaslow's, she could safely see him out of the store—and out of her life.

She ignored the tiny pang that thought gave her.


They got off on the sixth floor. The store was still mostly deserted, with only a few salespeople milling around. They took the escalator, now operating, down through the spine of the store.

Claire stood on the rung ahead of Matt, giving him a view of the top of her head. As they rode down, he examined the neat part in her hair, pulled back and tucked into a neat chignon. When she turned back to speak to him, she caught him staring. Their eyes met, tugged briefly, and then Claire's gaze veered off as she began to speak, taking her role as tour guide seriously.

"The escalators will be replaced by newer, wider versions. Forty-two inches instead of the usual thirty-six," she told him. "That way, couples can stand next to each other or parents can stand next to children."

They reached the next floor, and Matt let her go on talking. "We're constructing a model home here in the furniture department. 'The Twenty-First Century Home.' We'll have products from the other departments strategically placed throughout—coffeemakers, lamps, linens, designer fashions casually left on the bed—that sort of thing."

"Sounds like set decoration."

Claire nodded. "Yes, the retail industry is very much like show business. In fact, we plan to tie in future promotions with local opera and theater productions on the Avenue of the Arts."

Matt ran his hand over the smooth marble column next to the escalator well. "This place is something else. When was it built?" he asked, prompted more by a desire to see the animation her face took on when she talked about the store than historical curiosity.

"The present building, in the eighteen nineties. The first building was destroyed by fire. Hence the ghost stories you may have heard."

"Aren't they true?"

She shrugged. "People swear they've seen the ghost of Eudora Peabody in the ladies' lounge. She was killed in the fire. But I think it's just a rather inventive marketing gimmick on the part of our founder. 'See the ghost at Kaslow's and then check out the sale on winter coats,'" she mocked.

"It's been owned by Kaslow's from the beginning?" They rounded the corner and stepped onto the escalator, this time Matt on the rung below, his gaze level with Claire's.

"That's right."

"That must have been daunting. Coming in after a century of family control."

She met his eyes briefly, then looked away. "There have been a few tense moments."

He didn't comment, and she went on with the tour. "We'll have computer terminals on each floor, near the escalators, which shoppers can use to quickly locate a specific item. Customers want to be able to get in and get out, especially at the downtown location, where many are stopping by on their lunch hour."

Matt made an appreciative sound, watching their progress in the mirrored escalator wall. Claire was wearing a chic little suit, a plaid wool jacket in fuchsia shades, over a charcoal skirt. The color suited her, though Matt guessed she didn't dress in such shades very often.

"Aisles are being widened and rerouted to move traffic through each department. Department store floor plans operate on the 'hub' concept," she explained. "The trick is to prevent it from becoming a hopeless maze, where the customer gets lost."

"It sounds like you know a lot about this. I mean, you don't just sit up in your office and call in overdue accounts, do you?"

She looked surprised. "Of course not. I've studied the retail industry. Before I went to work for Connor, I worked for a department store in Arizona. That's where I met him, in fact."

"Connor? You mean Forrest? That's the new owner, right?" Matt tried to ignore the unaccustomed twinge of jealousy.

She nodded. "The Forrest Group, technically. They're an investment firm — mutual funds, primarily," she explained. "Based in San Francisco."

"And that's where you lived before moving out here," he said, putting the pieces of her life together.

"That's right." She returned to guidebook mode as they skirted a work crew busy polishing the marble floor. "Not everything in the store is being replaced. This floor, for instance, is Lasso white marble imported from Italy when the original store was built."

He let her go on with her travelogue. For the first time, he was seeing a touch of passion, a glow of pride on her face as she pointed out the architectural features of the store. He wondered if she only cared about buildings. Was there no one in her life to cause such an outpouring of affection?

The girl — the woman — she'd been ten years ago, had given him her affection pretty freely, hadn't she, and as a result, her name — even if it wasn't her real name — was smeared in the press, her motives impugned.

Maybe she'd learned a lesson. But, in Matt's mind, it was the wrong lesson. That, he decided, was an overdue account he intended to call in.

When they reached the first floor, Claire led Matt through the labyrinth of cosmetic counters, eerily darkened now, and ended up in the rotunda. It too would undergo a facelift, though mostly only the lighting would be enhanced to reflect off the sparkling fountain in the center.

"Tell me, what's the story with this lady?" Matt asked, taking a seat on the edge of the tile fountain and studying the impassive figure in the center.

"She's supposed to represent the Roman goddess Fortuna. Earnest Kaslow brought her back from Italy, where he rescued her from a fountain in Tuscany. Days after she arrived here, an earthquake destroyed the village where she had resided."

"And I suppose that was blamed on her departure."

"That's one way of looking at it. The other is, she was rescued. From her own fate, so to speak."

Claire gazed at the goddess, who, like the rest of the store, had aged gracefully. She preferred the latter version of the story, having been spared from the whims of fate herself.

Matt's voice intruded in her reverie. "Penny for your thoughts."

Before she could castigate him for the corny line, she noticed the quarter he held in his hand. She smiled. "Inflation?"

"Figured your thoughts might be worth it. You had that look on your face."

"Oh? Which look is that?"

"Like you've just watched some horror flick, and now you're telling yourself it was just a movie."

She shot him an admonishing look. "You've got a vivid imagination."

He shrugged. "Comes in handy in my profession." Then he asked, "Do you ever think, Claire, what your life would have been like if you hadn't disappeared? If you had stayed in Hollywood? It's a given you would have been offered more parts, once the scandal died down."

"No, I never think about that. I told you, I wasn't interested in a film career."

"Oh, come on, you don't regret it at all? Trading the bright lights for the boardroom?"

She bent her gaze from his too-knowing green eyes. She hadn't often imagined how it might have been, the glamour of a Hollywood career. As a twenty-one-year-old, she had barely allowed herself to dream, preferring even then the certainty of the business world to the vagaries of a film career. That, and she was sure she could also do without the very public nature of the film industry. But it was more than her own tiny aspirations she had put behind her—it was Matt himself that she had given up. For the first time, she wondered if cutting him out of her life, out of Tripper's life, had been the best course.

Even the thought seemed dangerous, as if he could read her mind. She glanced at him, but he was staring at the quarter in his fingers. "What do you think, Claire? Should we try it?"

"Try what?" she asked, momentarily taken aback.

"Lady Luck." Without waiting for her reply, he gave a flip of his wrist, sending the coin flying across the water to land with a tiny *plunk* exactly under the watchful eye of the goddess.

Claire frowned. "Don't tell me you buy that."

"Sure, why not?" He grinned. "Don't you believe in fairy tales? Miracles? Wishes in fountains coming true?"

"Not for a minute," she scoffed. "You're in the business of make-believe. You should know better than anyone it's all special effects." She shrugged in dismissal. "Lighting, makeup, smoke and mirrors—"

"Claire," he chided. "Don't you ever just let yourself believe in something you can't see?"

"Of course. I have all the faith in the world—in gravity, atomic theory, cyclical stock markets—"

"Those can all be proven." He dismissed them with a shrug, then eyed her with a speculative glint. "What about love? There's no proof that exists, yet people experience it every day."

She gave him a tight smile. "Do they? I always thought it was hormones."

"For some people it is." He tilted his head, staring at her inquisitively. "How about you? You ever been in love, Claire?"

She flushed, looking away. "No. Never."

"I thought I was, a time or two. Turned out to be hormones." An eyebrow quirked upward.

Claire started to tell him "I told you so," but before she could speak, his gaze trapped hers.

"They're starting to act up again," he said, his voice an octave lower. "They keep urging me on, while my good sense is telling me to steer clear."

She stiffened and looked away. She didn't answer, couldn't immediately come up with a way to turn the conversation back to safer ground.

She could feel his eyes on her, on the pulse beating in her temple. She felt like a butterfly pinned to a mounting board, wings beating furiously in a vain attempt to escape the inevitable.

"You should listen to your good sense. This time," she managed to get out, hoping he would make this easy for her.

Then, from the other side of the foliage, she heard the murmur of voices, the light tread of footsteps. With a relieved sigh, she stood up. "We'd better leave," she said, and then she heard Marcus's deep voice:

"You say she's not in her office? She must be around here somewhere. We could always have her paged."

"Someone must be looking for me," she said with relief. She was expecting an estimator from the contractor's office to stop by later. She turned, catching a glimpse of Marcus's gray head over the palms. "Marcus," she called, her voice echoing in the empty chamber. "I'm over here."

"Is that you, Ms. Porter? There's a young man here to see you."

Before Claire could react, Marcus and Tripper appeared at the opening in the foliage.

"Hey, Mom, I tried to call you! You forgot to sign my permission slip yesterday. David's mom is taking us to practice later—Mom?" Then his eyes traveled to the man standing next to her. Marcus gave him a little salute and turned to head back toward his post by the entrance.

Claire could only stand frozen, on legs that shook like saplings, and stare at her son as if he were an apparition.

But Tripper was too busy examining the man beside her to notice her reaction. "Hey! Aren't you—"

"Matt Grayson." Matt stuck out a hand. "And you?"

"Tripper—I mean Trevor—Porter."

"Well, Tripper-I-mean-Trevor, it's nice to meet you. Claire, you didn't tell me you had a son."

Claire was struck mute, unable to speak over the buzzing in her head, a cacophony of lies, all wanting to break out in a symphony of self-preservation.

Tripper shifted in his sneakers, a self-conscious grin on his face. "Tripper's just a nickname. My real name is Trevor, but no one calls me that." Oddly, it struck Claire that he didn't usually bother telling anyone his real name.

"Trevor," Matt repeated. "Porter, you said? Like your Mom?" he asked, and Claire knew the pieces would soon fall together, unless she forced a lie from her frozen lips.

Then Matt seemed to notice Tripper's outfit. "Basketball practice? Aren't you a little short to play for the Sixers?"

Tripper smiled, a shy, closemouthed grin that usually broke Claire's heart. But the block of ice she had become thankfully had no emotions.

"My mom just bought this for me to wear. It's not my uniform or anything. We play for a league at the Y." He glanced at Claire. "It's called 'Basketball Bridges.' It's so inner-city kids and kids from the suburbs can play on the same team — isn't that right, Mom?"

She struggled to locate her voice. "That's right. Do you have your permission slip? I'll sign it." Her voice sounded like a layer of thin ice that threatened to crack at any moment.

"Need a pen?" Matt reached in his pocket and pulled out a ballpoint. Claire stared at it, afraid to reach for it with her shaking hands. "Claire? You okay?"

She grabbed the pen, pulling herself together. "Yes, I'm fine." She even managed a little smile to prove it. "David's mother must be waiting. You need to hurry—"

"She's waiting at the door. They wouldn't let her in. Marcus said it was because of the movie people."

"My fault." Matt shrugged.

Claire knew his interest was piqued, the inevitable questions piling up. Her throat dry, she wished she could simply press pause and rewind the film. But instead the action continued, surely damning her more with every moment.

Matt crossed his arms casually and sized up Tripper. "You must be about, what? Ten, twelve years old?"

"I'm nine."

Matt's eyebrows lifted ever so slightly. "Tall for your age, aren't you?"

With a tiny touch of pride in his voice that pierced Claire's heart, Tripper told him, "I'll be ten in March. March tenth."

It took exactly nine seconds for the smile on Matt's face to turn sickly. "I see." And then it was his turn to be struck dumb.

Claire scribbled her name on the permission slip, silently cursing herself for forgetting when he had asked her earlier in the week. This she couldn't blame on the gods.

"Okay, honey, you'd better run. Candace is waiting." She gave him a weak smile, silently urging him to go.

"And I need a check for thirty dollars, remember?"

"I'll have to get it from my purse." She seized the excuse as a drowning woman grabs a rope. "It's in my office. We'll have to go upstairs," she added, relief coloring her voice.

"Can I stay here?"

"No—"

"Sure," Matt said, the agreeable tone a tad too hard to ring true. "You go on, Claire. I'll wait here with Tripper. We'll talk basketball." The look he gave her was bland, impossible to read. Then he turned to Tripper. "So what position do you play?"

Claire didn't know how she managed to walk away, but she heard her footsteps on the cool marble floor, the sound echoing in rhythm with the heavy thudding of her heart against her chest.

# CHAPTER ELEVEN

When she returned fifteen minutes later, check in hand, Matt and Tripper were talking like old friends. But Matt, she noticed, avoided meeting her eyes.

She handed Tripper the check, and with a grin and a wave of farewell for Matt, he hurried toward the front entrance.

When he was gone, Claire braced herself for the inevitable.

"You've got some explaining to do," Matt said quietly.

She stared at the fountain, the water silent and still now. All the excuses she had invented during her brief escape to her office — the lies — came creeping to her throat, where they snagged on a vestige of honesty.

He let the silence spin out, while her lies decomposed.

"You gonna tell me that kid's not mine?" he finally said, his voice oddly neutral.

"Would you believe it?" she asked, daring to glance at him for a reaction.

"Not without a blood test."

"I'm not putting him through that!"

"Right now, what you want is not my primary concern," he said, arms crossed as if reining himself in. "I've got a strong suspicion that kid's my flesh and blood, and you haven't bothered to inform me of that in almost ten years. And that, lady, makes my blood boil. All this crap about not letting us in here to film—that was just to cover your lovely little ass, wasn't it? You didn't want me getting near enough to find out your ten-year-old secret—"

"Stop it!" Claire hissed, alarmed. "Someone will hear you!"

"I don't give a damn if that statue there turns into a tabloid reporter and starts taking notes! You lied to me, and you're gonna start explaining right now!"

"For God's sake, please!" she said, her voice shaking. "Do you want him to find out, this way? Do you want him to read it in the paper, or worse, hear it on the playground, that his father—his mother—" She broke off, desperately afraid she would give in to the tears that threatened.

"He has no idea who his father is, does he? What did you do, lie to him too?" He looked at her in disgust. "What kind of mother are you?"

Despite her agitation, she bristled at his words. No one had ever called into question her abilities as a mother. In fact, throughout the years, she had grown accustomed to shrugging off the figurative pats on the back from her harried colleagues, struggling to raise kids in two-parent households. She alone was responsible for Tripper's upbringing, and she wasn't about to take a hit, no matter how well deserved, for a lack in that department.

Gratefully, she seized the anger that bubbled to the surface and let it rout that old urge to cringe, to flee and hide where nothing could reach her. Her gaze hardened as she answered him. "I'm the kind of mother who'll protect her son at all costs. Yes, I lied to him, and to you, and to whoever I had to, because to tell the truth would have meant ridicule. For my child. For an innocent little boy, whose only sin was being born to parents who should have known better. Don't you see what a field day they would have had? The papers, the TV, those horrible things they said…It would have reflected on him. On my son." Her voice caught. "Matt, please—"

She stopped, trembling, staring at him, the anger dissipating into stark terror. The thought of public exposure, for her son this time, was infinitely more upsetting than anything that had been done to her.

But she was seeking understanding from a man who regularly had his life dissected by the press. How could he comprehend her maternal fear, a fear that had held on to a secret that affected him equally?

He seemed to be trying to get a grip on his own emotions, undoubtedly too ripped apart to comprehend hers right now.

"My son, Claire. That kid is my son." He said it as if now there were no doubt. "You've kept my son from me. All these years, that kid was growing up, not knowing who his father was, while I hadn't a clue there was a kid somewhere running around with my genes." His voice steadily raised. "You know what you've done to us—to both of us, Claire? Do you have any fucking idea how I feel right now?"

She flinched.

"That's right. I'm angry." He pointed a finger at her. "I'm pissed as hell. And that's exactly why I'm not going to talk to you about this right now." He gave her a grim look. "Because I'm not a very nice guy when I'm angry."

He let that hang and then turned and said over his shoulder, "You'll be hearing from my attorneys soon. Don't go anywhere."

Claire stood as if turned to stone while his footsteps echoed faintly in the rotunda. Thank God the foliage had muffled their voices—otherwise, anyone could have overheard.

She struggled to organize her thoughts. Briefly she considered, then rejected, a plan to escape, to run, just as he had warned against. Matt would find them. Or worse, the hounds of the press would.

Attorneys. She would hire a lawyer, the best one she could afford—as would he, she realized. There was no way she could beat him on legal grounds.

That left appealing to his better nature. She was sure he had one. Right now he was angry, justifiably so, but the stakes were too high to allow him to react out of anger toward her. Somehow she had to make him see that Tripper would be the one to lose from any animosity he felt.

She simply had to convince him of that. But first she had to get herself in control, stop this weak-kneed trembling.

She stiffened her shoulders, then went upstairs to her office, mentally crossing off her options along the way.

Matt blinked the sweat from his eyes and increased the speed on the treadmill. Through the wide windows, he could see another round of snow falling, but inside the gym it was hot as a jungle.

It suited his mood. Today he wasn't running for fitness but to outrun the anger that had boiled in him ever since three hours before, when he had come face to face with Claire's lie.

A lie in the form of a son. A living, breathing, flesh-and-blood replica of himself. A child who had been growing up, forming a personality, learning about the world, all without his input.

Damn it, the kid was probably as uptight as his mother. Had she raised him alone all these years? Then an unpleasant thought struck him: Had she marched a series of boyfriends through the poor kid's life, in an effort to provide "male role models?" Or worse, had her bitterness toward the male gender been reflected on the kid? Or did she reserve that only for him?

It was no good wondering. He would find out for himself what kind of son she had raised. And if she didn't like the idea, too bad.

His lawyers would eat her alive in court. He smiled. Claire may have managed to get the best of him while negotiating the location fee, but that had only been a minor skirmish. This time, he would call the shots.

After all, he was holding the trump card. A word from him could expose the executive charade she had been living all this time, a charade he knew was important to her.

But feeding her to the wolves wouldn't solve anything. His muscles began to protest the pace he was setting. He slowed down, his anger reduced now to a simmer.

Maybe he should wait and hear what she had to say before he called his lawyer. Things would only get messier if this scene was played out in a courtroom. And now that the urge to strangle that pretty neck of hers had lessened somewhat, he was in a mood to listen.

But damned if she would outgun him this time.


Later that night, too keyed up to sleep, Claire got up, went downstairs, and fixed herself a cup of herbal tea. She curled up on the couch, determined to face the issue she had been avoiding ever since the morning's encounter with Matt.

She wondered what he was thinking. How much he must hate her, despise her for keeping this secret from him all along. She tried to reconcile the Matt who had dwelt in her mind all along with the new version she had become acquainted with during the past few weeks. Though in the press he came across as a happy-go-lucky cowboy who had just wandered into Hollywood by mistake, in reality he possessed a streak of sobriety, a maturity that had grown over the years. All in all, even she had to admit he wasn't bad father material.

But Tripper had come this far without Matt in his life, and as she well knew, there were worse things than growing up without a father.

But it was all a moot point. There was no way Matt would agree to just forget about his son, and she was sure he believed that Tripper was his son. Could she even try to convince him that he wasn't the father? He could demand a blood test…

She sighed. Somehow, she would have to convince him to do what was best for Tripper. She set her cup down, picked up a pencil and notepad, and began to list her talking points. Meticulous preparation had won her more than one boardroom battle, and now, with her son's future at stake, she wouldn't overlook a single reason why Matt should stay the hell away from her child.


She had to wait until Monday morning for the opportunity. When she arrived at work, she had a message from Matt. She returned his call.

"Meet me in my trailer in half an hour." He didn't give her a chance to object. Then he gave her directions—they were filming nearby—and hung up. Obviously he had decided that this time, the battle would go down on his turf.

Fine. Her talking points would be just as potent, regardless of the setting.

When she arrived, an assistant led her to his trailer, rapped on the door, and left when Matt opened it. A phone to his ear, he tossed out instructions to whoever was on the other end. He glanced at Claire, then wrapped up his conversation.

He nodded toward the couch. "Have a seat. If you can find one."

From the leather couch, Claire lifted an assortment of papers—dog-eared pages of the working script, a few coffee-stained call sheets, and a copy of the latest tabloid, she noted with disgust. She set them on a nearby table, where a half-eaten bagel had been abandoned, then took a seat on the couch, feeling vulnerable as she sank into the soft cushions.

Matt picked up a straight chair, turned it backward, and sat facing her. He looked tired, and she wondered if he too had spent a sleepless night. His brown hair had been trimmed into a neat conservative style, and gone was the stubble that had shaded his chin for the last week. His usual jeans had been replaced by a light brown suit and sport shirt.

She decided she much preferred her adversaries clad in denim.

He folded his arms and gave her a belligerent stare. "Are we going to start with the assumption he's my kid? Or are you going to argue that point? Because I won't hesitate to ask for a blood test, you know."

"I'm sure you won't. Although, for someone in your position…"

"What the hell does my position have to do with it?"

"I would think you would be happy to avoid a paternity suit."

"You thought wrong. Don't tell me that's why you neglected to tell me this for ten years."

She shrugged. "It's true I didn't think you would exactly welcome the news."

"It's still no reason to keep that boy from knowing his father. Was there any doubt in your mind who his father was?"

She looked at him sharply.

"Was there someone else, Claire? In the same time frame, who could have been — who you thought…"

"No. I never…I was always sure," she said, aware the words indicted her.

He nodded, then eyed her with something like chagrin. "I recall we didn't use birth control. And back then I still believed I could outrun Mother Nature." His mouth twisted in a rueful grimace. "Someone ought to inform the locker room there's been a research breakthrough."

Claire vaguely remembered his promises long ago to "pull out." At the time, it had only been some foreign phrase she knew instinctively was meant to protect her. Unfortunately, she had trusted her instincts and trusted Matt.

But now she was much more worried about saving her skin — and Tripper's — than in censuring Matt for failing to use protection. "We could both plead ignorance," she told him, willing to absolve him of blame if he would do the same.

"All right, we got that much out of the way. Then tell me why — why you never felt you could come to me? After the publicity died down, why didn't you come then?"

She swallowed carefully. This was the question she had dreaded for years, rehearsing it occasionally in the silence of the night.

"I…" She hesitated. "When I found out, I was afraid. Afraid of the publicity. What had been done to me was still…fresh. I couldn't face it again, and I knew it would just add to the scandal. So I thought I would wait, get through the pregnancy."

She paused, remembering. "And then, after he was born, while I was still in the hospital, in fact, I was offered a job. A pretty good job, working in the accounting division of a department-store chain in Arizona. And my grandmother was able to take care of him during the day, at least until I found a good daycare." It had been a struggle, but Gram had been supportive.

"I knew I could make it financially," she told him, "without your help."

"And you never thought he just might need a father? Never mind what I needed to know; he deserved to know the truth."

"At what risk? The risk that his very existence would be questioned, by you, by the public? I couldn't bear to have his picture splashed in the tabloids, the 'love child' of Matt Grayson and the tramp he took to bed. I would have spared him from that, regardless of the cost. And he hasn't suffered, I'll swear to that. He grew up knowing he was loved, and wanted, and—and a valuable human being, regardless of his birth." So unlike her own upbringing, when love had been a mere abstract.

Matt spoke patiently. "I can see that, Claire. I'm not saying you didn't do everything you could for him. But the press could have been handled—"

"How can you say that? Even now, you can't handle your own press! By last count, you've had dozens of affairs in just the last month! You've had countless encounters with aliens; your diet consists of raw eggs that supposedly give you superhuman strength…" She picked up the paper near her and shoved it toward him.

He glanced at the headline and made a face. "And here I figured you preferred *The Wall Street Journal*." Then he shook his head. "Come on, Claire, you know better than anyone those rags are full of lies."

"How could I subject an innocent child to that—that scrutiny?" She spit the word out, horrified.

"Celebrities have children every day. Some of us even manage to live normal lives. How can you use that as an excuse for what you did?"

"I know you can't possibly understand. And I'll admit, if I had come to you in the beginning, it may have been easier. But…" She paused, searching for words and knowing she was in an impossible situation. "I was frightened. Not just for me, but for him. I could only imagine what would be done to him. And I was…feeling so guilty myself, I thought I probably deserved everything that had been done to me. But he was just an innocent child."

He sighed. "All right. I'll accept that you were scared, alone. You weren't sure how I would react, much less how it would play in the press. But now it's a different matter. We need to tell him the truth, get things worked out between us."

"No! Absolutely not. Don't you see? Nothing has changed. Just because you know he exists—"

"Of course the situation has changed!" he exploded, rising from the chair and pacing across the room that felt too small to contain his anger. "I'm not about to walk away from the knowledge that I've got a son who's growing up without me."

That was exactly what she had feared. In the middle of the night, it had seemed reasonable, logical, that he would agree to walk away and leave her and Tripper to live their lives in peace. But now, from the set expression on his face, she could see convincing him of that was hopeless.

"Aren't you concerned about what this will do to him? He's just a little boy; he's got enough to deal with right now," she pleaded. "We just moved here. He misses his friends in San Francisco, and fourth graders can be…well, his teacher refers to it as the 'fourth-grade proving grounds.'"

"All the more reason to have his father around," he said, a stubborn look on his face—a look she had seen often on her son.

"You can't possibly think to just spring a father on him after all these years."

"Why the hell not? And just who exactly did you tell him was his father? Or does he think he's the product of an immaculate conception?"

"Of course not! I explained to him that things didn't work out between his biological father and myself. That we were incompatible. He knows plenty of other kids whose parents are divorced."

"Only difference is, his parents never got a chance to know each other, much less split up."

"Well, at least I've spared him the heartache of a broken home," she pointed out.

He settled on the chair again, too near, too perceptive. "You think it was inevitable, that you and I wouldn't have made it?"

She stared at him, incredulous. "Of course. There was never anything between us." She glanced away. "Except sex."

"That's not such a bad start." A wry grin spread on his face. He seemed to have tamped down his fury at her deception, though she could see it still simmered just below the surface.

"I want to get to know him, Claire. You owe me that much."

She looked at him doubtfully. "I don't think that would be a very good idea."

"It's a great idea," he argued. "I'm here for another six weeks or so, and I intend to see him every chance I can. Which won't be that often, with the schedule we're on, but I can make some time."

She weighed her options. If he was willing to settle for a few visits and would agree that Tripper didn't need to be told the truth, then perhaps she could go along. At least she would have time to figure out another plan.

Like moving to Antarctica.

"All right. You can see him. But under absolutely no circumstances are you to let him know of our relationship. He can't even know we were acquainted once."

"Wait a minute. You want me to lie to him?" He crossed his arms, pinning her with a stare.

"There's no need to lie; he'll never think to wonder if his mother is—was—involved with you, unless you tell him."

He studied her for a moment, clearly not happy, but she held the trump card: She was Tripper's mother, had single-handedly raised him until now. He couldn't—wouldn't—go against her wishes.

"All right. I won't breathe a word to him. But we'll have to arrange some reason for me to see him."

She thought quickly. "You could come to our house. We'll tell him it's business."

He shook his head. Then, with a wicked gleam in his eye, he suggested, "Why don't we tell him I've got the hots for you and we're dating?"

But Claire shook her head. "No. He'll never believe that."

"Why not?"

"He just…won't," she told him, not bothering to point out that for her, a date came around about as often as a lunar eclipse.

Matt just shrugged. "We'll think of something. Most evenings I'm tied up, so we'll have to make it this weekend. I'll give you a call and let you know what time."

Claire agreed, then returned to her office, not sure if she had won that round or not.

# Chapter Twelve

True to his promise, Matt called the next day and arranged to join them for dinner on Sunday afternoon. Claire spent Saturday searching her repertoire for a suitable recipe.

She wanted to feed him arsenic; she settled for chicken.

Now, as the carrot she was attempting to julienne slipped from the knife yet again, she wondered if Martha Stewart was available for a consultation. Maybe she should have picked up Chinese instead. With only Tripper's palate to please, her cooking skills had remained in the adequate range, though she did occasionally like to experiment.

After five attempts, the carrot finally cooperated, slivering into neat strips that would even make Martha proud. Claire held the knife aloft and smiled, triumphant. This was the best brand of knife Kaslow's sold, and now she could attest to its effectiveness.

The doorbell rang, preceded by the quick thud of footsteps running to the door—Tripper must have been watching from the window. So much for his attempts to be "cool" about Matt's impending arrival, she thought, her heart giving a funny little flip. If Matt ever disappointed him…she would slice him to ribbons, she told herself, whacking the next carrot with more force than was necessary.

The door to Claire's house swung wide. As Tripper greeted him, Matt noticed the eager look on his face, a look he was clearly trying to hide. As the boy stood there, shyness battled with fascination, striking him dumb, and he could only stare up at Matt.

Matt was used to dealing with hero worshipping nine-year-olds, but the last thing he wanted was for this particular kid to see him as a celebrity. A tiny part of him did acknowledge, though, that he wouldn't mind playing the role of hero to his son. "Hey, there, sport," he said with a congratulatory look. "Heard you guys won your first practice game yesterday."

Tripper's face lit. "Yeah, we creamed 'em at the free-throw line. We have this guy Jamal; he's, like, six feet tall and he's only twelve."

As he went on to recount the most exciting moment in sports history, at least in his young life, Matt relaxed. Not until he knocked on the door had he even been aware of the flicker of apprehension he felt. What if his son shared Claire's opinion of him? It was possible her bitterness had rubbed off on the kid, without her knowledge perhaps, but still, winning over the mother was proving to be a hard enough task.

As Matt followed Tripper through the house, he took in the surroundings, curious. For the last few months, he'd thought of Claire as existing in the vacuum of her seventh floor office, a woman without a home. But this was where she lived, along with their son.

And they hadn't exactly been living in poverty, he noted with relief. The smell of new construction still clung to the walls of the spacious interior. Off to one side of the entry hall, he could see a formal living room, seemingly reconstructed from the pages of *Metropolitan Home*. Rich garnet draperies framed the front window behind a spotless off-white sofa.

Not a couch a kid would want to kick back on with a glass of Kool-Aid. He mentally envisioned the words "Don't touch" written all over it—just like its owner.

The hall opened up to a den, less formal than the living room, with a cozy fireplace on one wall. He could almost imagine Claire relaxing on the plaid couch, maybe even dropping that cool air of formality she wore like armor.

But he was here to get to know his son, not to critique Claire's decorator.

He followed a still chattering Tripper into the kitchen, where Claire, a determined look on her face, expertly wielded a ten-inch knife.

He eyed it warily. "Have you got a license to carry that thing?"

The look she shot him started out exasperated, then changed to surprise as she caught sight of the flowers in his hand. Momentarily speechless, she finally managed to retort, "I should ask you the same thing. I hear some women consider flowers a lethal weapon."

"Oh, I've got more lethal weapons than tulips, trust me." He gave her a leer, because, heck, she deserved it.

The look she shot him could have frozen the Mohave.

She pointed the knife in his direction. "You're not getting one more day of filming in Kaslow's. Not even for tulips."

He looked offended. "Did I say anything about filming? Besides, you saw the footage we shot. It's great." Still distracted by the knife, he added: "Maybe you should put that thing down — real slow, now, we don't want any casualties."

The knife clattered in the sink as Claire cast a sidelong glare at Matt. "Tripper, could you grab a vase from the china cabinet? And then why don't you take Matt into the family room and…talk basketball or something, until I can get this on the table."

She seemed intent on reminding him the reason he was here was to get to know his son, not to flirt with her. But flirting with Claire was more fun than he'd had since he was sixteen and feeling up Kassie Smith in her parents' driveway.


During their meal, Claire figured she could have served braised shoe leather for all the attention the two males at the table gave the meal. She had already come to the conclusion that Matt would eat anything that didn't flop around on his plate, and Tripper was so busy pumping Matt for information that he didn't notice he was eating sticks of zucchini along with his carrots.

Matt described his ranch in Montana, which he claimed was the real thing, not like one of the outfits displaced Californians bought in a lame attempt to play cowboy by raising buffalo and llamas. His foreman saw to the day-to-day operation, while his sister-in-law kept an eye on the books — when she wasn't busy raising four kids and working part time as a nurse at the county hospital. Supermom, the western version, Claire mentally dubbed her, silently resenting the woman sight unseen. His brother Mark, Matt added, coached the local high school football team.

"And my sister Carolyn is a bug doctor in Minneapolis," he told them, helping himself to another serving of rice pilaf. "She and her husband both teach at the university there."

"She's a what?" Claire stared at him, not sure she had heard correctly.

"She's an entomologist," he explained. "She studies bugs. She's always going off to South America, looking for some exotic species."

Tripper's eyes lit up. "Cool!"

"You have another sister, right?" Claire asked, remembering he had talked of his family at length ten years ago.

"Yeah, Sarah. She lives in Livingston, has two kids, and teaches second grade."

"And your parents?"

"They're right there in Great Falls. Dad retired from the feed store a couple of years ago and spends the day fiddling with Lionel trains in the garage." He glanced at Claire over the platter of chicken, and she quickly lowered her gaze. She understood all too well the point he was making. He had just taken pains to "introduce" his family to them, for the express purpose, she supposed, of letting her know that Tripper had a complete set of relatives he had never met.

One more strike against her. It had never really occurred to her that by depriving her son of his father, she had also deprived him of aunts, uncles, cousins, and grandparents.

She tried to wipe the sick look off her face.

Matt pressed his advantage. "Listen, if your mom says it's all right, I thought maybe we could catch a Sixers' game one weekend. They play the Lakers in a couple of weeks. I've got a pal who's getting me tickets."

Tripper's face lit up, and Claire suppressed the urge to kick Matt under the table. She settled for throwing him a look that promised further discussion and a noncommittal murmur in Tripper's direction.

Then, smiling brightly, she changed the subject. "How about dessert? I made Tripper's favorite — peanut butter pie." If Matt wanted to play dirty, she decided she could too; after all, she did have a ten-year head start.

It turned out Matt loved peanut butter pie, too. After cleaning their plates, they both cast hopeful looks in her direction, twin sets of verdigris eyes turned innocently on her.

Claire's heart lurched. The two of them were as alike as a pair of vases, molded from the same clay. Scooping up generous helpings of pie, she wished she *had* opted for Australia, rather than face Matt Grayson over chicken and pie and their son.

After lunch, Claire decided the male bonding had gone far enough for one day. A subtle hint to Tripper had him heading off to David's to finish the snow fort they had begun earlier, but only after Matt had promised he would be back soon. Surprisingly, Tripper didn't seem to find the idea of a return visit from Matt odd, though Claire expected he would pester her with questions later.

But right now, it was time to lay down ground rules.

She turned to him and said firmly, "Matt, you simply cannot make plans without consulting me."

"If you're talking about the basketball game, I did consult you—"

"Right in front of Tripper! And now I have to be the bad guy and tell him he can't go."

"Actually, I was sort of hoping you would say yes."

"I can't let him be seen in public with you! My God, the press would have a field day with that!"

He sighed. "I told you, I can handle the press—and it's just a basketball game. People will be more interested in seeing Kobe Bryant sink a three-pointer than in watching to see who's in the crowd."

She gave him an exasperated look. "Matt! You attract cameras the way a loss leader attracts bargain hunters!"

His eyebrows shot up. "A loss leader? You're comparing me to a loss leader?"

"It's when—"

"I know what it is. I'm hurt, Claire, that you think of me as a discounted houseware." The glint in his eyes wasn't hurt, though. It was satisfied. Amused. He thought this was a game, but she wasn't about to assist his three-point attempt.

"I can't let you take him to a public event." She gave him the same warning look that usually worked with Tripper.

"You're being paranoid." Amusement turned to annoyance. "No one would find it the least bit unusual that I'm escorting a beautiful woman and her son to a Lakers' game."

She crossed her arms in stony silence, refusing to acknowledge the compliment.

He shrugged. "It's not for a couple of weeks. We'll talk about it later." Having planted the idea, Matt seemed to know when to retreat. He glanced at his watch. "I need to get back; I've got a meeting with the production staff in an hour."

But as they reached the door, he offered another compliment, one Claire was much more touched to receive. Pausing, he gazed at her sincerely and, in his deep Western drawl, said, "Pretty smart kid you got there. I guess he gets that from you. At his age, I think the only three-syllable word I used regularly was 'hamburger.'"

Her gaze dipped. She was more relieved that he was leaving than to hear the compliment, but then he continued. "Seriously, I was afraid…oh, hell, you know, growing up without a father around, he could have turned out…" His voice trailed off as he searched for the politically correct word.

She frowned. "You mean you thought I would have raised a sissy."

A slow grin spread over his face. "Actually, now that I think about it, I guess that was pretty silly. There's nothing at all sissy about you. In fact," he added, a considerate look on his face, "I'd put your balls up against just about any guy I know."

He tipped an imaginary hat, then walked out the door. "I'll call you next week," he promised, and Claire breathed a sigh of relief as the door shut behind him.

The irony hit her: For years she had searched out role models for her son, and now that the perfect one had arrived on the scene, she wished him a thousand miles away.

It was the effect he had on her, not her son, which set off alarms in her mind.

Just a word of praise from Matt meant more than any job promotion, a feeling she wasn't at all sure she liked.

Or deserved, for that matter.

# Chapter Thirteen

Later that night, in his bed surrounded by notes, Matt tossed down the copy of the script he was trying to read. It was no use; there was no way he could concentrate on the action he was planning to film tomorrow.

Now that his anger with Claire had died down, he couldn't get over the fact he was a father.

He leaned back against the pillow. His son was a nice-looking kid, too. The resemblance to himself at that age was unmistakable, though Tripper's hair was a little darker, his features a little sharper. He also bore a striking resemblance to Ben, Mark's son. Of course, they were cousins. In fact, Tripper had a total of seven first cousins he had never met, plus aunts, uncles — and grandparents.

He was certain of his parents' reaction when they eventually found out. Harold and Joyce would welcome a new grandchild, no questions asked. As firmly grounded as the rugged mountains to the west, they had raised all four of their children with strict Lutheran values, and though his scrapes as a youngster had often tried their patience, their support had never wavered.

His fame had failed to impress any of them. When he screwed up, they were the first to tell him. They were immensely proud of him, but he often suspected they would have felt the same way if he had stayed in Montana and run his dad's feed store.

Whenever the inflated egos and plastic values of Hollywood got to him, he escaped to Montana. The fact that he arrived in a private jet made no difference; once there, he was simply another rancher in a four-wheel drive.

He picked up the phone on his nightstand and punched the code for his brother in Great Falls.

His sister-in-law answered. Matt returned her greeting. "Hey, Mel. It's me."

"Matt! How are you? Stacy! Go get your dad out in the barn. Tell him Uncle Matt's on the phone." Matt could almost see Mel in her big kitchen, directing dinner cleanup with her usual efficiency. "How's the movie going? Mark said you just about had the exterior shots wrapped up."

"They're all in the can now. From here on out, it's indoor recess."

"Well, that's good, I guess. By the way, we were out at your place this past weekend. Randy's going to have the new fences put in as soon as the weather breaks."

"Maybe I'll get out there by the time the snow melts. So far we've stuck to our shooting schedule. Unless post production holds us up," he added, wondering if he could get Tripper out during spring break. But the thought of Claire's reaction nearly killed the idea.

He heard Melinda's voice, directed away from the phone. "Ben! Don't let that dog in unless you give him a bath first!"

Matt was used to the constant activity at his brother's house. His own home seemed lifeless compared to their Montana version of the Brady Bunch.

"Here's Mark. I'll talk to you later, Matt."

Mark's quiet voice came on the line. "What's up?"

"Just need some advice, big brother. It was either you or my lawyer. I figured you had more experience when it came to fatherhood."

There was silence on the other end. "Mark? You there?"

"Yeah, I'm here. I'm just recalling that talk I had with you out in the barn, right before you took Susie Campbell to the freshman dance."

"I thought it was behind the feed store, before homecoming with Valerie Parker."

"Must've had to do it more than once. You want me to run through it again, or have you got the particulars straight now?"

"They're straight, all right. In fact, you had me too scared to touch a girl for about six months after one of those talks."

"Glad to know it worked. I had one with Andy the other day. Hope he got the message as well as you did."

"I don't know if I'd say that." Matt chuckled. "I had a little bit of a surprise the other day. Maybe I should say a big surprise—about the size of a nine-year-old boy, as a matter of fact." He paused to let that sink in, picturing his brother's face.

He heard a heavy sigh. "Maybe you should call your lawyer, after all. If you're being sued, I can't help you much."

"I'm not being sued. In fact, she didn't want me to know at all. I found out by accident." He explained the whole story, only leaving out exactly who the mother was.

Mark's reply was measured. "It sounds to me like you're ready to take responsibility here, whether the mother wants you to or not."

"This kid is my son. It may be a little late to start playing daddy, but he deserves at least to know who his father is."

"Maybe so, but that's a lot to spring on a kid. You might want to go slow with him. I know you, Matt. Yesterday is always too late for you. Give the boy some time. Give the mother some time. Sounds like she hardly knows you."

"Yeah, well, other than in the biblical sense, I don't really know her either. She's changed a hell of a lot since I was involved with her."

"Then you want my advice? Get to know her and your son. Leave the lawyers out of it. If this kid is really yours—"

"He's really mine." Matt couldn't say why he was so sure, other than the family resemblance. It was a gut feeling, maybe, but one he'd stake his life on.

"Then," Mark reassured him, "I expect things will work out."

Matt hung up the phone, then noticed Sadie looking pleadingly up at him. As he walked downstairs to let her out, he realized he had the perfect excuse to see Tripper on a regular basis.

He just hoped Claire liked dogs.

Claire didn't know which made Tripper more excited: the news that Matt was dropping by again this evening, or that he was offering Tripper a job dog sitting.

He had called her at work, and she had tentatively agreed to his plan. She wanted to discuss it with Tripper first, though, to make sure he was up to the responsibility.

Tripper had no qualms. "You did say we could maybe get a dog."

"I said a 'pet.' A rambunctious golden retriever isn't quite what I had in mind." She set her briefcase on the desk in the kitchen. The reports she'd brought home to read could wait until after Tripper went to bed.

"Please, Mom. I'll take good care of her. You'll never even know she's in the house, I promise." His hopeful expression would have moved Scrooge, and the idea of having another female companion around, even one of another species, was oddly appealing.

When Matt appeared at the door twenty minutes later, a sack of dog food in one hand and a leash in the other, Claire could see the matter was settled.

"Come on in," she told him, opening the door wide to accommodate them. At the sight of the dog, Claire could feel her heart melting. With a coat the color of cookie dough and chocolate puddles for eyes, Sadie was comfort food on four legs.

Tripper immediately dropped to a worshipful pose in front of her, and Claire was left to deal with Matt, who stood grinning down at her.

"Okay. What's the verdict?" he asked, and Claire was sure he knew full well he had won another round in the battle they seemed to be continually waging. But this time the spoils might just go to her.

She nodded toward the floor, where her son was on the receiving end of the ancient canine friendship ritual. She hoped it was true that dog saliva was harmless. "She can stay. I can't say no to true love, can I?"

He smiled approvingly. "You're learning."

Matt went back to his car, a four-wheel drive he'd rented, to get the water bowl and food dish. When he came back in, she was on the floor, stroking Sadie's head. "She's really beautiful, Matt," she said, glancing up at him. "I'm sure Tripper will take good care of her. He's been wanting a dog for some time. I told him we'd think about getting a pet this summer."

Tripper scrambled to his feet and took the food from him. "My friend David has a dog, so I know a lot about taking care of them already. How often do you think she'll need to go out?"

As Matt and Tripper discussed the specifics of dog care, Claire filled the water dish in the kitchen. She found a convenient spot for it next to the refrigerator.

When she stood up, Matt was in the doorway, watching her with a satisfied look on his face. "This will be a perfect excuse to come out here occasionally to see him, but personally I liked my first idea better."

It took her a moment to figure out he was referring to his plan to "date" her. She frowned. "I don't think you'd find me very good at playing that particular role anymore." Then she glanced past him toward the living room. "Where's Tripper?" she asked, fearing he would overhear their conversation.

"I sent him out on a walk. I wanted to talk to you, make sure this is really all right."

"Of course it is. I would tell you if I had any objections."

He quirked an eyebrow. "Having had my ass blistered with your objections before, I have no doubt of that."

Claire resisted the urge to tell him perhaps she should have objected a little more frequently in her past dealings with him. Instead she smiled and said, "Actually, I like the idea of having a dog around. We had a cat in San Francisco, but she died shortly before we left."

He leaned against the counter. "A kid needs a pet or two hanging around. One day I'd like to get him his own horse. My niece Jenny keeps one out at my place, rides it when they come out. There's plenty of room to keep a couple more. Maybe when you all come out for a visit this summer—"

"Hold it." She held up her hand. "Aren't you getting the cart a little ahead of the horse, so to speak? I haven't said we were going anywhere this summer, and he's only nine years old. Much too young to have his own horse, no matter who his father is or how big your barn is." Her voice rose as her heart tripped on the idea of her son spending more time with Matt.

"Calm down," Matt said, putting a placating hand on her shoulder. "I'm not about to spoil him rotten just to make up for the years I've lost. That's what you're afraid of, isn't it? That I can offer him more than you can, and he might come to prefer his long-lost dad?"

"Don't be ridiculous!" She glared at him, not willing to admit there might be a grain of truth in what he was saying.

He looked away, dragging his hand through his hair and standing the short strands on end. Just like Tripper's, Claire realized, right after he got out of the shower.

"Claire, I'm trying to reassure you, not piss you off. There's not a chance in the world he's going to see me as anything but an absentee father, regardless of how many basketball games I take him to or how many pets I give him. You're his mother, and you've been there for him from the beginning. That won't change when he finds out I'm his dad."

Claire gathered her arms around her chest, protecting herself from his words, from her fears…

He reached toward her, but she turned away. She didn't want him reading her, didn't want his sharp director's vision seeing the fear she couldn't tamp down.

"You promised Tripper wouldn't find out anything right away," she said to the refrigerator in the corner. "You can see him whenever you want, just don't let him suspect. Please."

"It's hardly likely he'll suspect anything. He thinks you and I just met."

"Then you'll have to be careful not to let on you knew me before."

"That shouldn't be hard to do. You hardly seem like the same person."

She glanced back at him and saw his gaze rake over her.

"I still can't get over how much you've changed," he said. "It's as if you went and got a whole new identity from the witness protection program."

Her face hardened. "You've changed a lot yourself. The difference is, you've had yours documented in the media. I've managed to avoid that, but when they discover who I am, my life will be a living hell. You've got to give me time to figure out a way to deal with that." She swallowed, close to panic.

Matt sighed patiently. "I've got a publicist who gets paid to generate publicity about me and likewise keep my name out of as many tabloids as she can. That will include you and Tripper, when the time comes. I intend to make this as painless as possible, for all of us."

She gave him a bitter smile. "The truth is bad enough, Matt. There's not a lot anyone can do to cover the fact that I kept your child from you for ten years."

His mouth twisted in a grimace of regret. "No, and there's not a lot anyone can do to hide the fact that I wasn't a very responsible human being back in those days. I got you pregnant while I was practically engaged to someone else, then let you dangle in the ill wind while I holed up in Montana. I think we'll come out about even in the court of public opinion, don't you think?"

She gaped at him. "So you think we can just forgive and forget? Just like that?"

"I'm not holding a grudge. I thought I made that clear." He met her gaze squarely, and in his green eyes she noticed something she would almost label tenderness.

She shook her head. "No, I don't—" but before she could finish the sentence, he had covered the distance between them and tilted her chin up to face him.

His eyes seemed to take in every detail of her face as he spoke to her. "You see, I have this strange inability to feel hatred at the same time I feel something else. I don't know what it is between us, Claire, but it's there, pulling us together every time I'm around you. Whatever it is nearly destroyed us ten years ago, but I'm a lot smarter now. Believe it or not, I've learned a thing or two about the value of patience. I want you, just as much as I ever did, but I intend to wait this time. When I'm sure no one will be hurt by what we do together—and that includes our son—then I'm going to put moves on you, lady, that you've never seen before." A dangerous glint of passion had replaced the tender light in his eyes, a look she couldn't mistake any more than she could take a breath.

She stared transfixed, as his face came closer and his mouth captured hers in the most gentle of kisses.

She didn't move, not a muscle, while his lips gently explored hers. Warm, inviting, reminding her of something she had made herself forget.

The front door slammed, and Claire jumped.

"Hey, Mom! Matt!" Tripper's voice echoed in the hall, accompanied by the sound of paws clicking on the wood floor.

Matt lifted his head, though his gaze still held hers. He gripped her arms lightly, his thumbs tracing little circles on the ribbed knit of her sweater.

Her eyelids dropped. Her skin felt over-sensitive where he touched, burning her through the sweater. "Stop it!" she hissed. "I refuse to be your—your plaything while you're here!"

Matt just grinned. "We're in here, Tripper," he called.

Sadie's nose had already told her where to find both her master and her feeding dish, and she came bounding into the room. Claire recovered her poise, unobtrusively removing her arms from Matt's grasp just as Tripper walked into the room.

If he noticed the flush she could feel on her face, he said nothing. "Hey, Mom, can Matt stay for dinner?" he asked, aiming a hopeful look at her.

"Sorry, kid, I can't." Matt squeezed his shoulder, then explained, "I've got to go view the dailies in an hour. But I'll take a rain check." He glanced at Claire, a grin dancing in his eyes. "What about this weekend? I was hoping I could come over some time, maybe take a run with Sadie. I noticed there were some jogging trails around here."

"Sure," Tripper volunteered before Claire could speak. "I have basketball practice Saturday morning, but you could come over after that."

"Actually, I was thinking about Sunday. You guys go to church or anything?" He looked at Claire as he spoke.

She found her voice at last. "No, we'll be here. Call before you come, though." She gave him a warning look, one he couldn't fail to interpret.

"Sure. I'll call you—soon," he promised. Then, touching her arm in an oddly intimate farewell gesture, he turned, nodded to Tripper, and left.


After Tripper was in bed Claire made herself a cup of tea, then settled on the couch in the family room. An iPad was tucked, forgotten, in one corner of the couch. She had bought it to entertain Tripper during their long trip cross country, but instead, the hours had been filled with endless questions, some of which Claire had been hard-pressed to answer. Though she could forecast financial futures with some degree of accuracy, the geological origins of the Badlands were beyond her scope.

Tripper had forgiven her lack of knowledge, she remembered now with a smile. She had felt so close to him during those days spent on the road. Closer than she had ever felt to anyone.

Even his father…

She sipped the tea, then wrapped the string of the teabag around her finger and let it drip into the cup, as long-buried memories trickled back into her consciousness.

She had trusted Matt Grayson once. No, it was more than trust. She had looked up to him, admired him. Their brief friendship contained more than a hint of hero worship. Then the friendship turned to desire, on both their parts.

The quickness with which she had fallen into Matt's arms made her shudder in embarrassment now.

Though she had purposely blocked the memory of their time together, she knew he hadn't seduced her. That was the worst part. She had been willing, all too willing. The names she had been called ever since she could remember had been accurate. *Slut, whore…*

Her hand shook as she placed the cup of tea on the table beside the sofa. Those words clung to her memory like bits of tissue paper, bitter reminders of every wrong thing she had ever done, some as innocent as wearing cosmetics for her senior portrait.

She still remembered how Reverend Porter had punished her when he saw the proofs, sent to his office at church.

Her face had been bruised, her hair streaming wet from the near-drowning he'd forced on her in the church baptismal, but her mother hadn't asked any questions. Deborah Porter supported her husband Roy's efforts to cleanse their adopted daughter of her sins.

A cold shudder twisted inside her. She drained the last swallow of tea. She wasn't about to dredge up any more of the fecund sludge that constituted her childhood memories. It had all been buried years ago, when she boarded a bus at the end of her senior year in high school and left Paradise, Texas, behind her forever.

# Chapter Fourteen

Arriving at Claire's house a few weeks later, Matt found her sitting at the kitchen table, surrounded by piles of neatly folded clothes. Her head was bent, and her dark hair fell loose to her shoulders, the ends curling slightly. She wore stretchy ivory pants and a sweater that looked as if it were covered in wisps of cat hair.

She turned to greet him, and the domestic look was abruptly shattered. Silver wireframes were suspended business-like on her nose, and a stack of printouts was piled on the table beside a brace of perfectly aligned towels.

Catching sight of the seven-digit numbers that marched across the columns of the page, he frowned. "I hope that's not our bill," he said, taking a seat across from her.

She looked up at him. "No, it's our earning projections for next year, broken down by store. We've got sort of a competition going on, to see which store can increase their sales the most. Personally, I'm rooting for our Market Street location," she said, tapping her pencil on the first column. "The improvements we're making there should bring in the customers in droves."

He tilted his head, admiring the utterly charming picture she made. He found it hard to view her now as the hard-bitten executive who had pounced on him in Kaslow's boardroom. The reading glasses made her eyes appear slightly larger, and he wondered if he was the only one who ever noticed the touch of vulnerability there. Certainly she tried very hard to hide it, but his director's vision was honed to see the faintest hint of an expression. Beneath the cool smile she presented to the world lurked the pain of a wounded animal, constantly on guard for further abuse.

That thought surprised him. Had he really inflicted that much pain on her years ago? Inadvertently, of course, but nevertheless, abandoning her to the press must have seemed like the ultimate betrayal to the young woman she had been.

A familiar feeling of tenderness washed over him, and just as he resolved to make it all up to her, she looked at him and said tartly, "If you're memorizing that in hopes of doing a little insider trading, I should remind you the conviction carries a long prison sentence."

He jerked his thoughts back to the present and smiled. "The only punishment I'm going to get today is out on the jogging trail. Looks like the last traces of snow have melted. I thought I'd take Sadie with me — and Tripper can follow along on his bike, if there isn't too much mud." He turned to Tripper, who had joined them, having finally managed to rein in an exuberant Sadie. "How about it? Can you guide me through those trails out there?"

"Yeah, and I know a shortcut through the woods. I can show you the fort David and I made!"

"Cool. I used to make forts," he told Tripper. "I'd hide my sister's dolls there and make her pay ransom to get them back."

He glanced at Claire, who gave him a bland smile.

"Remind me to lock up my dolls — I haven't budgeted for ransom this year."

Ten minutes later, the two of them set off for what Claire knew would be another father-son bonding experience. They were becoming common these days, as Matt spent as much time as he could with them. Fortunately, Tripper now viewed him with less awe, though he still thought it the ultimate in cool to have a friend who could get him into the Lakers' locker room.

Claire had relented, allowing Matt to take Tripper to the game last weekend, after being assured that no camera would make it past Matt's bodyguard. Tripper needed to spend time doing the "guy" things she had never really gotten the hang of. If it had been anyone else, she would have been grateful for the attention Matt was showing Tripper.

He instinctively seemed to know how to relate to kids, viewing the world with a boyish pleasure, which Claire found oddly enchanting. No amount of boyishness, however, could mask the seductive glamour of his grin. Or the sharp intelligence that lurked just under the "aw shucks" demeanor, a perceptiveness Claire was learning to avoid. She sometimes had the feeling he could see right through her, a thought that sent shudders along her spine. Some secrets weren't meant to be shared, especially not with glamorous movie stars.

Sighing, Claire dragged her thoughts back to her work.

An hour later, the trio returned, covered in mud. Thankfully, they had left their shoes at the front door, Claire noticed as Matt and Tripper padded noisily into the kitchen where she was preparing dinner. Spotting the muddy calves just inches from her spotless floor, she frowned, raised one hand, and said sternly, "Hold it right there. No one gets in my kitchen until they've passed inspection." She pointed her broccoli spear in the direction of the bathroom. "Out."

Matt looked down sheepishly. "Sorry about that. We'll clean it up; I just wanted to see if it was all right to give Sadie a bath in the downstairs bathroom."

Claire glanced down at the mud-flecked dog, greedily lapping up water from her bowl. "Of course you can. Tripper, find some towels — better yet, get that old blanket in the spare room," she said, inwardly cringing at the thought of those muddy paws traipsing over her carpet. The extra money she had paid for stain proofing was turning out to be a wise investment.

Twenty minutes later, she looked up again as the damp dog emerged prancing from the bathroom, followed by two equally damp males. They had both stripped to the waist, and Claire couldn't control a quick jolt of appreciation upon seeing Matt's trademark torso. For years she'd avoided the sight of all that tanned skin stretched over rock-hard stomach muscles in magazine layouts, and now here it was in her kitchen.

She swallowed and said to the chicken sprawled in the Pyrex dish: "If you'd like to clean up, Tripper can show you where to find extra towels and shampoo. Oh, and you're invited to dinner." She risked a glance and found a knowing glint in his eye.

Tripper looked up from the floor where he was toweling a wriggling Sadie. "She's making chicken with orange sauce. That's her best thing. You'll like it," he promised.

Claire smiled. "Tripper's our resident food critic," she said. "I'll warn you, though, his tastes lean toward peanut butter and jelly on toast."

"I was going to offer to take you two out, but a home-cooked meal sounds better." Then, glancing at the title of the cookbook open on the counter, Matt added, "Although I wasn't aware French cooking was the sort of thing executives specialized in these days."

She laughed. "It's not. Sunday just happens to be my day for cooking. The rest of the week we rely on convenience foods." She opened the door of the oven and slid in the dish, hoping the heat from the oven would account for the flush on her face. "This will be ready in half an hour," she told them. "And Tripper, I'd like you to take a shower as well. That will save you the trouble tonight."

"Oh, Mom, can't I just go swimming later?"

"No, I don't have time to watch you this afternoon," she said, wishing Matt would hurry and remove his chest from her line of vision.

"But Matt could come with me," Tripper said hopefully, gazing up at Matt. "Do you like to swim? There's an indoor pool here, but Mom doesn't know how to swim," he explained.

"You don't swim, Claire?" Matt asked, surprise in his voice.

Claire's mouth tightened. "I never learned," she said shortly. "Now, if you two would kindly remove yourselves from my kitchen, I would appreciate it. Now. Scoot," she warned, giving the two her best no-nonsense look.

Matt just grinned and said to Tripper, "Moms have issues when it comes to dirt. Let's get cleaned up, then I'll race you in MotorStorm."

"You're on!" Tripper whooped, and they both disappeared.

Claire sighed with relief. Between Tripper's casual confidences and Matt's partial nudity, her nerves were well on the way to being cooked.


Matt lingered after dinner, enjoying the rare chance to relax. As he threw another log on the fire, the photographs on the mantle caught his attention. "When were these taken?" he asked as Claire joined him, a bowl of popcorn in her hand.

"Let's see," she said, glancing up at the wood-framed photos of Tripper. She pointed to the one on the end. "That one was from his fifth birthday. He learned to ride his bike the very day he got it," she said, a soft note of pride in her voice. "And this one I took when he was just three months old. I used to dress him in Felts Brothers bubble suits I'd buy at the department store where I worked."

Matt stifled a grin. In his opinion, the dainty smocking didn't suit Tripper as well as the Lakers' sweatshirts he currently favored, but the thought of Claire dressing her son with such maternal pride touched him.

"I don't know why I didn't think of it before," she said, bending down and removing a set of photo albums from the bookshelf that flanked the fireplace. "They're just snapshots, but you might enjoy looking at them."

They sat side by side on the couch while Claire shared with him the early years of Tripper's life. Most of the photos had been taken by Claire, but Matt was startled to see her in one of the earlier shots, holding her infant son, her dark hair cut short against her nape.

"You cut all your hair off," he said, surprised.

"Yes," she murmured, one hand reaching unconsciously toward her hair. "I never liked it long anyway. It's only lately I let it grow longer."

Matt studied the photo critically. The short cut emphasized her delicately rounded cheeks and huge eyes. She had cut her hair in an effort to disguise herself, he realized, shaken by the telling evidence of her humiliation.

Then, on the last page of the book, another photo of her holding Tripper and looking over her shoulder gave him an even greater jolt. This one was obviously professionally done, a black-and-white soft focus that gave her a dreamy Madonna look. He sucked in a breath, stunned by the sight. The woman in the photograph was hauntingly beautiful. Part woman, part angel, completely female.

"Claire." His voice was rough as he spoke, "I think you missed your calling. You should be in front of a camera. With a face like this—"

She snatched the book from him and snapped it shut. "Don't be silly," she said. "Make-up and retouching can perform magic. Now, have you seen enough, or would you like to see the other book? Oh, and there's also a few years' worth of video, if you're really in the mood for nostalgia."

He gave her a measuring look. It would take him approximately two minutes, he figured, to convince her she was the most beautiful woman on earth. But right now wasn't the time.

Instead, he insisted on seeing the video recordings, even though she warned him they tended to get rather boring. "We can fast forward over the boring parts," he promised. "I want to see how well you've captured your subject on video," he said with a wink at Tripper, who had just joined them.

Claire popped the first video in the DVD player, explaining that it had been made on Tripper's first birthday.

The action needed little narration. It featured a one-year-old baby, with solemn green eyes alternately looking into the camera and back to the gaily decorated cake before him.

Then the image on the screen cut to the same toddler, totally bemused by the giant caterpillar his mother had given him to ride on.

Matt swallowed a lump of regret. He'd missed too much of his son's life, missed too many birthdays. He wouldn't miss any more, he vowed.

Sitting on the sofa beside Matt, Claire smiled at the memory, glancing at Matt to see if he was enjoying the humor. He was gazing at the screen, a poignant expression on his face, his green eyes moist in the corners.

She jumped up. "This is awfully long. We should spare Matt the rest of this, Tripper." Punching the pause button, she continued. "It's getting late anyway. You need to finish your homework and get into bed. Tomorrow's a school day, remember?"

"Mom," he started to protest, but she insisted, and her son knew better than to argue with her when it came to homework and bedtime.

When Tripper was gone, Claire gathered the glasses that littered the coffee table. She glanced at Matt and found him staring at her with a chagrined look on his face. "You didn't have to stop the video," he said. "I could have handled it."

"I'm sure you could have, but…it was starting to get boring. I've seen it a dozen times, and believe me, there's only so much messy birthday cake a mother can take." She attempted a smile, but inside, she ached for him. All the years he had missed…

"Can I borrow the recording? I'll make a copy of it and return it to you."

She hesitated, then nodded. "Of course. And I'll be happy to give you some of the photos if you'd like." She had plenty of extras, as there had never been anyone to give them to before.

"That would be great. There's a real family resemblance in a lot of those. He's got my dad's ears, you know. They stick out."

"They do not!" she protested. "I had them surgically pinned when he was five!"

Matt groaned. "Poor kid!" He shook his head regretfully. "Good thing Dumbo's mother never thought of that — or Mickey's. Just think where Disney would be."

"The other kids were starting to laugh at him!" Though it seemed a minor thing, she had sworn her son would never face ridicule from his classmates.

Matt followed her to the sink and began handing her the clean dishes from the dishwasher. They worked in silence for a while, though Claire could feel Matt looking at her occasionally with a thoughtful expression.

Reaching over her head to place the last glass in the cabinet, he mused aloud, "Ever wonder what would have happened? If we had stayed together?"

"I don't believe in playing 'What If.'" She turned off the tap, wanting to stop his words as easily.

"But sometimes it's fun," he insisted, turning to face her. "For instance, what if Hayley had gotten help instead of killing herself? What if you had come to me when you found out you were pregnant?"

"And what if baby elephants could fly? There's no point in speculating what might have happened. Besides, I don't have any regrets." But that wasn't true, she realized. She did regret that Matt had never known his son, that Tripper had never had a father he could respect, love…

Afraid Matt would read her confusion, she turned away, but he reached out and untucked her hair from behind her ears, watching it fall against her face. "No regrets, huh? Not even for your long-lost hair?"

She tucked her hair back in place.

He chuckled. "Not exactly wild abandon, but sexy just the same. I like it like this, but you shouldn't have had to cut it all off."

She kept her gaze pinned to his chest. "I liked it short," she said stiffly. "Matt, we had an agreement—"

"I seem to be in the mood for nostalgia. You wouldn't care to indulge me?"

"Certainly—there's a vintage video store on your way home. They have a whole section labeled 'nostalgia.'"

"Our video won't be there. It would have been too hot for an R rating anyway," he said, allowing his wayward finger to trail lower, dangerously near her throbbing heartbeat. "We were good together, Claire. Proof of that's upstairs right now. Wouldn't you care to give it another shot?"

She batted his hand away. "I've told you, I'm not available." Then she added nastily, "Surely there's no shortage of women who are?"

He lifted a lazy eyebrow. "As a matter of fact, I canceled a weekend in Atlantic City with a hot redhead so I could come here." Then he grinned wickedly. "And it's a sure bet we wouldn't have spent the whole time at the blackjack table."

She frowned. "Well, you've come to the wrong place to recoup your losses. I've told you, I'm not interested in a relationship with you. We've been there, done that, so to speak." She sighed. "How can I make that any clearer?"

His gaze narrowed. "I'm beginning to think I'm not the one you're trying to convince."

She refused to look at him. But her feet also refused to move her out of the line of fire. And she did feel as if she were under attack, by his nearness, by the clean smell of him…by his tenderness when he looked at the pictures of their son…by the little traces of fire that ignited along her nerve endings whenever he touched her…

He was right. It was her body that was betraying her, and until she got it under control, he would take full advantage. She stepped back, just a little movement, but he checked it by putting an arm around her waist.

"Convince me you feel nothing for me. I'll bet anything you can't…"

Then he lowered his mouth to hers, slowly, giving her plenty of time to pull away, but she stood her ground, determined to prove him wrong. Telling herself she could resist this one time, she held herself stiffly, letting his lips touch hers—the memory of last time fresh in her mind, preparing her for the incredible longing that surged through her, sharp and sweet, just at the moment his lips made contact.

She closed her eyes, trying to concentrate on anything but the nearness of his body. The papers she should look at before tomorrow…the sandwich she needed to make for Tripper's lunchbox…the weather in Tanzania…

But it felt so good to be touched like this—by an experienced, confident man, not some fumbling business-suited Lothario trying to impress her with his bucket-seat moves.

She should relax and enjoy it. Not every woman is so lucky, she told herself. In all her life, she had only met one man who made her feel this way…

And there was the rub.

For it was this very same man who had awakened her once to passion, who had taught her everything about the incredible closeness that a man and woman could feel, who had touched her—exactly like this—before, and when her body had betrayed her then, the price she had paid was too steep.

With a sharp intake of breath, she pulled away. Before he could protest, they both heard Tripper's voice.

"Hey, Mom, I forgot to take…Oh." It was obvious from the confused note in his voice he had caught the tail end of their embrace.

But Matt grinned at him reassuringly. "Hey, don't worry. I'll take Sadie out before I go."

"I don't mind—"

"Yeah, but your mom mentioned something about a strictly enforced bedtime before she would agree to the whole dog thing," Matt said with an ironic glance at Claire.

The gently worded admonition seemed to work, and Tripper headed back to bed, after first wishing Matt another good night. True to his promise, Matt slipped out to take Sadie for one last walk.

Fifteen minutes later, he returned to find Claire in the kitchen, two pieces of bread and an open lunchbox on the counter in front of her. He watched as she dabbed a generous portion of peanut butter on a plate, then began swirling honey into it.

He stopped just behind her. Reaching around, he slid a finger into the concoction she had prepared, then stuck it into his mouth. "Mmmm," he said. "Peanut butter and honey was always my favorite too."

Ignoring his pilfering, Claire pivoted, facing him squarely. "What happened before was totally out of line," she said, her eyes hard as concrete. "We're adults, not adolescents with raging libidos. Now we've given Tripper the wrong idea—"

"No, we've given him exactly the right idea. What's wrong with him knowing we have feelings for each other?"

"We don't! Not the way you mean," she amended.

"Why are you so eager to deny that we're sexually attracted to each other? We're consenting adults; neither one of us is attached at the moment—"

"So you want to fill in with me until you find something more permanent?" She brandished the butter knife, as if defending her space. Matt stepped back, then took the knife from her hand. She continued, weaponless. "Meanwhile, Tripper is getting the impression that you're about to become a permanent fixture in his life."

"I *am* about to become a permanent fixture in his life! And in your life, as well." He gave her an amused look as he licked the remaining peanut butter from the knife. Placing it in the sink, he decided to approach the argument logically. "Why should we ignore a physical attraction just because we happen to share a child? It seems to me that's the best reason of all to explore the possibilities."

"The last time I 'explored the possibilities' with you," she countered, her voice low and controlled, "I ended up pregnant and alone. I refuse to have—"

"Oh, come on," he interrupted. "I would hope we've both learned a thing or two about birth control since then. You've managed to avoid any more unwanted pregnancies."

Her face flushed pink, and she turned away. Matt stared at her in silence a moment, then reached out a hand and turned her face toward his. "Haven't you?" he said, his eyebrows lifted inquiringly. "Surely you've had sexual relationships since then." He searched her face, but her gaze remained locked on his clavicle, her lips pressed firmly shut.

"My God, you haven't been with anyone in…over ten years?" He released her, then raked a hand through his hair. "Hell, Claire, was it that…painful…an experience? Did it turn you off the idea of sex entirely?"

"My sex life is none of your business."

"I think it *is* my business if I'm the reason you haven't been getting any for the last ten years. For God's sake, that isn't natural."

"Don't flatter yourself. I simply had no time, in between raising a child and working sixty-hour weeks. And besides, who are you to tell me it's not natural to not jump into bed at every opportunity?" she countered bitterly. "You've no doubt got a different woman for very night of the week."

"That's not true," he protested, wishing now he had refrained from mentioning Annie. "In fact, I'm currently in a dry spell. It's been…weeks," he said.

"Oh, so you've decided to quench your thirst at the most convenient watering hole? What's the matter? Isn't your co-star receptive to your advances?"

He shook his head. "There's nothing going on between Laura and me except friendship. And we're not talking about me here, though that was a clever attempt to turn the tables." He crossed his arms across his chest and leaned against the counter, giving her a confident half-smile. Although Claire could probably cut him to shreds in a boardroom, when it came to this particular topic, he knew his stuff.

"And as for you being a 'convenient watering hole'…Well, the food's great, but my water glass has been dry since I got here." He let his gaze drift down. "Of course, after ten years in the deep freeze, I guess those extremities," he said, glancing up at her nose, "are starting to get a little frostbit."

Giving her a wicked grin, he drawled, "And if I'm the reason for that, I figure it's my duty, ma'am, to warm you up."

Before she could protest, he folded his arms around her, lifted her easily until her feet left the floor, and sat her on the counter. A little gasp slipped from her throat, but he settled his mouth on hers before any further sound could escape.

This time, he kissed her intimately, deeply, with more heat than before, determined to break through the icy barriers she had erected. His tongue explored her mouth, tasting honey. She had obviously dipped into the honey jar herself, and it made his blood race to know that she too could be tempted. Like a chemical reaction, he felt lust surge through him. His loins tightened, and what had been a teasing challenge became more urgent.

One hand slipped inside her sweater. Her skin was surprisingly warm underneath. His fingertips explored every inch of her back, her shoulders, halting at the bra strap that pressed into her soft flesh. In seconds he had it unhooked. He heard her gasp but ignored it.

Until he heard the word "no," he planned to take this as far as he could.

Far from protesting, however, Matt could swear she was enjoying this. Her arms clung to him, and he could feel her pulse throbbing in the veins in her neck. He kissed the spot tenderly and felt her shiver in response. He moved his mouth to her ear and was rewarded with another shiver.

She started to back away, and Matt took advantage by slipping his hand, now nicely warmed by her skin, around to her stomach. "You've got the softest skin," he murmured, wishing he knew something to compare it to that wasn't corny. But his mind was incapable of creating analogies at the moment. His body—particularly the lower half—was in control now. It directed his hand to her breast. He cupped his palm around its weight.

He felt her tighten in resistance against him. It had been ten years, he reminded himself. Better to take it slow. His fingers danced over her nipple, and he heard her moan. In a heartbeat, his mouth was on hers, seeking, exploring, encouraging a response he was now sure he would find.

Every instinct he had urged him into her. The blood pounded in his veins, and sensation replaced thought. He wanted nothing more than to lay her across a horizontal surface…

But then Matt felt her stiffen against him, heard her gasp in protest. Not a no, but somehow he knew he had to let her control the pace.

He sucked air into his lungs, willing his racing heart to slow. The throbbing tightness in his jeans was another matter, one that craved the recently broken contact. Resisting the urge to flatten himself against her softness, he braced himself against the counter, breathing in the scent of her hair.

He let out a shaky breath and murmured softly against her hair. "God, it's good with us, Claire. Do you know the first time I made love to a woman after you, I thought something was wrong with me? It didn't work nearly as well."

She gave him a sharp look. "If you think I'm buying that line, you're—"

"It's not a line," he said, laughing softly. "If it was, I'd insist on a rewrite—it's a pretty bad one." Then he sobered. "It's true. It's never been the same. Not with anyone."

It *was* true, Matt reflected. Though he had been searching ever since, unconsciously, for a woman who brought him to the same level of gut-wrenching passion, he had never found one. Instead, he had settled for sexual expertise rather than true feeling. The implications of that…he would think about later, he decided. When wide gray eyes weren't staring at him skeptically with just a hint of need in their depths.

"It was your imagination. You had to justify what happened by building it up into something it wasn't."

"This coming from a woman who ended her sex life due to the same experience?" He raised an eyebrow.

She looked away and broke the last remaining contact. Reaching behind her, she struggled to refasten her bra. Matt nudged her hand away, turned her slightly, then made quick work of the clasp.

He could feel her fury coming off her in waves.

"Regardless, I'm not interested in repeating the experience," she said, facing him. "It may have been life altering for you, but personally, I can live without the complications."

He laughed. "Complications?" He shook his head. "If that's all you feel when I stick my hand up your sweater, I've lost my technique." He smiled ruefully, then glanced at his watch in regret. "And unfortunately, I've got to be on the set at five a.m., or I'd stick around and give it another shot."

Before turning to leave, he gave her a wink, saying, "Thanks for dinner—and the video. I'll have it copied and get it back to you."

# Chapter Fifteen

Claire carefully stepped around an outcrop of scaffolding and glanced down at the copy of the floor plans in her hand. The eighth-floor theater was beginning to resemble a daycare center. In one corner would be a kitchen, for staff to prepare snacks brought in from the restaurant downstairs. An indoor garden would bloom underneath new skylights, an opportunity for the kids to learn about nature. The stage area would be carved into three separate playrooms, including one just for infants.

Claire couldn't wait to show the plans to Joan. She'd be glad to know that when she came back from maternity leave, her baby could come with her and be well looked after in the bright new space.

Having been the board member to propose it, Claire thought of the childcare center as her baby. She smiled at the pun. In some small way, she felt she was giving back to all those who'd helped her when she struggled to raise her son alone, with no one but her aging grandmother to help look after him. Gram had been a lifesaver, in more ways than one.

But the past was over, and Claire had no need for her grandmother's help, either financially or as a refuge when she was escaping from the reverend and his wife—she refused to think of Roy and Deborah Porter as her parents.

She stepped off the stage, which had once hosted fashion shows in Kaslow's heyday, and almost ran into Evan, tapping at his mobile. He stuffed the phone in his pocket and glanced around at the scaffolded walls, frowning.

"What a waste of perfectly good cash. Kaslow's is bleeding money, and you want to turn this into a luxury theme park for rugrats."

Claire braced herself for another skirmish. Evan was the one person on the board who'd never accepted the fact that Kaslow's was no longer a privately held corporation and no longer controlled its own destiny. "I'm sorry you feel that way. But the theater wasn't being used anymore, and the board approved the renovations. The childcare center will help Kaslow's attract top-notch employees."

"Kaslow's never had any problem attracting top-notch employees." Written on his face were the words "until you came along."

Claire swallowed her retort. It was best to ignore Evan and the enormous chip on his shoulder, she'd found.

But he wasn't done. "I understand congratulations are in order."

"Excuse me?"

"The Bendel account. They selected Kaslow's. Tell me, what did you offer Monsieur Lemond to sweeten the deal?" His gaze lowered to the scalloped collar of her blouse.

Claire clutched the floor plans tighter. "Nothing other than the quality that Kaslow's is known for," she said sharply.

"Apparently the video you sent influenced the old bat. I'm not the only one wondering what you had to do to get it. After the way you screwed Matt Grayson in the location negotiations, you'd think he'd want nothing to do with you." He let that sink in, then added with a hard smile, "Or are you, literally, screwing him now?"

Claire didn't flinch, though inside she cringed at Evan's crude suggestion. Instead, she fixed him with the cool stare she'd perfected when harsher words than Evan's were hurled at her. "Keep your playground taunts where they belong, Evan." She turned to go, but his next comment stopped her.

"Lee Ann says she saw you talking to him in the rotunda."

Claire turned. "Lee Ann?"

"My secretary."

Lee Ann, Claire remembered, was known more for her too short skirts than her speed at typing.

"She must have been mistaken." Claire kept her voice calm, despite the fact her stomach had lurched in a dead drop. "I've had nothing to do with—"

"Oh, there you are!" Jackie Prescott appeared from behind the scaffolding, her heels echoing in the cavernous space. "I've been wanting to congratulate you on the Bendel account. I've got some ideas for promotion—oh, hello, Evan." She gave him a look that Claire suspected wasn't entirely as guileless as it came across. "Weren't you working on that account?"

"Yes, and if my mother hadn't chosen that day to break her hip, I'd have been the one to secure the deal."

Jackie ignored his expression. She was no doubt used to his sour moods. "Well, the main thing is Kaslow's will benefit. The exposure will be tremendous. Isn't that right?" She turned to Claire. "I'm loving what's happening with the childcare center! I can't wait to get some photos so we can place a piece in the local papers, hopefully get some national press on our renovations."

Claire couldn't help a smile. Jackie had the air of a ditz sometimes, but underneath her chic blond bob was a shrewd publicity hound.

Evan aggressively flicked a piece of lint off his sleeve. "I'm sure the national press has better things to report on than what's happening on the eighth floor of Kaslow's. Right, Claire?" He gave her a secretive smile, a reminder of their recent conversation.

Claire wanted to wrap his Hermes tie around his skinny neck but instead she pinned him with a cool stare. "At least they're not reporting our same store sales," she replied. "I've got some ideas about improving sales at the Cherry Hill store we'll have to discuss when you've got a minute, Evan. I'll have Joan contact you."

He slid his hands in his pockets and smiled blandly. "I'm all ears when it comes to your plans, Claire."

As he walked away, Jackie turned to her and said with a serious look on her face, "Watch out for him. He'd sell his own mother if there were a run on the commodity market."

Claire smiled at her description. Since their first skirmish in the boardroom, she and Jackie had developed a sort of friendship. "He's still upset about the Atlantic City store," she explained. "He seemed particularly fond of the plans for some reason."

"Yes, well, he holds a grudge. He got a board member fired last year when he nixed Evan's bonus."

They stopped at the back entrance to the theater, next to the elevator. Jackie leaned toward Claire, her voice low. "And his secretary Lee Ann will do his dirty work. She's his eyes and ears. He planted her on the *Lyin' Hearts* set, just in case any worthy gossip came her way. Although frankly, I think she was there to offer her 'services' to Matt Grayson." Jackie laughed. "As if he'd want anything to do with her!"

Claire stepped aside as several workmen walked past, hoping Jackie would change the subject, but unfortunately Jackie seemed to be in the mood for sharing.

"I don't know why Bernard Kaslow puts up with him," she continued as they got on the elevator. "He feels he owes it to his brother, I guess. But if he knew Evan was screwing his secretary on the side, he'd cut him out of the will. Bernard's a bit…old-fashioned."

Claire smiled tightly and pressed the button for the seventh floor, wishing she had taken the stairs. Anything to avoid a gossip session with Jackie and especially the reminder about Bernard Kaslow's old-fashioned values. If he ever found out that his financial officer was once a notorious homewrecker, he'd toss her out on her ear along with his nephew.

Somehow, she had to get Matt to agree to keep their past a secret. How, she didn't know. Instead of being pacified with a few visits with Tripper, he was growing more determined to be a part of his son's life, of their lives.

Claire swallowed the fear in her throat. She just had to convince Matt that there was too much at stake and that their past was best buried and forgotten.

# Chapter Sixteen

"Is this Alicia Howard? From the *Inquisitor*?"

"That's right. Who's calling?"

"I don't want to give you my name. But I've got some interesting gossip. Do you still pay for tips?"

"That all depends. If we use it, sure." Alicia was used to anonymous sources. She also knew that most of the news they bore was either well-known gossip or total fabrication. Of the two, she preferred fabrication. At least it had the ring of originality.

"So, who's been abducted by space aliens out in your neck of the woods?"

"You know Matt Grayson is here in Philadelphia filming a movie?"

"So I've heard." Alicia perked up, though she was pretty sure she could guess the contents of this latest "tip."

"Look, if you're calling to tell me he and Laura Hayes are shacking up, it's old news. That was in my column last week, and neither party denied it."

"No, it's not Laura Hayes I'm calling about. It's a woman at the department store where he's been filming. Claire Porter. She and Matt Grayson have been spending a lot of time together. He's been phoning her office, and a couple of people have seen him drop by there during the day. He even sent her flowers."

"Big deal. You know how many women he's sent flowers to in the last month? More than there were days." Alicia was ready to ring off, when the voice on the other end became urgent.

"You don't understand! Claire Porter is the Kaslow's executive who wanted to keep him from filming here. Those two were practically at each other's throats during the contract negotiations for the location shoot. All of a sudden, he's looking at her, well, sort of like he looked at Jennifer Garner in *Time Bomb*, just before they escaped from that building."

Alicia's eyed a copy of last week's column, the one where she had hinted at the latest blonde in Matt Grayson's life. "If he's exchanging gooey looks with this executive, then what's he doing sharing space with Laura Hayes?"

The woman gave a superior laugh. "Decent living space is at a premium in downtown Philadelphia. Nothing more than convenience." From the tone of her voice, Alicia sensed she was dealing with a comrade in the insider-information trade.

"Another thing. I know for a fact that he's made several trips out to her place. Supposedly her son is watching his dog."

"She has a son? Is she married?"

"No, according to the personnel file at Kaslow's she never was married. And she never mentions the kid's father. Or the kid, either, according to the few people she deigns to talk to." A sneer accented her voice.

Alicia was about to write off the gossip as an in-house grudge, when the woman said something that piqued her interest. "I know he usually dates blondes, but there was that woman about ten years ago — what was her name? The one he was having an affair with when Hayley James…?"

"Clarissa Peters." Alicia's mind was a virtual storehouse of facts, a necessary attribute when one's profession called for skirting them on a daily basis.

"Well, Claire Porter has dark hair, too, though she's got a lot more class than that tramp. Sort of untouchable, if you know the type. Which was why it was so surprising to see her cozying up to Matt Grayson. I mean, a few weeks ago, she was acting like she was too good for Hollywood. It was because of her they had to triple their offer."

Alicia's eyes lit up as she pictured the headline. *Hollywood's Hunk Bested by a Corporate Delilah?* Though she doubted it was true, it would sell magazines. Matt Grayson was hot right now. If she could bring him back down to earth, her Page Two column would once again be the avenue for first-rate gossip.

"Why don't you give me more information? And would you happen to have a photo of this Claire Porter?" Alicia flipped through her contact list until she found the number of another East Coast informant who had reliably supplied her with information in the past. If there was anything to the story, she would know in a couple of days, just in time to include it in next month's column.

She loved it when celebrities screwed up in time for a deadline.


Claire listened to the *thunks* of the basketball hitting the driveway as she got an early start on spring cleaning. Occasionally, a masculine whoop of joy punctured the crisp February air, eventually coaxing her outside, where Matt and Tripper were tossing a basketball at a portable goal Matt had had delivered from a sporting goods store. An early birthday present, he had called it, and she hadn't had the heart to protest.

When she finally joined them outside, she felt a smile of contentment spread on her face, surprising her. Two months ago, she never would have thought she would be watching her son play basketball with his father and actually enjoy it.

Part of her wished this could have taken place long ago, but she hadn't forgotten the reasons she'd never told Matt about his son. She shivered, a reaction that had nothing to do with the chill in the air.

The ball landed in front of her and bounced neatly into her hands. "Your turn, Claire," Matt called from the makeshift court in the driveway.

She demurred. "No, basketball isn't my game."

Her protest fell on deaf ears. Matt stalked toward her, worn jeans hugging his hips, his shirt tail hanging out, a rumpled sexy look that would appear right at home in the pages of a fashion magazine. His green eyes were filled with challenge. Claire's heartbeat quickened.

"Come on. Let's see what you can do."

She eyed the ball in her hands, then gave the basket a measuring look. Frowning, she aimed, tossed, then hid a grin as the ball slid through the net. She lifted her shoulders in a "nothing to it" shrug, even though she had spent the better part of an hour the day before practicing her hoop skills.

Tripper punched the air. "Way to go, Mom!"

Matt whistled appreciatively. "Obviously a woman of many talents," he said, catching the ball as it bounced. "Tripper tells me you've got a killer serve. Want to try to score some points on the tennis court?"

She shook her head. "My backhand's a little rusty. I haven't played since last summer."

He gave her a perceptive look. "Don't like to play unless you can win, huh?"

"Something like that," she agreed, knowing they were talking about more than sports. "Are you guys hungry?" she asked. "I made some fresh salsa. Tripper's favorite."

They went inside, where Claire had set chips and salsa on the pine table.

"We should wrap up filming next week," Matt told her as she handed Tripper a napkin.

She glanced at him in surprise. She hadn't realized they were so close to completing the location work.

"And then what?"

"Then I've got to go back to LA. Frank's already got a start on editing, but I have to be there to go over it with him." He cracked a chip in two, dipped it in the salsa. "We'll spend about a month cutting it down to size, and then we should have something ready to show John DeSoto—he's writing the musical score."

"I've heard of him. He wrote the score for *Private Lives*, didn't he?"

"Sure did. Won an Oscar for it," Matt replied, tipping his beer bottle to his lips. Claire had begun stocking her refrigerator with his favorite local brew. "We're lucky to have him on this project—he's pretty busy these days."

And Matt's own time was at a premium, Claire knew. "What about your next film? Won't you need to start the research on it soon?"

"Yeah, I'm working on that already. Pam's trying to line up a stint in a state prison for me sometime in April—"

Claire froze. "What did you say?"

"It's a prison film," he explained. "Based on the book *Outrage* by Jessica Beaumont—you know, it was a bestseller a couple years ago?"

Claire remembered the book—a true story about a Louisiana man wrongly accused of murder and imprisoned for ten years; but the thought of Matt spending any time in a penitentiary caused her heart to lurch.

"You aren't honestly going to have yourself locked up like a criminal, are you?" she asked, frowning.

"Sure. It's the best way to prepare for the role," he said, popping a chip into his mouth.

Claire turned away, not sure she wanted him to see the concern in her eyes. "Can't you just interview the subject of the book? I'm sure he could give you an accurate picture."

"But I want to know firsthand what it's like, to hear the doors clang shut in my face, to smell the loneliness, the despair she talks about in the book."

Claire closed her eyes, swallowing the sick taste.

"If they can work it out, I plan to spend some time in solitary confinement—"

She rounded on him. "So go lock yourself in a closet! Rattle some chains. You don't have to risk your life!"

"It's the contact with the people there I need," he explained patiently. "I want to know what it's like to live with that hopelessness every day."

A wave of fury washed over her. That Matt could so calmly plan to immerse himself into the kind of hell she could all too easily imagine…

"You plan to risk your life, all for the sake of art." She slammed the refrigerator door, hard enough to startle Sadie, who was lying next to her water dish. "Surely you're not so naïve you think you can just walk up to a convicted murderer and have him share his deepest feelings with you."

Matt looked annoyed at her lack of confidence. "I'm flattered that you're worried, but believe me, I can take care of myself."

"Now you're conceited as well as—as naïve," she scoffed. "The people in those places are killers, Matt. Rapists and murderers and psychopaths! They'd probably earn a merit badge for offing a celebrity like you."

His lips twitched, as if he were holding in laughter. "There'll be guards around at all times, just in case any boy scouts are working on that merit badge."

She struggled to calm down, to erase the image of him locked in a solitary hole. Matt was a grown man, fully capable of taking care of himself. But the danger was more than physical. He needed human companionship, more so than she did. Her heart twisted at the thought of him locked away. "Joke all you want, but I warn you, when you get stabbed with a homemade knife, I'll be the first in line to say I told you so."

Then he did laugh. "As long as you show up at my bedside, honey, I don't care if you tattoo 'I told you so' on my rear end," he said, glancing toward Tripper, who was listening to every word with interest. "Didn't you say you were cooking steaks? Come on, Tripper. I'll show you how to light the grill."

Claire remained silent throughout dinner, but Matt deliberately kept up the conversation with Tripper, hoping he wouldn't notice his mother's silence. Afterward, Matt enlisted Tripper's help to clean up the dishes, while Claire settled on the floor in the kitchen, brushing out a freshly bathed Sadie. The dog sat patiently, occasionally lifting her face to acknowledge the attention with a lick of grateful pleasure.

"Not worried about dog germs, Claire?" Matt asked, coming to sit beside her.

"If you aren't worried about getting a knife in the back, I'm not worried about a few germs."

Matt propped his chin in his hand. "You really are worried about this."

"Not at all," she answered coolly. "You were right. I'm sure you'll charm the entire prison population into remaining on their best behavior."

"I'd be more interested in charming you."

She glanced down, pressing on the wire bristles of the brush, flexing them in to the spongy rubber base with her thumb. "I told you—"

"Yeah, but can't a guy dream?" he interrupted, keeping his tone light, but beneath his words was a thread of seriousness.

"I'm not the woman of your dreams. I never will be."

Undaunted, Matt framed her face with his hands, then brushed her hair back with the same gentleness she had shown with Sadie. His eyes flickered over her face, her skin so pale, so flawless, as if it rarely felt the touch of the sun. "Sooner or later, you've got to risk getting burned."

Her gaze wavered, but she didn't pull away. His fingertip slid over the scar at the edge of her temple. Not flawless, after all. Something—or someone—had already marred her. The thought of her being hurt—deliberately—caused his jaw to clench. "Who hurt you, Claire? Tell me. Give me a name. I swear I'll tear him apart."

She jerked her face from his hold. "Don't be ridiculous," she scoffed. "It was an accident."

He didn't believe her. But before he could question her further, she stood up.

He let it go, for now. One day, Claire would learn to trust him, he was sure. Until then, he could be patient. He intended to do everything in his power to convince her that he was in for the long haul.

Because, insecurities and all, he wanted her, not just in his bed, but in his life, making him earn her love every single day—a challenge he couldn't wait to meet. He wanted to make up for all the hard knocks life had dealt her.

But he had only one more short week, ten days at the most, to convince her she couldn't live without him. Remembering her concern at the thought of him in danger, he decided there was plenty of reason to hope.

The email arrived two days after Alicia's source in Philly had confirmed some of the details of her conversation with the anonymous informant.

She clicked on the attachments, which must have come from the store's publicity department. She pursed her lips in silent approval.

The ax-grinding colleague was right. Claire Porter was a very classy-looking woman. An executive type. That was what was so unbelievable about the story. Matt Grayson didn't usually hang out with financial types, unless it was his own accountant. But this woman was certainly a looker, Alicia thought, noting the slight resemblance to a younger Jaclyn Smith. And there was something else about her, something vaguely familiar…Kristen Stewart, maybe? No, that wasn't it.

She frowned, saving the photo to her hard disk. She would come up with it later. She clicked on another photo. This shot of the storefront should accompany the title: "Hot Times in Philly: Matt Grayson lights a fire in the boardroom of Philadelphia's staid department store."

Too long? She'd give that some thought—she wanted plenty of room for the photos. Her readers especially liked visual aides to accompany their gossip.

# Chapter Seventeen

"'A hint of *Scandal*' will be the promo," Jackie announced to the gathered board, surveying their faces for reaction.

The slogan would draw them in, Claire agreed, sniffing the little packet of perfume Jackie had distributed.

Jackie was also handling plans for Mme. Bendel's upcoming visit. It was the first time she had come to the U.S. in a decade, so the retail press would cover the event with all the aplomb of visiting royalty.

As Jackie outlined the details for the promotion campaign, Claire made a note to make sure the contractors had the renovations completed in time for the debut. It would cost more in overtime, but in the long run, the publicity would be worth it.

She glanced up as Joan tapped on her shoulder. One look at her worried face, and Claire jumped up, prepared to phone 9-1-1, or at least Labor and Delivery.

But it was Tripper. His school had just phoned, Joan said in a whisper.

Before she could finish, Claire had rushed out of the room.

Tripper had been involved in a fight, the secretary at school had explained as soon as Claire phoned. But as she drove out to Tripper's school in the suburbs, she decided it must be a mistake.

Tripper wasn't the sort of child to resort to violence. But, she remembered grimly, his new hero, Matt Grayson, was well known for his exploits with his fists, at least on the screen.

She edged above the speed limit, the thought of her son sitting in the principal's office sending a wave of pity through her heart. Fortunately traffic was light at this time of day, and thirty minutes later, she was walking into the school's office. Tripper slumped in a chair near the door, a bleak look on his face.

"What happened?" she asked, hoping her voice sounded nonjudgmental.

His face flooded with relief as he looked up, but then he lifted his shoulders in a shrug and returned to contemplating his sneakers. She didn't know whether to interrogate him or hug him.

Mrs. Harper, the principal, came out of her office, followed by a stocky man in a brown suit and a boy holding an ice bag over one eye. Henry Kuntz glared as introductions were made, not lifting his hands from his son Justin's shoulders.

The principal's voice was brusque. "Why don't you both come in my office while we get to the bottom of this?"

Claire listened in disbelief as Mrs. Harper explained. According to the teacher on duty, the boys had been playing basketball, when suddenly Tripper had fired the basketball at point blank range straight into Justin's face.

"The kid's a menace!" Mr. Kuntz stuffed his hands in his pockets and jangled his change aggressively. "He's got no respect for authority. Just stared at me when I asked him to apologize to Justin." He jabbed a finger toward Claire. "If Justin's vision is affected, you'll be hearing from my lawyer."

Claire met his glare with a cool look. "I assure you my son is not a violent child, Mr. Kuntz. Whatever he did to your son was undoubtedly done with provocation." Remembering the surly glower Justin had directed toward Tripper from under the icepack, she had no doubt that was true. "I'll be happy to pay whatever medical bills result from this incident, but I warn you — stay away from my son. If Justin deserves an apology, I'll be the one to extract it from Tripper, not you."

She didn't lower her gaze, and finally he blinked and looked away. Claire turned to the principal. "If that's all, I'd like to take Tripper home now. Perhaps he'll share more details with me later." She offered a brief smile to the principal, then turned and left the room, firing a last warning glance at Justin's father on her way out.

But at home, her son was no more forthcoming. "Tripper, I know he must have said something to upset you. Won't you tell me what it was?" At his silence, Claire continued, determined to get to the bottom of it. "It must have been something that hurt you terribly. You must know whatever it was, it isn't true." At the risk of sounding cliché, she added, "'Sticks and stones can break your bones'—and I might put basketballs in that category—but words are harmless. Whatever Justin said was—"

"Just leave me alone!" Tripper shouted, jumping up from the couch where she had pinned him down for questioning. "He deserved it, and his father's a big fat idiot too. I'm not going to apologize, never. So just stop talking to me!" Two spots of color highlighted his cheekbones as he stood facing her.

Claire was completely at a loss. Tripper had never been prone to outbursts like this; normally he exhibited the same easy-going personality of his father. But she knew he also had inherited her sensitivity and hadn't yet developed the hard shell necessary for protection.

Resisting the urge to give him a hug, she picked up his schoolbag and handed it to him. "I'd like you to go upstairs now and do your homework. When you're ready to talk, I'll be happy to listen, but you will not speak disrespectfully to adults."

He took the bag, a look of relief relaxing his features. Sadie, who had been watching with ears raised throughout their exchange, followed him up the stairs, sensing her favorite playmate needed her protection.

When he was out of sight, Claire lowered herself onto the couch, surprised to notice she was shaking. This certainly couldn't be classified as one of the joys of parenting.

She had an overwhelming urge to share the burden, get Matt's take on Tripper's outburst.

But Matt made his living knocking off villains and despots, though as far as she knew he had never employed sports equipment while exacting justice. There was little chance Tripper would be influenced to apologize after a talk with Matt.

Still she debated calling him. Maybe this was one of those situations where a man's perspective was needed. She refused to use the word "father"; as far as Tripper knew, Matt was nothing more than a family friend. One he obviously respected, though. Perhaps she *should* call him…

In the end, the decision was made for her when she answered the phone to hear Matt's voice. "Hey, I just called your office. They said you had to pick Tripper up at school. He's not sick, is he?"

"No, it's worse than that. He was in a fight on the playground, and he hit another boy in the eye with a basketball—deliberately. Apparently they were having some kind of argument."

Matt gave a reassuring chuckle. "Boys get in fights all the time. This will probably blow over—"

"Don't give me that 'boys will be boys' garbage!" she blurted. "The other boy has a black eye, and his father is threatening to sue. And worst of all, Tripper won't apologize or even give a reason for his behavior. It's just not like him."

"Calm down, Claire," Matt said, his voice reassuring. "My attorney will eat him alive in court, no contest—"

"Matt!"

"Sorry. Just trying to lighten the mood."

Claire clutched the phone. "Actually, I was hoping you could try talking to him—to Tripper, I mean. He's not communicating with me at the moment."

"Sure. As a matter of fact, I was calling to see if I could come out. I had Heather pick up another bag of dog food—I noticed you were low the other day. How about if I drop by—" he paused, then added "—in an hour or so?"

Claire agreed, hoping Matt would be more successful than she had been in dealing with a recalcitrant nine-year-old.


Matt called Jackson and put off the meeting they had scheduled to go over the next days' shooting schedule. Handling his first crisis as a parent was more important, he figured. From the sound of Claire's voice, she was more than a little worried. Plus, he had to shamefully admit, he wasn't above racking up a few points with the normally self-sufficient Claire by offering support and comfort. She obviously didn't realize playground fights were a guy thing.

When he arrived at her home, neither Tripper nor Sadie showed up at the door to greet him. Claire opened the door alone, the smell of a high-class bordello clinging to her.

He wrinkled his nose. "What on earth is that?"

"It's called *Scandal*," she said, a little smile slipping onto her lips, despite the worry that shadowed her eyes. "We're launching it in a major promotion, starting next week."

He lifted his eyebrows. "You're promoting scandal? Here I thought you did your damnedest to avoid it."

"At least it smells better than the last one I was involved in." Then she nodded toward the stairs. "I hope you can get more out of him than I did. I promised Justin's father he'd have an apology."

"I'll give it a shot," he promised, then went upstairs.

A poster of bats decorated Tripper's door, along with a "No Trespassing" sign. Matt rapped his knuckles on the wood and, at Tripper's listless bidding, entered the room.

He was sitting on the bed, twirling a red-and-blue basketball on the tip of his finger.

"Hey, sport," Matt said. "What's up? Your mom said you had a little trouble at school."

Tripper glanced at Matt, lifted his shoulders in a small shrug, then returned his gaze to the ball.

The gesture struck a familiar chord in Matt. In his own youth, he had often been called on the carpet for similar misdeeds. He joined Tripper on the bed, then took the ball from his hands. "Maybe I should teach you how to use this thing. Normally you aim it at the hoop, not someone's face."

Tripper frowned, not appreciating the joke.

Matt eyed the ball, signed by several of the players for the Sixers. "So what really happened?" He waited patiently.

"I just wanted him to shut up," Tripper said at last.

"Why?"

Stubborn silence greeted the question. Matt probed a little deeper. "He wasn't dissing your hook shot, was he?"

Tripper's eyes met his briefly, and Matt could see he was tempted. Whatever the kid had said, Tripper had obviously felt it justified a bouncer in the face.

Matt was inclined to go with Tripper's judgment.

"You want to get it off your chest? I can keep a secret, you know."

"He's just a jerk, that's all."

"There're better ways of dealing with jerks. Your mom probably has a few pointers there. I've seen her in action, and believe me, it's not a pretty sight!"

Tripper raised a curious gaze, his green eyes almost a carbon copy of his own. He seemed to weigh his words. Finally he said, "Matt, can I ask you something? About my mom, I mean?"

Matt hesitated, not sure where Tripper was heading. "What is it you want to know about your mom?"

"Do you think she's…well, do you like her?"

Matt was startled at the turn the conversation was taking, but he replied gamely, "Sure, I like her. You know that. Your mom and I are friends."

"If somebody said something bad about her, would you hit them?"

Matt almost choked. "What has someone said about your mom?" he asked, ready to punch whoever had planted any ideas in Tripper's head.

"They said I was lying about you coming over here. They said I just made it up because I don't have a dad or anything."

"But you do have a dad," Matt felt compelled to point out.

"Yeah, I know, but he's one of those deadhead dads, the ones you see on TV who don't pay their child support." Matt suppressed a grin, but Tripper's next words erased all desire to smile. "I'm glad he doesn't come around. I think my mom's afraid of him. She gets a funny look on her face when I ask her about him, and she even keeps a gun in her closet. I saw it once, when I was playing hide-and-seek in there."

"Jesus Christ," Matt muttered. "Listen, Tripper, I think we ought to talk to your mom about this. She could probably set you straight—"

"No! She told me I shouldn't talk about you coming over here to the other kids at school." Tripper's face registered alarm. "She said other people wouldn't understand. She was right."

"It's true some people get all weird about celebrities. I told you that, didn't I?"

"Yeah, but all I did was tell them you took me to the basketball game."

"Well, there's the proof of that." He nodded toward the basketball in his hands. "Why don't you take that to school and show them?"

"My mom won't let me. I already asked. And I can't tell her what they said—about my dad and all. She would get all upset."

"I think she might be even more upset if you keep hitting guys in the face with a basketball just because they accuse you of lying. Maybe she could even understand why you did it."

Matt understood, perhaps better than Tripper did himself. With no father to brag about, the kid had to improvise occasionally. Surely Claire would agree that it was time to tell Tripper the truth, though Matt was beginning to share her apprehension. Obviously Tripper had come to the conclusion he was a "deadhead" dad—one who went around hitting women with abandon. It would be up to Claire to set him straight on that—but at her own expense, he realized.

The whole situation was muddy as a melted snowdrift. But the fact was, one little boy was confused, and hurt, and regardless of the difficulty of explaining all the intricacies to him, he deserved to know the truth.

But Tripper was giving Matt a pleading look. "Don't tell her, Matt. You promised!"

"Tripper, I know you want to protect your mom. I do, too, but she needs to know why you got into a fight at school."

"She'll just say I should ignore it—'sticks and stones' and all that stuff."

"I think she might understand better than you realize. She's not exactly immune to words either."

Tripper kicked his sneakers against the bed frame, contemplating Matt's advice. "Some people are just jerks," he said. "They deserve to get black eyes."

"You may be right there," he said. "But recess monitors usually take a dim view of that approach." He spun the basketball over his fingertips. "And I speak from experience."

Tripper gave Matt a sidelong glance, taking his measure. "We were shooting free throws," he finally said, "and I was making more baskets than Justin. So that's when he started calling me names. He just does that, to everyone."

"He's a bully," Matt supplied.

"Yeah. He called me a loser, and then he said my mom was too. Because my dad didn't stick around and marry her."

"That's ridiculous."

"I know, but ever since open house, Justin's been bragging about how his dad does stuff with him. I think his parents are getting a divorce and they're, like, fighting over him."

"Makes sense," Matt replied. "Kid's still a bully."

"I told him my mom just didn't want to marry my dad, but then… then—" Tripper hesitated.

Matt had a feeling the bad part was yet to come, though at this point, he already wanted to see Justin get his just deserts.

Tripper ducked his head. "He said that was just what she told me. He said she was lying and that I'm lying about knowing you." He glanced up, swallowing what Matt felt sure were more tears.

"He said you're a big star, and you wouldn't be hanging around me and my mom. He said…he said my father didn't even want anything to do with her."

Matt tightened his fist, refraining from hugging his son. More than anything, he wanted to reassure Tripper that Justin's words had no bearing to the truth. But it wasn't his truth to tell.

Tripper looked up, his eyes brimming with tears. "Then he said she was a freak like me. And that's when I hit him. I just couldn't let him say things like that about my mom."

"Jesus." Matt wanted to lob a basketball at the kid too. But somehow, agreeing that his son had done the right thing by giving his tormenter a black eye would probably earn him a flunking grade in Parenting 101.

"Listen, Tripper, none of what he said was true. You know that, don't you?"

"Yeah."

"Your mother—"

"Don't tell her what he said! Promise!"

Matt set the ball down and met his gaze squarely. "Look, I agree, it might make your mom sad to hear all that stuff, but she needs to know the gist of it. Why don't you just trust me to explain the situation to her? Remember, I want to protect her as much as you do." He dropped a hand onto Tripper's shoulder. "I think I can get you off the hook and at the same time not upset her too much. How about it?"

Tripper gave him an assessing look. "Okay," he agreed. "But be sure and tell her Justin deserved it!"

"Don't worry. Justin will definitely be cast in the role of Bad Guy," Matt promised.

But on the way downstairs, Matt wondered if central casting hadn't screwed up and given Justin his own part.

Christ, he dreaded being around when Tripper found out the truth. For abandoning his mother, Tripper would probably like to lob a boulder at his face.

Claire hung up the phone just as Matt walked into the kitchen. "That was Justin's father," she said, picking up a cup of coffee. "I told him to send me the bill for the doctor visit, though nothing was really wrong. Just a black eye. It should heal in a week or so."

Matt sat at the table, his eyes on her as she poured him his own cup. She'd taken off her suit jacket, but now she wished she'd left it on, for protection from his too knowing leer.

"Maybe someone should have a talk with Justin," he said. "Sounds like he's the playground bully."

Claire glanced at him, the sugar spoon held up in her hand, but he wasn't paying attention to the coffee she was fixing. She added two teaspoons, figuring he could use a bracing dose of sugar after dealing with her son — their son, she reminded herself.

"Claire, do you keep a gun in your closet?"

Her eyes widened as she set the steaming mug in front of him. "A gun? What on earth are you—" Then the implication hit her. She sat down across from him. "Did Tripper tell you that?"

"Yeah, he claims it's proof you're terrified of his father showing up one day. Mind explaining where he got that impression?" Matt gazed at her over the rim of his cup.

She gave a bewildered shrug. "I honestly have no idea. I certainly never told him that. Whenever he's asked, I've been very vague. Maybe too vague," she conceded. "It's true I used to own a gun, but I got rid of it when we moved here. It belonged to my grandmother. I had no idea Tripper even knew it was there."

Matt swallowed his coffee. "You're telling me your grandmother was some sort of pistol-packing granny?"

"She owned a gun for protection. You're from the Wild West… Surely you don't find gun ownership all that unusual?" She gathered her mail from the desk and began opening it.

"No, but I would have pegged you as the pacifist type."

She just shrugged and said with an air of indifference, "I didn't know what to do with it after she died, so I just kept it in my closet, unloaded."

"I see," he said, but he seemed far from convinced. "By the way, in addition to being a potential wife beater, he also thinks I'm some sort of 'deadhead' dad." His lips twitched. "I don't think he means a Grateful Dead fan."

Then he sobered. "I think it's time to straighten him out. The kids at school have been teasing him. That's what the fight was about today. Apparently Justin got wind of the fact that Tripper hasn't got a father at home and insinuated it was his fault."

"Oh, no!" All indifference gone, Claire gave him a stricken look.

Matt set his coffee cup down and leaned across the table. "I don't want him thinking he's worthless just because his father deserted his mother."

"He doesn't think that! I've told him that it was my choice to leave his father. Whatever the kids are saying, it will only get worse if the truth gets out."

"Just what *is* the truth?"

"The truth? The truth is we had a sordid, sleazy affair and drove a woman to kill herself. What child wants to know he was conceived that way?"

"It wasn't the sordid sleazy affair you think it was. Believe me, I've had plenty of those. I know the difference."

"I just bet you have!" She turned away, but she knew Matt had seen the disgusted look on her face. Anger flared, a white hot arc between them. He sprang from the chair and swung her around. "I have sex, Claire. Good, hot sex with women who are ready, willing, and able. You, on the other hand, have turned yourself into an icicle because of one rotten experience."

She yanked her arm from his loose grip. "You have no right to judge me. No right at all. Just because I won't hop into bed with you—"

"Hell, this isn't about sex! It never was! I cared about you then, and I care about you now. God knows why—you're about as easy to love as a prickly pear—but I want to anyway."

Claire gave a brittle laugh. "Well, that's too bad. Not even big movie stars get everything they want."

She knew it was a low blow, but she had her own wounds to tend. "Just leave me alone, Matt. Please. My life is complicated enough."

"Unfortunately, your life and mine are already more tangled up than a roll of baling wire. That kid up there—" he gestured toward the ceiling "—needs the support of both his parents. And as much as you want me to, I'm not going to walk out of his life just because it would make your life easier." He leveled his stubborn gaze on hers, his words drawing a figurative line in the sand.

She could only stare back at him, fear pleating her gut.

He sighed. "I know you've been hurt, and not just by me. Tripper's told me enough, and you've been conspicuously silent on enough occasions, that I've been able to put two and two together. I know you must've had a pretty rotten deal growing up." His voice grew rough with concern. "But whatever your life was like, the important thing is not to let it affect our son."

She bristled. "Are you accusing me of letting my—my…" she sputtered.

"Insecurities," he supplied.

"I don't have any insecurities!"

He laughed. "Come on, Claire. You're the fucking motherlode of insecurity!"

Claire ground her teeth. Sticks and stones, she reminded herself, though right now she wished she had a stone the size of Dallas—or at least a Spaulding—handy.

Instead she braced herself with a deep breath and aimed squarely at his heart: "Since you seem to be the resident psychologist, why don't you analyze this, Matt? The first woman you loved went suicidal on you. Now you say you want to take the chance with someone like me—a poster child for neuroses. If I'm so insecure, aren't you afraid I'll lose it one day, go to pieces right in front of you?"

"Hell," he protested, scraping a hand over his face. "I didn't say you weren't a strong woman! It's obvious you've had some hard knocks, but you're not like Hayley."

"You're right, I'm not. What you think is insecurity is caution. And yes, I learned it the hard way. I pulled my life together more than once, and I'm not about to let you destroy it, just so you can play Long-Lost Daddy.

"When I think Tripper's ready for the truth, I'll tell him," she continued. "Until then, you get the starring role of his friend." Then she sighed, remembering her son upstairs. "He needs that more now, anyway."

"And you? What do you need?" Matt asked quietly.

She turned away, her pulse gradually returning to normal. "Maybe I need a friend too," she admitted. "But not a psychologist. And certainly not a lover. Not now, not…you."

"Sure," he said, shrugging his shoulders as if it made no difference to him. "I can be a pretty good friend. And hey, like you say, sex is always available—elsewhere. No strings attached, just like I like it." His voice was mocking. "And if she wants to blow her brains out afterward, hey—" He gave another what-do-I-care shrug, then reached for his jacket.

"Matt, I'm sorry. I shouldn't have said that—"

"No, I'm the one who's sorry," he said lightly, tugging his jacket over his arms. "I made the mistake of giving a damn."

As he walked out the door, Claire ignored the urge to rush toward him and tell him again she was sorry. A grown man, after all, had no use for a plastic Band-Aid.

And that was all she had to give him.

# Chapter Eighteen

The scent of *Scandal* sweetened the air, as throngs of people milled about the rotunda. Deep purple carpet led from the main entrance to the cosmetic counter in the rear of the store. From the ceiling, purple and gold banners announced "The latest *Scandal*." Sparkling champagne flutes surrounded an ice sculpture in the shape of a perfume bottle. The kickoff had turned into a party, celebrating the opening of the newly refurbished flagship store as well as the launch of a new perfume.

From her spot near the elevators, Claire glanced around, unable to squelch a feeling of pride. Tonight Kaslow's shone, from the marble floors to the mahogany panels above the fountain. An ecclesiastical air filled the old building. A hint of bergamot wafted from the *Scandal* sachets piled on a display table, while strains of Bach, as lovely as hymns, poured from the piano in the corner.

Perhaps the comparisons were a tad bit sacrilegious, Claire thought: they were selling perfume, after all, designed to inflame the passions of men…But then, wasn't that exactly what religion did? Claire's thoughts curved back to long ago, sitting on a pew while Roy Porter lashed out at his attentive congregation, each and every soul determined to repent before the sun had set on their sins. Yes, she decided, inflamed passions could certainly account for much of what went on in her adoptive father's church.

She watched as someone threw a silver dollar into the fountain. Instantly she thought of Matt standing there, offering her a quarter for her thoughts…right before he found out what secrets her thoughts concealed.

And he still didn't know all of them.

Claire ignored the sickening thud that pounded between her ribs. Not even she was aware of all the secrets hiding in the dark corners of her mind, and tonight she refused to think about them.

Around her, the hum of the crowd grew expectant, as the Bach rolled into a rock beat. Bendel's signature model strolled across the carpet, just ahead of a more dignified Mme. Bendel, followed by a string of reporters with flashing cameras. For an instant, Claire froze, reliving the time when the flashbulbs were all aimed at her. But tonight, the reclusive Mme. Bendel was the object of their frenzy.

At the fountain the eighty-year-old perfumier paused, then inclined her head slightly, one grande dame paying her respects to another. Jackie leaned toward her and interrupted the moment of reverie. Probably reciting the legends, Claire guessed from her spot twenty feet away.

Then the turbaned head of Mme. Bendel turned. Her gaze swept the room, finally landing on Claire. As the woman approached, Claire ignored the sudden impulse to curtsy. The Queen of England herself probably hadn't generated as much excitement when she appeared at Bloomingdale's years ago.

As introductions were made, Claire's high school French came in handy. Though Mme. Bendel seemed to understand English, her replies were heavily flavored with French. With a wave of her hand, she encompassed the whole store with the words "*C'est magnifique! My perfume and your store…a perfect match, n'est-ce pas?*" She nodded toward the fountain. "Surely, she will smile on us both, *oui?*"

"*J'espère bien,*" Claire answered, a vision of climbing stock prices dancing in her head. Then she blinked as a flash went off near her.

Mme. Bendel, having made her pronouncement, swept forward to where Bernard Kaslow and his wife waited for an introduction. An excited flush stained Bernard's cheeks as he posed for a photo next to the legendary perfumier.

Just behind his uncle lurked Evan, a smile pasted on his face. In a display of continental flair, he leaned in to kiss the woman's cheek, despite the scowl that seemed entrenched on her face. An impervious hand stopped him mid-way. His smile faltered, and then the sea of onlookers followed Mme. Bendel toward the merchandise display.

Claire felt an almost imperceptible tug at her attention. Turning, she noticed the reclining figure of the goddess, and for a moment, Claire could have sworn the bronze lips were curved in a knowing smile.

The next morning, a photo of Mme. Bendel appeared in the business section of the *Philadelphia Inquirer*. Claire would have been pleased with the publicity Kaslow's coup had garnered, but for the fact that she herself was shown in the photo, greeting Mme. Bendel, the goddess Fortuna reclining in the background.

Sipping her coffee at her desk, Claire wondered just how much the goddess would fetch on the clearance table.

Her phone buzzed, and Jackie's animated voice floated into the room. "I just heard: *Advertising Age* has picked up the story; they want to interview me! Oh, and Claire, a reporter called from the *LA Times*. Something about Matt Grayson's film. They had your name wrong, though. By the way, did you know Nordstrom had the West Coast *Scandal* account?"

She prattled on for a moment, and then Claire's other line buzzed. "That'll be the *LA Times*," Jackie said. "I told her you could answer her questions."

Claire punched the button and heard the reporter's voice.

"This is Lesley Burnett, *LA Times*. Could you comment on the story in today's *Inquisitor*?"

"Actually, Jackie Prescott can give you more information on the *Scandal* debut."

"Oh, no, I'm not talking about the perfume. The story I'm referring to is the one in Alicia Howard's column…"

Claire listened, one eye on the figures in front of her.

"In light of your recent association with Matt Grayson, I was wondering, has the romance between you two rekindled? And if so, are you planning to—"

The pen Claire was holding dropped to the desk. She swallowed, but a sick feeling of dread stuck in her throat. "Just exactly what story are you referring to?"

"According to the *Inquisitor*, you were once involved with Matt Grayson…on the set of *Bed of Roses*." She paused.

Claire's hand tightened on the phone.

"It is true, isn't it? You're the former Clarissa Peters?"

Claire didn't answer.

"Hello? Ms. Porter?" The reporter's voice struck silence again.

Claire hung up the phone, the figures forgotten. Only one thought filled her mind: She had to get to her son.


Matt watched the best boy take down a c-stand, folding the contraption like a Tinkertoy. This was the next-to-last scene they would film in Philadelphia. Provided everything went well this afternoon at the mansion where they were shooting the scenes with Jane's father, most of the filming would be complete.

Later, voiceovers would be taped in the studio, but that would occur in May, after a major portion of editing had been completed.

An assistant director paged him on the walkie talkie he wore around his neck. "Matt, your publicist has been trying to get you since five a.m."

Matt swore. The call wouldn't have been put through. With the tight schedule they were on, his assistant was under orders to shield him from any but the direst emergencies.

He punched in Sharon Rogers's number on the cell Heather handed him.

"You're not going to believe this," she told him, "but the *Inquisitor* thinks you've met up with an old flame there in Philadelphia."

His mind still on the afternoon's schedule, he started to shrug off the news; then, as the realization hit, he halted mid-way to his trailer.

"What are you talking about? What old flame?"

"The woman from that aborted *Bed of Roses* film — what was her name? Clarissa? That's right; it's here on their web site. The print article hit the stands this morning."

"Oh, shit."

"I figured it wasn't true, but I wanted to verify it with you before we issued a denial. The article claims she's now some executive at the store where you're filming."

"Oh, *fuck*." Someone had figured it out — *son of a bitch!*

"Matt? Should we even bother to deny this one?"

He rubbed his jaw, thinking hard. Claire would be frantic—provided she'd heard. Her first thought would be Tripper, protecting him from hearing the truth from some kid on the playground.

"Matt?"

"No. Don't deny a damn thing. If you get any questions, just act coy—keep them guessing. Meanwhile, I'll prepare a statement—" He looked at his watch. "Shit. I can't cancel this afternoon's shoot without screwing the schedule…" His mind leaped to possible solutions. "Listen, call my pilot, have him get the plane ready to fly to Montana. Leaving from—from Brandywine Airport, in Chester County," he said. No one would look for her there.

With an apology for asking her to make arrangements he'd normally have his assistant make, Matt rang off. His first priority now was Claire, making sure she didn't get the same treatment she had received the last time her name had been linked with his.

He called her work number. She had left a half hour ago—in a hurry, her assistant informed him—and she had no idea when she would return.

He tried her cell, but she didn't pick up.

She had obviously heard the news. She'd be with Tripper, shielding him the best way she could—most likely with more lies, he thought grimly.

It was past time to tell him the truth, but now, a sudden attack of stage fright knotted his gut. What if Tripper decided Matt was to blame for everything that had befallen his mother? Would he ever be able to forgive him for not protecting Claire, for not being a part of his life?

Their relationship was hardly off the ground, and already Matt had plenty of explaining to do. Opening the door to his trailer, he swore to himself. He'd rather face a bar full of mean drunks than his son right now.

Inside, he tried Claire's cell again. When she answered, he gave her instructions, ignoring the trace of panic he heard in her voice. "Go home and pack a bag for you and Tripper. Don't worry about Sadie; I'll have someone pick her up later. My plane will be at the Brandywine Airport—" he glanced at his watch "—in an hour. I'll send a car for you, and a couple of security guys."

"Brandywine? The commuter airport?"

"Yeah, it'll be the last place they'll look. I'd come with you, but by the time this breaks, they'll be all over me like mold on cheese."

"But, Matt, we can't—we can't just go to Montana. What on earth would your family say?"

"Don't worry about them. I've already told Mark everything. He'll meet you at the airport."

"You've told your family? Everything?" Her voice was skeptical.

"I told them Tripper was my son. That's all that matters to them. Trust me, Claire."

"I can't go to Montana. I—I have work to do. Tripper has school…" Her voice trailed off. They both knew it was only a matter of time before the tabloid reporters discovered where Tripper went to school and aimed their zoom lenses on the playground.

"He's out next week for spring break. Taking a few extra days won't matter. And you can work from my ranch—believe it or not, we've got Internet out there now."

There was silence on the other end. Matt wasn't sure if that indicated agreement. "I'm going to straighten this mess out, one way or another," he vowed. "All you have to do is keep Tripper from hearing anything from anyone other than you or me."

"Right," she said, her voice guarded. "That should be…a snap."

"Right now, they only know who you are—or were. They have no idea Tripper was born nine months after our affair."

"It won't take more than a day for that to become public knowledge." He could hear the note of despair in her voice.

"Just stay calm, Claire. I'll fix everything," he assured her. "Just get him to the airport in an hour. Okay?"

"All right," she agreed, though there was still a note of uncertainty in her voice. Matt knew her well enough to know she didn't like to be cornered.

He heard her sigh over the phone. "I suppose it's better than moving to Australia."

"You were going to move to Australia?"

"Yes. I hear the weather's better there than Antarctica."

He laughed, applauding her gallows humor. She was a tough cookie, but even tough cookies crumbled sometimes.

Damn the press for putting them in this position, he thought, ending the conversation. He would have preferred to choose his own time for telling Tripper the truth.

Like maybe when he announced he was marrying his mother.

# Chapter Nineteen

Claire looked down on the state of Montana while the plane began its descent. The mirror lake below reflected the fluffy clouds, but the sight didn't lift the gloom that had settled around her. Next to her, though, Tripper was beside himself with excitement. She had told him Matt had reissued the invitation to join him in Montana and she had decided to take him up on it, using the age-old excuse that she had been working too hard. It wasn't exactly a lie, and Tripper believed her, with a trust that stabbed at her heart.

Matt had promised to meet them at this brother's house that evening, as soon as he had a handle on the rumors that would certainly be flying now. She didn't know how, could not even begin to focus on the mechanics involved with dealing with the media. She just knew Matt wouldn't let them down.

His brother, Mark, met them at the tiny Great Falls airport. Claire recognized him right away. With hair barely a shade darker than Matt's and a neatly trimmed beard, just tinged with gray, Mark was exactly as she had pictured him. A more sober, and older, version of Matt. Mark accepted the presence of Claire and her son in the brisk air of Montana as if nothing were amiss, greeting them like old friends rather than refugees.

Claire, whose nerves were still jangling from the morning's near brush with notoriety, felt the first stirrings of relief sweep through her system.

"This it?" Mark asked, hefting their bags as if they were filled with popcorn.

"Yes," Claire replied. "I wasn't sure what the weather was like here, so I packed everything."

He chuckled, the sound more subdued than Matt's laugh. "This time of year, the only certain thing is we'll have some…weather," he clarified. Then he glanced at her leather pumps. "Mel's probably got some boots you could wear, if it comes to it."

Claire smiled stiffly. "Thank you, but I don't plan to be here long." She glanced at Tripper, tagging along beside them, her carry-on bouncing against his legs. "Tripper brought his snow boots and pants, though. Matt did mention spring blizzards weren't all that uncommon."

Mark nodded. "That's right. Out here, Mother Nature doesn't pay much attention to the calendar."

As they walked out of the airport, she noticed Mark's eyes lingering on Tripper, but he didn't comment. They stopped in front of a white pickup. Claire hesitated beside the door, daunted by the height of the seat. She could count on one hand the number of times she had ridden in a pickup truck.

But Mark was as gallant as his little brother. After throwing their bags in the rear, he held out his hand for Claire, assisting her into the cab after Tripper had scrambled into the backseat.

Any awkwardness Claire would have felt during the drive was dispelled by Tripper's excited questions.

"How far is it to Matt's ranch?" he asked, taking in the streets of Great Falls, as if expecting to see honest-to-god cowboys on every corner.

"It's about an hour, but we're stopping by our place. Matt called earlier; he's catching a flight in this evening. Said for you guys to hang out with us until he gets in. He keeps his truck at our place when he's out of town, and one of us ferries him from the airport."

As they drove, Claire stared straight ahead, resisting the urge to bite her fingernails. Anxiety brewed in her stomach. Matt's family would probably hate her on sight, though he had sworn they would accept Tripper, no questions asked.

She hoped that was true.

They pulled up in front of a spacious cedar-sided house. The driveway was loaded with testosterone, in the form of three mud-flecked four-wheel drives.

A barking retriever, a darker gold than Sadie, bounded up to greet the truck, followed by a trickle of children of various ages. Claire cut a worried glance toward Mark when he opened her door.

He correctly interpreted her concerns as he helped her down. "We told 'em Matt had invited a couple of friends out to the ranch," he said casually, letting her know Tripper's cousins had no idea of their relationship.

But it would be impossible to keep the secret much longer. Desperately she wished for Matt's arrival, though at the same time, the thought almost made her stumble.

Introductions were surprisingly easy. "Hey, I'm Hannah. Who are you?" was the forthright greeting of the smallest, a girl of about six, with blond curls streaming down her back. Before Tripper could answer, a boy about his age — Ben, Claire remembered — sauntered toward them, an animal that looked suspiciously like a rat on his shoulder. "Hey. You want to see my pet rat? His name is Streaker — see, 'cause he's got that stripe on his back," he pointed out, breaking the ice with the efficiency of a ten-year-old.

"Oh, that's cool," Tripper replied nonchalantly, casting an interested look at Streaker — and at Ben. Claire detected just a hint of nervousness in his voice. These children were, after all, Matt's family. For the first time, Tripper would be forced to share his hero's affections. Claire took a deep breath. One more lie, this time a lie of omission: These children were her son's cousins, this man his uncle. And his mother had kept them from him all his life.

Melinda was drying her hands on a towel when they walked in. "Hi, I'm Melinda — Mel, to most folks. Just hang your coats there." She continued to issue orders with an authority Claire couldn't help but admire. "Hannah, wash your hands; you've been playing with the dog. Ben, let Tripper get his shoes off before you drag him upstairs to play with that rat. Mark, your brother called. He wanted you to call him as soon as you got in." The last request was accompanied by a none-too-subtle look.

Thirteen-year-old Stacy helped them hang up their coats, darting a shy smile at Claire. After Melinda had sent her off to practice piano, she introduced her last child in absentia.

"All that's left is Andy—he's got a job out at our neighbor's place after school. He's sixteen," she explained, ushering Claire toward the kitchen where she could smell coffee. "And Harold and Joyce—Matt's mom and dad—live in town. He'll probably want to take you by there later."

Claire didn't respond to that. She wasn't ready to meet Matt's parents—Tripper's grandparents.

"Sit down. I'll pour you some coffee." But Claire, recognizing a protective instinct when she saw one, knew the coffee would be served with questions along with the cream.

"Actually, I was hoping I could rest—it's been a long day." She met the frankly curious gaze of her hostess head on.

Mel set the coffee pot back on the burner. Sharp blue eyes seemed to take quick measure. Claire imagined she looked like hell, a fact that was confirmed when Mel's face turned sympathetic.

"There's an apartment downstairs you can use to freshen up. Matt uses it when he stays here, though he usually just heads on out to his place. As you can see, it's a madhouse around here," she told her. "I'll tell them to keep it down. We usually eat around six thirty. If you're asleep—"

"I'm sure I won't be; I just need…" Claire paused. Sleep was exactly what she needed. She felt as though she had just survived a battle—a narrow escape into territory she was beginning to think was controlled by the enemy.

And tomorrow's skirmish was still to come.

In the room downstairs, Claire couldn't rest. A thousand thoughts ransacked her brain. What if Tripper became suspicious? What if the reporters tracked them down? What if Melinda, who obviously knew the whole story, let something slip?

She rose from the too soft bed. Traces of Matt were everywhere. A photo on the dresser, of Matt and a flaxen-haired cowboy—Mel's brother? she wondered, remembering Matt's tales of his adolescent exploits with Jay. A pair of creased boots, neatly placed in the opened closet—probably by Melinda, she thought, remembering the casually kicked-off boots Matt used to leave on her own floor.

And hanging from a rack on the closet door, a denim jacket, with the smell of hard-working male clinging to it.

Just for a moment she closed her eyes and pictured Matt. If only he were here now—here to ward off the curiosity of his well-meaning family; here to reassure Tripper he was still his best bud. *Here to hold her*, she thought longingly, feeling a sting of tears against her eyelids.

And then, spurred by the imminent emotional breakdown, her defenses kicked in. She had gotten this far, hadn't she, without Matt's help? It had been a momentary weakness that had made her agree to accept his protection, like some medieval wimp.

The thing to do was to face the threat herself.

Now, with plenty of time to stop and think about her situation, she realized she had acted precipitously. She should have stayed and fought her battle on her own turf. Holed up here like some Wild West bandit, she had given up control of the situation.

Unaccustomed to the feeling, her breathing came quicker as panic threatened to overload her sensory circuits. Her hands knotted on the sleeves of the jacket, and it slipped from the hook, into her arms.

She hugged it around her body, grateful for its fleece-lined warmth, then lowered herself into a stuffed chair. She tucked her legs under her, and minutes later, her mind slipped into exhausted sleep.


When Matt found her three hours later — tucked into the chair, wearing Jay's jacket — he stopped and stared. For one moment, he had an urge to pick her up and carry her away to his stone fortress, where she would never have to be frightened again. It might be corny as hell, but still he couldn't resist the old-fashioned thrill it gave him to come to her rescue.

He had spent the day marshaling forces. With a carefully worded statement, he had confirmed the identity of the woman he had been seeing for the past few months as the same woman he had been briefly involved with early in his career. And he had made clear the fact that he was also the father of her son. He had given few details, knowing from past experience the more you told them, the more they slobbered for information. But he had, in no uncertain terms, let it be known that Claire Porter had his utmost admiration and support.

And anyone who wanted to mess with her could come through him first.

She sighed in her sleep, looking oddly vulnerable. So unlike the image she presented to the world — a carefully maintained façade, he now knew. He'd seen her soft spot, for her son, and even for him — her fierce objections to his upcoming "imprisonment," the tender way she'd provided him with the DVD of their son's early years, the portfolio of photographs she'd sent him the next day.

His feelings for her had turned into something protective, he realized, something permanent. He didn't know when it had happened—maybe the first time he'd seen her, looking so sweet, so out of place on the movie set—but now he wanted to spend the rest of his life taking care of her. He wanted to sleep with her; wake with her; show her God's greatest work of art, the state of Montana.

But first they had to get through the next few weeks, which, for her at least, were sure to be hell. She wasn't used to the cameras, the notoriety, to seeing her face featured in gossip columns.

He leaned down, placed a light kiss on her pale forehead. She didn't stir. Giving in to the urge to hold her, he picked her up, moving slowly so as not to wake her. She curled into his arms. He savored the feel of it for a second, then laid her gently on the bed, stretching out next to her, his shoulder pillowing her head. Dark hair fanned over his chest, the scent of her shampoo filled his nostrils, and his thoughts took a salacious leap. For just a moment, he envisioned her naked, writhing underneath him.

He let out a sigh of disgust. God, if he felt this way after a whiff of her shampoo, what on earth would he do at the sight of her in those lace-edged panties he'd once caught a glimpse of, before she'd slid them under a pile of folded laundry?

He tensed involuntarily, his hold tightening. Next to him, she gave a start.

"Matt?" Her voice sounded strained, unsure.

He rubbed his hand against her shoulder. "Yeah, it's me. How you doing?"

Her heart quickened against his chest, like a yearling foal faced with a saddle the first time. *Take it slow*, he told himself. The last thing Claire wanted—needed—was a quick shag in the sheets.

He swallowed his lust. Superman could keep his cape on, at least until the girl was properly rescued.


Claire felt his voice through his shirt, a reassuring thrum deep in his chest. She stretched, intending to move away, but his arm clasped her firm around her waist. She stopped breathing, mid-stretch. All thoughts fled her mind like a wind gust—her body suddenly, urgently, without preamble, aroused.

She strained for composure, willing her breathing to slow, her heart to stop racing. If she held herself very still, surely this would pass. Surely sanity would return, and this warmth that was flooding her body would go away…

"Claire?"

"Hmmm?" It came out a high-pitched squeak.

"We should talk about—"

Her hand covered his mouth, stopping the words. She didn't want to talk. For once, she just wanted to feel.

Her fingers moved of their own accord, exploring his lips, his face. The stubble of his beard tingled like an electric charge against her fingertips, bringing alive dormant nerve endings. Desire, denied for so long, now reared up with a vengeance. *I want this man*, she thought wonderingly. *I want to be a part of him*! Stunned by the force of her body's hunger, she stretched against his length and heard him groan.

With a little twist, she flipped on top of him, her legs moving sinuously against him.

She was throbbing all over. Places she had forgotten existed heated up deliciously as she stared down at this most wonderful example of the species. God, what had she been thinking, pushing him away all these weeks, keeping him at arms' length, depriving herself of this wonderful warmth?

She kissed his neck, tasting the saltiness, wanting more, wanting all of him. She curved against his hard angles, wanting nothing more than to be closer to this man who made her *feel*—so alive, so desired, so loved.

For the first time in ten years, Claire lost herself to passion, the thought of consequences shadowed by primeval need.


Matt's heartbeat quickened beneath her. His body responded, hardened at the feel of her. Not a single thought clouded his head as he brought his hands up under the jacket, holding her close, sliding against the silk of her shirt, near those enticing curves…

She moaned. An honest-to-god moan, from deep in her throat, that almost sent him over the edge. But gamely he held on, deciding the best way to answer her was to cover her mouth with his.

She latched on like he was manna from heaven and she was a starving Israelite. And, bless Moses, he was mighty tired of being lost in the desert himself.

Passion soared, there on his brother's bed. He pried the jacket from her arms, arms that wanted to scale his chest, jerking the sleeves over hands that were busy unbuttoning his shirt.

*God, Claire was unbuttoning his shirt!* He almost chortled with glee over the sudden victory that seemed his for the taking…except she was the one doing the taking.

She pressed her mouth to his chest, roaming, with little nibbles here and there…and then she found his mouth again. He satisfied her hunger, keeping her tongue busy while he slid his hands under her silk blouse and unhooked her bra.

And then those beautiful breasts were in his hands, filling his palms, and he wanted her more than he had ever wanted anything.

Above him, she raised up to allow him better access, eyes closed, mouth trembling, inching toward his, as if she couldn't decide if she were sated. He certainly wasn't. He shifted. Lowering his mouth to her breast, he gave in to the urge to make her melt with his tongue.

She writhed in pleasure above him.

*Heaven.* He had found it, here in his brother's bed…in Claire's arms.

And then a knock sounded on the portal of heaven, and the voice of his sister-in-law came through the door: "Matt? You guys hungry? You'll want to get it while it's hot."

*What an understatement!*

He groaned as he felt Claire stiffen against him. She refused to meet his gaze as she scrambled off him, fumbling with her bra and grasping at buttons.

After he answered Mel, Matt lay with his hands tucked behind his head, silently observing her distress.

He loved the way she looked, flustered, her hair falling around her face, the apples of her cheeks stained with a pink glow.

He grinned. "If I clear my plate, do I get dessert?"

Shooting him a look, she clipped her hair, her wanton image dispelled—except for the lock of hair that refused to bend to her will. "Don't get any ideas," she warned in a voice that held only a few residual tremors. "God knows, your sister-in-law already thinks I'm some kind of tramp."

"No, she doesn't. Mel knows everything. I told her…" He stopped. He had told Mel he was in love with Claire, that he wanted to marry her, but he didn't think Claire wanted to hear that right now. "I told her the truth," he said instead.

"That's bad enough."

"The fact that we have a child out of wedlock is hardly—" he began, but she cut him short.

"It's the fact that I've got the nerve to show my face here, after keeping you in the dark for so long. It's obvious the woman—your whole family—thinks you're in need of protection. From women like me."

She'd buttoned her shirt wrong. He reached over and moved her fingers, refastening the buttons. "My family, Claire, if you only knew…" He shook his head. "To them, I'm still the same kid who used to torture his sister's Barbie dolls."

"Well, I'm not a Barbie doll," she said, illogically, and Matt resisted the urge to laugh. *God, he loved Claire Porter when she was flustered!*

"Damn good thing," he said, "Otherwise, I'd have painted you with fake blood, tied you up, and had GI Joe stage this rescue operation."

"Ah," she said, sliding her feet into her shoes. "Wasn't that basically the script for *Jungle Fever?*"

He laughed. "Yeah, even as a kid I got off on playing the hero." Then he sobered. "But it's a hell of a lot easier when the bad guys aren't after someone you love."

Claire dropped her gaze. "We'd better go upstairs. Before Melinda sends reinforcements."

# Chapter Twenty

Claire stood in the living room of Matt's ranch house, gazing out the window at the snow-capped mountains that outlined the horizon. Matt's ranch was larger than she had thought, stretching as far as she could see. Last night she hadn't been able to appreciate the view of the ranch, or the house itself, but this morning she could admire the care someone had taken to create a luxurious yet cozy retreat.

A big stone fireplace stretched along one wall, the mantle filled with a selection of family photos, some of whom she recognized. The painting hanging above the fireplace was by Charles Russell, famed Montana cowboy artist, a fact Matt had told her with a touch of pride in his voice.

Comfortable leather sofas flanked a wide table, covered with an assortment of magazines and books on subjects ranging from ranching to film. The wide window showcased a view worthy of Hollywood. Claire could see why Matt often referred to Montana as "God's backyard."

"There's a couple thousand acres," he had told them when they reached his house last night. "Small, by Montana standards. But it suits my purposes."

Claire glanced at him, wondering what it was about chambray that looked so incredibly sexy. "What exactly is that? You mentioned this was a working ranch—just what does that entail?"

"It entails a few hundred head of cattle, a couple ranch hands, half dozen horses, a couple rigs—"

"A couple what?"

He smiled. "Trucks. Four-wheel drives. Two-ton ponies," he elaborated. "Every year we sell off a hundred or so steers. Though we do hang on to one or two—we keep 'em in the freezer," he added, grinning as Claire winced.

There were some aspects of ranching, she had decided, that she didn't want to know.

Through the window, a horse came into view, her son perched on the saddle. Tripper was having his first riding lesson. He must have risen at dawn, eager for the ride Matt had promised. Claire had been asleep, helped by the sleeping pills Melinda had handed her before they left last night. At first she had refused the offer, but Melinda, noticing how she jumped every time the phone rang, had insisted she needed a good night's sleep.

It had helped. Now, as she sipped the coffee Matt had left for her, she could feel her battle gear slipping back into place. Last night's weakness was a momentary aberration; this morning, the battle seemed definitely winnable and the world just a little brighter.

As Tripper and the horse slowly circled the corral, her heart warmed another degree.

Her city boy already seemed at home at his father's ranch. He would be happy without her here for a few days, weeks even, until she had faced whatever needed to be faced. There was no better place to shield him. Matt had shown her the security system last night, assuring her it was guaranteed to keep out cattle rustlers as well as the paparazzi.

As Tripper turned the horse, he glanced up, catching sight of his mother. She returned his wave. When he motioned for her to join them, she smiled, then stuck her thumb up in agreement.

She headed upstairs to change. Hopefully the boots Matt's sister-in-law had lent her would fit; if not, the opportunity would be worth ruining her Italian leather loafers.

She swallowed the lump that suddenly appeared in her throat. This might just be her last chance to enjoy her son's company. Soon he would know the truth, and Claire knew it would be a long time before he forgave her.

Horse riding was one of those skills that was harder than it looked, Claire decided an hour later. Beside her, Matt chuckled when the horse refused to move at Claire's sternly worded command.

"Forget it—and don't bother sending a memo, either," he added. "Horses respond to physical cues…a tug on the reins, a squeeze of the knees."

He put a hand on her knee to illustrate, giving it a squeeze. Claire felt the heat through the denim, along with a stirring of last night's lust that apparently was still simmering just under the surface. She swallowed, then noticed his gaze had landed on her knee. When he looked up, a wicked gleam lurked in his green eyes.

Suddenly the horse moved, and Claire was too busy hanging on to wonder at the direction of his thoughts. After a turn around the muddy corral, where their tracks were making short work of the layer of snow that had fallen the night before, she let herself relax. She just might get the hang of this after all.

"That's good, Mom," Tripper encouraged. "You've got a pretty good seat—doesn't she, Matt?" Head tilted, he looked up at his father, obviously echoing the praise he had heard earlier.

Claire hid her grin; then, realizing her "seat" was going to ache tomorrow unless she cut the lesson short, she started to ask Matt to explain the proper way to dismount.

But she tensed at the sound of gravel crunching.

Matt placed a reassuring hand on the saddle. "It's probably just Randy."

But it wasn't Randy. A few minutes later, Matt's sister-in-law, Ben, and Hannah appeared, accompanied by an older woman. Matt's mother, Claire realized, dismounting with Matt's help.

She wanted to run and hide in the barn. Instead, she squared her shoulders and prepared to meet yet another member of Matt's over-protective family. But she would willingly face the "firing squad" at point-blank range, as long as their protection extended to her son.

Later, inside, as they all sat around the pine table eating the muffins Mrs. Grayson had brought, Melinda gave Claire an apologetic look. "I couldn't stop her," she said with an undertone. "She would have come out on her own if I hadn't brought her." She glanced toward Tripper, who was refilling his milk glass at the refrigerator. "I figured the least I could do was bring Ben to provide a distraction."

The strategy had worked. Busy entertaining his new friend, Tripper hadn't even noticed the thorough examination Matt's mother had given him over her cup of coffee.

Or the pointed glances she directed at Claire.

"How long did you all live in California?" she asked, and then before Claire could answer, she looked at Matt. "You'd think, living so close…"

"Ma, San Francisco isn't exactly in the same neighborhood as LA."

But Joyce just shrugged. "It's all the same state, isn't it?"

Matt gave Claire a dry look. "She thinks California is just one big drug den."

Claire wiped her mouth delicately on a napkin. "These are delicious."

"The blueberries came from Matt's grandmother's yard. I put them up last summer."

Claire glanced at Matt. "Your grandmother is still alive?"

His mother answered for him. "Yes, but she's in her nineties. She won't live forever." She gave Matt a sharp look, her meaning clear.

He shifted uncomfortably in his chair.

Claire cleared her throat. "Matt tells me you direct the children's choir at church. That must take up a lot of time."

"Oh no, there's just a few kids—and three of them are my grandchildren," she told Claire with another pointed look, this time at the two boys who, from the looks of the kitchen, were preparing for a siege.

Claire seized the opportunity to redirect the line of questioning. "Tripper, where are you planning to take all that?"

He looked guilty, but Ben had an answer. "We're going to the barn. We're gonna make a fort in the hayloft."

Mel spoke up, the voice of authority. "Go ahead, but remember we're leaving in thirty minutes."

True to her word, they didn't overstay their welcome, and when they were gone, Claire slipped into Matt's office, intending to phone her office. It was Saturday, and though no one would be there, she could still check her messages.

She had barely glanced at the room when Matt had shown it to her last night; now she took the opportunity to look around. Feed bills lay on the desk atop a pile of movie scripts. Along a shelf, a few anonymous videotapes were shoved among various awards and football trophies. Inside the glass-front bookcase were novels: Ernest Hemingway, Henry James, and the latest Jodi Picoult.

Claire was impressed. None of the articles she had read about Matt Grayson over the years mentioned his penchant for reading, but the bookcase bore a well-used look. A stereo cabinet contained a rack of CDs — again, an eclectic assortment: Kenny Chesney, The Killers, and several soundtracks.

The fax machine hummed behind her. She noticed it had been busy, and as the fresh page unrolled to the full tray, it fell to the table beside her. Claire picked it up and couldn't help noticing it was from Matt's publicist.

It was a copy of the statement Matt had released to the press. As Claire read it, an ache pierced her heart. Matt was trying to shield her. The statement implied that he had known of his son's existence all along and had ignored it.

The next two pages that fell out of the fax were a wrap-up of yesterday's coverage of the story. Though the publicist explained in her note that the aftermath wasn't as bad as they had feared, the coverage of the story was still extensive. With *Jungle Fever* still in the top ten at the box office, any news involving Matt Grayson — especially the news that the single star was a father — was bound to titillate the public. Not only had the gossip rags, including those in Europe, picked up the story, but the cable programs devoted to Hollywood gossip had led with the news. It had even rated a mention on the *Today* show.

And posted on the unofficial Matt Grayson web site, maintained by fans, was a photo of Tripper: "The son Matt Grayson never told anyone about."

*Oh God,* thought Claire. At any moment, Tripper — or one of his newfound cousins — could log on and discover the news of his parentage.

She couldn't put it off any longer. He had to be told.

Swallowing her dread, Claire picked up the phone and punched the number to check her messages. Work was something she could handle.

Motherhood, on the other hand, had suddenly become more complicated than the most intricate corporate merger.

In the end, it was Tripper himself who brought the discussion to a head.

The three of them were seated at the pine table having lunch when Tripper recounted his conversation with Ben.

"Ben's pretty lucky. He's got a pet rat *and* a horse."

Claire hid a smile. But Tripper's next words erased all urge to laugh.

"He thinks I'm deprived or something. I mean, not only do I not have any pets," he explained, "but I don't even have a dad. He thinks that's really weird."

Claire's heart flipped. "But, Tripper, honey," she reminded him gently, "you do have a dad."

"I know, but—"

She took a deep breath, and then the words came as if washed ashore. "Matt is your father."

Tripper's eyes grew wide, and then a grin dawned on his face. "You mean you guys are going to get married?" he said, a hopeful expression lighting his eyes.

"No. I mean Matt is your real father. Your biological father."

Tripper stared at her for a moment, then his gaze slid from his mother's face to Matt's. What he read there confirmed her words, yet Claire could still see his confusion.

She knew the questions were piling up in his mind. Bracing herself, she attempted to answer them. "You see, Matt and I met a long time ago. Before you were born, and even though we only knew each other a short time—"

But Tripper didn't let her finish. "You mean Matt is my dad? And you knew all this time? And you didn't tell me?" His voice rose as tears threatened.

Matt spoke up. "Tripper, there were a lot of reasons—"

"Did you know?" his son demanded. "Did you know I was your kid?"

Matt met his son's gaze squarely. "No, I didn't know. Not until I met you a few weeks ago. But—"

His words were lost as Tripper bounded up from his chair, shouting at his mother, "How could you do this to me? You never even told me! You—you took my father away from me!" He gave her an accusing look that stabbed at her heart, robbed her of words.

"How could you be so mean?" His face crumpled, his eyes red with tears. The confusion on his face ripped Claire in two.

But then the confusion solidified into anger. The green eyes focused on her filled with rage. In a voice ragged with tears, he shouted, "*I hate you, I hate you!*" and then ran from the room, leaving behind the echoes of his screams.

Claire stared blankly at the spot he had vacated. Her son had meant every word he threw at her. She understood all too well the anger a helpless child felt against an all-powerful parent.

She ached for him, for herself, knowing the relationship she had valued more than anything on earth was permanently damaged.

She wanted to cry, but a familiar numbness was settling over her, insulating her from the pain.

Matt tried to reassure her. "I'll go talk to him. I'll explain."

But Claire knew this wound could never be healed by words. Her son had good reason to hate her. No explanation would make it easier for him to understand why she had deprived him of a father, of a family, all these years.

She had prepared herself for this all along, and now she knew, in her heart, that she had just lost her son.


In the barn, Matt followed the muffled sound of sobbing and found Tripper huddled between two bales of hay, his head pillowed in his arms. Matt knelt down, put out a hand, and stroked his son's head, hoping he didn't blow this first official test as a father.

"Hey, buddy," he said. "Don't you think you were a little hard on your mom?"

"No! She should have told me!" he cried, his head still buried. "I didn't even know you! I thought my father was some creep."

"Listen, Tripper, she had her reasons. Reasons you don't know anything about right now."

His head poked up, his face wet with tears. "There's not any reason for not telling me about my father! I never even saw you before! Not in person, anyway."

"I know, and I'm sorry about that —"

"It's not your fault! It's hers!"

"Maybe it's not, Tripper. There were things I should have done —"

"She still should have told you! And I'm her son—she should have told me."

In his mind, there was only black and white, Matt realized. Discerning this particular shade of gray was beyond the ability of a ten-year-old. Hell, it had even been beyond his own ability at first, hadn't it?

Claire had been right. Explaining to their son all the complexities of their relationship would be impossible.

Rubbing a hand over his face, he sighed. He'd give it a shot, anyway. "You see, Tripper, when I met your mother, she had just arrived in Hollywood, for a bit part she had been given in a movie, and didn't know anything about making films. I got the impression she didn't even want to be there." He carefully chose the words, glossing over the past. "Even though I was involved with someone else, I was attracted to your mother…but I should have broken off my relationship with Hayley, before—before doing what I did."

In the nearby stall, Jenny's horse snorted, agreeing with him.

Tripper wiped his face on his sleeve, his sobs quiet now.

"Your mom was scared, son. Scared for both of you. Those things they said about her…even though she didn't deserve them, it still hurt. And she didn't want to see you hurt…the way you're hurting now."

Tripper lifted his tear stained face, and Matt's heart nearly cracked. "But I wouldn't have even known you!"

Matt didn't have an answer for that. The thought that he wouldn't have known his son if it hadn't been for a twist of fate still kept him awake at night.

No, sometimes there weren't any answers, Matt thought. He wrapped his arms around his son and held him for the first time in his life while he sobbed all his misery and bitterness onto his dad's denim shirt.

# Chapter Twenty-One

att couldn't sleep that night. He lay awake, staring at the fire glowing in the big stone fireplace, wishing he could be with the two people he cared about most in the world. But they weren't speaking to each other. Tripper had made it obvious he couldn't bear to be in the same room as his mother. Matt knew better than to try to force a reconciliation, though the bruised look in Claire's eyes nearly drove him mad.

He was caught square in the middle, torn by sympathy for Tripper, the son he hadn't even known two months ago, and for Claire, the woman he had come to love.

Tripper's anger was understandable. It was a hard thing, to realize your heroine had faults. All his short life, Claire had tried to protect him; in the process, she must have appeared like Superwoman to a young boy—Claire the Invincible, Tripper's very own Zena the Warrior Princess.

And now, her armor was tarnished.

He wished he could shoulder the blame for this whole mess, but it wasn't that easy. He felt just a tiny bit angry at Claire himself.

For so long, he had tried to make her feel something—anything, even anger—and she backed away. Her feelings were in a perpetual holding pattern, an orbiting satellite preferring the coldness of outer space to a painful reentry through the earth's atmosphere. He wished he could show her that they could have a safe landing with him at the controls—but then, he wasn't so sure himself. They had crashed and burned the last time, hadn't they?

He sighed and put his drink down. He might as well go to bed, get some sleep. As he went through the hall, he heard a sound over the intercom. A tiny rustling, a whimper, then a louder gasp. His first thought was Tripper—Claire had mentioned he was prone to the occasional asthma attack.

But asthma attacks weren't accompanied by blood-curdling screams.

The sound sent spikes of fear racing up his spine. It was coming from the bedroom upstairs, where Claire slept.

He took the stairs two at a time, then threw open the door to her room.

"My God, are you all right?"

She was sitting bolt upright in bed, her hand on her mouth, staring straight ahead.

He went to her, took her stiff body in his arms. "Claire…sweetheart, wake up. Are you hurt?" He smoothed her hair, damp with sweat. "You must have had a bad dream. Tripper told me you have nightmares."

He felt her shudder in his arms.

"You're okay now; it's all right."

"The water…drowning…" she whispered, so low Matt thought he hadn't heard her correctly.

"You were dreaming you were drowning?" He kept his voice low, soothing, though his own heart still pounded against his ribs.

She didn't respond, and Matt had a funny feeling she didn't know he was there. "You're not drowning, Claire. You don't even like to swim, remember?"

"I'm sorry—I'm so sorry," he heard her whisper.

"It's okay, honey. He'll forgive you. Tripper knows you love him. You only did it to protect him."

"No," she said, her voice clearer now. "I didn't do it to protect him…" Her body shook in his arms, and he held her tighter. "It was me, Matt. I wanted to protect myself. I was so scared!"

She sobbed, a rusty gasp that almost broke his heart. "It's okay. You did what you thought was best—for both of you."

She shook her head. "No, he would have been better off with you. You would have known what to do…"

"Known what to do about what?"

But she didn't answer, blinking as if she had just realized what she had said.

He could feel her returning to consciousness. Yet that familiar stiffness was gone, her guard down.

She shivered, and he held her tighter. The thin nightgown she had worn to bed was hardly enough to keep her warm in the night chill. He ignored the enticing curves just below the neckline. A woman in distress, he reminded himself, was not a target for lust. "It was just a nightmare," he said, stroking her back. "After all you've been through, I guess that's not surprising."

"It was just a—a little one." Her voice quivered, and he could feel her heart racing against his chest.

"Well, for a little one, it sure got you spooked." He stroked her hair, tugging a lock away from the scar on her forehead. "I could probably rustle us up some cocoa. Might help you sleep." His saint-like intentions were rapidly dissolving as he felt her pressed against him.

Her breath grazed the hairs on his chest, left exposed by his partially unbuttoned shirt. "No, don't bother. I—I'm not really hungry."

"How about a drink, then? I've got some whiskey—one hundred proof, guaranteed nightmare repellent."

He glanced down and saw her smile against his chest. She seemed content to have his arms around her. Her scent filled his nostrils. Ivory soap? Or some pheromone invented by the gods to drive men wild? Him, in particular…

In his arms, Claire let the sweet relief of consciousness flood through her, bringing life back into her numb limbs. But this time it was accompanied by a warmth, a strong chest, comforting arms. Never before had the presence of another human made her feel so cherished, so loved…but she didn't want love and all its accompanying complications—did she?

But this felt so good, she couldn't bring herself to complain. She just enjoyed, letting the feeling creep back into her limbs, stretching into the warmth…letting it suck her down…and the drowning feeling she had had before returned, only this time the arms holding her were salvation, not damnation, and she let herself sink into the safety of Matt's arms.

She shivered again, and Matt held her tighter. "You're cold," he whispered against her hair. "Let me get you back under the covers."

"No." She leaned into him, slipping her arms up his chest. Tilting her head back, she looked into his eyes. They were warm with desire, with passion—and caution. He wouldn't rush her, wouldn't ask for anything she couldn't give…but she wasn't so sure she didn't want to give him everything he desired…everything *she* desired…especially if that meant an end to her fears.

She realized she had found the perfect antidote: Better than any sleeping pill, more secure than the most advanced security system, Matt's arms were a life raft, come to save her in the middle of the cold ocean. If the price of this was sex, it was a price she was willing to pay.

Somehow, putting it into terms she could understand made her feel it was the right decision. It wasn't a case of passion ruling her head, lust overcoming her good sense. This was the right thing to do. The smart thing.

Just to be sure he understood her intent, she raised up and kissed him, ignoring the tiny prick of doubt. She was determined to see this through. She had hidden long enough. No longer would she allow fear a hold on her.

There was something different in her kiss, Matt realized. He could taste her determination, feel it in the way she pressed her open mouth against his.

His body leapt in response, and for a moment, he lost himself in the sudden sweet pleasure, meeting her kiss with his tongue, probing, seeking the passion that simmered just beneath her cold surface.

He found it. She kissed him back, her tongue meeting his in a little dance of welcome, exploring his mouth eagerly. A spike of joy burst through his mind, sending rockets of desire through his body. But he had been in this scene before. Before passion could overtake his good sense, he pulled away, gazing down at the woman in his arms.

"Claire, honey…" She nibbled his neck. He swallowed, determined to hear it from her lips. "Do you want me to make love to you?"

But she was too busy unbuttoning his shirt to answer, licking and kissing her way down his chest. He laughed. "Sweetheart…" He stroked her hair, then reached down to drop a kiss on her temple. "Why don't I take you to my bed? I've got a fire going—"

She hushed him with her lips. It was as if she were making up for a decade of abstinence — which she was, he realized, gentling his kiss. As she pulled his shirt from his jeans, he vowed he would do his part to make her reentry into the world of passion a safe one. He rose in one smooth motion, picking her up and cradling her in his arms.

"This is my grandmother's room. If I'm going to make love to you, it'll be in my bed." He waited for her to protest.

But she simply met his gaze and nodded. Her eyes were clear. She wasn't still asleep, or drugged, as he'd half-feared. She knew what she was doing. In the morning, there'd be no regrets.

Claire tightened her arms around his neck, a smile on her face as he carried her down the stairs and into his warm bedroom.

Firelight glowed from the wood stove in the corner, but Claire hardly noticed as Matt laid her down on his huge bed. No longer cold, no longer aware of the terror that had sent her in blind search for comfort. She had found it, she realized. A safe harbor in a sea of emotion.

Matt would chase away all her cold fears and warm her heart once again.

She held his gaze as he lowered her, surprised to see a flicker of uncertainty there. He was as nervous as she, and the notion gave her a heady feeling.

She reached up and kissed him lightly, committing herself to the act as surely as if it were scored in blood.

Matt returned her kiss, deeper this time, exploring.

He groaned, tearing his mouth from hers to look down at her. A fresh surge of desire swept through her, but still she wanted to shut her eyes, hide whatever she felt.

"I love you — you know that, don't you?" he murmured.

She put her mouth against his to stop the words. Sex, she could deal with. Love was another matter, an item for another meeting's agenda.

For now, she simply wanted to feel. It had been so long, so long since she had felt this coursing of emotion through her veins. A wave of tingling awareness filled her, as if her nerves were awakening, one by one, building into a tidal wave of feeling.

Claire closed her eyes, giving herself up to the joy, the wonder of the moment.

Slowly, Matt slipped the nightgown from her shoulders, inching it down by degrees. She wanted his hand to caress her bare skin, his tongue to savor—more than she'd wanted anything in her life.

The earlier urgency they had felt in each other's arms melted into languor. Their bodies moved of one accord—a touch, a whisper, a glance, like the ebb and flow of tide. Never had Claire felt so treasured, so desired. Never had she wanted anything so much, the teasing hint of fulfillment just over the edge of the joy that threatened to engulf her.

And when the doubt circled, pulling her back from the edge, it was Matt's needy exclamations that propelled her forward again…

Matt slid his shirt off his arms, and Claire traced a finger over his shoulder, glistening in the glow from the fire. Skin to skin, they warmed each other's bodies, moving in sync, as if they were lovers for decades rather than moments.

Matt paused to open a drawer next to the bed and pull out a foil packet. "No unexpected consequences this time," he said, then ripped it open with his teeth.

Claire gave him a grateful smile; birth control had hardly entered her mind. Never, during the last few weeks, had she imagined she would find herself in this position, so close to letting go. Never had she dreamed she could throw off years of caution, years of suppressed desire, and eagerly look forward to total immersion in pleasure.

When he bent her leg up, searching for better access, she welcomed it, with only a tiny gasp of surprise that changed into a sigh of gratitude. His fingers made their slow way to their destination, finding her moist and trembling, ready for him—more than ready, she thought as he touched her, there. Oh, God, how she wanted him!

He lowered himself into her, slowly, holding back, giving her time to adjust. But the feel of him inside her, filling places she hadn't known were empty, gave her a chaotic joy. A tense excitement raced through her muscles, and she wondered how on earth she had ever lived without this in her life, this man…in her. With a shudder, she gave herself up to the rapture spreading throughout her body.

His teeth clenched, Matt dove into her again and again, filling her until he exploded in her arms, crying out her name as he went under.

Beneath him, she trembled through the last of her climax. Lying still, cocooned in the warmth, she felt a strange lethargy creep over her, turning her limbs to lead, her heart to butter.

"God, Claire," was all he said.

She didn't possess the strength to smile, though she wanted to shout—she had found it, that forgotten feeling, that forgotten warmth. No, not forgotten; never before had she felt this intensely, this acutely. A strange emotion made her want to cry, but she didn't dare put a name to it, didn't dare speak of it.

Above all, she didn't dare care.


The sharp edge of desire had dulled, but neither of them wanted to sleep. Matt, as if sensing her reticence, was unusually silent. Claire was grateful and let herself remain tucked against his side, enjoying the feeling of being treasured for a while longer.

In the corner, the wood stove warded off the cold reflected on the windowpanes, the firelight from its opened door painting a chiaroscuro glow on the walls. The only sounds in the room were the contented popping of the burning logs and the soft breathing of Sadie, curled up near the fire. A strange restlessness crept through Claire, as though she had been energized by the unfamiliar physical activity. Sex was better than tennis for relieving stress, she decided. She stretched languorously against the warmth beside her, flexing muscles that seemed suddenly alive.

Matt's body tempted her hands, like a museum piece one was suddenly allowed to touch. She let her fingers roam, over his face, his chest, lower…

He sucked in a breath, then reached for her hand and brought it to his mouth, pressing tender kisses to her fingertips.

Claire's lips curved in a smile. She could feel his heartbeat echoing against her own. She captured his fingers, took one in her mouth, and sucked lightly, wrapping her tongue around the tip and licking it like a confection. Matt groaned.

Then he turned, raising himself above her. He stroked her hair from her face, encountering the little scar, fingering it for a moment. He kissed it, letting his tongue skate along the edge of her hairline, sending a fresh batch of shivers through her.

She reached up and ran her fingers through his hair, the caramel-colored strands longer now—in preparation for his next role, he had told her.

Though it was his role as her lover that frightened her—in truth, she was the one in prison, he her liberator. But what would he demand as payment?

Then his gaze met hers, and she read the answer there. He wanted everything. He would take it all, every iota of passion she had to give. She closed her eyes.

Matt's voice cleaved the darkness. "Claire, I'm not going to ask you for something you're not ready for," he told her. "But—"

She stopped him with her lips, the best way she had found to halt her own doubts.

# Chapter Twenty-Two

When Matt woke, she wasn't there. He lay for a while, savoring the wonderful dream—no, the reality, he thought with a lazy smile, picking up the strand of dark hair on the pillow next to him.

Whatever their problems were, they could work them out. There was too much at stake, and after last night, surely she knew they were meant to be together.

He found her in the kitchen, the makings of breakfast scattered on the counter. His mother's old robe was belted tightly around her waist, and she was stirring something he hoped was pancake batter.

"Now this is a sight I could get used to," he announced. "Beautiful woman, barefoot, in the kitchen, making breakfast. Too bad there's no chance you could be—"

She thumped the bowl down. "I hope you like waffles," she said. "I found a waffle iron in the appliance garage, and there was a mix in the pantry."

Matt stepped behind her, slipped his arms around her waist, and began nuzzling her neck.

The spoon clattered against the bowl.

"What do you say we go back to bed, maybe forget the condoms this time."

"Matt," she began, but the cell phone on the counter interrupted what was sure to be a prim lecture, one he was prepared to bypass the most effective way he had found. Her neck, he had discovered last night, was particularly sensitive…

"Hello, Connor," he heard her say. "Yes, I did call. How was your trip to Japan?"

Matt sighed, a satisfied smile lingering on his face. Somehow the fact that she could be so damned proper during the day, then at night focus all that drive into passion, was exciting as hell.

She handed him the spoon, then disappeared down the hall to his office to finish her conversation in private. Later, Matt told himself, pouring the batter onto the hot waffle iron, he intended to finish his own conversation with Claire. It was past time they got their feelings for each other out in the open.

He had no doubt how he felt about her. And after last night, he no longer doubted her feelings for him. Claire didn't show that vulnerable side of herself to anyone—except her son.

That was another thing they had to talk about. Tripper would get over his anger, he was sure, as soon as he realized his mother had only been trying to protect him.

He stared at the batter oozing from beneath the lid of the waffle iron. The memory of her from last night, shaking from the nightmare, left a sick feeling in his stomach. He wasn't even sure just what terror haunted Claire. Was it the same nightmare she had been desperately trying to protect their son from?


When Claire ended her conversation with Connor, she used Matt's computer to check her email. As she waited for the connection, she noticed a copy of *GQ* among the opened mail, Matt's ruggedly handsome face gracing the cover.

She flipped to the article inside, smiled at the headline, then examined the accompanying photos of Matt: playing basketball on the desert set of his last film, shooting pool in a bar he owned in LA. She raised an eyebrow—he had never mentioned any of that. There was so much she didn't know about him: his "other life," as a movie star, the celebrity who made headlines just by taking a morning jog.

The man attracted women like an open box of chocolates. She had lost count of the number of names linked with his—the latest being Annie Cutler, the redhead he'd once used to taunt her. As

Claire pictured her wholesome image, another face popped into her mind: Hayley James, another woman who had loved Matt too much.

It would be so easy to let herself love Matt, to dig those feelings out of the cave she had hidden them in and dust them off. And so incredibly stupid. Emotions carried a high price. By the age of six, she had learned that feelings were fragile little things. Like the tiny black kitten she had found, hungry and cold. She kept it in her closet until the reverend had discovered her secret and made her watch while he tied it in a bag and threw it in the pond.

Another ancient memory surfaced, this one of her first-grade teacher, Miss Carlson. At least she hadn't ended up tied in a bag. Instead, Reverend Porter had pulled Claire out of the public school and taught her at home, enforcing his lessons with the rod he never spared.

Claire squared her shoulders. She figured everyone was allowed a momentary weakness—once every ten years wasn't really such a bad record. And this time, if she was lucky, the only thing bruised would be Matt's ego.

Glancing down again at the magazine, she gave a little laugh. A man who looked like that should have little trouble finding a remedy for a bruised ego.


Matt was mucking out a stall in the barn when Claire came around the corner, her boots crunching the hard-packed snow. She'd skipped breakfast, and he knew it was because she didn't want the strain of sharing another meal with Tripper, who'd stared sullenly at his plate last night while Matt had tried to make the tension disappear.

"Can you drive me to the airport this afternoon?"

He gazed at her in surprise. "You want to leave?"

She nodded. "I'm meeting Connor Monday morning in Philadelphia. He plans to speak with the other board members himself. Let them know I've got his support, despite the bad press."

"I'm going with you."

"No. I'd rather you stay here with Tripper."

Matt gripped the shovel, not bothering to hide his displeasure. "I don't like the idea of you going back there by yourself."

"I'll be okay. The worst of it has blown over. Connor also gave a statement to the press. Blurring the picture enough so that his judgment isn't called into question."

"What do you mean, 'his judgment'? Doesn't the guy have any faith in his employees?"

"Of course he does. But this is business. There are millions of dollars resting on something as delicate as the perception of propriety."

"To hell with Forrest's reputation." He tossed the shovel against the wall. "It's you I'm worried about."

"Well, I can't hide out here any longer. I have to face the music sooner or later." Claire glanced back at him, her expression set in the hard line with which he'd become familiar. "I'll be fine. Connor's hired a guard and driver to escort me to work for the next couple of weeks."

"I could've done that," he said impatiently. Then, with hands on his hips, he added grimly, "Better yet, anyone who wants a piece of you should have to go through me first."

She shook her head. "You'd draw enough of a crowd on your own. Besides, I need a favor from you."

"Whatever you want, but I still think — "

"Can you keep Tripper here? For a few days? Just until this blows over. He's out of school this week anyway, for spring break. I think he'd like to spend it out here, getting to know your family better."

"Sure, you know he can stay. I've got to go to LA next week for a couple days, but he can stay with Mark and Mel." He tilted his hat farther off his brow. "We need to talk — about what happened last night."

She turned away. "Not now."

He grabbed her above the elbow, preventing her from leaving. "Then when? There are things we need to get out in the open."

But she remained stubbornly silent, focused on the mountain peaks in the distance. She looked about as chilly as the March wind. He gave a bitter laugh. "You don't want to hear it, do you? What I can't figure out is why. Because you don't feel the same way, or because you don't know how to handle the fact that you do?"

She ducked her head. "Matt, this isn't the time. I've got too many things going on in my life right now, plus there's Tripper to consider."

"You're damn right there's Tripper to consider. Don't you think what he needs now is for his parents to be together?"

"Oh, come on. I've told you before that's a lame excuse for… for — "

"Then how about the fact that we have great sex?"

She gave him a cool look over her shoulder. "Was it? I really wouldn't know. I haven't had much experience."

"Then you'll just have to take my word for it. It was fantastic. Mind blowing. Out of this world. The earth moved." He laughed, releasing her at last. With the toe of his boot, he kicked at a snow clod. "Hell, and to think I used to envy Robert Jordan."

"Who?"

"You know, the guy from *For Whom the Bell Tolls*. Not only does he get to blow up bridges, but he gets his girl too."

"Doesn't he die in the end?" Claire pointed out, ever practical, as she turned to face him again.

He grinned wickedly. "Yeah, but he still got a great fuck out of the deal." Then he sobered. "Is that all I'm getting here? One night with Claire, and then it's back to blowing up bridges…" He made a sound of an explosion.

"What is it you want, Matt?" she said with an exasperated sigh. "Two great fucks? Three? I told you, I don't have any experience in that department."

"You think that matters?" He shook his head, disbelieving. "I'm telling you, if you had tried any harder, I'd be in worse shape than poor old Robert Jordan."

Spots of embarrassment stained Claire's cheeks. "I suppose I was…a little…aggressive."

"It's okay, honey." He grinned. "I didn't mind one bit."

"It's not okay. I never should have—"

He broke in. "What, the sheets haven't even dried and already there's recriminations? What we did wasn't wrong. We're two people who happen to care for each other. I would use the word 'love,' but you seem to have some aversion to it."

"You don't love me, Matt. You just want to marry me. You think you can put things right for you and Tripper by marrying his mother."

"That's not true," he protested.

"Yes, it is. You don't even like me very much," she pointed out with an air of irrefutable logic he found endearing.

"Babe…" He shook his head, laughing. "What I feel for you goes way beyond like." As long as he was putting his heart on the line, he decided to go all the way. "You're a part of me, Claire. I can't take a breath without thinking about you on the downswing. I picture your face, and I get this funny little tug, right here…" He jerked his thumb toward his chest. "If that's not love, I don't know what is. Hell," he added with a rueful grin, "I don't even feel that way about Sadie."

Claire didn't reply. She sought out the frozen peaks in the distance, again, as if lured by their impassiveness.

"Tell me you feel nothing for me, after last night. You can't."

"Last night was just sex. That's all it was for me. I'm sorry I gave you a different impression, but—"

"You're sorry." He shook his head, amazed. "Jesus, Claire. Why don't you write me a thank you note while you're at it? 'Dear Mr. Grayson, thanks for getting my rocks off. It was really swell. Another fine performance—'"

Claire rounded on him. "Right! I suppose you're used to gratitude from every woman you take to bed. But as I said, I'm afraid I really don't have enough experience to judge the performance. Perhaps I should get some, then get back to you with a score."

The look in her eyes reminded him of a wild animal, an arrow piercing its heart. He had the feeling she was fighting for her life, while all he wanted to talk about was love.

But now she didn't give him a chance. She took a gulp of cold, dry air and spoke again, her voice harsh. "We're not filming a remake of *Love Story* here. This is real life." She turned to him. "And right now, I've got to return to Philadelphia and try to salvage what's left of mine."

Matt watched her walk away, hands shoved in his pockets to keep from reaching out to stop her. Like a lovestruck fool, he had led with his heart. He had said the wrong thing, but then, he was beginning to suspect everything he said to Claire was the wrong thing.

If only he knew the words that would change her mind, make her look at him differently. He'd sure as hell run them by her right now.


At the airport that afternoon, Tripper still didn't say a word to Claire. Matt started to intervene, but Claire shook her head. This was between her and Tripper, after all.

But she couldn't resist touching him, placing a gentle hand on his head as she told him goodbye. He held his head stiff beneath her fingers. He wouldn't be ready to forgive her for a long time, if ever.

Then she turned to Matt. His eyes were searching, asking her silently if she was sure she wanted to do this.

She smiled back reassuringly, absurdly grateful to him for keeping Tripper out of harm's way. There was a strange kind of relief in her heart, knowing that Tripper was no longer her sole responsibility. Now there was someone bigger, stronger, to take care of him, to answer his questions, to teach him things she never could. Never before had she considered just what sharing parenting responsibilities could mean, but she was willing to admit there were advantages.

The tired smile Matt gave her before she turned to board the plane almost broke her heart, until she told herself the hurt look in his eyes was caused by the harsh Montana sun reflecting off the snow outside.

# Chapter Twenty-Three

There were only a few reporters waiting outside Kaslow's entrance when Claire arrived Monday morning, and the security guards kept them at bay. Though they were more respectful this time, the sight of them brought back memories of ten years ago, when she had been hounded by the media. Just thinking about it gave her a queasy feeling, and she was very glad she had left Tripper with Matt.

This morning, though, she hadn't even read the paper. She had bigger worries. Before meeting with Connor, who was flying in from New York, she had to face Bernard Kaslow. She had debated the form her apology should take. A memo? A formal letter? But in the end she decided this was something she had to do in person.

She crossed the rotunda, still quiet and dim, waiting for the store to open. Today the figure in the center of the fountain didn't meet her gaze when she passed. Instead, Claire imagined, the goddess looked contrite.

She ought to be, Claire thought. Then she stepped into the open elevator and punched the button for the seventh floor.

Claire stood in front of Bernard Kaslow's desk, her carefully worded apology still fresh in the stale air. Her attention focused on the man behind the desk, who stared at her with a grave look on his face. "You realize this is a very serious situation we have here. A financial manager who deliberately hid her past, a person who should inspire confidence in our lenders…" Bernard Kaslow stumbled for words.

Claire didn't bother pointing out that Connor Forrest was the only lender they needed to worry about, and he had complete confidence in her.

Then Evan, who, to Claire's dismay, had insisted on being present for the early morning meeting, supplied the words Bernard couldn't locate. "For someone who claimed to have the good of Kaslow's as her first priority, it's surprising that there was never any mention of this…this incident." Evan plucked a piece of lint off his jacket sleeve.

"Mr. Kaslow, I'm certain the whole thing will die down soon. I've issued a statement, admitting past mistakes — of a personal nature, I might add — that should set any minds at ease."

"Still, the negative impact on Kaslow's will be tremendous." Evan licked his lips delicately, reminding Claire of a cat who had wallowed in too much cream. "We'll be the laughingstock of financial circles."

Bernard frowned. "Evan's right. With a stain like this on our reputation," he began, and Claire couldn't help but remember that Bernard had shown little concern for Kaslow's reputation when Gray-Wolf had dangled money — and publicity — in front of him.

A knock on the door interrupted him. At his booming "come in," his secretary came into the room, a worried look creasing her forehead. Silently, she held out the morning's newspaper in her hand. On the front page, just under the fold, a headline read: "Kaslow's Smells a Scandal."

Bile rose in Claire's stomach.

Bernard grabbed the paper. His face flushed red as he scanned the article. Throwing it to his desk in disgust, he turned to Claire. "Do you see what I mean? The entire store will be affected by this… this garbage. And the Bendel account — who the hell could have known?" His voice grew raspy with anger. "Except you." He pointed a finger accusingly at Claire, and for a moment, she was back in her father's church, accusations of *Slut* and *Whore!* ringing in her ears.

But Bernard was much too refined to use such language. Instead, with Evan looking on almost gleefully, he rose from his chair and sputtered, "This could be compared to corporate espionage! I won't have it! I simply won't have an employee who can't keep her priorities straight."

The secretary gave Claire a pitying look as she walked out the door. Claire swallowed. Offering her resignation seemed the only recourse. Just as she was about to suggest it, the door opened and Connor Forrest walked in.

A hush fell over the room, as every eye was immediately trained on the man who owned Kaslow's—lock, stock, and tie rack. He stood over six feet tall, with piercing blue eyes and the coal-black hair of his Irish ancestors.

It was rumored he had smiled once, after winning an amateur tennis championship match against the governor of California. Tennis, Claire knew, was the only activity in which he could be considered an amateur. In every other arena he entered, Connor Forrest played for keeps.

"Hello, Claire, Bernard." He nodded toward each, then briefly let his cold gaze settle on Evan Kaslow before he turned back to Claire. "I'm sorry I'm late. Last-minute events in Europe delayed my departure from New York."

She gave him a weak smile, trying not to look as grateful as she felt. He was the one person who had always had complete faith in her. She had forgotten how much she missed his quiet support.

"I trust things have settled down here." He glanced sharply toward Evan, then at Bernard, who was leaning back in his chair now, mopping his forehead. Satisfied, Connor turned toward Claire and said in a low voice, "I understand the press has been lying low. My contacts have explained that may be due to the influence of Matt Grayson. Apparently he threatened to boycott any media whose coverage got out of hand." His lips tightened in a line of distaste. He had a well-known aversion to the media himself. "The threat seems to have had some impact, on the tone of the coverage, if not the amount. I doubt the story will linger more than a couple of days."

Claire started to smile with relief, but she remembered the headlines in today's paper. Connor must not have seen it—and then it hit her what he had said. Matt had threatened to boycott the media? She knew how much movie studios depended on the vast publicity the media delivered each time a new film opened. That Matt would even consider giving that up—she took a quick breath. The implications of that she would consider later.

When her own job wasn't on the line.

Connor tucked his hands in his pockets, a stance Claire had seen often—just before an opponent received a killing blow. "Now, with that disposed of, I'd like to discuss other issues." Looking dispassionately toward the two men in front of him, he continued, "The proposal to open a branch of Kaslow's in Atlantic City."

This time, his gaze stopped squarely on Evan Kaslow. Claire was surprised to see Evan look nonplused. She would have expected the mention of his pet project to be met with interest. Instead, he nervously looked toward the door.

Connor didn't waver, however. "Recently, it's come to my attention that the contractors approached in regard to the possible construction of the Atlantic City store have been under investigation by the federal government. In fact, the Feds expect to file charges soon — on racketeering and collusion."

It took Claire only a second to realize the full implication. Suddenly, she understood why Evan had been so eager to have his way with the Atlantic City project. A healthy kickback from the contractor would have gone a long way to replacing the bonus he had lost when Forrest bought out the company. It would have been easy enough to steer the contract the way of his favored builder. Though the project would have been put out to bid, there was no requirement that the lowest bidder be hired. It would have been at the board's discretion to hire the contractor — on the recommendation from the VP of Stores.

Her stomach knotted again at the thought of dealing with contractors with close ties to the underworld. Apparently, Bernard had reached the same conclusion she had. "Were you aware of this?" he demanded of his nephew.

"Of course not." But Evan wasn't a good enough actor to pull off the innocent look. Dread pulled at his cheeks.

His uncle turned away, his glance resting momentarily on the figure in the portrait on the opposite wall. The look on Earnest Kaslow's bearded face seemed grim.

But Connor wasn't finished. "An investigator I hired has further informed me that there were several deposits made to your account recently, of a total which approximately matches that of your gambling debts to Atlantic City casinos."

Bernard turned and faced Evan. "Is this true?" His voice was low and ominous.

"Of course not! And…I don't know where this information came from but…but this is a violation of my civil rights!" Scraping a hand through expertly scissored hair, he managed to look offended as he muttered, "You can bet I'll be talking to my lawyer about this!"

But Connor brushed off his threat. "The information will be public knowledge by this afternoon. If it's your reputation you're worried about, I would recommend you resign. Because I intend to cooperate fully with the investigators—as will everyone here at Kaslow's."

A sneer appeared on Evan's country-club features. "That won't happen—this is a family-run store! Kaslow's loyalty is to its own."

"No, Evan, it *was* a family-run store." Bernard looked at his nephew with censure in his tired brown eyes. "And before we were forced to sell to Forrest—due to the wasteful projects *you* endorsed"—the accusing finger was now pointed at Evan—"the primary stockholder in Kaslow's was me, you might remember. I bought out your father shortly after he lost his shorts on the stock market."

Evan glared at his uncle. "He would never have gambled so heavily on stocks if you had loaned him the money he needed!"

"For his crazy schemes!" Bernard thundered. "He wanted to turn the business into a manufacturing operation. Can you imagine? Manufacturing hosiery right there in the rotunda!"

His tirade was interrupted by a knock on the door. Before the secretary could announce her, Jackie Prescott burst into the room, seemingly unaware of the tension that gripped the occupants.

"Mr. Kaslow. Hello, Claire." Jackie halted at the foot of Mr. Kaslow's desk. She noticed Connor and, with a flustered smile, added, "Hello, Mr. Forrest." Then she turned to Bernard, a smug look on her face. "I'm sorry to interrupt, but I just had to tell you…I figured out who spoke to the press about Claire's past. It was one of our employees. I caught her snooping around last week, asking my assistant for background info, photos we might have on file. You remember Lee Ann Ellison. She works for"—her gaze swung to Evan Kaslow, standing in the corner—"your nephew. It was his assistant—if you can call her that—who's the reason Kaslow's had this round of bad publicity."

Claire was the first to react as Bernard grabbed his chest. She rushed to his side, suddenly remembering his heart condition. He struggled to speak, then finally, just before his head slumped to the desk, he managed to get the phrase out: "You're fired."

No one in the room had to ask who he meant. Before Connor had finished punching 9-1-1 on his cell phone, Evan had slipped out of the room, with a last glance at the newspaper lying forgotten on his uncle's desk.

# Chapter Twenty-Four

"If you're prepared to accept the presidency of Kaslow's on a tempo-rary basis, I think I can almost guarantee an eventual permanent appointment."

Claire hesitated. With Bernard Kaslow in the hospital recovering from a heart attack, she agreed it was necessary to appoint an interim president. Yet she had only been here a few months. Doubtless there were other qualified candidates among the board members, ones who hadn't recently had their faces splashed across supermarket tabloids.

"I appreciate the offer, but aren't you worried about the fallout? I mean, not only has my past just been the topic of gossip columns all over the country, but I would also be one of the youngest people to ever head up a department-store division. And though I certainly feel I've got the experience, there are people here who would disagree."

Connor listened patiently to her objections, then did exactly what he intended to do all along.

"I have complete confidence in you," he told her, and Claire knew that confidence would carry a lot of weight in financial circles. When Connor Forrest spoke, Wall Street listened. The man *The Wall Street Journal* had once claimed could "backstroke in waters too turbulent for Warren Buffett" never second guessed his decisions.

And the truth was, Claire had been hoping all along the presidency would someday be hers. She just never expected to have the reins in her grasp so soon, and so soon after her public exposure. For ten years, she had dreaded being found out as Clarissa Peters; now, with Matt's support, and Connor's, she was beginning to believe she could weather the scorn that had been half-heartedly tossed her way. Even the article in the local paper had been much less lurid than the headlines made out. A couple of hours ago, she had been ready to resign; now, it looked very much like she would be getting a promotion.

Connor read her hesitation as acceptance. "I'll make the announcement today. I don't see any need to postpone it, and the sooner we get started, the sooner we can go over a few ideas I've been mulling over. I think you'll find them interesting."

And so it was done. By that afternoon, Claire was effectively the head of Kaslow's. But she had no time to enjoy the perks of the new position. She and Connor spent the afternoon holed up in the conference room, going over plans for both Kaslow's and the Forrest Group's other business dealings.

It was almost like old times, talking shop with Connor. Claire had never found anyone else who shared her enthusiasm over business trends and economic principles. Their minds in tune, each often finished the other's thoughts, a situation that also repeated itself when they played doubles on the tennis court.

But, despite the fact that she and Connor had much in common, she had never experienced with him that shiver of excitement she felt when Matt merely glanced her way, his green eyes teasing — or warm with desire. Or that rush of warmth to her belly when he grinned at her with that sexy smile, the same one that turned millions of women into Silly Putty. She was determined to put thoughts of Matt on hold, though. She had a company to run now and no time for sexy smiles.

The next few days were filled with meetings, plans, and late nights laying out the future direction of Kaslow's. Claire had been pleased when the rest of the board had voted to accept her appointment. Her main detractor had turned in his resignation. Claire was already eyeing Bernard's assistant, Christine Gillis, as a possible replacement for Evan. Christine had worked behind the scenes at Kaslow's for years, and Claire knew she was more than capable of moving into a board position. There were several other women who, in Claire's opinion, had been overlooked for mid-management positions.

Coming to work every morning, Claire realized she hadn't felt so much energy since she had first gone to work for Connor years ago. He used to stop by her office on Saturday mornings to find her at her desk, a three-year-old Tripper playing quietly by himself in the corner.

She had hardly had time to miss Tripper. He still wouldn't speak to her on the phone. Matt tried to insist, but Claire told him not to push.

She spoke to Matt every day, however. She had tried to thank him for throwing his weight around, protecting her from the media—she knew he didn't normally stage Hollywood ego trips—but he brushed off her thanks. She realized that he truly didn't care if his next movie bombed without media support if it meant lessening the heat on her.

And it had worked. The story was already yesterday's news. Except for the sleaziest of the tabloids, the story had died after a couple of days—and with the star himself lying low, there was little to feed the flames.

Though they stayed away from him while he was in Montana, no doubt he would be assaulted with questions when he went to LA on Friday. He offered to cancel his meetings, but she knew he needed to wrap up post-production on *Lyin' Hearts* before his next film began shooting.

"Tripper will stay with Mark for the day or so I'm gone," he'd reassured her. "He and Ben are getting to be pretty good buddies."

"I'm glad. Tell him David's called a few times."

"Why don't you tell him yourself?"

"No." She swallowed her maternal instincts. She didn't want to risk hearing her son refuse to talk to her again. "I've got to go. I'll see you in a week," she told him, then hung up the phone.

She knew Matt thought Tripper's reaction was harsh, but she had learned one thing well growing up: Punishment was never intended to fit the crime.


A few days later, music pounded from the speakers in Matt's candy-red Porsche as he maneuvered the machine automatically through the smattering of cars on the freeway.

His conversation earlier this morning with Dr. Greenfield, the psychologist he had lined up to speak to as part of his research for *Outrage,* kept replaying in his mind. The character he played came from an abusive home, and Matt had arranged to speak with an expert in the field of child abuse in an effort to understand him better. Matt's own awareness was limited to the dozens of shock stories that had been all the rage a few years back—stories of repressed memory, startling statistics, and the talk-show revelations of various celebrities.

Matt had listened as Dr. Greenfield described the lasting impact of abuse, the emotional toll taken on its victims years after the abuse itself had stopped. Fear of commitment, lack of trust—all to be expected when the most important figures in a child's life bring nothing but pain, both emotional and physical.

"Abused children often have trouble making commitments as adults. They pull back in their relationships, preferring to stay on the sidelines. This stems from a basic lack of trust in human attachments. They're reluctant to express feelings, afraid they'll be shot down for having any.

"They often put up a good front. The tough guy on the playground, for example, is often an abused child."

Matt had an image of Claire. She was tough, gutsy, always packing the first punch. She used words, instead of fists, killing looks instead of blows, but constantly she remained on the defensive, never letting her guard down, not for an instant.

But then, she had once, with him. Ten years ago. She had let him in, and as a result, she had been shamed, abandoned, and left to care for a child.

"Is it true they grow up to be abusive parents themselves?" he asked the doctor.

"Certainly, sometimes the pattern does repeat itself. But an abused child is equally capable of becoming a loving, caring, emotionally involved parent. Often, they may be determined for their child to have the love and support they never had. And, of course, a child is emotionally bound, in a way—guaranteed to return the love, so it's a risk-free environment for testing those loving feelings that have been repressed all along."

The consultation with Dr. Greenfield was no longer about the character Dylan McAllister; it was about Claire. The signs had been there all along. He remembered the way she flinched when he touched her, the guarded way she kept her feelings under wraps.

Tripper's words came back to him: "Mom even keeps a gun in the closet," and his assumption that his mother was afraid of his dad coming back.

He felt a chill chase down his spine. It wasn't Tripper's dad she was afraid of. Was the thought of her own father so frightening that she had once kept a gun, in case he ever showed up?

But then he remembered the flat sound of her voice when she had told him her parents were dead. Was that the truth or a convenient lie to explain why they weren't a part of her and Tripper's lives?

He would ask her, as soon as he saw her, remembering his last question for the doctor. "How do you go about getting them to open up—if you're the one having the relationship with them?"

"That's a good question," Dr. Greenfield had said, thoughtfully stroking his beard. "Patience is the key. Patience and understanding. They need to know they won't be abandoned emotionally. The physical scars will have healed, but emotionally, they're very fragile. It may take years to build a trusting relationship."

Years. *Jesus.* They had already wasted too much time.

Matt slammed on his brakes as a BMW cut in front of him.

In real life, the job of hero was not as straightforward as it was in front of a camera.

Somehow, he vowed, he would make Claire open up, make her realize that shedding light on the past would chase off the shadows and dissolve her nightmares.

Though it had been a nightmare that had sent her into his arms that night at the ranch, he didn't want to simply play the role of ghostbuster. He wanted her to come to him without fear. More than anything, he wanted her to trust him—not just to keep her safe, but with her heart.

Because he had already entrusted his heart to her.


Claire took off the day Tripper was expected home. She cleaned with a frenzy, some part of her mind thinking her son would appreciate her housecleaning savvy and forgive her for every time she had lied to him.

Matt was dropping him off on his way to Louisiana, where he was expected to start serving his prison "sentence." Claire had given up objecting to his method of research. After all, she had no right to care if he risked his life, as she herself had made perfectly clear in Montana.

When she heard them at the door, she pasted a smile on her face, hoping the trepidation in her heart was well hidden.

But her smile faltered when she opened the door. Matt handed her flowers, and for an instant she felt like crying. She suspected he had done it, however, to take the focus off Tripper's lukewarm greeting. He barely glanced her way, and Claire hid her disappointment. She had known it would take more than a spotless house to redeem herself in her son's eyes.

Matt tried hard to gloss over the tension, but they were both relieved when Tripper excused himself and went to his room.

Claire watched him disappear up the stairs, swallowing the lump in her throat.

"Give him time."

"I lied to him, Matt. He's not going to forgive me for that."

"How do you know?"

"I know my son —" she started to explain, but he cut her short.

"Tell me…Did you ever forgive your parents? For that lousy childhood they gave you?"

She looked away. "It's not the same."

"No, it's not. You were trying to protect him. What your parents did to you —"

"We're not talking about what my parents did to me," she said with what she hoped was a note of finality, laying the flowers on the table near the door.

"And why is that?"

In the mirror above the table, Claire could see a dogged expression on his face. She braced herself for another verbal skirmish.

"Because it's not relevant. It's Tripper who —"

"Tripper's behaving like a spoiled brat."

Spinning around, Claire gaped at him, shocked into silence.

"Face it, Claire, for years he's been the focus of your life. Suddenly he finds out he could have had two parents, instead of one, doting on him all these years, and he's a little angry. Who wouldn't be? But that's not a good reason to punish the one parent who cared enough to keep him safe the only way she knew how."

Claire wanted to laugh. "Listen to yourself. You're the one who wanted to sue me for everything I had only a few weeks ago!"

"I've changed my mind." He crossed his arms across his chest.

"What's the matter? Now that your son turns out to be 'spoiled goods,' have you decided fatherhood isn't all it's cracked up to be?" She glared at him. How dare he imply Tripper was spoiled!

"No, not at all. In fact, it's turning out to be a hell of a lot better than I ever could have imagined. I love that kid, no question about it." Her anger dissipated. She had to believe him, especially when he added, "And he isn't spoiled; he's just acting like he is. Momentarily. With encouragement from you."

"Me!" She stared at him in disbelief.

"He'll get over it as soon you quit acting like you deserve to be a finalist for worst parent of the year."

"What are you talking about?"

"Come on, Claire. You might as well shave your head—like you did before, when you blamed yourself for Hayley's death."

"I didn't blame myself for her death."

"Then why the hell did you run off so fast? Just like you did two weeks ago. Rather than deal with your son—and deal with me—you left the scene of the crime. Convenient, isn't it? Running away from those pesky little emotions. Guilt, love, anger—just push it all under the rug and forget about it." He leaned in, his gaze too knowing.

She laughed bitterly. "I see you've picked up a degree in psychology. Congratulations."

"As a matter of fact, I *have* talked to a psychologist. About adults who were abused as children, for the role I'm playing—"

"And now you've decided you can use your 'expertise' on me? How dare you—how *dare* you?" she repeated, wanting to aim daggers at him.

"Listen." His voice calmed. "I know it's a serious subject, one you don't like talking about."

"You're exactly right." She kept her voice hard, propelled by carefully contained fury. "I don't talk about it. I don't even think about it. And if you think I'm going to open up to you, just so you can understand your character better, you're seriously mistaken."

"God, is that what you think?" He shot her a look of disbelief. "That's not what this is about."

"Isn't it? Isn't that how all this got started anyway? We took our roles just a little too seriously and ended up in bed."

"You don't believe that any more than I do. The truth is, we both want each other so much we melt cement. You push me away because you're terrified of what I make you feel."

"I don't feel anything for you."

"We both know that's not true."

She kept her face a porcelain mask. A challenge, she realized too late.

"Prove it to me, Claire. Convince me you can't stand the sight of me." His eyes lit with the confidence of someone who knew he could elicit passion from a lump of concrete.

Claire braced herself, like a sailor standing firm against the waves that crashed at the sides of the ship. This time she wouldn't bend. He pulled her into his arms, and she didn't move a millimeter as his mouth roamed over her lips. His hands, tracking hungrily over her waist, her stomach, and her breast, failed to stir so much as a shiver. But when he groaned against her throat, her breath caught.

"Damn you, Claire, don't shut me out!"

She heard the pain in his voice and could feel herself weaken. She pushed against his chest, but he didn't budge. Panicked now, she struggled harder, some primeval force rearing up and giving her a strength she didn't know she possessed.

She wrenched her face away, pushing at his shoulders, and cried out, "Matt! Let me go!"

From the corner of her eye, she saw Tripper, at the bottom of the stairs, staring in the scene in the hall with alarm on his face.

Then with the force of a speeding basketball he hurled himself at his father. "Don't you hurt her! You creep! She didn't do anything to you!" he yelled, pulling at Matt's arm. "Leave her alone!"

Tears streamed down his face, his fists merciless pistons against Matt's broad chest. "You leave my mom alone! Don't hurt her, you big jerk!"

Claire wrapped her arms around his waist, pulling him back. "Oh, no, Tripper! Stop! Matt wasn't hurting me! Oh, honey!"

He let her pull him off, finally, though he continued to glare at Matt. Claire wanted to erase the confusion and tears from his face, but she had lied to him about a father he barely knew. He turned and buried his head in her shoulder.

"I thought he was hurting you!" he cried, anguish ripping through his voice.

Claire fought back her own tears. "Oh, honey, your father didn't hurt me," she said. "He would never do that." As she stroked his head, her gaze met Matt's. His eyes were filled with remorse, his face ashen under his tan.

"God, Claire, I didn't mean to come on like that."

"You didn't," she said firmly. "I panicked. It's okay," she said to both of them. "Everything's going to be all right."

And as she smoothed Tripper's hair back from his damp face, she knew it would be.

Matt was right. She had allowed Tripper to harbor his resentment toward her, inadvertently furthering the impression that he had every reason to hate her.

But deep down, the bonds between mother and son were stronger than she had imagined. Tripper would still take on a lion if he thought his mother was in danger — and, maybe, could even understand why she had gone to such lengths to protect him.

Another, more startling notion made its way to the surface. If her son was capable of forgiving her, was it even possible she could forgive herself?

Matt wasn't able to stay long, he told them regretfully. He was due in Louisiana to begin his "incarceration." More importantly, he knew Claire and Tripper needed some time alone, to reestablish the bonds that had been so strong before they were severed by the sharp edge of truth.

He was glad Tripper had come to his senses. Not only was he talking to his mother again, but after he realized he had misinterpreted what he had seen, he had apologized to Matt for trying to punch his lights out.

"No problem, son," Matt replied easily. "The bruises will make me look tough in prison."

Claire had turned away, but not before Matt had seen the look of worry on her face.

He tried to reassure her, but she simply smiled brightly and wished him a good trip.

Matt sighed. One day she would be ready to face her feelings, but for now, the last thing she needed was him breathing down her neck.

# Chapter Twenty-Five

Matt sucked in his first clean breath in two days and blinked, his eyes still sensitive to the bright morning sunshine. The humidity of Louisiana in the spring was suffocating, but not nearly as stifling as the atmosphere inside Angola, where he had just spent the last twenty-four hours in solitary confinement. Though the prison officials had at first tried to give him the star treatment, Matt had made it clear that for the duration, he was to be subjected to the same conditions of a hardened criminal — though security guards had continued to watch at a distance.

Still, Matt knew Claire would have been horrified if she had known how exposed he had been as he mingled with the other prisoners.

He paused to wipe the moisture that clung to his brow. She cared about him, he was sure, more than she was willing to admit.

And now that he had an idea — or thought he did — of what Claire's childhood had been like, he could understand why she didn't want to risk having her heart torn to pieces.

Meanwhile, his own heart was getting used to running on empty. Since leaving her house, he had felt as if his left ventricle had been torn off. Although he was glad she and Tripper were on speaking terms again, he hated the thought that she didn't trust him enough to open up.

But he'd done a lot of thinking while locked in a cell without so much as a pet cockroach for company. He was a patient guy — he'd wait her out. Sooner or later, she'd come to realize they deserved a shot at happiness.

Matt's bodyguard opened the door of the car that would take him to New Orleans, where he had a meeting with the author of *Outrage*. He had chosen not to meet the real Dylan McAllister, knowing he would give a better performance if he imagined Dylan wearing his own skin.

The film would open with Dylan fighting for his life in a prison brawl. This time, the scar on his arm that makeup techs often attempted to hide would be appropriate for the part.

"Matt? Matt Grayson?" At the sound of his name, Matt turned and saw the glint of sun on a camera. Another reporter. He had hoped the visit to Angola would pass unnoticed by the local press.

"I'd like to ask you a few questions." As he spoke, the man lowered the camera from the strap around his neck, and Matt noticed a small tape recorder in his hand, along with a large envelope.

"Call my press agent," Matt said impatiently. Most of these guys knew that interviews were scheduled by press agents, who also handled routine questions.

"Yeah, but this story — it's scheduled for tomorrow's paper. I'd like to get your reaction." The guy was young — mid-twenties, Matt guessed — with a nervous edge that usually went along with a weasel personality.

"What story?"

"It's about Claire Porter."

Matt bristled. Another bottom feeder. "Don't you guys have anything better to rag on?" He turned and stepped toward his car.

"I'm talking about the fact that she was raped ten years ago."

Matt halted dead still, jerking back to skewer the reporter. "What did you say?"

"There's a police report, from Stillwater, Oklahoma, where she was living at the time. Claire Porter was assaulted, not long after Hayley James killed herself. No charges were ever filed."

"Oh my God." Matt wiped a hand over his face. Just the thought knotted his gut.

"I take it you weren't aware."

"Hell no. I had no idea." He couldn't contain his shock, despite the fact the reporter was latching on to the scoop. No, he hadn't known. Claire wasn't one to disclose information — he should know that better than anyone. "How do you know about this? And what do you mean, it's going to be in tomorrow's paper? What happened ten years ago is old news, buddy."

The guy shrugged. "I was digging into her background, now that she's been appointed president of Kaslow's. I wondered how a former bimbo rose to the top so quickly. Turned up a case of possible rape."

"What do you mean, possible?" Matt stifled the urge to hit the guy.

"She was found in the bathtub, nude. Any evidence had been washed away, and according to the report, the victim had no memory of the assault."

"Jesus." Matt clenched his fist, too stunned to protest the invasion of Claire's privacy just now. Rage warred with concern, but uppermost was the need for more details.

The reporter seemed to know he had his full attention. He waved a large envelope in his hand, which Matt supposed contained the results of his digging. "We're also running a related story about her childhood. She grew up right across the state line, in a little spot on the map called Paradise, Texas. Apparently her father, the Reverend Roy Porter, is some sort of religious nut who founded his own church — 'the Blood of the Lamb Church of the Redeemer.'"

"Did you say 'is'? Her father's alive?"

"He was yesterday. I talked to them both for the story. I tell you, the guy's a nut case. Called his daughter the 'spawn of the devil,' crazy shit like that." He shook his head, and Matt had a sickening feeling every word would be printed in the smut rag he worked for.

Matt's gaze hardened. "Call your paper. You're not running this story."

"Hey, buddy, it's our First Amendment right—"

"My lawyers will crawl all over your First Amendment rights."

"But the records are open to the public—"

"Rape reports aren't public records." Before the man could protest, Matt reached out and ripped the envelope from his hands.

"Hey, chill. We have copies anyway," the guy said with a smirk.

"Yeah? You got an extra face, too?"

His eyes widened. "Now, listen—"

"'Cause you'll need one when I'm finished with yours." The last two days among hardened lifers lent an extra menace to the glare he gave the reporter.

The guy put his hands up and backed away. "Hey, man, talk to my editor. I just write the story."

Matt took a step forward. "Get this straight: Tomorrow's paper had better not even mention the name Claire Porter. Because if it does, the next day's will feature your name, right next to the other victims."

The reporter swallowed, then tried one last time. "Look, man, it's a legitimate story. She's a public figure."

"You want a legitimate story? I'll give you a scoop." Like lightning, his fist came out and landed squarely on the reporter's face. "How's that? 'Celebrity Hits Sleazebag,'" he finished as the man reeled, blood dripping down his chin and onto his white shirt.

Matt turned and, without another glance at the reporter, slid into the waiting car. He didn't give a damn if the guy pressed charges. As far as he was concerned, he had done what any red-blooded male would do to protect the woman he loved. He just hoped he had hit the guy hard enough to make him think twice about printing the story.

He glanced down at the envelope still in his hands. With an unsteady hand, he opened it. A set of black-and-white photos fell out. At first he didn't recognize the face—bruised, eyes almost swollen shut, a clot of blood on her forehead, right where there was a scar now. His stomach churned as he accepted the fact that the battered woman in the photo was Claire.

Looking at the bruises on her face, on her body, Matt felt rage sluice through him. Even though the hurt was ten years old and the bruises healed, he still wanted to go a few rounds with the person who did this to her.

But according to the police report that he found in the envelope, they had never identified the attacker. No other similar crimes had been reported in the area, leading the police to suspect it may have been an acquaintance. There was no mention of the brief notoriety Claire, as "Clarissa," had endured, but Matt figured it was possible that the police had no idea who the victim was. Her appearance, distorted by the bruises covering her face, would certainly not have held a clue.

More disturbing than the bruises were the details of the police report. The victim had been in the bathtub when they found her, semiconscious and near drowning, which had apparently destroyed any evidence of rape. When questioned by police and hospital personnel, however, she had denied that a sexual assault had occurred. Without evidence, the police had been forced to believe her.

But Matt knew Claire's powers of denial. She could have blocked it from her mind.

Then the realization hit him like a blow to the gut: If a rape had occurred, so close to the time she had conceived, the identity of her child's father would have been in doubt.

Matt leaned his head back on the seat cushion, swallowing the bile that burned his throat.

Suddenly Claire's reasons for not informing him about Tripper's existence were much clearer.

Matt canceled his trip to New Orleans. Instead, he instructed his pilot to file a flight plan for an airport near Houston, then arranged for a rental car. The police may not have figured out the identity of the attacker, but Matt had a sickening hunch. He intended to find out the truth, and after he finished with the man who had done that to Claire, his next incarceration might be for much longer than two days.

Three hours later, Matt pulled into the one-stoplight town that was optimistically called Paradise. The sun was high in the sky, filtered through the dark-green kaleidoscope of pines that lined the road.

*Drive friendly*, the sign on the state highway warned, but Matt didn't feel a damn bit friendly. The image of Claire's face, as it looked in the photos on the seat beside him, filled him with cold fury.

The attack had undoubtedly been provoked by the notoriety over their affair. She had been helpless to stop her attacker. The words of Dr. Greenfield came back to him. "Abused children feel they deserve what happens to them." Surely not even Claire, a master at harboring guilt, could feel she deserved such a punishment.

Maybe he was making a mistake, coming here, exacting revenge for a crime he wasn't even sure had been committed.

After all, Claire said her parents were dead—and hadn't she mentioned she was adopted?

But he had to know the truth. If he and Claire were ever to have a chance, he had to understand what kind of demons haunted her, made her terrified of stepping into the deep end of a relationship.

And if his darkest suspicions proved true, then no force on earth would stop him from tearing Roy Porter into tiny pieces. He smiled grimly. The dragon that raged in Claire's nightmares was about to meet its match.

Gravel popped under his tires as he pulled into the parking lot of the Blood of the Lamb Church of the Redeemer. The name was bigger than the whole building—the church didn't seem to believe in erecting architectural monuments. Just four square walls of putty-colored brick, with double doors set square in the middle. The place looked more like a cardboard box than a church building.

Behind the main structure was a house, made of the same washed-out brick as the church. Matt saw no cars around, and he hoped the Reverend Roy Porter wasn't out tending his flock. He didn't want to delay the confrontation he was itching for.

He decided to try the house first. Shaded by a line of pines in the rear, the house had a deserted look.

At his knock, Matt saw a curtain flicker in the front window, then a shadow behind the tiny window in the front door.

For the first time, he remembered his appearance—it was less than reassuring. A two-day beard, plus the unmistakable "eau de prison toilet" that clung to his clothes, would probably lead whomever was behind the door to assume he was some bad-news bandito.

The door opened. The woman who appeared could have been mistaken for a time traveler—a settler's wife from the old west, when moisturizer and haircuts were equally scarce. A thick braid of gray hair fell to her waist, and her dress was made from something that looked homespun.

"Can I help you?" Her voice was soft, the accent reminding Matt of Claire's when he had first known her.

"I'm looking for Roy Porter."

"He's not here right now."

"When do you expect him back?"

"He's out doing the Lord's work—and that's never done." A smile creased her weathered face.

"You're his wife?" Maybe it was a good thing the reverend wasn't around. He could get more information from this woman.

She nodded. "I'm Deborah. Is there something I can help you with?" Her voice was eerily benign. "You're not lost, are you?"

"No..."

"I mean in the spiritual sense. The Lord sends lost souls here all the time, the ones the others just give up on. There's never been a soul too far gone for Roy to save," she said, and then her face clouded. "Except once—but that was a long time ago."

She stepped aside before Matt could comment. "Why don't you come in? I can get you some tea. You like iced tea, don't you?"

Matt didn't hesitate. "Yes, I'd like that. Actually..." He smiled as benignly as he could. "I was hoping to ask you some questions... about your husband's work."

"Oh, are you a servant too?" she asked.

Matt gave a noncommittal sound, fighting the feeling he was way out of his depth. She obviously didn't recognize him, nor seem to care about his unkempt appearance. He followed her into a spotless kitchen, not exactly the stuff of nightmares. A faint odor of bleach hung in the air, a marked difference to the prison stench he had been breathing the last two days.

She pulled a tall glass from a shelf and filled it with tea from a brimming pitcher. "I make a new pitcher every morning for Roy. If that man has a vice, it's his iced tea. Never drank a drop of liquor, but when it comes to my sweet tea..." She shook her head, chuckling. "Here you go, Mister—what did you say your name was?"

"Call me Matthew," he said, taking the glass from her. Matt was beginning to feel a little uneasy with his deception. Maybe he was completely off base here. "And you could probably answer my questions," he said, thinking carefully how to phrase them. "I have a friend—she's from this area. She might be a relative of yours. Her name is Claire Porter."

"Oh my stars!" Deborah's hand flew to her mouth. "You're talking about Mary Claire!"

"Then she *is* your daughter."

A dark look passed over her face. "Our adopted daughter. We weren't her parents—her real parents," she told him. "We tried, but raising that child took all our strength. After what Delores — her mother — did…" She looked away, shaking her head. "It was such a tragedy. But easy to see how it happened."

Then she leaned in, as if letting him in on a secret. "It was the Devil, you know, who tempted her beyond all power to resist. She showed up here one night — Halloween, it was — her belly about to pop. Roy knew all about her — he just knows things like that. And the baby…well, we thought we could save it. But it wasn't to be."

Matt was confused. "The baby died?"

"Oh, no, not that night. Mary Claire — that's what her mother named her, on the birth certificate — she was a fighter, all right. The baby came early — no one even knew Delores was with child! Except Roy, of course. He had talked to her, offered to show her the way if she would only…" A faraway look came in her eyes. "But the Devil was too strong. He had such a hold of her, Roy finally had to give up altogether. And later, we heard she put a gun to her head. Just couldn't face the life she had chosen." She shook her head, a look of regret in her faded eyes.

"And the baby? What happened to her?"

"Oh, Delores didn't care if we kept her." She said the words as if it were a rag doll they were discussing. "Roy thought — he thought he was strong enough to keep the Devil from coming near that child."

Matt had a sick feeling. "And did he? Keep the devil away from… Mary Claire?"

"Well, if you know her, you must know! Has she come to you for help? Is that it?" She laughed. "Let me tell you, Roy's done nearly everything he could to rinse the stain off that black soul. I never saw a child so determined to resist salvation."

"What…methods exactly did the reverend employ?"

She gave him a strange look. "I thought you said you were a healer too. Doing the Lord's work, like Roy."

Matt blinked. "I could never be like your husband, I'm afraid. His reputation precedes him."

She smiled. "Yes, it does, but he doesn't do it for the glory, you know. No, his place in Heaven is waiting, and he's planning to bring as many lost souls with him as he can."

Kicking and screaming, Matt added to himself. But he still hadn't found out everything he wanted to know. "I take it Mary Claire was resistant to the idea? Of salvation at the hands of your husband."

"Well, that's a way of putting it," she said. "Many's the time Roy would have to take the switch to her backside, just to get her into the doors of the church. Now you tell me…" She pointed a finger at him, as if sure of his agreement. "What kind of creature likes her sins so much she hangs on to them tight, with both hands? Even with the pure blood of Jesus just waiting to wash away her sins?"

"You're talking about a child. A child you raised."

Deborah didn't seem to hear him. "And after her mother went and gave her life to that old Devil, you'd think he'd have been satisfied. But no, he had to get his claws into Mary Claire. We tried—Lord knows, we tried—but sometimes, the Devil just won't let go. Especially when it's one of his own to begin with."

Matt felt like he had been dumped into the middle of a horror flick and he didn't know his lines. "Surely you're exaggerating. She was just a little girl."

A hard look came into her eyes. "Don't let her fool you. She was as much a harlot as her mother. Look what happened to her. Only difference is, she got away with what she did. God hasn't got around to punishing her for her sins yet."

Matt wanted to gag, but he forced himself to finish the charade. "What about what happened in Oklahoma? After…after her return from California?"

She gave him a surprised look. "You know about that?"

"Yes." Faking a flash of insight, he added, "It was Roy, wasn't it? He was trying to…punish her."

"Why yes, for the Lord of course. But—"A look of pain came over her face. "The Devil interfered. He was just too strong that time. To think, my very own mother—she invited the Devil right into her heart. Although, Momma was never too strong to begin with, not like me."

"So your husband never got around to punishing Claire for the sins she committed…in California."

"I told you, he was interrupted." Before Matt could ask how, she continued. "But Roy will get around to it, never you fear," she told him. "He always does such a good job for the Lord. Don't you think?"

This time, Matt didn't bother to hide his disgust. "Where did you say your husband was?"

Deborah frowned. "After that reporter stopped by yesterday, he set off for the bus station. A Greyhound stops right here in town."

The heat in the house was stifling, but suddenly Matt felt chilled to his bones. "Where was he going?"

"I told you—to do the Lord's work."

Matt resisted the urge to shake her. "Where?"

"I think he said Philadelphia," she told him, but Matt was already heading out the door.

# Chapter Twenty-Six

Matt tried to call Claire's office on the way to the Houston airport, but she wasn't in. Her secretary told him she was touring the Cherry Hill store, meeting with the store managers there. She wasn't expected to return to her office that afternoon. He debated what to do. He didn't want to scare the wits out of her, but he wanted to keep her safe. She had canceled the bodyguard that Connor had hired before Tripper arrived, not wanting to alarm him.

He contacted the service that had provided security during filming in Philadelphia. It would be an hour before they could position their personnel at Kaslow's and at her house in West Chester.

He hoped that would be soon enough. Once he arrived, he'd stick to her side like adhesive until Roy Porter was stopped.

Matt's pilot was waiting at the airport, and within minutes of arriving, he was on board. Fortunately, they didn't have to wait for clearance and were in the air before the afternoon traffic had filled the freeways below.

Matt phoned the Philadelphia police once he was out of Houston airspace. As he had suspected, though, there was little they could do without evidence of a crime. Even if they could find Roy Porter, they could only question the man. They did agree, however, to send an officer to the bus station to look for him.

He called Claire, but her cell went straight to voice mail. She would probably go straight home from Cherry Hill. By then the security team would be in place.

Turbulence rocked the jet, but Matt didn't notice. He leaned back and closed his eyes. Images of Claire, battered and bruised, filled his mind.

If sheer rage could power the aircraft, they'd slice through the clouds and land in record time — in time, he hoped, for him to get to Claire before Roy Porter did.

Claire glanced at the clock at the entrance to the building, then made her way toward the elevators. Her tour of the Cherry Hill store had gone well. Sales were still lagging, but she was convinced it was a matter of demographics, not lack of effort from the staff. She would have marketing work more closely with their buyers to ensure that the tastes of suburban shoppers were considered.

She just needed to stop by her office and pick up a couple of folders she'd left in her desk. Estelle was staying with Tripper until she returned. She hurried into the elevator, wishing Joan were back from maternity leave. Her temp had left the door to her office unlocked yesterday when she left.

She was worried about Matt. She'd checked her phone, but the battery had died during her outing today. He had promised to phone her as soon as he was out of the prison. Maybe he'd phoned and the temp had forgotten to give her the message. Or more likely, Matt hadn't left a message. During the last couple of weeks, he had been following her wishes and not drawing attention to their relationship.

If what they had could be defined as a relationship. Claire was on shaky ground there. She missed him. During the day, she found herself thinking about him, longing to hear his voice on the phone. And at night, she longed for his touch — an ache she had never felt before.

But sexual desire wasn't enough on which to build a lasting relationship. There had to be trust, commitment…love.

The elevator stopped at the seventh floor, and she got off, hurrying down the hall to her office.

Did she love Matt? She honestly didn't know. He thought he loved her. But magazines were full of stories of celebrities who fell in and out of love like teenagers. She couldn't believe that Matt's feelings weren't based simply on convenience, that he was more enamored by the fact that she was his son's mother.

Even she had to admit, it would certainly be convenient to fall in love with her son's father. She knew Tripper wanted more than anything for his parents to be together. It wasn't fair to deny him time with his newfound father. He and Matt had grown close during the two weeks in Montana. Matt had invited him to spend a month there this summer, before he began shooting on location in July.

She frowned as she entered her office. As she had suspected, the door had been left unlocked. She made a mental note to ask security to double check it from now on.

Quickly she found what she needed, then looked through the telephone log. Yes, Matt had called, she noticed, relieved. Twice. But predictably, he had declined to leave a message.

Then she noticed the call from the Philadelphia police. She frowned and picked up the phone to return the call.

Before the police could answer the phone, Claire heard footsteps outside her office. Perhaps it was Matt, she thought, knowing every-one else had left for the day. He had probably flown in to surprise her and to finish the discussion they had barely begun the day he dropped Tripper off. She replaced the phone, and with a hopeful smile on her face, she looked toward the doorway.

But the face that appeared wasn't Matt's.

It was the face from her nightmares.

A gasp escaped her throat as Roy Porter walked in. He was older now, but she'd never forget that face, that straw-colored hair, those washed-out eyes filled with righteous indignation.

He glanced derisively around her office. "The Devil rewards his own, doesn't he?" His harsh laughter was an echo from her child-hood, a fanfare of fear.

Though her bones wanted to curl protectively, she forced herself to sit motionless in the chair. She was in no danger, she told her-self—security was only a phone call away. With trembling fingers she picked up the phone…and then dropped it onto the cradle with a crash as Roy withdrew a gun from his jacket.

Terror clutched at her throat. She placed her shaking hands palms down on the desk. Forcing her gaze off the dull-gray metal, she met his eyes. They were feverish and wild, brimming with hate. Roy had obviously stepped over the edge since she had seen him last.

"I see you've come prepared," she said, her voice somehow calm, despite the memories assaulting her…memories she'd repressed for so long.

"Of course, even though that she-devil isn't around to protect her cub. Whatever happened to the old woman, anyway? I assume she's resting comfortably—in Hell!" He chuckled at his own joke.

Claire barely heard him. Her mind was busy sorting the possibilities for escape. The building was full of innocent people who might inadvertently stand in his way. She couldn't let him leave the office.

A new dread slid through her consciousness. Thank God he had come here, not her home, where Tripper…

The gray pistol in Roy's hand wavered, while bits of memory came oozing back to Claire.

Suddenly she remembered another gun. A prop—but then not a prop gun after all. Pointing at her, at Matt…and at Hayley James. Then there was blood everywhere, blood smattered on her hands like scarlet finger paint…

She blinked, pushing the thoughts away. Right now she had to figure out a way to escape.

She had no weapon with which to defend herself, and the huge office hadn't come equipped with an escape hatch. But negotiating her way around opposition…she had done that before. Maybe she could stand a chance—if fear didn't paralyze her first.

She licked her lips, her throat dry, and forced herself to speak. "It must have been a long ride over here. Why don't I get you something to drink?" She nodded toward the bar in the corner.

He laughed, low in his throat. "Always were good at temptation, weren't you?" He mocked: "'Here, Daddy—I made you a glass of tea.' Like I didn't see through your wiles."

Claire swallowed the bile that had crept into her mouth and forced a thin smile. "Well, I'm fresh out of wiles now. And probably iced tea as well. Maybe I could call for something?" It was worth a shot—

He lifted the gun an inch higher. "The only thing you're going to call for is mercy." He laughed. "But not even your false idols can save you now. You think I don't know about your depravity, don't you? You think you can hide—just like always."

Another memory—in a closet, darkness swirling around her, hiding from Roy Porter. Claire shook her head, dispelling the images.

She had to be in control this time, with her life on the line…*Tripper's life*…"No, I never could hide from you, could I? I always knew you'd find me—sooner or later."

Even as she spoke, her mind raced, searching for a way out. She could seek cover under the desk, but she rejected the thought before it formed completely. She had to get the gun from him, incapacitate him somehow…but for now, she had to keep him talking.

"Your work—you must have been very busy these last few years."

"Of course. Sin doesn't stop for a sandwich, you know." Pleased with his quip, he glanced around, his eyes coming to rest on the frame on her desk. Claire sucked in a breath as he reached for Tripper's photo. The thought of those hands anywhere near her son sent a chill racing down her spine.

*Oh God*, what if he went for Tripper—after he finished with her? What would stop him from walking out of her office and going to her home? Would anyone hear the gunshot and try to stop him?

From over the photo, Roy's cold gaze narrowed. "I should have known you'd follow in her footsteps. You always were just like her." He waved the frame in the air as if it were a Bible from his pulpit. "She lay down with the Devil too, and look where it got her. She's living it up in hell now, ain't she?"

An idea came to Claire. "You told me my mother killed herself. My real mother."

Suspicion clouded his eyes. "She died covered in shame. You don't want to be like her. You can have your sins forgiven, right here and now. You know that."

Claire swallowed and strived to look contrite. "Actually, I'd prefer… to just end it. It's a coward's way out, I know." She gave a little shrug. "If you would let me have the gun, you could leave and no one would ever know…"

His laughter cracked the quiet. "That's what you think? Even now, when you should know you can't outrun your sins?"

He looked at her as if what he said made perfect sense, and Claire knew he was a madman. He had hid his lunacy from the town, practicing his vengeance on select members of his congregation—sinners whose shame was so great they were willing to face Reverend Porter's particular brand of punishment in exchange for salvation.

He went on talking, while Claire desperately inventoried her dwindling options. "You never would go willingly, would you? You had to fight it. I should have known even then you were headed straight for hell." He aimed the gun at her, as if it were an accusing finger. "You're nothing but a slut, a whore just like the woman who bore you."

The words slapped at her: *Slut. Whore.* Only it was Hayley's voice, accusing Claire, as the memories flooded back with the force of a raging river. Hayley's trembling hands holding a gun, pointing first at Matt, then Claire, while she recited a heartfelt soliloquy. At first they'd thought she was improvising, the lines were so perfect, coming from the heart of a spurned wife — or lover. But she'd deviated from the script, the script Claire had so painstakingly memorized with Matt's help.

And then she'd turned the gun on herself. The sound of the shot rang out like a clap of thunder, and then there was blood, so much blood…

Claire flinched. No, that was a memory — she was in her office, and it was Roy Porter who held the gun.

"What do you want from me?" she asked quietly.

"It's not what I want from you, you know that. If it were up to me, I would have let you go on your merry little way, cavorting with the Devil all you want. But it's the Lord. He's told me I must save your soul from your sins." He looked down at her, his eyes glowing with the excitement of saving another lost soul. "You must repent and be washed in the blood of the lamb."

It all came back to her, had never really left. The horror, the shame, the cold, sinking feeling — that she couldn't breathe, that she would smother under the water — her worst nightmare come true, again and again.

She closed her eyes. "You're insane," she whispered. But he didn't hear her. He was too far gone, too consumed with the passion that had overcome him as he began to impersonate his own version of God.

He stepped closer. His voice an octave deeper, eyes closed, he intoned: "I am the way, the truth, and the light, and he who cometh before me shall be saved — "

Claire lunged. She flew across the desk, the gun never leaving her vision. But he was still quicker, stronger, and halted her attack before she could knock the gun from his grasp. With one hand gripping her hair, he held the gun high above his head, out of her reach.

Forcing her head backward, he bared his teeth and muttered, "The Devil's not going to win, not this time. 'You're mine now, sayeth the Lord.' And there's no one to save you now but God."

All the fight drained out of Claire, and she sank to the desk, knowing she had lost, had never even stood a chance.

At last her destiny had caught up with her.

# CHAPTER TWENTY-SEVEN

Matt's limo pulled in front of Kaslow's in the wake of screaming police cars, yanking to a stop behind a line of dazed onlookers. After talking to Tripper, he knew Claire was still at the Philadelphia store—and still not answering her phone.

His heart pounded as his worst fears were realized. He was too late! Somehow Roy Porter must have slipped past the security he had arranged and gotten to Claire.

He put the gut-wrenching fear on hold and leaped from the car. Fighting his way against the crowd that streamed from the entrance, he finally reached an officer in a dark jacket. "What's going on?"

"Stay back, sir. We have a possible hostage situation." Another officer spoke into his walkie talkie, but Matt couldn't hear him over the sirens, as more squad cars blocked the street at either end of the store.

"Who is it?" he shouted. "Who's in there?"

"I can't give you that information—" Then the officer recognized the face behind the two-day beard. "Mr. Grayson, you'll have to remain back." A voice crackled on the radio, and Matt heard the news at the same time the officer did. "Positive ID on hostage. It's Claire Porter, Kaslow's president. No ID on the gunman. Repeat, no ID—"

"Jesus," Matt breathed. Then he turned to the officer and grabbed his arm. "You've got to let me in there!"

"Sir, you can't—"

"I'm her family, damn it! And I know who's holding her! Let me talk to your supervisor…anyone…" He broke off as someone in the crowd yelled behind him. Already Matt was drawing attention, away from the situation and on to him. A living, breathing celebrity was just as good as real-life drama.

After a brief consultation with his superior, the officer, who had identified himself as Dan Griggs, agreed to escort Matt through the east entrance. By now, most of the crowd had been cleared from the premises and were gathered behind the hastily erected barricades. Inside the store, the perimeter had been cordoned off, restricting access to the area outside the rotunda where the gunman was located, out of firing range. Officer Griggs briefed him as they walked, though there was little information he could give.

"Customers reported seeing the two get off the elevator at around seven twenty-five p.m. An older man, approximately sixty years of age, and a younger woman. No positive ID on the type of weapon, but it's assumed to be a small-caliber handgun."

"Where are they?"

"He's taken her to the fountain, at the center of the first floor. We've got sharpshooters on the way, but it'll be hard to get a clear shot with all the greenery."

Matt tried to forget it was Claire they were discussing, Claire who would be directly in the line of fire. Instead, he gathered his wits and told the officer what he knew.

"I know who the guy is. I called earlier, tried to warn you guys…" He swept a hand through his hair. It was futile to point out now that they should have taken him seriously. "It's her father—her adoptive father, Roy Porter. The guy's a religious fanatic, thinks he's on a mission from God. I just talked to his wife earlier today. They're both a couple of goddamned lunatics." His mouth tightened. He should have known, should have prevented this somehow. But now wasn't the time for recriminations; it was time for action.

Unfortunately, there didn't seem to be a damned thing he could do.

While the officer relayed the information on the radio, Matt looked around. He couldn't see the fountain, but he noticed a monitor set up a few yards away. It received a live feed from the video camera the team had positioned so that they could have "eyes" on the situation. Matt once played a member of a SWAT team, and his research had given him a good idea of what was going on around him.

They would be searching blueprints of the store, trying to find a way to surprise the gunman. But Matt already knew: Except for the foliage, there would be no solid cover to hide behind. The closest display counters were on the other side of the walls that divided the rotunda from the first floor selling space. The ceiling of the rotunda was four floors high—there was little chance of approaching from that direction.

He edged closer to the monitor, and in the confusion, no one noticed him.

He could hear the comments of the officers as they viewed the situation. "He's got his eyes closed—he's mumbling something. Think we could get off a shot?"

Matt's heart leaped to his throat. Then he caught a glimpse of the screen. It was Claire, on her knees in front of the madman. A gun was pointed right at her bowed head.

Matt's head swelled with white-hot rage. He wanted to rip the gun from Porter's hands, then tear him to ribbons with his fists. His blood pumped faster, loaded with the adrenaline that had been fueling him ever since he had seen the photos of her.

He slammed his fist into the wall that separated him from the open area where Claire was being held. The pain didn't register. Sweat poured from him as he realized the truth: It was Claire out there, in harm's way, and he was powerless to help her. This wasn't a movie, where the superhero comes charging in at the last minute to save the innocent hostage tied to the tracks. There was no director calling instructions from the sidelines, no makeup tech to wipe the sweat from his brow. This was real life, with real bullets in the gun Roy Porter held.

He paced the small area in which he was confined. There had to be something he could do, before the situation escalated, before the finger on the trigger grew antsy, before Roy Porter's mind slipped totally.

After his conversation with Deborah, Matt was convinced Roy Porter thought he was a one-man judgment team. God's enforcer. He was crazier than a loon. There was no reason to which he could appeal.

But maybe someone could appeal to his delusions, convince the guy they had bought into his game. No sane person would fall for it of course, but if the guy was out of touch with reality already, why not convince him he wasn't the only one playing make-believe?

Matt approached Officer Griggs. "Listen up. You've got to let me go out there. I think I can convince this guy to let her go."

But the officer only shook his head. "Not a chance. Civilians have to stay behind the line. You don't know when this guy's going to crack."

"That's exactly what I'm worried about! By the time you guys get your act together, it might be too late. Look, I'm no hostage negotiator, but I can convince this guy I'm whoever he wants me to be. With his mindset, he wouldn't be a bit surprised if God himself dropped in for a chat."

"Sir, I understand how you feel. If it was my girlfriend out there, I'd want to go busting in there myself." The officer looked at him pityingly. "We've got a family counselor on the way over. She's used to working with victim's families."

Matt's thin hold on control vanished. "Claire isn't a goddamned victim! That man's a lunatic, and unless someone can get to her in a hurry, he's going to snap! And then I'll have to explain to my son why I sat here and did nothing while his mother was…was—" Matt's throat constricted.

"We can't let you approach the area, sir. We just can't. The best thing you can do is stay out of our way and let us do our jobs."

Matt turned away, disgusted. If there was nothing he could do, he'd be damned if he'd do it in the designated waiting area.

He pushed his way through the gathering swarm of black-jacketed officers. He had one advantage: After spending seven nights filming in this place, he knew his way around better than any of the SWAT team.

He slipped past a pyramid display of *Scandal* bottles. When the officer nearby looked away, Matt broke into the aisle, beyond the point the police had cordoned off.

Ignoring the shouts behind him, he loped past a display of handbags, toward the center of the rotunda. He slowed as he reached the planters bulging with spring bulbs and huge tropical plants. He edged around them until he could see the side of the fountain where Roy Porter stood, his eyes closed, intoning scripture. He seemed to be in his own world, totally unaware of the crisis he had instigated, unaware even that he was no longer alone with his "penitent." The gun in his hand wavered with the rise and fall of his voice.

Matt didn't dare glance at Claire. One look at the fear in her eyes, and he would lose his cool and charge the bastard. Instead, he focused his attention on Roy Porter.

The man needed a reality check, but Matt wasn't going to give it to him.

"I see you're holding a baptism here. Without me." He forced himself to chuckle devilishly. "What a shame. I always like to be around when these things happen. After all, you never know when one might slip." He pasted an evil grin on his face.

He heard Claire's gasp, but he ignored it, totally focused on his character now.

Roy opened his eyes. He stared at Matt over the top of Claire's head. "What do you want? Can't you see I'm trying to bring about God's justice?"

Matt lifted an eyebrow. "Oh yeah? Well, it looks like you've got the wrong sinner this time. I'm the one you want. I was the one who taught her everything she knows." He gave Roy a sincere grin. "Why don't you perform your little ceremony on me, instead? I could use some salvation."

Roy looked at him, mistrust blazing from his blue eyes. "You're that actor, aren't you? What are you doing here? You're supposed to be out in Hollywood—that sinner's paradise."

"Hey, I get around," Matt said, his expression open, trusting. "Right now I'm interested in hearing what you've got to say."

"My business is not with you."

"Hey, come on! How often do you get a chance to save the Big Guy himself?"

Roy's gaze faltered as he focused on Matt. "Who are you?"

"Why, don't you know? You've been after me for years. You just haven't seen me up close and personal—until now." Matt gave him an evil leer Jack Nicholson would have been proud of.

Roy Porter took the hint. His eyes lit with an unearthly light. "Get thee from me, Satan!" he implored, his voice stark.

Matt laughed. "You really think I'm gonna fall for a cliché line like that? Come on, Roy," he sneered. "You can do better than that!"

Roy turned a wavering hand in his direction, the one that held the gun, muttering the cant of religious fervor all the while.

Matt smiled. He felt all powerful, as if his shirt were made of Kevlar instead of rayon, capable of stopping a speeding bullet.

"Come on," he taunted. "You can't even hold that thing steady, can you? I always knew you'd be terrrr-rified in my presence!" His laugh was pure evil and pure Hollywood.

"No! I won't let you interfere with the Lord's work! This one is mine! I raised her! The Lord led me here; he ordered me to do this, don't you see?" Roy's eyes glowed with fanatical logic, sweat beading in the furrows of his forehead.

"How you gonna stop me? With that little popgun you got there?" Matt came in closer and closer. From the corner of his eye, he saw Claire twist, yanking the plug of hair still held firm in Roy Porter's grip.

"Go away, Matt," she pleaded. "Please, go away. Let me handle this!"

He ignored her, only praying she would take the opportunity to run when Roy Porter became fully occupied with his newest target. "Come on," he taunted. "Give it your best shot!"

In his peripheral vision, he saw her move an instant before Roy reacted, knocking the arm that held the gun just enough to throw off his aim.

Matt was already lunging. He barely felt the sting in his shoulder as he tackled the man, bringing him to the ground and knocking the gun away as if it were a football—he only hoped Claire recovered the fumble.

With Roy Porter underneath him, Matt somehow resisted the urge to pummel his face into the marble floor. Instead, he grabbed him by the collar and looked him square in the eye, dead serious now. "You listen to me, you son of a bitch," he growled, shaking Roy Porter's scrawny neck. "You think you know what hell is like? You touch her again—you so much as think of her—and you'll go there, I promise. First-class ticket, no stops—courtesy of me."

He glared at Roy Porter, no trace of Hollywood in his eyes. Then he watched as blood dripped onto Roy Porter's face, splattering onto his wire-framed glasses.

"*Oh God*, you've been shot! Oh God, Matt!" Claire's voice came from somewhere behind his shoulder.

"I'm okay, honey," he said, breathing heavy. "Just a flesh wound."

*Damn, he'd always wanted to say that.*

# Chapter Twenty-Eight

By the time Claire left the police station, it was midnight and she was ready to collapse. She had answered question after question, her voice sounding rusty even to her ears. It had been so long since she had even uttered the names of Roy and Deborah Porter, since she had even allowed herself to think of their brick house in Paradise.

She had been shocked when the police had asked her questions about the attack in Oklahoma City. Somehow they knew more than Claire herself did, more even than she wanted to know. When they asked her to confirm that Roy Porter was the man who had attacked her ten years ago, she shook her head. "I have no memory of what happened that day," she told them, and it was the truth. Her mind had covered up the worst of the ordeal.

The odd thing was, she remembered every detail of the last five hours. Every minute since Roy Porter had walked into her office, like a figure from hell. She had known he would reappear eventually, once the publicity about her reached the outskirts of Paradise. But unlike those times in the past, when sheer terror had caused her mind to go blank, a self-protective cocoon of emptiness, she had remained in control the whole time, aware of the situation and capable of reasoning, even fighting for her life. There had been no need for Gram to come charging to her rescue, bearing a borrowed rifle. And there certainly had been no need for Matt to risk his life.

She leaned toward the front seat of the car and spoke to the driver. A guard had shown up from somewhere, the same one who had provided escort a few weeks earlier. She had been too grateful for his presence, amidst the gathering media attention, to ask any questions. Now that the police had been satisfied with enough information to ensure Roy Porter remained in jail until he was tried, convicted, and locked in prison indefinitely, uppermost on her mind was the need to get to Matt. She had to see for herself that he was all right.

"The front entrance of Philadelphia General is on Spruce Street. I don't know how long I'll be there," she told him, then settled back in the seat and rehearsed what she planned to say to Matt.

She found his room with no trouble. Apparently someone had thought to leave her name on the official visitor list, along with the names of his immediate family. She knew from the information the police had given her that the bullet had exited his shoulder. With no surgery necessary, Matt should make a full recovery, in plenty of time to begin filming his next picture.

It was sheer luck that the bullet hadn't pierced a vital organ. When she thought how close he had come to being killed, she shuddered.

What had possessed him to take a bullet for her? Was he living out his fantasy of live-action hero? Saving the endangered heroine despite the fact the gun was real, not a prop?

She pushed open the door to his room. A dim glow from the street lights outside came through the window. On a bed that seemed too narrow for him, Matt lay asleep, an IV connected to his arm. His tan seemed to have faded, washed away by the loss of blood.

She approached the bed quietly, her legs shaking. A white bandage encased his left shoulder, disappearing underneath the sheet. She drew up a chair, prepared to wait until the morning when he woke, grateful that she had made arrangements for Estelle to stay the night with Tripper.

Matt stirred, and for a moment, she was afraid he would awaken. She wasn't sure yet what she would say to him.

Part of her wanted to read him the riot act — what was he thinking, walking into the path of a bullet with no protection? But another part of her wanted to hug him to her breast, smooth his hair back from his face, and tell him she loved him, more than life itself.

The thought almost knocked her over, arriving with a tidal wave of feeling she hadn't expected, hadn't guarded herself from. It was an ache, deep in her heart, deep in her soul, a joyous, tender pain. Like a fever that burned while it healed.

The last remaining drops of adrenaline drained from her, leaving her weak and shaking. She suddenly realized how close she had come to losing him. As he had walked confidently forward, arms spread in a challenge to Roy Porter to take his life—in order to spare hers—her life had seemed worthless.

She didn't notice as the first tears slipped from her eyes, the first real tears she had shed since she was a young girl, alone in a house that smelled like fear.

But while she had been locked in the dark closet for hours on end, her mind had spun fantasies. Fantasies that she once thought would never become reality. A white knight on a steed would never come crashing through the piney woods of Paradise to save Mary Claire Porter.

Through her tears she gazed at Matt, lying still as death, bandaged and dosed with painkillers. He was no fantasy knight, but a real, flesh-and-blood hero. It was real blood that he had shed, for her.

And real love he offered, if only she had the guts to take it.


Matt woke slowly. It had been thundering before he fell asleep. The nurse had said something about a storm…The thunder was louder now. Shaking his bed…

If he knew where the damn light switch was, he might be able to see. Fumbling around, he finally found the button the nurse had shown him earlier. Florescent light shuddered on.

The first thing he saw was Claire's dark head, bent over his bed, her shoulders shaking as soft sobs poured from her throat.

His heart leapt into his throat. Claire was crying! Something must have happened to Tripper. But he'd talked to Tripper just before he'd arrived at the store, hadn't he? The damn drugs were making his mind fuzzy.

"Claire, honey—" He reached out to stroke her hair. But she was so lost in grief, she didn't hear him, didn't feel his hand on her head, smoothing back the hair that fell over her face. He wished he could summon the strength to pull her into his arms, but they didn't seem to be working just now. If he could get her attention, maybe she could climb up here herself.

Her sobs became great heaving shudders as she struggled for breath. Alarmed, Matt searched for the button to call the nurse. Claire could be in shock—

And then it all came back to him—all that had happened today, all that he had learned. All that he had seen.

His hand gently gripped her chin, tilting her head up. "Oh, sweetheart," he said, wishing he could erase all the hurt she had felt, wishing he could undo the damage.

She opened her eyes and gazed wetly at him, her face taut with anguish. "What were you thinking?" she accused him through her tears. "You could have been killed!"

He gave her a weak smile, glad to see her spunk. "Nah, I'm a lot tougher than that."

She raked her soggy hair back from her face, her mouth set in a furious line. Eyes glowing like rain, she vented her fury. "In case you weren't aware, those were real bullets in that gun. A real gun, not some stage prop. You may get paid to face fabricated danger at every turn, but in real life, you aren't invincible. Goddamn it, Matt, you could have…you could have been—" But then her face screwed up and another sob rushed out.

Matt tried to soothe her, wiping a tear with his finger. "It's okay, honey. I wasn't hurt too bad. It was just a little bullet, not even the size of a marble."

But she batted his hand away. "I could have handled it! Don't you think I know how to handle my own father? How do you think I survived so many years? I didn't need you to save me then, and I don't need you now!"

She covered her face with her hands and sobbed. Great throat-tearing sobs that ripped at his heart and gave lie to her words. "Sweetheart, I know it was hard for you—"

She shook her head behind her hands. "No, you don't know anything!"

"Yes, I do know. I talked to your mother. To Deborah. In Texas."

Her breath caught on a sob as she listened.

"I went there from Angola. I had to find out—" He took a breath, then started over. "There was a reporter at the prison when I got out. He told me about…what happened in Oklahoma. The attack. He also told me about Roy Porter. Apparently this guy had talked to him—in fact, he was the reason Porter took off for here. God, when I think how close…" He raked his hand over his face, still stubby with beard. "Jesus, Claire, I couldn't get here fast enough."

"Did it ever occur to you to simply call the police? It *is* their job."

"Yeah, I did. I got the royal runaround. I even called the mayor's office. He was out of town. I tried to call you, but your cell wasn't working and I didn't want to leave a message."

"The battery was dead. My secretary forgot to recharge it before I left." She sighed. "But that doesn't mean you had to risk your stupid life! My God, Matt—"

"Claire, sweetheart, don't you get it? If anything had happened to you…do you think my life would have been worth a goddamn breath? If he had used that gun on you—"

She shook her head. "He wouldn't have." With a bitter laugh, she added, "And lose my soul to hell? His ego's too great. I could have convinced him, eventually, that I was the penitent soul he wanted to see." Closing her eyes, she took a shaky breath. A wave of sorrow passed over her face. "God knows I have enough sins to be forgiven for."

"What sins are those, Claire?"

She shook her head, frowning. "It's over, Matt. I don't want—"

"The sin of omission maybe? The fact that you didn't tell me about Tripper? Is that the sin you're talking about?"

She didn't say anything.

"I know, Claire. I know about the rape."

Her eyes widened.

"It was Roy Porter, wasn't it? He raped you in Oklahoma City."

She shook her head. "No. He never raped me."

"Claire, the report said—"

"I don't care what the report said! It wasn't rape!" Her hands fisted the corner of his bedsheet. "Don't you see? He did the same thing then he always did. He stripped my clothes off and forced me into the water. To cleanse me. If the River Jordan wasn't handy, or the church baptismal, he'd use whatever he could find. A bathtub. A fountain." She shuddered. "He's insane, but he managed to hide it from most of the town. He preyed on the weak, the weak in spirit." The tears were coming again, mingling with her words. "The sinners, people like my mother. My real mother. She must have been so ashamed!" A great sob racked her body.

"Like you, Claire? When you found out you were pregnant?"

She shook her head. "No. I wasn't a-ashamed. I was happy. So happy, to be having your baby. I wanted something for myself…a part of what we had. Oh, Matt, can you understand that?"

Matt did. And it shook him to the core that she had felt for him then what she couldn't admit now. She had never known love, the kind of love he had been given all his life. Instead, she'd received nothing but condemnation, punishment that, judging by his experience with Roy and Deborah Porter, couldn't have been anything but cruel. It was no wonder she had developed such a tough skin, though he knew better than anyone the woman underneath was soft as butter.

The harsh words of the press would have been doubly damaging to her all those years ago, and more recently, her son's anger when he found out her lies — Matt had seen how hurt she was, hurt enough to turn to him for comfort.

"You were trying to protect Tripper from him — from Porter, weren't you? You were afraid he'd find you both, subject him to the same treatment he had you—"

"No! I would never have let him near Tripper! Never." She gave him a fierce look through the fresh tears, and then her voice calmed as she continued. "I even had a will drawn up, naming you as guardian should anything ever happen to me. And if you hadn't wanted him, I had friends lined up. His soccer coach in San Francisco. I told him just enough about the situation, enough so that he agreed." She wiped at her cheeks, but the tears kept falling, as if from a frozen water pipe that had finally burst.

Matt regarded her, his head raised slightly from the pillow. "Claire… have you ever thought, maybe you should get counseling? The doctor in California—"

She bristled. "I don't need a shrink!"

"Abuse is nothing to be ashamed of."

"I'm not ashamed!"

"Then why did I have to hear about your parents from a damn reporter? You told me they were dead."

"They *were* dead," she insisted. "To me. I never intended to have anything to do with them."

He held her gaze. "What he did to you was unforgivable. The abuse — I saw those photos. He should have been prosecuted."

She looked away, then scoffed, "This, coming from the man most likely to forget where he placed his grudge? I don't intend to forgive…just forget," she said firmly.

He wanted to argue—every time he thought of what had been done to her, he wanted to rip into Roy and Deborah Porter with his bare hands.

But she had learned to deal with it her own way. By presenting that tough-as-nails exterior, by guarding her emotions, parceling them out like candy on Beggar's Night, she had warded off the normal wear and tear of life.

She had refused to let anyone close who could hurt her—except once, when he had slipped past her guard. He was pretty sure she had begun to let it down again, just a little. A little more, and maybe he'd have a chance.

From the look of the damp sheets next to him, it certainly looked as if a thaw was in the works.


A nurse came in, took Matt's temperature, and reminded him to get some sleep, giving Claire a stern look. She started to leave, the fight drained out of her, but Matt motioned for her to stay. His family would be arriving soon, he told her. As soon as they had heard the news, Mark and his mother had taken off for the Great Falls airport. They should arrive at any minute.

She settled back in the chair, pulling her feet under her. As soon as Matt's family arrived, she would leave, but until then…until then she would stay.

After her unaccustomed cry, she felt as if a flood had finally abated, leaving her dry, but replenished. She was still shaky with emotion but blessedly aware. No longer numb. Aware of Matt, beside her on the bed, the bandage pristine against his skin.

He had no white charger, his suit of armor was invisible, but he was still her hero. A love so overwhelming surrounded her, wrapping around her like a blanket, warming her heart, repairing her spirit that had been so nearly broken, filling her with a blissful sense of peace.

She wanted him in her life, and if that meant taking a risk, the rewards were well worth the emotional investment. She didn't need a balance sheet and a calculator to tell her that.

She closed her eyes, the florescent light shattering into patterns against her eyelids. For so long, she had tried to hide from her feelings, unconsciously protecting her fragile emotions. But now she realized they weren't in any danger. There was no need to run from what she felt. Matt's love was a sturdy thing, not easily broken, not easily destroyed. Strong enough to hold her and Tripper.

Roy Porter had tried to cleanse her of sin, but the real sin was what she had done to herself. Keeping her love under lock and key, only letting it out in small doses.

It was time to set it free.

The thought settled over her tired mind as she realized she had forgotten to ask Matt how his prison stay had gone; she hoped he had all the research into troubled pasts that he needed. Hers, she could shove back into the dark closet of her mind. She had read once that nightmares were only terrifying until they were shared. By sharing hers with Matt, her dreams had lost their power over her.

An incredible feeling of joy washed over her, and she wanted to shout with it, but she could only manage a tired smile as she gazed at Matt. He was losing the struggle to keep his eyes open. She leaned over and switched off the light, then kissed him lightly on the lips, his whiskers tickling her chin.

"Get some sleep, Superman. We'll talk tomorrow."

But the next day, she realized she had another priority. Her secretary called her at home. Maria, the temp who had taken over for Joan, was overwhelmed. With all the excitement yesterday, the phones were jammed with inquiries from all over. Associates wanting to know if she was all right, if Kaslow's was undergoing another change of leadership. Claire tried to calm her but then agreed to come in. The employees needed to see her face, in person, rather than the image of a frightened victim shown on the late news.

Before she went in, she decided to make a quick stop at the hospital. It was only a few blocks away, and she wanted to see Matt again. She hadn't even thanked him, she realized, she had been in such a state of shock last night. After a few hours' sleep, she felt more like herself, the tears of last night seeming to have come from another person.

But inside, she still felt like a great weight had been lifted. She hurried up the steps to the hospital, hardly able to contain a smile as she entered the elevator.

When she reached his room, she was surprised to find Laura Hayes there, looking like she had come straight from a photo shoot—which she had. A press shoot for *Lyin' Hearts* had been scheduled for that morning, Claire remembered.

She was sitting on the end of his bed, her feet, clad in the slimmest of sandals, dangling over the edge. Matt lay under a sheet, a sling protecting his arm and a six-inch gauze pad just below his left shoulder. His face had been shaved, but his hair stuck out in disheveled spikes. He looked rumpled and sexy, a warrior after the battle, ready to sample the morning-after spoils.

Which came in the form of cookies—an open box from Reading Market lay on the bed.

Laura brushed crumbs from her hands. "Hi. You must be Claire. I'm Laura." She turned her warm smile on Matt. "I stopped by to see how my roomie was doing…and to bring him some magic pain-relieving cookies." She pointed to the box. "Have one. They're chocolate chip pecan, his favorite."

"No, thank you. I have to go to work. I just stopped by to see how Matt was—"

Matt eyed her sharply, his lids dragging low over his eyes. "Matt's great," he replied, his tone sarcastic. "Strung out on drugs, surrounded by pretty nurses and magic cookies. What could be better?"

She swallowed, unsure of his mood. "Well, that's nice."

"What's this about you going to work? I thought the store was closed today."

"It is. But the administrative offices are still open. And I've got a pile of correspondence to answer—"

He scowled. "Why do I get the feeling the store could be burning and you'd still be answering your email?"

Laura gave him a wide-eyed look. "My, someone sure is grumpy. Maybe that nurse needs to come back with that enema bag."

"And maybe someone needs to take a day off. Come on, Claire. You were a hostage not twenty-four hours ago. Hell, even Terry Anderson took a year off."

She gave him a tight smile. "Yes, well, I'll start on my memoirs tomorrow. Today I have a store to run."

"I'm leaving for Montana later today. As soon as the doc signs my release papers."

She gaped at him. "But you can't! You've — you've got a hole in your shoulder! And the police want to talk to you," she added.

"They were here this morning. They said an attorney's been appointed for Porter. I expect the guy will plead insanity. Son of a bitch should be locked up for life."

Claire looked away. She didn't want to discuss Roy Porter. And Matt certainly didn't seem to be in a mood to discuss their future together. Maybe he had changed his mind. Maybe he wanted a woman who could be at his beck and call twenty-four hours a day, who could accompany him to film sets, even co-star in his next film.

Maybe he preferred blondes.

Laura reached over and picked up a cookie.

Blondes bearing cookies.

Suddenly, all the old insecurities flooded Claire, and she was twenty-one again. And Matt was turning away from her, like the day at the police station after Hayley died.

She glanced at the door. "Well, I'm glad you're feeling better. I'd better be going. I had the driver wait for me."

"Hold on—" he began.

Laura looked sheepish. "Actually, I was just leaving," she began, while Matt called, "Wait!"

But Claire was already at the door, dragging her insecurities with her.

She almost ran into Matt's mother on the other side.

"Claire, I was hoping I'd see you. Matt told us everything that happened." She shook her head, a soft pitying look in her green eyes. "You poor thing. You must have been scared to death."

Claire couldn't answer her. Matt had told them everything? All of his ugly suspicions, about the rape — about the doubts concerning Tripper's paternity? Of course he had. His family was the most important thing in his life. It was to them he owed his loyalty.

And she was just an outsider, a woman whose passions involved spreadsheets.

In the cold light of day, she realized how silly the idea was. That she and Matt could have a relationship, could manage to work around their vast differences in personality, in lifestyle. Sure, they had their share of passion-filled moments. But when the sex was over, she still had responsibilities — responsibilities she wasn't willing to give up, and he still had his films to make.

What had she been thinking?

Joyce put her hand on her arm. "Why don't you stay? Have some lunch with us. We'd like to see Tripper while we're here."

"Of course, Mrs. Grayson. I'll bring him by after school. But I can't stay. I really have to get back to the office. I've got a meeting."

She didn't notice the tears slipping down her face.

Laura gazed at Matt earnestly. "She loves you, Matt. It was written all over her face!"

His mother walked in before Laura could finish the lecture he could see coming. "What on earth did you say to make that woman rush out of here like the place was on fire?" she asked, coming to a stop at Matt's bed.

"I didn't say anything. She's got some damn fool notion to go to work today, when it's obvious she's been through hell and back."

He was beginning to wonder if the woman who had cried her eyes out on his bed last night had been real or just a character from his drug-induced dream. Despite what Laura said, he had battled with Claire enough to know she was an expert when it came to dodging her emotions, and she would relax her guard when hell froze over. Last night, if it had occurred, had been the result of shock.

"Well, I think it's high time you put a ring on that woman's finger and made an honest woman out of her."

He snorted. "Mother, the last thing she wants is to get married for Tripper's sake."

"Then what about hers? She needs you, Matthew. And Lord knows you're head over heels in love with her."

Like part of a matchmaking tag team, Laura backed her up. "He is. You should have seen him on the set. Once or twice, when we were filming at Kaslow's, he thought he saw a glimpse of her, and suddenly, Mr. Suave and Debonair became a sixth grader again. It was really cute, Mrs. Grayson."

"Cute?" he exclaimed. "Don't you read my press anymore? What the hell happened to the 'Quintessential Guy'?"

She smirked. "He's in love and scared to death she doesn't feel the same way. I think it's adorable. I mean, here you are, a big star and all, and you're afraid to ask the girl of your dreams to the prom."

Matt blinked. Was she right? Was he so afraid of offending Claire that he had backed off too soon? Had he been too afraid of pushing her, in her vulnerable state, to convince her he was serious?

Maybe she needed some pushing. Though she was a fierce fighter in the boardroom, underneath those chic, armored suits was a scared, shy little girl who had been told repeatedly by her parents that she was worthless.

And now, when she was most vulnerable, what she needed wasn't a superhero taking a bullet for her. She needed a man, willing to love her through thick and thin, no matter the consequences.

And that was a role only he could fill.

He threw his legs over the side of the bed. "Ladies, I've got nothing on underneath this contraption. Unless you want an eyeful, you better hit the door. Now," he barked.

Laura squealed and made a beeline for the exit, but Joyce stood her ground, lingering long enough to issue a warning.

"There's a whole herd of reporters gathered at the front entrance. If you want to get out of here, especially dressed like that, you'd better take a different route. I'll have Mark meet you at the back entrance."

She turned, then added over her shoulder. "And there's a jewelry shop just across the street. I bet you could find something nice there."


When Mark dropped him off at Kaslow's, Matt went straight to the freight entrance. He had borrowed Mark's jacket. Underneath, he wore nothing but a bandage and the pair of Levi's he'd found hanging in the closet.

He had to ask where her new office was, but finally he found the corner office that used to be Bernard Kaslow's.

Her secretary escorted him to the inner office door, where she hesitated. In a worried voice, she informed him, "She's just not herself. I tried to make her go home, but she insisted she had work to do."

"Yeah, she gets like that sometimes. Hardheaded as that damn statue in your fountain there, but I love her anyway."

He didn't care if she quoted him to the media hounds that were clamoring for a tidbit. He had caught just enough of the morning news to know he'd be a hunted man for the next few days at least.

He opened the door and quietly slipped inside. He shut the door behind him, then saw her. Her head was wedged between her hands, dark hair cascading over her face, and she was crying. This time, it wasn't the great, throat-clearing sobs that had possessed her last night, but dainty little tears. They rolled down her cheeks and dropped to her desk, and he realized why they called it a desk blotter.

He approached her desk, but she didn't look up.

"I guess taking a bullet isn't enough these days to convince a woman you love her," he said in a lazy drawl that barely hid the emotion he felt. "So I thought maybe this would do the trick." He held out the ring he had bought on the way over. A three-carat diamond, set in platinum. Not too fancy, but nice. Classy. A lifetime investment, the guy at the shop had told him.

She lifted her head and looked up at him, love and tears in her eyes. "Oh God, Matt, I'm so stupid! You were right. I'm the most insecure woman on earth! I — I've been looking in the phone book, trying to find a therapist." She pointed to the open phone book in front of her, and then she caught sight of the ring he held in his outstretched hand, the one that wasn't in a sling.

Slowly, she reached out and took the tiny box from his hand. "You — you're serious?"

"Hell, yes, I'm serious. What do you think I've been after all this time?"

"Not sex?"

"Of course n — Well, yeah, that was part of it," he agreed. "But only with you. From now on. Ever since I came here, there's been no one else. There never will be. You believe that, don't you?"

She nodded. "I believe you. But Matt, we're so different."

"Yeah, I noticed. In fact, I kinda like that about you."

She gave him a weak smile, but there was still a question in her eyes. He realized, analytical thing that she was, she needed to hear the facts. Why he loved her, in a four-point plan with all the i's dotted and t's crossed.

"You see, it's like this. The first moment I saw you, all those years ago, I knew right then you were different from all the women I had known. I thought you were perfect: funny, smart, sexy. I wanted to get to know you better, see if my instincts were right, 'cause they were screaming this was the real thing between us.

"But unfortunately, we didn't get that opportunity. Things happened, too fast for either of us, and when it all blew up, I just chalked

it up to bad timing. But I was wrong. We *were* meant to be together."
He sighed. "Hell, I don't know, some cosmic force or something
must have preordained it, because when I'm around you I feel like
I've found the other half of my heart, the other half of my soul." His
voice became a little clogged, but he didn't pause.

"I love you Claire, so much it hurts sometimes. I know there're a
few problems we need to work on—we both have careers, we both
have scars—" He glanced at the one at her hairline and swallowed
the emotion that rose in his throat. "But all I want in this world is
to be with you, spend the rest of my life taking care of you. Making
you happy."

With a little cry, Claire slipped off her shoes and jacket and in
seconds had climbed across the desk to him. His uninjured arm
stretched to come around her in a protective hold.

"But there's so much I have to learn. About—about love. I n-never
knew." She lifted her gaze to his, and the shadows Matt had become
used to seeing in her gray eyes were gone. In their place was something
he knew was love, shining like dawn slipping over the mountains.

"Just answer one thing: Do you love me, Claire?" He needed to
hear her say it, finally.

She nodded. "Yes. Yes, I love you. I always have. I thought it was
silly, all those years ago."

"Then let's nail this down: Will you marry me?"

She drew his head down and kissed him, a soul-shaking kiss
that scuttled the last of the drugs from his system. And then she
murmured, against his mouth, "Yes, I'll marry you. Let me get out
my calendar…"

# Chapter Twenty-Nine

Later that evening, Claire found herself alone in the upstairs bedroom at Matt's ranch. It hadn't taken much for him to convince her to come out for a few days while he recovered, though until now, they'd had little time to themselves. His family had all hovered solicitously upon their arrival in Great Falls, but this time, Claire was included in the protective wrap of their love and support.

They would soon be her family, too, she realized, wondering how on earth she would know how to be part of a family—a normal family.

But for Tripper's sake, she would learn. During the plane ride out, he had been full of eager questions, though the news of their engagement hadn't surprised him a bit. He simply lifted his shoulder in an unconcerned shrug, as if he had known all along his parents would one day get married.

Claire still had some doubts. She wouldn't give up her job, she had told Matt, but he had replied that he didn't expect her to. "I'm gone a good bit on location, and though I'd love to have you join me, I know you'd hate it. The store means a lot to you—I know that better than anyone, and believe me, no one was prouder than I was when you were appointed president."

"And what if we have more children?"

He shrugged. "We'll find a good nanny. And I've got a flexible schedule, remember. I can take a year or two off, play Dad full time." And he had looked almost eager at the prospect, though she couldn't imagine him giving up his promising new career as a director.

It was almost too perfect.

But now, as she got ready for bed, she acknowledged another problem. Her ignorance in the bedroom was a worry she couldn't ignore. She was a neophyte compared to him. Despite his insistence that things had been perfect before, she was very much afraid she would disappoint him.

Maybe she could find a book on the topic…Were there journals published? On sexual technique, perhaps?

Downstairs, she heard him whistle for Sadie. Claire's things had been brought to the room where she had slept the last time she was here, but tonight, she didn't want to sleep alone under his grand-mother's log-cabin quilt.

She wanted to be with Matt, but the thought of walking down those stairs and into his big bedroom terrified her.

Claire sighed, impatient with her timidity. After all, didn't she regularly gobble up ornery executives for breakfast?

Then she frowned at the sturdy cotton pajamas she had laid out on her bed. She didn't even have the proper outfit. Matt was probably more accustomed to women in silk negligees, like the ones she had admired in Kaslow's lingerie department the other day. If only she had thought to have one wrapped up and charged to her account.

Claire sat on the edge of the bed, contemplating her options. She could walk into his bedroom, announce she was ready for sex, and hope he took his cue. Then another objection occurred to her. He was recovering from an injury. The last thing on his mind would be physical exertion.

But that, she realized, was perfect—she could be with him, with no expectations on either part, nothing but their feelings for each other. They could just snuggle and talk.

Before she could lose her nerve, she threw on her pajamas and hurried down the stairs. Outside his bedroom, she paused, the closed door momentarily daunting.

She knocked lightly, and when she didn't hear an answer, she assumed he must be asleep. She opened the door, intending to slip into bed beside him, but the sight that greeted her almost took her breath away. Matt was just coming out of the bathroom, wearing nothing but jeans and a stark-white bandage, a contrasting appliqué against his tanned skin.

Her throat went dry. She tried not to stare at the exposed skin where his stomach curved inward, at the hard, carved expanse of his chest. His hair was damp, as if he had just washed behind his ears. A wave of tenderness washed over her, mixed with a sexual desire that almost made her knees buckle.

"I—I thought I'd check and see if you needed anything."

For a long moment he didn't say a word, just gazed at her with a starved look in his eyes. Finally he spoke, his voice ragged. "Yeah, as a matter of fact, there's one thing I could use."

She waited, but he said nothing, just continued to stare at her, his eyes luminous in the dim light. Silently, he held out his arm, inviting her to the very place she wanted to be.

Her feet flew across the carpet, and in seconds, his arm was wrapped around her, holding her tight against him. "I had a feeling you'd be too shy to come down," he murmured against her hair. "I thought I'd have to come and get you, and I wasn't sure I could manage the Rhett Butler routine."

"I *did* almost chicken out," she admitted, breathing in the sweet-sharp male smell of him. "But then I thought…" She swallowed. "I thought you might be too tired for any strenuous activity. So I decided to just come and…and…" She smiled against his chest. "Provide some company."

He nuzzled her head. "Company? I could've had Sadie for that. I want you for more than company—and for more than sex, too."

She lifted an eyebrow, then smiled, just a bit wickedly. "That's too bad, because I was hoping…there's a problem I need to work on, right away, if you don't mind."

"What's that?"

"Will you show me how to make love to you?"

He gave her a look that was equal parts love and desire and said softly, "I'd like nothing better."

Claire sighed. Her fears floated away, like clouds chased by the sun. But there was still one…

"Your arm—I don't want to hurt you."

"I'm tougher than I look."

Glad that he was confident enough for both of them, she took his hand and led him to the bed.

She sat on the edge, then looked up at him as he stood in front of her. Slowly, she began unbuttoning her pajama top, gauging him for reaction. When she got to the end, he swallowed, his eyes lingering on the gap she'd created.

"God, Claire, flannel pajamas could only look sexy on you."

"I thought it might be cold—I wasn't sure you'd have the fire lit." Her voice came out strangely husky—hormones? "It's getting a bit…too warm." She shrugged the pajama top off her shoulders, exposing her breasts to his hungry gaze.

Then she started on his Levi's, slowly managing the buttons, her fingers brushing the denim.

He groaned. "I don't think you need any lessons."

A satisfied smile curved her lips. "You seem to be…in some pain." She slid her hands over his hard length, caressing, cherishing.

"I'm in a great deal of pain now. I'd better lie down."

She leaned back on the bed, inviting him with her eyes.

He didn't need a second invitation. He stretched out on the bed beside her—they were sideways on the huge bed, but Claire decided geometry didn't matter.

"Your arm…"

"That's not the part that hurts, Claire."

She helped him pull off his jeans, then slipped off her pajamas and slid against him. Their mouths met, tongues dancing, teasing. Then her tongue went on an exploration—she kissed his neck, licked the salty moisture, tested her teeth against his earlobe.

His hand, and then his mouth, focused on her breasts—a heavenly feeling, she decided, momentarily distracted.

Somehow, she found herself on top of him, arcing over him, imitating the goddess of Fortune who, she reminded herself, she still needed to thank.

Fortune had never felt this good.

Even with one arm out of commission, Matt still managed to find all the right spots, teasing her with his fingers until she begged him to stop.

"Matt, please! I want you, now."

"Take it, babe. You're in the driver's seat."

Claire decided she really, really liked being in the driver's seat. She bore down on him, filling the need she'd had for so long…and he responded, as if the same need drove him.

Together, they reached climax, Claire shuddering above him as he gasped, holding her tight, one arm around her back.

"Matt, I love you. I love you." Tears gathered behind her eyelids as emotion threatened to overwhelm her—hormones again. "Oh, God, I've loved you—ever since the first time," she admitted, lowering her mouth to his, kissing the face she'd dreamed about—but this was no dream.

He gathered her close, tucking her in against his good arm. "It's been a long time coming."

Contentment eased over her, and all the old fears, the old insecurity, vanished as somewhere, the dawn gathered and Fate's bronze lips cracked in a smile.

# Epilogue

Claire watched as her son and his father splashed in the pool. Sadie, who'd taken a liking to Claire, preferred to rest at her side, stretched out alongside her redwood lounger.

"That's two points for our side, buddy!"

"You cheated, Dad! No going into the deep end!" They were playing basketball in the pool, substituting a beach ball for the regulation ball and making up the rules as they went along.

"Hey! I already spotted you five points. What more do you want?" Matt complained, then called out to his wife, "Hey, Claire, your son's definitely got your negotiating instincts. He's already talked me out of five points, he's up by six, and he wants me to roll over and play dead. If this were a boardroom, I'd be losing my shorts right about now."

She just smiled from the sidelines. It might be the only thing he had inherited from her, she thought. Every day he looked more and more like his father, and soon the girls at school would notice as well.

A drop of water landed on the page of the *Business Week* she was reading, and she felt a shadow cool the skin on her arm.

"I think it's time you got your hair wet."

She looked up in alarm. "No, Matt, I told you, I don't want—"

But her words were cut short when he lifted her up. "It's okay, honey. I swear, I won't let you go. All you have to do for now is get in and get wet."

She stared into his eyes, her own hidden behind sun shades. He had proposed the idea before, but she had always found a convenient excuse.

"It's time to let it go," he said softly, walking across the smooth tile toward the crystal-clear pool.

He was right, she realized. And there would never be a better time, with the two guys she loved — and trusted — here to catch her.

She glanced at the water, and for a moment, the old fear caught her.

"One step at a time — deal?" His voice was warm, persuasive, his eyes magnetic, the color of the sea at dawn.

"Deal," she agreed, her voice hardly wavering.

He led her to the edge of the steps that led into the pool. Her hand in his, they made their way, inch by inch, into the pool, until she was standing in three feet of water.

"See? It's not so bad," he said, still holding the fingers that clutched his more tightly now.

Tripper tread water nearby. "See, Mom? There's nothing to be afraid of. It's just water," he pointed out, as if she had mistaken it for quicksand.

She gave him a wobbly smile. "You're right. Just water. Cold water," she amended as a shiver passed through her.

"Come on. A few more feet, and you'll be done for the day."

"No, I want to go all the way." She eyed the far end of the pool. Eleven feet. Drowning depth.

But it wasn't the actual depth that caused a curl of fear to knot in her stomach. It was the thought of suffocating under the weight of it, the fear of never being able to surface once she lost her footing. But the hands at her side were strong, steady, and supportive against her waist.

As she slowly walked toward the center of the pool, the water exerted pressure on her chest, and conversely, she felt a freedom, a lifting of a weight that had held her down.

And then Matt was supporting her, his height adding inches to hers so that she floated freely in the deep end.

She leaned back, faced the sun, and closed her eyes. The water bobbed gently around her, and she felt cleansed. For the first time.

Matt's hands were strong beneath her, his warm chest inches from hers. Tripper circled like a dolphin around them.

Gulls screamed overhead. An ocean breeze scuttled the clouds, and when Claire opened her eyes, for an instant she thought she saw God's face. The face from her childhood, the God she had wanted to believe in but had eventually given up on.

It was time, she realized. Time to let go of the fears, the memories, and the guilt. And time to share the news she had been clutching close like a life preserver.

She turned her head slightly to avoid the sun's rays. "Matt," she murmured. "I have to tell you something."

"You want to try scuba diving," he said, gazing down at her with an expression that didn't match his joking words.

"Maybe later. After the baby's born."

He stood completely still for a moment, while the words sank in. "The baby?" he said, his voice pitching slightly upward at the end.

"That's right. You're going to teach her to swim, aren't you?"

His arms tightened around her, and then he tilted her up until she was facing him, her legs wrapped securely around him.

"You're pregnant." He stated the words as if to nail down the fact.

"That was the idea, wasn't it?" She gave him an indulgent grin.

"You talked to the doctor?"

She nodded. "Just before I left Philadelphia."

"Oh, Claire." His voice was husky, and his lips met hers in a kiss before he pulled her to him, hugging her there in the middle of his pool.

Claire laughed, squeezing him back. She felt so totally free, totally alive. A weight lifted off her shoulders, and for a moment, she thought, if she had wanted to, she could float above the water.

THE END

# Acknowledgments

Thank you to my editor, Milli Davis, for understanding when I announced to her that I'd be moving across the Atlantic before the end of the summer, and adjusting her schedule so we could finish those last few edits on *Redemption*. We made it!

# About the Author

Kathryn Barrett reluctantly put aside childhood dreams of becoming an author and took a more practical approach, majoring in Business Administration in college. But after marrying an Air Force officer, she realized a career in high finance didn't suit an itinerant lifestyle. She happily returned to her first love, writing stories that feature larger-than-life characters, family relationships, and of course, a happy ending.

Having lived all over the United States, Kathryn and her family have recently relocated to northern Virginia, after ten years in the United Kingdom. She enjoys long walks with her squirrel-obsessed dog, traveling to tiny European countries, cooking vegan feasts, and, only occasionally, she still reads the *Financial Times*.

## New Adult Romance

*Three Daves* by Nicki Elson
*Streamline* by Jennifer Lane
The Shades series: *Shades of Atlantis* & *Shades of Avalon* by Carol Oates
The Heart series: *Beside Your Heart, Disclosure of the Heart* & *Forever Your Heart*
by Mary Whitney
*Romancing the Bookworm* by Kate Evangelista
*Flirting with Chaos* by Kenya Wright
The Vice, Virtue & Video series: *Revealed, Captured* & *Desired* by Bianca Giovanni
Granton University series: *Loving Lies* by Linda Kage

## Paranormal Romance

The Light series: *Seers of Light, Whisper of Light* & *Circle of Light* by Jennifer DeLucy
The Hanaford Park series: *Eve of Samhain* & *Pleasures Untold* by Lisa Sanchez
*Immortal Awakening* by KC Randall
The Seraphim series: *Crushed Seraphim* & *Bittersweet Seraphim* by Debra Anastasia
*The Guardian's Wild Child* by Feather Stone
*Grave Refrain* by Sarah M. Glover
The Divinity series: *Divinity* by Patricia Leever
The Blood Vine series: *Blood Vine, Blood Entangled* & *Blood Reunited*
by Amber Belldene
*Divine Temptation* by Nicki Elson
The Dead Rapture series: *Love in the Time of the Dead* by Tera Shanley

## Romantic Suspense

*Whirlwind* by Robin DeJarnett
The CONduct series: *With Good Behavior, Bad Behavior* & *On Best Behavior*
by Jennifer Lane
*Indivisible* by Jessica McQuinn
*Between the Lies* by Alison Oburia
*Blind Man's Bargain* by Tracy Winegar

## Erotic Romance

The Keyhole series: *Becoming sage* (book 1) by Kasi Alexander
The Keyhole series: *Saving sunni* (book 2) by Kasi & Reggie Alexander
The Winemaker's Dinner: *Appetizers* & *Entrée* by Dr. Ivan Rusilko & Everly Drummond
The Winemaker's Dinner: *Dessert* by Dr. Ivan Rusilko
*Client N° 5* by Joy Fulcher

### ←———→ Historical Romance ←———→

*Cat O' Nine Tails* by Patricia Leever
*Burning Embers* by Hannah Fielding
*Seven for a Secret* by Rumer Haven


### ←———→ Anthologies ←———→

*A Valentine Anthology* including short stories by
Alice Clayton ("With a Double Oven"),
Jennifer DeLucy ("Magnus of Pfelt, Conquering Viking Lord"),
Nicki Elson ("I Don't Do Valentine's Day"),
Jessica McQuinn ("Better Than One Dead Rose and a Monkey Card"),
Victoria Michaels ("Home to Jackson"), and
Alison Oburia ("The Bridge")

*Taking Liberties* including an introduction by Tiffany Reisz and short stories by
Mina Vaughn ("John Hancock-Blocked"),
Linda Cunningham ("A Boston Marriage"),
Joy Fulcher ("Tea for Two"),
KC Holly ("The British Are Coming!"),
Kimberly Jensen & Scott Stark ("E. Pluribus Threesome"), and
Vivian Rider ("M'Lady's Secret Service")


### ←———→ Singles and Novellas ←———→

*It's Only Kinky the First Time* (A Keyhole series single) by Kasi Alexander
*Learning the Ropes* (A Keyhole series single) by Kasi & Reggie Alexander
*The Winemaker's Dinner: RSVP* by Dr. Ivan Rusilko
*The Winemaker's Dinner: No Reservations* by Everly Drummond
*Big Guns* by Jessica McQuinn
*Concessions* by Robin DeJarnett
*Starstruck* by Lisa Sanchez
*New Flame* by BJ Thornton
*Shackled* by Debra Anastasia
*Swim Recruit* by Jennifer Lane
*Sway* by Nicki Elson
*Full Speed Ahead* by Susan Kaye Quinn
*The Second Sunrise* by Hannah Downing
*The Summer Prince* by Carol Oates
*Whatever it Takes* by Sarah M. Glover
*Clarity* (A *Divinity* prequel single) by Patricia Leever
*A Christmas Wish* (A *Cocktails & Dreams* single) by Autumn Markus
*Late Night with Andres* by Debra Anastasia
*Poughkeepsie* (enhanced iPad app collector's edition) by Debra Anastasia